## CONNECTION TO A KILLER

"I can hear Justice," Laura said.

"Hear him?" Harrison asked. "How do you mean?"

"What I mean is that I can hear his voice scraping at my brain. He talks to me."

"What does he say?"

"He says, *'Sssisssterr,'*" she rasped. "He says it with a menace so strong, it actually scratches across my brain and I know he's coming for me. I've sensed him all my life. He's sent messages off and on for years, although I didn't really get what they were about until I was older. I only really fully understood the last when he was on his mission."

Harrison's face was sober now, his eyes darkening gravely. "His mission of killing people? A few years back? That's what you're talking about?"

She nodded. "Justice is after my family. I don't know why exactly. He wants to kill us all."

"And he's sending you messages to that effect?"

"Yes." Then, "I know what it sounds like." She rubbed her face hard, wishing she hadn't started this, knowing there was no backing out now. Besides, she needed someone to know that she had contact with Justice, though she supposed trusting a reporter like Harrison wasn't the best idea. "His voice is really strong right now. He knows where I am. I'm on his radar."

"You think he wants to kill you."

*And my baby.* "Oh, yeah."

Of this she was certain. . . .

## Books by Lisa Jackson

SEE HOW SHE DIES
FINAL SCREAM
RUNNING SCARED
WHISPERS
TWICE KISSED
UNSPOKEN
IF SHE ONLY KNEW
HOT BLOODED
COLD BLOODED
THE NIGHT BEFORE
THE MORNING AFTER
DEEP FREEZE
FATAL BURN
SHIVER
MOST LIKELY TO DIE
ABSOLUTE FEAR
ALMOST DEAD
LOST SOULS
LEFT TO DIE
WICKED GAME
MALICE
CHOSEN TO DIE
WITHOUT MERCY
DEVIOUS
WICKED LIES
BORN TO DIE

## Books by Nancy Bush

CANDY APPLE RED
ELECTRIC BLUE
ULTRA VIOLET
WICKED GAME
UNSEEN
BLIND SPOT
WICKED LIES
HUSH

**Published by Kensington Publishing Corporation**

# LISA JACKSON

## Wicked Lies

# NANCY BUSH

ZEBRA BOOKS
KENSINGTON PUBLISHING CORP.
http://www.kensingtonbooks.com

ZEBRA BOOKS are published by

Kensington Publishing Corp.
119 West 40th Street
New York, NY 10018

All Kensington titles, imprints, and distributed lines are
available at special quantity discounts for bulk purchases for
sales promotion, premiums, fund-raising, educational, or institutional use.

Special book excerpts or customized printings can also be
created to fit specific needs. For details, write or phone the
office of the Kensington Special Sales Manager: Attn. Special Sales Department. Kensington Publishing Corp., 119
West 40th Street, New York,.NY 10018. Phone: 1-800-221-
2647.

Zebra and the Z logo Reg. U.S. Pat. & TM Off.

ISBN-13: 978-1-4201-0339-7
ISBN-10: 1-4201-0339-3

First Kensington Books Hardcover Printing: February 2011
First Zebra Books Mass-Market Paperback Printing: June
2011

10  9  8  7  6  5  4  3  2  1

Printed in the United States of America

# CHAPTER 1

*I can smell her!*
*Another one whose scent betrays her!*
*Even inside my cell, I can smell her sickness. Her filth. Her lust.*
*There have been others, too, while I've languished here. Others who need to be avenged. Others who, with their devil's issue, must be driven back to the deadly fires from which they were spawned!*
*Oh, sick women with your uncontrollable needs.*
*I am coming for you. . . .*

Laura Adderley leaned a hand against the bathroom stall, clutching the home pregnancy test in her other fist, unable to look. She didn't want this. Not when her marriage was newly finished—a divorce she'd wanted as much as her newly minted ex, maybe more. Byron had already taken up residence with another woman, and he would undoubtedly cheat on her as much as he'd cheated on Laura. It didn't matter. Their marriage had been ill-conceived from the beginning; it had just taken Laura three years to recognize that fact.

Ill-conceived . . .

Grabbing on to her courage, she slowly unfurled her fist, staring down at the two glaring pink lines of the home pregnancy test.

Positive.

She'd known it would be.

*Oh, God . . .*

Squeezing her eyes closed, Laura inhaled a deep, calming breath. She'd ignored the signs for as long as she could, but there was no keeping her head in the sand any longer. She was pregnant. With her ex-husband's child. They'd signed the papers that very week, though Byron had tried to stall because he simply didn't want to give Laura what she wanted: freedom from lies and tyranny.

*But now what?*

Dr. Byron Adderley was an orthopedic surgeon at Ocean Park Hospital, and she, Laura, was a floor nurse. They'd moved to this smaller facility along the Oregon coast about a year earlier, leaving one of Portland's largest and most prestigious hospitals for a slower-paced life. Laura hadn't wanted the move, had been adamantly against it. For reasons she didn't want to tell Byron, she wanted, needed, to stay far, far away from Ocean Park and the surrounding hamlet of Deception Bay.

But as if he'd somehow divined her secrets, he'd announced he'd taken a position at the smaller hospital and they were up and moving. Laura had been stunned. Had told him she wasn't going. Simply was not going. But in the end he'd gotten his way, and though she'd dragged her feet, she'd reluctantly made this move in the vain hope that she could get her dying marriage off life support, though she knew she no longer loved him, maybe never really had. But with a new start, it was possible something could change. Maybe her heart could be rewon. Maybe Byron would want just her. Maybe everything would be . . . better.

Then he was discovered groping one of the Ocean Park

nurses in an empty hospital room. The hospital tried to chastise Byron Adderley, but he wasn't the kind of man to be chastised. The nurse was summarily dismissed and the incident swept under the hospital rugs . . . and Laura filed for divorce.

At first he'd argued with her. Not that he wanted her; it just wasn't his decision and so therefore it couldn't *be*. She didn't listen and he changed tactics, humbly begging for a second chance. Laura was suspicious of his motives, aware he might be acting. But she looked down the road of her own future; and it was decidedly bleak and lonely; and one night, three months ago, he'd sworn that he loved her, that he would never cheat on her again, that he would seek help for past mistakes. She had wanted to believe him so much. Needed to. Shut the clamoring voice in her head that warned her to be smart, and one thing led to another and they ended up making desperate love together. A second chance, maybe a last chance that Laura had to take.

And then another nurse came forward, complaining that Dr. Adderley had made inappropriate advances toward her. Byron vehemently denied the charge, but Laura, who had abilities that he didn't understand—some she didn't understand herself—knew without a doubt that he was lying through his miserable white teeth.

She let the divorce proceedings run their course, and being Byron, he took up with another woman. This time Laura didn't look back. She was through with Byron Adderley, and until today, she'd been determined to move back to Portland and find employment far, far away from Ocean Park and Deception Bay.

But now . . .

The door to the bathroom opened. "Laura?" Nurse Perez called.

"I'll be out in a minute," Laura said, flushing the toilet and wrapping the telltale wand in toilet paper and shoving it in her purse.

"We need help in the ER. We've got a head trauma coming in."

"Okay."

She heard the door close and let herself out of the bathroom. Washing her hands, she looked hard at her reflection in the mirror. Serious blue-gray eyes stared back at her; and she could see the beginning of her own dishwater blond hair reappearing at her hairline, the longer, darker tresses trying to escape their ponytail and curl under her chin, a strong chin, she'd been told, that, along with high cheekbones and thick lashes, gave her a slightly aristocratic look, something far from what she really was.

A familiar pressure built inside her head, and she mentally pushed it back, visualizing a twenty-foot-high iron gate to withstand the force coming at her. This was an automatic response that clicked in almost unconsciously when particularly strong, unwanted—*bad*—thoughts attacked her. For years she thought everyone had this ability but then slowly realized that it was unique to her alone. It was like someone, or ones, was knocking at her brain, trying to get inside, and she would push up a mental wall to keep them out. But this time was different; there was more urgency and determination. As if this someone were pounding a metal hammer at her wall. At her brain.

*Sisssterrrr!*

Laura jerked to attention and glanced around, half expecting to see who had spoken. But there was no one. Nary a soul. And the voice had been decidedly male.

Her eyes widened; she watched the autonomic response happen in the mirror as realization dawned, a realization she wanted desperately to deny. He was back.

Shutting her lids tightly, she squeezed at her brain, holding the wall firm until the hammering turned into a tinny, little *ping, ping, ping* and was gone.

By the time she reached the ER, the ambulance was screaming up the drive. It was 8:30 p.m. Late June, so it was still light out, though she could see the shadows forming beneath the gnarled branches of the scrub pine that lined the asphalt. Red and white lights flashed in opposite rotation and the *woo*-woo . . . *woo*-woo . . . *woo*-woo of the shrieking siren seemed to vibrate the very air.

With a squeal of brakes the ambulance jumped to a halt. EMTs leapt out and ran to the back of the vehicle. Doors flew open, and a victim was rushed in on a gurney, head surrounded by a white bandage that was dark red with blood.

One of the residents sucked in a breath. "Jesus, it's Conrad!"

"Conrad?" Laura repeated in shock, gazing down at one of Ocean Park's security guards: Conrad Weiser.

"What happened?" one of the trauma surgeons demanded.

"Attacked at Halo Valley," the EMT responded. "He was on the way there to pick up a patient, and one of the crazies beat the hell out of him and escaped."

"Halo Valley?" Laura repeated through lips that barely moved.

"Yeah, the mental hospital," Dylan, the EMT, clarified soberly.

"Let's get him in here," the trauma surgeon ordered as a second victim on a gurney was off-loaded from the ambulance.

"You okay?" Dylan asked, frowning at Laura.

"Fine."

Bringing herself back to the present, Laura helped guide the second wounded man's gurney into the ER. He was awake but his throat was wrapped and he clearly couldn't speak. His dark eyes glared at her, and Dylan said, almost in an aside, giving her a second shock, "This is Dr. Maurice Zellman from Halo Valley. He was stabbed in the throat."

"Also by the escapee?" she asked.

"Looks like it."

She watched as Zellman was hurriedly wheeled through the double doors to the ER as well, and was unable to control a full-body shivering that emanated from her very soul.

Halo Valley. The mental hospital for the criminally insane.

*He* was there.

Wasn't he?

Or, was that why he'd just tried to breach the wall in her mind? He'd escaped!

And he was coming after her.

*Oh, God, no! Not now!* She thought of the baby and her heart nearly stopped. Fear crawled up her spine and nestled in her brain. *No, no, no!*

Blindly, pushing back that horrid snaking fear, she turned to one of the other nurses. "Who did this?" she asked.

"Don't you wish we could ask Zellman and find out?" Nurse Carlita Solano answered flatly. "Some nut job, for sure."

*Please, God, don't let it be him.*

But she knew it was. Justice Turnbull had escaped the walls of Halo Valley Security Hospital, and he was free to take up his murdering ways.

Laura watched the doors behind the injured doctor slowly close with a soft hiss and wondered how this had happened.


The day had started out like many others.

Dr. Maurice Zellman, one of Halo Valley Security Hospital's premier psychiatrists . . . maybe the premier psychiatrist, if you'd asked him . . . had begun his morning with a piece of dry wheat toast, a soft-boiled egg, and a slice of cantaloupe before driving to the hospital and arriving punctually at 7:15 a.m. He had several consults before lunch, called his wife, Patricia, at noon and learned that their sixteen-year-old son, Brandt, had gotten in some kind of trouble at school and was facing detention for the rest of the week. With a snort of disgust, Zellman told Patricia that Brandt would be facing some serious punishment from his father as well, and then, ruffled, he visited a number of his patients in their rooms—cells, really, though no one referred to them as such—throughout the rest of the afternoon, his mind on other things.

By six o'clock he was finished with work, except that he hadn't yet visited with his most notorious patient: Justice Turnbull, a psychotic killer who had tried to kill his own mother and had proven to be obsessed with murdering the group of women who lived together in a lodge called Siren Song along the Oregon coast. These women were whispered about by the locals as members of a cult dubbed the Colony and were reclusive, brooding, and odd. What Justice's personal beef was with them remained a mystery, one Zellman had sought to crack in the over two years of Justice's incarceration but hadn't quite managed yet. Justice was also responsible for several other murders and was an odd bird by anyone's definition.

No one at Halo Valley knew what to make of him, and they certainly didn't know how to treat him. The other doctors just didn't have it, as far as Zellman was concerned. They were adequate, in their way, whereas he, Maurice Zellman, was extraordinary. He actually *cured* patients instead of resorting to mere behavioral modifications.

And Justice . . . well . . . Maurice had made significant progress with him. Significant. Yes, the man was still obsessed with the Siren Song women, but that was because Justice was apparently related to them in some way. At least he thought he was, though that had yet to be proven. Maybe the women were a cult; maybe they weren't. They were certainly paranoically reclusive and, in appearance, looked as if they came from another century. Zellman was inclined to think they should be left alone to their own devices. Everyone found a way to live in this world and there was no right way or wrong way, although getting Justice to see that point was a work in progress. For reasons of his own, Justice Turnbull seemed determined to snuff them all out.

But . . . there had been progress, Zellman reminded himself with a mental pat on the back. Initially, when Justice had first been incarcerated at Halo Valley, he'd bellowed long and loud that he would kill them all and their devil's issue! The staff hadn't known whom he meant, at first, but he made it clear that he wanted to wipe out all the *ssissterrss* at Siren Song. With the help of time and antipsychotics, he'd all but recanted this mission. He still was agitated about them; he couldn't completely disguise it when Zellman would mention the women of the lodge, just to see. But Justice wasn't nearly as single-minded as he had been at first. Was he cured? No. Would he ever be? In Justice Turnbull's case, unlikely, though Dr. Maurice Zellman was definitely the man for the job if there was a chance.

And Maurice understood Justice was tortured by demons of his own making, which didn't matter to his colleagues one whit. They had locked the man away for the next few decades with no chance of getting released. Paranoid schizophrenic. Sociopath. Psychopath. Homicidal maniac . . . Justice Turnbull might be a little of all, but he was still a patient in need of care.

With a glance at his watch, Zellman noted the time: 6:45 p.m. He had a surprise for Justice, one Justice had been asking for and Zellman had finally been able to put together, though not without much resistance. With a satisfied smile on his face, he headed for Justice's room. It was at the end of the hall by design as no one wanted to visit him. In fact, no one ever did, outside of hospital personnel. He was considered weird by the other inmates, which was saying a lot, as they were criminally insane themselves, every last one. But every group had a pecking order, and Halo Valley Security Hospital was no exception. As one of the hospital's leading physicians treating some of the most notorious patients—killers, sadists, rapists, to name a few—Maurice Zellman was intimately aware of how mentally unstable and deranged the men and women were on this side of the hospital, the side that housed those convicted of serious crimes. They might be excused from regular prison by reason of insanity, but it didn't mean they weren't the worst kind of criminals. That was why they were housed on Side B, as this sterile section of the hospital was euphemistically called. Side B. The side for the irredeemable. Connected to Side A, where the mentally ill without criminal tendencies were lodged, by a skyway, surrounded by a tall chain-link fence and razor wire, which were partially hidden by a laurel hedge, all the better to make everyone think the hospital was a warm and cozy place. In truth, Side B was little more than a prison for the criminally insane.

Dr. Zellman was high in the pecking order of the specialists on Side B. He understood the criminal mind in a way that both fascinated and horrified the less imaginative doctors. Well, that was their problem, wasn't it? he thought with a sniff. Dr. Maurice Zellman did his job. And he did it very, very well.

With a tightening of his lips, he picked up his pace. He was running late, and checking on Turnbull was going to make him later still, but he really had no choice as Justice was his patient and was patently feared by the rest of the staff. This fact half amused Zellman, who'd worked with the strange man ever since he'd been brought to Side B, because Justice was really no more frightening than any other psychotic. He was just a little more directionally motivated, focused on women, specifically these Colony women.

Just as Zellman reached Justice's room, the door flew open and Bill Merkely, one of the guards, practically leapt into the hall. Merkely didn't immediately see Zellman, as he was looking back into Justice's room. "So, long, schizo!" he yelled harshly, his beefy face red. He yanked the door shut and checked the automatic lock as Zellman cleared his throat behind him. Merkely jumped as if prodded with a hot poker, his already red face turning magenta. "Fucker told me I was going to die!" he cried as an excuse.

"You can't listen to him."

"I don't. But he sure as hell predicts a whole lot of shit!"

"What were you doing in his room?"

"Picking up his tray. But I had to leave it in there. Hope the food rots!"

He stomped off toward the guards' station, which divided Halo Valley Security Hospital's Side B from Side A, the gentler section, which housed patients who weren't considered a serious threat to society. Zellman thought of Side A as an Alzheimer's wing, though he would never say so aloud as they considered themselves to be a helluva lot more than institutional caretakers. He shook his head at the lot of them. Perception. So many people just didn't get it.

He had a key to Justice's room himself, and he cautiously unlocked the door. Justice had never attacked him; he'd never attacked anyone since he'd been brought to the hospital, but the man had a history, oh, yes, indeedy he did.

Now the patient stood on the far side of the room, disengaged from whatever little drama had occurred between him and Merkely. Justice was tall, dusty blond, and slim, almost skinny, but hard and tough as rawhide. He didn't make eye contact as Zellman entered, but he flicked a look toward the meal tray, which had been untouched except for the apple.

"That man is afraid of me," Justice said, now in his sibilant voice. Always a faint hiss to his words. *An affectation,* Zellman thought.

"Yes, he is."

"He always leaves the tray."

Zellman had a clipboard with a pen attached shoved under one arm. There were cameras in Justice's one-room cell, tracking his every move. Zellman didn't need to watch reams of film to remind himself of the content of each of their meetings. He wrote himself copious notes and typed up reports, which he suspected no one ever read. They all wanted to forget Justice Turnbull and his strangeness. When first brought to Halo Valley, he'd referred to the women he sought to harm as "Sister," in his hissing way. "*Sssiissterrrs . . . ,*" he would rasp. "*Have to kill them all!*" he'd warned. But a lot of that dramatic act had disappeared over time.

Not that he wasn't dangerous. Before his incarceration he'd killed and terrorized a number of women. He had also cut a swath through some peripheral people and had nearly slain his own mentally ill mother. She now lay in a twilight state in a care facility with no memory of the attack and not a lot of connection with the real world.

"Justice," Maurice Zellman said now in a stern, yet friendly, voice, one he'd cultivated over the years. "You've finally got clearance to have those medical tests run at Ocean Park Hospital. The van's on its way here now. I'm warning you, though. If this stomach problem proves to be just a means to get out of Halo Valley, you'll be further restricted. No more walks in the yard. No being outside and staring toward the sea." Zellman heard his faintly mocking voice and clamped down on that. "No privileges."

Justice turned to look at him through clear blue eyes that were almost translucent. He was extraordinarily good-looking except . . . there was just something unnatural about him that made one hesitate upon meeting him. A reaction to something he emanated that Zellman had never quite put his finger on. Now his mouth was turned down at the corners and he winced slightly, as if he were in pain.

Over time and in-depth sessions with him, Zellman had come to realize that some of Justice's deeply rooted problems were because he'd been rejected and scorned. Rejected and scorned by women. Maybe even his own mother. The women of the Colony particularly bothered him. They might not be his sisters, per se, but he seemed to think they were. Was there any shared genetic makeup between them? Zellman thought it unlikely. Justice's world was all of his own making.

Still, Justice definitely believed the Siren Song occupants were the Chosen Ones, while he was kept outside the gates. Locked out. Barred. Left with a mother who had been spiraling into mental illness most of her adult life, Zellman guessed. Who knew about his father? Certainly not Justice or anyone Zellman had ever talked to.

Not a great childhood by any stretch of the imagination.

"Can we go now?" Justice stared at him hard.

Zellman nodded. Justice wore loose gray pants and a white shirt, the regulated outfit for the patients on Side B. "I need to get the handcuffs, first. Sorry."

Justice asked softly, "From the guard?"

"Yes."

"I won't try to escape."

"It's hospital policy."

A spasm crossed his face, and he clutched a palm to his stomach. "This pain is killing me."

Zellman considered the man. Inside the van Justice would be chained around the waist and locked to the side of the vehicle for the ride to Ocean Park. The handcuffs were merely an extra precaution. Sure, it would be against protocol to give him this small freedom as they made their way to the van—against the most basic rule of the hospital. But the stomach pain Justice had been complaining of was definitely worsening, and anyway, Zellman knew when someone was telling the truth and when they were lying. It was just . . . his gift. Justice was telling the truth.

It would take time to get the damned handcuffs, time and effort. And Maurice disliked Bill Merkely almost as much as Justice did. "Come on, then," he said. "Hurry up."

Justice's expression brightened a little, the most anyone could ever scare out of him. He was in gray felt slippers, and he eagerly walked through the door ahead of Zellman. There were precautions overhead in the hall: big, glossy, mirrored half circles that housed hidden cameras. Justice looked up at them as they passed, and Zellman smiled to himself. There would be hell to pay later when the handcuff protocol breach was noticed. Dr. Jean Dayton, a mild-mannered little brown bird with a permanent scowl, would scream her pinched-tight ass off.

They walked along the hall together and, side by side, clambered up the utilitarian metal stairway that led to the ground level. At the top it was a short walk toward a set of gunmetal gray, locked double doors with small windows filled with wire netting—doors that led to the outside. They stood together just inside, looking through the windows, waiting while a white hospital van with the Ocean Park logo pulled under the portico beyond. Daylight was disappearing, the fading sun fingering stripes of dark gold along the grass that fanned out on the far side of the portico, night still an hour or so away.

As Zellman watched, the driver, an orderly from Ocean Park, jumped from the van. The man would be expecting Justice to be handcuffed, and with a faint feather of remorse touching his skin, Zellman turned to Justice and opened his mouth to . . . what? Ask him to be good?

Swift as lightning, Justice snatched Zellman's clipboard and pen away from him. The clipboard clattered to the floor, and while Zellman goggled in surprise, Justice jammed the pen deep into Zellman's throat and out again. Twice.

Blood spurted in a geyser.

"Wha? Wha? Wha?" Zellman burbled.

The door opened and the driver stepped in. Justice grabbed the man by his head and slammed it into the metal door. Once, twice, three times. More blood. Pints of it.

"Keys," Justice demanded.

"Van . . . van," the man mumbled, his eyes rolling around in his head.

And like that, Justice was gone.

Shoved aside and tossed to the floor like a rag doll, Zellman clutched at his throat helplessly, blood squeezing through his fingers. Shocked and outraged that Justice had lied. About the stomach pain. About needing to go to the hospital. About *every damned thing!*

And he, Dr. Maurice Zellman, a doctor of psychiatry, a member of Mensa, had believed him. Worse than the sting of pain at his throat, the bite of his own damned pen, was the knowledge that he, Dr. Maurice Zellman, had been wrong, after all.

# CHAPTER 2

*Ssssissssterrr...*
*Whore...!*
*With Satan's evil incubus growing inside you...!*

The voice rasped against Laura's brain again. She flinched and nearly stumbled as she thrust up the mental wall against him again on her way to surgery to check on Conrad's condition. But her worst fears were confirmed: it *was* Justice.

*And he knew she was pregnant??? How?*

The frisson that shivered down her spine was an old friend. She'd felt it before many times, but not since Justice Turnbull had been captured, convicted, and locked away. Not like this. Not with this harsh hammering into her thoughts.

Outside the doors to the surgical ward she glanced around, always a bit uncertain that someone else couldn't hear him as well, though she knew from experience she was the only one. She could block him from digging into her thoughts and feelings, but she could not prevent her own mental receptors from hearing him.

He was a devil. A scourge. A sickness that frightened them all. He was—

"Laura?" Her ex, Byron Adderley, broke into her thoughts, causing her to jerk as if goosed. "What's wrong with you?" he demanded instantly. Frowning, he stripped a pair of surgical gloves from his hands and tossed them into a trash receptacle. His eyebrows rose, as if he were waiting for her to answer.

*Like an obedient puppy,* she thought sourly.

He'd just come from surgery, she realized. Of course she would run into him. Of course. Murphy's Law. Pulling herself together, she ignored his question. "How's Conrad? Do you know?"

"Who? Oh. That security guard?" He shoved a thinning shock of coffee-dark hair from his eyes. "We drilled into his head to relieve the pressure in case of a subdural hematoma. Hope he has a brain left. Someone beat him half to death." He actually smiled, as if he'd said something clever. "That what you wanted to know?"

"I was just concerned."

His smile fell away and Byron gazed at her hard. "You like him?"

"I barely know him," she shot back. "I just want to make sure he's okay."

"Yeah, well. 'Okay' is maybe not the word for it." Byron yawned. He stretched his arms over his head in a move she remembered, one she'd once thought was sexy. No longer. "God, I gotta get some sleep," he admitted. "I was out late last night, and this morning came early."

Like she cared.

"What about Dr. Zellman?" Being a floor nurse, and not part of the surgical team, Laura was forced to get information secondhand.

"Jesus. He's lucky to be alive! That fuckin' psychotic stabbed Zellman, too. Got his voice box but good." Byron actually sounded a little concerned. "Could be, Zellman never speaks again."

"Oh, I hope you're wrong." She glanced past him toward the double doors that led into surgery. "That's what they're saying?" she asked.

He shrugged. "Too early to tell."

"The psychotic who did this . . . ?"

"No surprise there. You remember the one. Justice Turnbull." Byron shook his head, his unruly forelock falling forward again. "A whole new kind of crazy." He stifled another yawn. "Think Turnbull'll come back to his old stomping grounds and go after those cult freaks again?"

Laura went completely still. Tried not to look as if his remark had hit a nerve. "The sheriff's department will find him," she said with an effort.

"Oh, yeah." He barked out a laugh. "Count on them."

Ever the cynic.

Laura had heard enough. "I've gotta get back to work." She turned on her heel.

"Hey. Laura." She didn't so much as look over her shoulder and set her jaw. How had she ever found him attractive, and why the hell had she married him? Her thoughts strayed to the child growing within her, *his* child, the baby that Justice seemed to sense, and her insides went numb. "When are you going to stop dyeing your hair?" Byron called after.

She ground her teeth together, angry at him and herself for ever thinking they could build a life together. She'd known he wasn't her kind of man from the get-go, hadn't she? She'd suspected he was self-centered and narcissistic. How had she let him convince her to leave Portland for this stretch of coastline and Ocean Park Hospital, when she'd known it might not be safe? God, she'd been a fool to let him talk her into anything so idiotic. She hadn't wanted to move. She certainly hadn't wanted to relocate *here,* of all places. The house they'd rented together in Deception Bay, about six miles down Highway 101, until he'd moved out wasn't much to write home about, and the apartment he'd subsequently moved into was even less impressive, but that was just icing on the cake of her unhappiness.

*Why did you marry him?*

At a corner, she hazarded a quick glance over her shoulder, but Byron had already turned away. He couldn't really care less about the horrific events that had taken place at Halo Valley. If he wasn't the center of the universe, then the universe itself didn't matter.

*Because I wanted to believe someone loved me.*

And she'd been stupid enough to buy into his good looks, his easy charm, his success . . . what a fool she'd been and now . . . Automatically her hand strayed to her abdomen and the life beginning to pulse within her. She couldn't keep this baby. Byron's baby. She couldn't. Yet, it was a child . . . *her* child. . . .

Nurse Baransky, middle-aged, brusque, was coming down the hall toward her. "Are you checking on Mrs. Shields?" she asked.

"I'm on my way to her room now." Laura tried not to appear like she was hurrying, but inside she was running, running, *running*. From Byron, from her marriage, from the strangeness of her childhood, from Justice . . . *from the truth* . . .

"Were you at the ER?" Baransky asked.

"Just coming from outside surgery. No word yet on Conrad or Dr. Zellman."

Baransky nodded. "It was that madman who escaped, wasn't it? The one they captured in the shootout at the motel a few years back? Can't think of his name. Justin something?"

"Justice," Laura reminded carefully, the taste of his name on her tongue bitter, the sound of it striking a chord of terror that shuddered through her. *Sssiisssstterr.* His hiss echoed through her brain. Dear God.

"They were bringing him here for testing because he was complaining of stomach pain off and on, apparently."

"He was faking," Laura said automatically.

"They told you that?"

Laura nearly bit her tongue trying to take the words back and was instantly sorry that she'd blurted out something she didn't really want to discuss. "I'm just going on an assumption," she backtracked as a patient, a thick-in-the-middle woman with a wan expression, walked tentatively down the hall. Her plump fingers were clenched tight around the pole of a rolling IV stand.

"You need help?" Baransky said, and the woman offered the ghost of a smile as she shook her head, determined to walk on her own. "You said that Justice Turnbull was faking his illness?" Baransky asked, turning her attention back to Laura.

She didn't know how to answer that she knew Justice was faking. She sure as hell wouldn't be able to explain that Justice had started banging against her brain, something that had begun when she was young, though its strength had waxed and waned over the years, and had practically been nonexistent since he'd been incarcerated, had come back with a vengeance. That she still could manage to hold him out, but there was always a tiny iota of time before she could effectively throw up her mental wall, an infinitesimal moment where he left traces of his own thoughts, scraps that were available to her. So, yes, she knew he'd faked the stomach pain because, in effect, he'd told her as much. More like an overall realization than the needle-sharp words he sent to her.

And she also knew he'd been planning this escape a long time.

And she knew that he was hunting her now. . . .

*How does he know about the baby?*

"Laura?" Baransky suddenly demanded, eyeing her

closely. She had a big voice and little or no tolerance for anything she deemed to be nonsense.

Laura could tell her face had lost color. "I'm just overly tired. Didn't get good sleep last night."

"Maybe you should sit down. I can check on Mrs. Shields."

"No, no. I'm okay."

Laura forced out a smile as she walked past her. She was feeling nauseous, but it was less about the pregnancy and more about the realization that Justice Turnbull had escaped. When the events of his rampage had taken place a few years earlier, she'd kept the wall against his thoughts up solidly high. Before then, he'd never been seen as a serious threat to her and the others he'd targeted by either herself or her family. But then suddenly he was after them all! Threatening the very foundation of her family, her ancestors, anyone even remotely related to her, all those who lived at the huge lodge shielded from the world by massive iron gates. Her sisters.

*Sissterr* . . . How he'd given the word a horrid sound. Her flesh crawled as she remembered the sibilant sound of his voice, a hiss that grated, like talons running down a blackboard.

Justice was bent on destruction and chaos and killing, and though she hadn't been before, Laura, within the sterile hospital walls, sensed she was definitely in his sights now.

Mrs. Shields was sitting up in bed, her beady, dark eyes regarding Laura with avid curiosity as she walked into the room. She was in her fifties and had been through knee replacement surgery. "How many times do I have to push this button?" she demanded. "I need painkillers, Nurse Adderley. Where's your husband?"

"My ex-husband," Laura said for about the tenth time.

"I need more pain medication. I'm supposed to keep 'on top of the pain,' that's what I was told, to not be at a 'ten on the chart,' right?" She was referring to the pain manage-

ment chart that had been pinned to her wall, a row of smi-
ley faces where the smile disintegrated to a frown as the
level of pain increased. Zero was pain free; ten was excruciating, the face on the chart twisted in serious agony, a far
cry from Mrs. Shields's primarily ticked-off expression.
"Right now, I'm at about a level twenty!" she insisted and,
when Laura didn't respond quickly enough, added, "I need
*Dr.* Adderley . . . stat!"

"You're on the medication levels he prescribed," Laura
said calmly as she tried to take the woman's temperature.

"It's not enough!" Mrs. Sheilds said, around the thermometer.

Her voice had risen, and it brought Nurse Nina Perez to
the doorway. Nina, an attractive woman in her forties, was
Laura's immediate boss, and she was fiercely devoted to her
job. She also was fair and could assess a situation quickly.
"Everything all right in here?"

"No!" Mrs. Shields had been scheduled to leave earlier
in the day, but she was one of those rare patients who
wanted to stay in the hospital as long as possible. She was
an attention seeker who had bullied her husband for so long
that he seemed to have no identity and no ability to make
decisions.

"I need more painkillers," Mrs. Shields declared as
Laura removed the thermometer and noted a reading of
98.6. Perfectly normal. "And here. Fill this up." Mrs.
Shields thrust her water glass at Laura, who took it from
her hand. Laura's fingers brushed hers, and a tingle fled up
Laura's nerves to her brain.

*Pancreas.*

The word pulsed across her mind. Vivid. Red.

She nearly dropped the glass.

Laura knew, with certainty, that Mrs. Shields would
contract pancreatic cancer at some future point and that the
disease would ultimately lead to her death. Laura received
these messages from time to time when she touched an-

other human's flesh, and it was this odd ability that had first steered her toward a career in medicine. She couldn't tell anyone about it, just as she couldn't tell anyone about her private communication with Justice Turnbull, but she trusted it implicitly.

"Let me see," Nurse Perez said. She turned toward the woman's IV and examined the drip. Laura suspected that it was all an act for the bristling Mrs. Shields. The woman was being given the proper amount of medication.

Laura asked her casually, "Does cancer run in your family?"

"No. Why?" She was suspicious.

"I thought I saw it in your medical file." She poured water into the glass from a near empty pitcher on Mrs. Shields's tray near her bed, then noted how much fluid the patient was taking in.

The older woman harrumphed, then admitted, "My father had cancer of the pancreas. Killed him in his fifties."

Nina Perez gave Laura a searching look; it wasn't usual for the floor nurses to pore over their patients' medical history. The doctors ordered the protocol, and the nurses followed through.

Laura, offering a smile she didn't really feel, said, "With all the tests you've had for this surgery, I'm sure you've checked that, too."

"I'm not sure of anything!" Mrs. Shields declared. Her nostrils flared slightly, and there was a definite purse to her lips. "Tell your husband to check on that, too!"

*My ex,* Laura thought, but nodded on her way out. She was grateful to Nina Perez for not questioning her too closely, but now that she'd "heard" this information, she wanted to follow through. So thinking, she had to search out Byron, catching him coming out of the staff room. That boyish smile she'd once found charming curved his lips, and his eyes definitely sparked as he joked with one of the nurse's aides—a girl with round doe eyes, pert nose, and was probably just into her twenties. Her face was bright and flushed as she looked up at him with an adoration she didn't bother to hide.

Laura didn't know whether she was disgusted or amused.

Byron's latest woman—definitely not this girl—wasn't the kind to take his flirting with a forgiving attitude.

Spying his ex-wife out of the corner of his eye, Byron stopped short, as if caught in a nefarious act.

*Serves you right,* Laura thought as the clueless aide wandered away, gazing back at Byron longingly and even waving her fingers coquettishly before catching a glimpse of Laura, frowning slightly, then rounding the corner to disappear.

*A ninny,* Laura thought, but bit her tongue. Who cared? It was surprising to find that she didn't.

*But you're pregnant. With his child.*

Ignoring that persistent and irritating voice in her head, she said, "I was checking on Mrs. Shields. She told me her father died of pancreatic cancer in his fifties, about the age she is now."

"I know her history," he bit out, obviously irritated. "Why?"

"I don't know. I just thought maybe it was something to recheck."

"What? Why?" he demanded, affronted.

"Due diligence."

"So now *you're* the doctor?"

She wasn't going there, wasn't going to be drawn into a no-win discussion, and Byron's pager erupted, anyway, and he stormed off. Fortunately, in the direction of Mrs. Shields's room. Good. He could deal with her.

She walked the other direction but felt him glance over his shoulder and give her an assessing look. The way he always did when she became a puzzle, something he couldn't begin to understand. His ex-wife just wasn't a square peg that fit snugly into the square hole he'd wanted to force her into.

Not that it mattered any longer.

Laura pushed aside all thoughts of him and, for now, her unexpected pregnancy. For now, she concentrated on doing her job and keeping Justice, the monster, at bay.

Thankfully, the rest of her shift was uneventful, but as she was driving to her house, her senses were on high alert. She hoped to hell they'd caught Justice already, but she suspected that hope was unlikely. If he were captured, she believed he would blast out a raging message to her, and since that last sibilant *sssssisterrrr,* he'd been quiet.

The house she and Byron had rented was a two-bedroom with white trim and gray shingles. One bathroom. Built in the fifties, renovated in the seventies, left to disintegrate over time. She and Byron had bought a condo in downtown Portland, and then the housing market had tumbled and they'd sold for a small loss. It had soured Byron on real estate; he hated losing anything. So, they'd chosen this rental for its proximity to the hospital and signed a six-month lease, which had turned into month-to-month as time had marched on. Once Byron had moved out, Laura was grateful for the cheap rent, even if it did come with a leaky bathroom faucet.

Pulling up to the back porch, she cut the engine and climbed from her Subaru. Byron drove a black Porsche, but Laura had preferred her dark green Outback. The Porsche was leased and Byron's affair; Laura owned the Outback in her own name. Another blessing.

Hurrying past the rhododendrons long past blooming, she heard the rumble of the Pacific Ocean and smelled the thick, damp scent of the sea as she walked along the cement walk to her porch. The neighbor's black cat slid under the porch as she climbed the two steps and unlocked the back door.

Once inside the small kitchen, she snapped on the

lights, then dropped her purse and coat on the counter. Its chipped Formica had been scrubbed to a shine when Laura moved in, and she'd repainted all the interior cabinets, trim, and walls herself. Tired it might be, but it was bright and white.

And home.

Her sanctuary.

She'd thought that she might feel a bit of nostalgia, a loss, when Byron had moved out, but all she'd really experienced was relief, a quiet peace.

Until today.

When Justice had reached out to her and reminded her that she was different. Growing up at Siren Song had made her so. Now she was vulnerable . . . so very vulnerable. Sighing, she sat down in one of the two café chairs surrounding the small glass table, put her elbows against the surface, and buried her face in her hands.

The baby . . . a baby . . .

She should go to the lodge and talk to Aunt Catherine, tell her that Cassandra's prediction had come true. But Justice was out there. Loose. Waiting for someone to make a move. And she, being outside the gates, was the logical choice.

Oh, dear God.

She shuddered. She'd never told Byron about her past. She'd simply said she was estranged from her mother and she'd never known her father. She'd been in her second year of nursing at the hospital where he'd been a resident when they met, and he'd just become a full-fledged osteopath when they'd started dating. She'd been starry-eyed and too eager, and he'd been intrigued by her ability to understand, practically diagnose, underlying problems with his patients that had nothing to do with the broken bones he corrected. He called it her instinct, and they both let it be an understood, and basically untouched, thing between them. Now she knew it was what had set her apart from the other young nurses and medical staff that cast admiring glances in his direction. When he'd casually suggested marriage, she'd jumped at the chance. She'd ignored his selfish traits. She simply hadn't cared. She'd wanted the whole picture: the house with the picket fence, 2.5 children, a dog, and a husband. She'd suspected Byron wasn't as deep as she was. The fact that he hadn't been all that interested in her family had been one clue, but she'd thought it wouldn't matter if she was more in love than he.

On that, she'd been wrong.

So wrong.

He was not only shallow, but he was unfaithful. And uncaring. And unrepentant. He'd wanted her for his wife. He was intrigued with her "instinct," but he wasn't going to be monogamous for anyone. That was simply the way it was. She'd tried to accept the rules but been unable. She'd tried once to make believe they could work their way back together, and that was a complete failure, for which she now was pregnant.

With Byron's child. For so long she'd wanted a baby, hoped for a child, and now . . . oh, God, now she felt a fierce love for this baby but didn't kid herself that raising the child—Byron's child—alone would be easy.

She sat at the table a long time, finally got up and heated water in the microwave and, when the timer dinged, dipped a packet of decaf tea into the steaming cup. As the fragrant tea steeped, she turned on the television and caught breaking news.

Her heart nearly stopped.

The narrow face of Channel Seven's Pauline Kirby, her short, slick dark hair blowing a bit in the evening breeze, was reporting that Justice Turnbull, a known murderer, had escaped from Halo Valley Security Hospital. Two men had been critically injured. One was fighting for his life.

"Oh, dear God." Laura stared at the screen.

"A madman is loose," Pauline was saying, and Laura

recognized the redwood and stone facade of the mental hospital in the background, filmed earlier this evening, and shivered to her toes.

Her tea forgotten, she watched the rest of the short report while her heart drummed in her chest and her worst fears were confirmed.

She wished suddenly, mightily, that there was someone out there who could find Justice Turnbull, dig him out from under whatever rock he chose to hide, expose him, and make sure he was locked away so deep that he could never hurt her or the new life growing inside her, a life she was already bonding with.

# CHAPTER 3

It had been a less than interesting day for Harrison Frost, but then they all were since he'd been fired, let go, canned, kicked in the ass, and ordered ten million miles away from the *Portland Ledger* and his old job. One day he was a respected investigative reporter; the next he was dog meat. All because he'd tweaked a few tails that didn't want to be tweaked. And he would do it again. His brother-in-law's death was a homicide no matter how many people wanted to shriek otherwise, and at some point he was going to prove that fact.

But tonight . . . tonight he was following another story, one with less drama but one that was a fascinating character study nonetheless. He was sitting at an outdoor café table, scrunched down in a half-lounging manner by design, staring across Broadway—Seaside, Oregon's main drag—toward a waffle cone stand as this surprisingly soft June day faded into night. His right arm was hanging loose, his fingers touching the fur of his sister's fuzzy mutt, Chico. He'd be lucky if the mean little bastard didn't turn around and bite him. The beast seemed to have an aversion to men of all kinds, but the dog sure as hell liked the girls, and that was exactly the reason Harrison had deigned to take him out. Harrison was on a story that involved teenagers, and he didn't want the young girls to think he was some creepy guy, so he kept Chico around to make him seem more approachable.

Now the dog growled low in its throat, so Harrison carefully removed his hand. No need to risk injury for the sake of his costuming. Chico had snapped at him enough times for him to respect the little bastard's space. Jesus. The only thing good about this assignment was it didn't require much in the way of self-realization and reflection. He could just move forward and forget—or at least put aside—the events that had led him here. It was a job. It didn't require anything from him but to be in the present.

Harrison glanced at his watch. It was 9:00 p.m. The girl Harrison currently had under surveillance was a sixteen-year-old thief with a bad attitude, a habit of chewing gum with her mouth open, and an enormous sense of entitlement. She and her girlfriends and a few guy friends appeared to have banded together and started stealing items from the more affluent families in their neighborhoods or schools. Not that they weren't affluent themselves. It was a lark, an exercise, a way to kill time. They were giddy and drunk with power and their own secrets. They were zigzagging toward something worse: home invasion. It would take only one time for a home owner to catch them in the act and the situation would turn from burglary to something far worse. The Seaside police weren't really aware of the crimes yet, as the victims had been unilaterally silent. Maybe they thought their own kids were involved? Maybe they even were. The bottom line was these kids weren't on anyone's radar but his, and Harrison had stumbled on the story rather than sought it out.

He'd moved from Portland to the coast, following his sister, Kirsten, and her daughter, Delilah, whom everyone called Didi, after Kirsten's husband, Manuel Rojas, was gunned down. Harrison hadn't meant to move with his sister. He'd intended to stay hot on the story and expose Manny's murderers for the brutal killers they were. But that hadn't happened; and when Kirsten, sad and broken, quietly asked if he'd come with her, he'd reluctantly done as she suggested; and now, over a year later, he'd just moved from her little bungalow into his own apartment, which was full of unopened boxes, a blow-up double mattress and sleeping bag, and a couple of camping chairs that could fold up into a sling for easy packing. Each sported a black, plastic cup-holder space in the chair's right arm. He'd set many a beer in that spot and nursed it on the front porch of his sister's place and now on the miniature side deck of his own.

His sister's husband, Manny, had been killed in a senseless shooting rampage when a kid opened fire on a group of people waiting to get into a nightclub before turning the gun on himself. Manny was in that line, trying to stop an argument that had arisen between two men over an anorexically slim blond woman who was smoking a cigarette nearby. Then the kid suddenly pulled out a .38 and sprayed several rounds into a madly fleeing crowd. Manny and one of the men were killed instantly, the other man and a woman and her boyfriend were critically injured and later died in the hospital, and the twenty-year-old shooter, who was underage and had never been allowed into the nightclub, turned the gun on himself and pulled the trigger. He was later found to be an unemployed high school dropout who was also a pharmacological repository. He was filled with enough meds to knock out an elephant. The anorexic blond woman was unhurt and had simply sauntered off. She was only known to exist because of the security cameras.

It was ruled a terrible tragedy. The blame rested entirely on the extremely high and screwed-up kid, who'd been dabbling in drugs since anyone could remember. But he'd never shown suicidal or murderous tendencies. He'd never shown aggression. When Harrison got a look at the security tape of the shooting, he saw the kid had pulled out the weapon and shot Manny point-blank. Then he seemed to wake up and realize what he'd done, and he just sprayed gunfire from left to right and took out whoever was in his arc of fire before he killed himself.

Manny's partner in the nightspot, Bill Koontz, obtained full ownership of the place, while Kirsten received a small insurance stipend.

Then Harrison got an anonymous tip from a cool female voice that suggested maybe the drugged-up shooter was somehow connected to the business partner.

The blond woman? Maybe. Or maybe someone else. But as soon as Harrison started writing pieces that contained more questions and conjecture about Bill Koontz than cold, hard facts, he was shown the door of the *Ledger*.

Which was just plain odd. A journalist was supposed to expose the truth, right? Even if it pointed to Koontz?

These thoughts passed across his mind in half an instant. Yeah, maybe he'd screwed up. His sense of impartiality certainly had taken a beating after Manny's death. He'd liked his brother-in-law, a darkly handsome man with flashing white teeth and a deep belly laugh who'd won his sister in less than thirty minutes upon one meeting over shared drinks. He had wanted to find the conspiracy behind Manny's death and had rashly chased imaginary leads and listened to gossip and conjecture and reported it as fact.

He'd really pissed off Koontz, who had friends in high places. For that he wasn't sorry.

And since that time he'd been forced from his job— well, technically he'd quit when they'd given him the "retract-or-you're-fired" speech—he had steered clear of conspiracies, major news stories, and anything that remotely resembled real investigative reporting, until this teenage thievery ring fell into his lap. Was the fact that he was interested in this story progress? Was he ready to give up the bullshit small stories he'd been delivering to the *Seaside Breeze* and make a run at the big time again? Maybe even try to dig into Manuel Rojas's death a little deeper again? On his own time, of course, and without involving the *Breeze* or anyone else? He had friends in high and low places himself, regardless of how he'd been treated in Portland. He sensed that if he were to ever step forward into the larger arena, he would be welcomed by some, reviled by others.

But did he really even give a damn? He hadn't for over a year. Yet . . . there was an itch beneath his skin he couldn't completely deny.

He shifted his weight and Chico growled again.

"Oh, shut up," Harrison muttered without heat, an order that Chico utterly ignored, as the growling continued on as if he'd been encouraged.

Night had fallen completely, and the shops along Broadway were decked out in bright white lights, giving it a carnival feel. Harrison glanced to his left, to the overhang of the coffee shop/gelato bar/gift shop, where his "quarry" was leaning forward and conversing rapidly with the girl behind the counter. Without looking, he could describe them both in detail: slim, dark-haired, practically nonexistent hips, expensive jeans or cutoffs for weather like today's, flip-flops, smirky smiles, eyes that exchanged glances with their friends as they made unspoken comments about the rest of the world. The one behind the counter had her hair scraped into a ponytail; the one leaning over the counter was wearing impossibly short cutoffs, so ragged they looked like they might disintegrate. Her hair was tucked behind her ears, and Harrison could see an earring that glimmered as she tossed her head. Diamonds? Fakes? Hers, or something she stole . . .

Harrison had followed the news and been aware of some unconnected robberies, though it was nothing that initially blipped on his radar. But then, one night while he and Chico were on a walk along the beach neither of them wanted to take, he overheard a girl—the one he was surveilling tonight—talking about hitting the Berman mansion with a group of friends. He'd noted the girl and her friends by habit and watched them get to their feet from the stone bench where they'd been sitting and amble toward Seaside's main drag, where bumper cars and stands that sold elephant ears stood cheek by jowl with trendy clothing stores, art galleries, and wine shops. The girl he was watching walked up to the counter of the hip gelato/coffee/gift shop and talked in whispers to a girl behind the counter whose eyes narrowed and mouth tightened into a cold, hard smile of relish.

Two days later the Bermans were robbed, the thieves taking money, jewelry, and expensive handbags.

And Harrison had thought, *Huh*.

The last couple of days he'd made a point of waiting outside the coffee and gelato store with Chico, passing time, his mind traveling of its own accord to Manny and the reasons behind his death. He'd gotten in trouble for suggesting his brother-in-law's death was more than a random killing, that Koontz, Manuel's business partner, one of those terminally charismatic salesmen who showed you a smile, a handshake, and not much else, was involved in some way. Both Koontz and Manny had known the boy with the gun as someone who'd tried to sneak into their high-end club with its lowbrow name, Boozehound, by showing fake ID more than once.

Something was just off with the whole scenario, but Harrison had been warned off, and so here he was, waiting and watching as life continued on.

And now he was experiencing a low-level excitement because this case intrigued him, the first since his brother-in-law's death. He had considered going to the police but had dismissed it. He hadn't really heard anything of substance and was playing a hunch. He'd been burned badly enough trying to ferret out the truth in Manny's death, hadn't he?

The girl with the glittery earring started to stroll by him.

He yanked on the leash a bit, and Chico, on cue, resisted, pulling away from him just as the girl tried to pass. The leash tangled in her legs and she started to fall.

"Hey!" she cried. "What the fu—?"

Harrison, on his feet in an instant, reached out and caught her arm, keeping her from actually hitting the sidewalk. "Sorry."

"Let go of me!" She managed to unwind the leash from her legs and yanked her arm away from him. "Jesus, can't you control your damned dog!"

"Usually, but he does have a mind of his own."

She rolled her eyes as if she was bored out of her mind with his explanation, then reached down and rubbed her bare leg where the leash had bit into her flesh. A thin red welt was developing.

"You okay?" he asked.

"No!" she said angrily, then straightened to narrow her eyes at him.

"Do you need a doctor?"

"What? No!" Then, some of her anger having dissipated, she added, "I'll live."

"Good." He turned his attention to the dog. "Chico! Here, boy!" Knowing she was still watching him, he picked up the dog and tucked him under his arm. Chico's eyes glittered in pure hatred, as if he realized that he'd been used as a pawn in some subtle game, but he didn't growl or snap.

"Cute dog," she admitted, giving him a long look.

"I guess." He ruffled the fur on the back of Chico's head.

"No, I mean it." She seemed to have lost most of her quick-fire fury. Which was good. This was the first time they'd made actual contact. "His name is Chico?"

"Yeah." Nodding, he said, "To tell you the truth, he doesn't like me much."

"Yeah, why?" she asked. "You beat him?"

"No. Not that he doesn't deserve it. Dogs, these days," he teased. "You feed them, love them, give 'em an education. Buy 'em a car when they turn sixteen, and whad'd'ya get? Grief."

She couldn't stop her sudden smile, even if she thought he was corny. Harrison half smiled back, aware he'd sunk the hook. He knew how to be engaging, although he rarely tried hard at it and basically used the skill only when he was working. The rest of the time he was, by his own admission, a loner. He didn't trust many people. Most, he'd found, lied.

And he couldn't stand liars.

"He's actually my sister's dog," Harrison said as he set Chico on the sidewalk again. "I take him for walks, but he really just tolerates me."

"Can I pet him?"

"Sure. Go ahead. He won't bite you . . . much."

She leaned in closer, hesitated, saw he was teasing, then reached forward. Harrison let Chico, who was busting at his leash and wagging his tail, get his furry head beneath her hand, sniffing and licking and wiggling all over. The little traitor.

At the same time Harrison leaned back in his chair, keeping a large distance between himself and the girl; he didn't want to scare her off. He was wearing jeans, sneakers, a black T-shirt with a worn plaid cotton shirt as a kind of jacket, the tails hanging out. His dark hair was longer than usual, brushing his collar, and purposely a bit shaggy. He was clean-shaven, and he'd taken off his sunglasses as the sun started setting. He hoped he was unthreatening. He wanted information.

"I've seen you here," she said. "You don't have a job?"

"I got this dog-walking gig."

"How do you make money?" she asked, ignoring that. Uninvited, she perched on the chair opposite him. Suddenly, it seemed, she was curious. Or just didn't have a place to go.

"I don't make much," he admitted. "How about yourself? You got a part-time job of some kind? You look like you're in high school."

"How old do you think I am?" She tilted her head and smiled, striking a sexy pose. Almost flirty. Her anger with him long forgotten.

"Eighteen?" He figured she was sixteen, seventeen maybe.

"Fifteen going on thirty," she answered smugly. "Or, so my stepdad says."

There were rules to interrogating teenagers, Harrison had learned. Unspoken rules. Rule #1 was pretend you want to talk only about yourself and watch what happened. "I used to work in Portland for a corporation," he said. "I was a cubicle guy. Go to work at eight. Off at five. Go home, have a drink. Watch the news. Eat dinner. Go to bed."

"God, I'd kill myself," she said.

"Got me a paycheck."

"Sounds mega-boring."

"It was." Okay, he'd never been a cubicle guy. He could lie when he was working, but not when it counted. When it counted, when it involved people he cared about, then the truth was all that mattered. There was no other option.

She tilted her head and looked at him from beneath deeply mascaraed lashes. "I go to school at West Coast High. You know it?"

Give a little information, ignore them, and *bam*. They couldn't stop talking about themselves. "The one they built after that upper-end housing development went in?"

"With the rich kids? Yeah. Only some of 'em aren't as rich

anymore. Their dads lost their jobs." She shrugged. "Too bad."

"What about your dad?"

"Stepdad," she corrected. "He still has his job. But my dad lost his. He got fired."

"Layoffs." Harrison made a face.

"Nope. He got involved with Britt's mom, and he used to work for Britt's dad, so that was no good."

"Sounds like drama."

"Shit, yeah. He can have them all," she said with sudden fury. "Britt's a bitch."

Harrison wondered if Britt was Britt Berman.

Chico whined, stood on his back legs, and dug at the girl's knees, craving more attention. She scratched his ears, then pulled back and brushed off her fingers. "Gross. Dog skin." She looked at her nails. "I do have a job . . . sort of . . ." A smile snuck across her lips. A sneaky little I'd-love-to-let-you-know-just-how-clever-I-am grin. "We kind of formed our own company, and it's not boring at all." She bit her lower lip, really trying hard not to tell him and yet unable to stop.

"A company," he repeated with a hint of skepticism.

She rose to the bait like a breaching whale. "Yeah, a company. Like we work together. We're an *alliance*."

*Alliance* came out sounding like she was tasting the word. It clearly wasn't one she was comfortable with. Something she probably heard watching a reality show. If she hadn't been able to see, he would've dug in his cargo pants pocket for his phone and started recording her. But her angle of sight would allow her to see him switching on the phone, so he had to wait.

"Who's 'we'? You and your family?"

"God, no." She threw him a dark look. "My stepdad is a butthead asshole. Worse than my dad. I'm talking about my friends and me." She glanced around, as if expecting some of those friends to appear.

"High school kids?"

"You ask a lot of questions," she declared, pushing away from the table. "You don't know what we can do."

Just then his phone started vibrating against his leg. He ignored it, but very few people had his number. His sister. His managing editor at the *Portland Ledger*. His new editor at the *Seaside Breeze*. He knew he should give it out more often, but he'd been in a kind of self-imposed exile.

"Okay, you got me there," he said. "I don't know what you can do."

She took it as a challenge. "There's a bunch of us who . . . get together . . . and do stuff." Her eyes sparkled as brightly as the neon lights winking in the town; she was proud of herself and excited, a sly smile teasing the corners of her mouth.

"You and your fifteen-year-old friends."

"Yeah. Well, and some older ones, too. Like Envy."

"Envy?" Harrison repeated.

"You know what envy means?"

"Got a pretty good idea."

"It's his initials. Get it? N. V. He says it's a deadly sin."

"Okay," Harrison said. His phone silently buzzed again.

"There are seven deadly sins."

"Mm-hmm. Like in the movie *Seven*."

"You know that one?" she asked in surprise. "It's really old."

"Morgan Freeman. Brad Pitt. Gwyneth Paltrow." *Really old,* Harrison thought with an inner snort, his hand easing toward his phone. But then this kid would have been barely a thought when it was released in the midnineties.

"We're not weird, or anything, like in the movie."

"You just do stuff."

"The seven of us," she said. "Guess which one I am."

"Well, what are your initials? If that's how it works."

"That isn't just how it works."

"So, okay, you don't look like gluttony. I don't really see you as wrath. Pride, maybe? Lust?"

Her own cell phone chirped and as if suddenly realizing she'd said too much to a perfect stranger, she jumped to her feet. She glanced around her shoulder again, looking like she wanted to take off and run, then glanced at a text message on the screen of the phone.

"I can't remember the other ones," he mused, but she suddenly racewalked across the street, as if she couldn't get away from him fast enough.

As soon as she was out of sight, Harrison dug for his phone. He grabbed it just as it finished vibrating. "Hello? Hello? Damn."

Glancing at the number, he didn't recognize it, but when he called it back, it rang only once before a woman's voice asked cautiously, "Frost?"

"Who's this?"

"Geena Cho."

"Geena?" Harrison's surprise was tinged with caution as well. Geena worked in dispatch for the Tillamook County Sheriff's Department. He'd met her when she was off work at a local dive, Davy Jones's Locker, and they'd hit it off, but Harrison was leery of getting involved right away. Every relationship he'd had with a woman flamed too hot before he ever got to know her. Then, as time revealed each other's foibles, baggage, and basic craziness, the heat was squelched fast. When Geena said she worked for the sheriff's department, it was enough to cool Harrison's blood even further. He'd kept her in the "friend" box with an effort, as Geena was angling for something more. She was one of the few he'd given his cell number.

"We got an escapee from Halo Valley," she said quietly, and he realized she was talking on her cell and giving him information the sheriff's department might not want to release just yet. "He injured two men, who were taken to Ocean Park. Half the department's at Halo Valley."

"Who's the escapee?" He was already on his feet, yanking a reluctant Chico from sniffing a newcomer, a fluffy white bichon who wanted to play. Chico just wanted to hump the female dog, which was embarrassing to the bichon's owner, so Harrison, needing the whole circus to end, dragged the reluctant Chico away.

"That guy from a few years ago who terrorized the cult."

Harrison remembered the story but not the man's name. "You got a name?"

"Hey, not yet," she said, suddenly reticent, as if she was already second-guessing her decision to call. He couldn't push her too far.

"So," Harrison prodded, "this unnamed assailant . . ." *And legendary wacko.* One he could track down on the Internet as soon as he got to a computer. His current cell didn't have those capabilities. "He attacked the two men at Halo Valley while he was trying to get away?"

"That's what it sounds like. I can't talk long. They all took out of here a couple hours ago, lights on, sirens screaming. Everybody thinks the psycho's coming our way."

"Who are the victims?"

"Hospital employees. That's all I know."

Probably another way of hedging.

"Okay."

"Gotta go," she said, almost as if she regretted her rash call. Then, not subtly, added, "Remember. We have a standing deal. I'm an 'unnamed source in the police department.'"

"That's right," he said, though he was certain if anyone really wanted to know, Geena's cell phone records would be a dead giveaway.

"Harrison?"

"Yeah?"

"You owe me."

That much he knew. "Thanks, Geena."

He wasn't really sure what to do with the information.

His job description, loose as it was, wasn't about deep investigative journalism for the *Breeze*. Not that they wouldn't run the story about this guy. A psycho escaping a mental hospital was big news, especially this psycho, who'd terrorized the area once before.

And Harrison had been given a jump on the competition.

*At what price?* his skeptical mind nagged. *Remember, payback's a bitch.*

Shoving his phone into his pocket, he ignored the questions, snatched up Chico, who nipped at his wrist, then headed swiftly back to his dusty brown Chevy Impala as a couple riding a tandem bike whizzed past and the smells of caramel corn and grilled hot dogs reached his nostrils.

His stomach rumbled, but he ignored it.

As he reached his low-profile, decade-old Chevy, he was nearly run over by a kid on a skateboard. The skateboarder screeched around a corner and jumped a bench as Harrison dropped Chico into his little car seat. The dog turned around and bared his teeth as Harrison climbed into the vehicle. Harrison bared his own teeth right back, and Chico curled his lip and emitted a *grrrr* that would only scare another dog of the same small size on a good day.

Checking the dashboard clock, Harrison figured it would be just over thirty minutes before he could drive south, drop off the mutt, and make it to Ocean Park Hospital. He didn't feel like fighting for attention at Halo Valley mental hospital with the sheriff's department all over the place—especially Deputy Fred Clausen, whom Harrison had already managed to get on the wrong side of—but Ocean Park, where the victims had been taken, would be a better bet. He could probably get some interviews there.

His teenaged Deadly Sinners were being allowed a momentary reprieve while he tackled a different kind of story. He liked that. The Deadly Sinners. Made for good copy, and it sounded like the kind of thing the group—or this

N.V. guy—had dreamed up, probably from watching *Seven*. Didn't anybody have any new ideas anymore?

But Harrison's mind was already switching off the thieves to the more immediate story. "What's his name?" he said aloud, trying to recall as much as he knew about the strange man whose obsessions had sent him on a killing spree in the area of Deception Bay, a usually sleepy little seaside town, where his sister and niece now lived. Had the guy escaped Halo Valley just to be free? Or, did he have some new sick plan in place?

Psychos were like that. They didn't just give it up as a rule.

Chico glared at him, and his little black lips quivered into a snarl.

"You're not as cute as you think you are," Harrison warned.

That earned him a series of full-fledged barks and bristling fury.

Ten minutes later, Harrison dropped off Chico with relief, shaking his head at the way the little fur ball leapt into Kirsten's arms and licked at her with wild love, his tail wagging, whole body squirming.

She was standing in the front door of her cottage, the smells of baking bread wafting outside to mingle with the salty scent of the sea. Seeing Harrison's expression, his sister said on a sigh, "I don't know what you have against Chico."

"Who says I have anything against him?"

She stared him down, and he gazed back at her with affection. She stood three inches shorter than he, with the same tousled brown hair, the same hazel eyes, the same lean body. She wore jeans and a dark blue T-shirt, and her feet were bare. Chico wriggled from her arms and ran into the house, probably in search of Didi, Kirsten's daughter, who, by all accounts, should be in bed by now, even though the sun hadn't quite set.

"It's the other way around," he assured Kirsten. "I love the dog."

She snorted as she closed the door. "Yeah."

"Really."

But he was talking to himself as he climbed back in the Impala. There was no accounting for what went on inside Chico's twisted little doggy brain, he decided, as he turned the car south toward Ocean Park Hospital. Kirsten's bungalow was on the north end of Deception Bay. The town sat on a bluff above the beach, spilling over onto both sides of Highway 101, and was about twenty minutes from the hospital.

Twisted little doggy brain. Twisted psycho-killer brain.

He would bet that Halo Valley Security Hospital's escapee was heading back toward his old haunts to pick up where he left off. That was how it was with a twisted psycho-killer brain. Almost instinctive, along the lines of demented decision making.

"What's your name?" he asked aloud, into the deepening shadows.

*And where the hell are you?*

# CHAPTER 4

The Vanagon had seen better days, Justice thought, eye-ing the vehicle as it limped to the side of the road. From his vantage point on the bluff, he had a bird's-eye view of the narrow lanes snaking below.

Volkswagen had stopped making them sometime in the '90s or early 2000s, a more modern rendition of the Volks-wagen bus, but they, too, had disappeared from the show-rooms, replaced by Touaregs and Jettas and Passats and others. In his younger years Justice Turnbull had been in-terested in all makes of cars. It had been a passion. But that was before his mission was revealed and he talked to God, who asked him—*ordered* him—to annihilate the armies of Satan, armies being incubated in the wombs of the whores who'd been spit from the depths of hell and who pretended their innocence. Whores. Every one. Satan's profligates.

They were locked inside a prison of their own making, one they believed was a sanctuary. Fools! Sick-minded, stench-riddled fools. Siren Song. With its wrought-iron fencing and gates. It could be breached. It could. It was only a matter of planning. And timing. He smiled to him-self as he thought of those inside and what he would do to them. Theirs, each and every one, would be a slow, torturous death. Each of the witches would learn what it meant to turn on him; they would feel his pain. . . . They would burn. . . .

In time.

One at a time.

His nostrils flared, and he felt a little curdle of recognition that things weren't as they should be. Not all of them were "safe" inside the walls surrounding Siren Song. Despite Catherine's vain attempts at locking them away, a few of the more stubborn and curious ones had escaped. They, women who straddled two worlds and elected to stay outside, would have to be taken care of first, before the onslaught he would wreak on their filthy prison, where they huddled, feeling smug and secure. Oh, how wrong they were.

Killing them all would be simple.

*Like shooting fish in a barrel.*

Who had said that? Old Mad Maddie herself. His upper lip trembled at a blurry memory that wouldn't quite come into focus as he thought of her. Palm reader? Visionary? *Fraud!*

Eyes narrowing, he decided that the Vanagon wasn't going anywhere soon. It seemed disabled, a flat tire, at the very least. Was this his sign from God? Was this his path?

He scented the air, his nostrils quivering. Their odor was like a pulse that he alone could smell. It came to him in waves, the scent of rotting meat. He felt almost faint with his last intake of breath; then he opened his eyes and gazed at the lights of the marooned Vanagon again.

Time to go.

As daylight waned, he moved carefully, near silently, down the hillside and through the gnarled pines and berry vines rooted in the soil. His mind settled upon the filthy witches he'd been asked to annihilate. He'd almost lost track of them during his incarceration because he'd been drugged and held inside a windowless tomb. And the concrete walls had made it difficult for him to track them. He couldn't see them. He couldn't even *smell* them at first.

Now, though . . .

They were easiest to smell when they were pregnant, and he'd caught the scent of those who'd lain with the devil and carried Lucifer's spawn within their wombs several times in spite of the hole they'd tried to throw him into.

But they couldn't contain him forever. He was sent to do God's bidding. And God wanted the devil's issue burned in the fires of hell. This was Justice's mission.

In a dream, a vision of sorts that had occurred while he was in the hospital, he'd seen himself faking an illness in order to escape the prison walls. It had come to him late at night, awakening him with a start, the remembered odor lingering in his nostrils. He didn't doubt that it was the word of God for a second and had followed the instructions he'd heard during a fragmented sequence of vignettes, images of exactly how he was to escape from the moment he'd arisen. His body had been covered in sweat, as if he'd actually done the deeds within the dream, and he never faltered.

It had almost been too easy. Dr. Zellman, that pompous idiot, had wanted to believe he understood him and the inner workings of his mind.

But Zellman had never suspected Justice's innate intelligence. Nor had Zellman, the egomaniac, understood Justice's intellect, his ability to read the doctor's motivations. More telling, Zellman hadn't counted on Justice's raw animal instincts, his prowess as a predator, his keen awareness of how to lure in his prey before viscerally attacking.

Justice, knowing Zellman's weaknesses, had pretended, and the idiot with his esteemed degree had bought it.

One less obstacle to worry about.

Now Justice approached the Vanagon quietly, ever watchful. Its owners apparently liked the psychedelic lifestyle most often associated with the Volkswagen bus and the '60s, as its sides were embellished with hand-painted peace signs, rainbows, and images of girls with long hair that turned into vines and became twigs for doves to roost upon. Justice had once had a small replica of a VW bus in his toy car collection, but it had not sported the artistic detail this vehicle did. The Vanagon's colors had faded over time, but it still flaunted its homage to the hippie culture.

As Justice appeared from the scrub pines at the side of the road, a long-haired dude with a headband and John Lennon glasses straightened from his perusal of the left rear tire.

"Hey, man," he drawled in greeting. The van was parked in a small turnoff, and there wasn't a lot of room for maneuvering unless you wanted to get a wheel in the ditch. The guy himself was smoking a joint and seemed to be considering his bald, deflated tire. He held out the joint to Justice, who simply said, "Marijuana."

"Yeah. Weed, man. Good stuff."

"No, thank you." The sickeningly sweet herb stench clouded Justice's sense of smell.

"Jesus, damn," the guy said, gesturing in the direction of Justice's prison and squinting behind his glasses as he let out a puff of smoke. "Did you see? The whole damn county sheriff's department went flying by thataway!" He hitched a thumb and shook his head. "Not one stopped, y'know." Then, as if considering the consequences if a cop had stopped and found his weed, he added, "Maybe that was a good thing." He took another long drag.

"Which way are you going?" Justice asked, talk of police making him anxious.

The dude pointed the opposite direction, west, toward the coast, and after a few seconds exhaled a pent-up cloud of smoke. "Where'd you come from?" he rasped.

Justice gestured in the general direction of the steep hill to the north. It was flat-topped, a mesa, basically, since clear-cutting had taken off its timbered top. He'd driven the hospital van up a muddy track along its eastern side, over sticks and small boulders. He'd nosed the van through a forgotten chain gate that had been there since the beginning of the decade and broke with little resistance as he'd gunned the engine. He knew the area and had planned where to go when he escaped, and so he'd driven straight to the hilltop and then partially down the back side, parking the hospital van on the edge of a cliff side. Climbing out, he'd grabbed the jacket the orderly had left, with its Ocean Park Hospital patch on the sleeve; then he put the vehicle in neutral, got behind it, and pushed.

The van had shot straight down into a gully, snapping off small trees on its way, crashing and blundering, splashing into a small stream at its bottom and turning onto its side. It made a horrendous amount of screeching noise— tree limbs grabbing at it—but it had made it all the way down and the whole noisy melee was over in the space of two minutes. Wary, ears straining, Justice had waited at the top of the mesa, squatting in the underbrush, hoping the van's noisy crash was a distant rending for anyone within earshot. He'd then seen the line of police vehicles fly by far below, lights flashing in the early darkness, sirens screaming. He'd watched them disappear, and he'd sat down on the top of the mesa and waited, unsure of what form God's next message might be.

Then, as if God Himself had answered, this psychedelic relic of a Vanagon had staggered to the side of the road. Without doubting for an instant that this was his destiny, Justice had trekked rapidly down.

"Can I get a ride?" Justice asked, trying not to cough at the vile smoke, a sense of urgency running through him. He couldn't leave himself exposed, not for any length of time, even though darkness was approaching.

"Can ya help me fix my tire?" the dude asked hopefully.

"Gotta pump?"

"Yeah, but there's a hole, man."

"Got a spare?"

"Nah . . . not one that works . . ."

"Get me the pump," Justice ordered. He heard the sound of a car's engine whining closer and fought the urge to scramble back into the bushes.

"Uh, okay." The guy looked him over again, and then, as if deciding Justice was just a little tightly wound, he shrugged and opened the rear of the van, rattling around through a bunch of baby gear—a Big Wheels, a Pak 'n Play, some kind of circular bouncing device with brightly colored knobs—until he found a toolbox and the pump.

The car's engine was louder, and Justice, pretending to be looking over the axle, hid on the far side just as the car, a rattling old Toyota, cruised past. He caught a glimpse of the driver, a red-haired teenager, a girl, who didn't so much as glance at the disabled Vanagon as she drove lead-footed toward the next town.

"I'm Cosmo," the dude said, as if he'd just realized he'd never introduced himself. He dropped the toolbox at Justice's feet. "You?"

"Bob."

Cosmo frowned. "Your name tag says . . ."

"Yeah, I know." Justice waved off the question and bent down to the box. If the guy got too suspicious, he'd have to take a hammer from the box and . . . His fingers curled over the smooth wood handle as he explained, "Had to borrow my buddy's today. Left mine in my car. Sometimes I'm a damned fool!"

"Well, Bob, if you can fix this thing, I'll take you anywhere you wanna go," Cosmo declared with an easy smile that showed a row of slightly crooked teeth. If he had any doubts about "Bob," they were lost in a fog of pot.

"You got any gum?" Justice asked, trying not to show his anxiety as he pushed the hammer aside and studied the rest of the contents of the box. Wrench, screwdriver, box cutter . . . all weapons he could use.

"Uh . . ." Cosmo ran his hands through a few pockets and pulled out a pack. "Bubble gum."

"I can pump the tire full of air, put some gum on the leak." Justice palmed the box cutter with its razor's head and stealthily slipped it into his pocket before he straightened again, his shadow lengthening over Cosmo. "Good for a few miles, I think. But you'll have to get it fixed in Tillamook."

"I can do that." Cosmo was nodding, a little more comfortable. "Sure you don't wanna toke? Or a beer? They're not cold. I had to leave my woman and the kids for a while. Big fight. Big, big fight. Got any kids? Babies." He shook his head, long tresses beneath his headband shivering. "All they do is cry."

Justice thought of babies. Of pregnancy. Of the unborns. But he didn't respond as he bent down and pumped up the tire while Cosmo finished his joint, then chewed up some gum.

All the while he thought of time ticking by, the cops. . . . Oh, God, had they reached the hospital and now were returning? His stomach tightened, and he told himself to relax, try to stay cool.

Gingerly taking the slick pink wad from the other man's fingers, Justice had discerned where the nail was and he stuck the gum over it in a thin and messy line. Might help. Might not. All he wanted was to get off this stretch of road and fast. Before the cops returned.

"Nice, man," Cosmo said, grinning widely as he surveyed the near-bald tire with its pink patch.

Justice knew cars. Engines. Boats. He knew about babies, too. The devil's spawn. His nose suddenly filled with the sweet, rotting scent of betrayal and deceit, a smell that was only growing stronger. One of them was nearby. The one that could hear him and shut him out! They all were cursed with some ability, and this one . . . she was close.

His skin crawled and the back of his mind went dry as he tried to call up her image. . . .

He snapped back quickly.

*Hurry! You're wasting time!*

Cosmo was saying, "My old lady, she got really pissed at me 'cause I said, 'Can't you shut him up?' which was kinda mean, for sure, but she just went nutso. Threw all my clothes out the door. So I took the van and all this kid stuff and just fuckin' took off. I love her, man. And the kids. But it was a bummer. You a hospital employee?"

The patch on the jacket again. Damn. Justice gave a quick nod. "I'm an EMT."

"Yeah? Like the guy whose jacket you're wearing? Huh."

Justice tensed up. Cosmo was putting two and two together. "Yeah, we work for the same company."

"So . . . what're you doin' out here?"

"Hitchhiking. Got my own problems with a woman," he improvised again, hoping to strike a chord with the man.

"Ahh . . ." He seemed to try and think that one over, but Cosmo wasn't really tracking all that well.

Justice glanced at the tire. "Won't last long."

"But long enough to get to Tillamook?"

"Depends on how fast the leak is."

"Well, get in, man," Cosmo said suddenly, as if he'd told himself not to look a gift horse in the mouth—another one of Maddie's old sayings. God, why was *she* coming to mind today? Cosmo threw the toolbox in the back of the Vanagon and slammed the door. "We're losin' daylight. Let's roll." He walked to the front of the Volkswagen and slid behind the steering wheel.

As Justice climbed into the passenger seat and cracked the window against the thick scent of marijuana, Cosmo fired up the engine of this less than discreet getaway vehicle.

In a few seconds, they were out on the road, bumping

along as the vehicle's shocks were shot, too. Justice was counting off the seconds in his head. How long before the sheriff's department started circling back? They had to realize which way he'd traveled after he turned out of Halo Valley's long drive to the two-lane highway that connected the Willamette Valley to the coast. He knew he had only a small window of time in which to disappear. He would have headed east, toward Salem, if he'd known the area better, but Justice was most familiar with the ins and outs of the Oregon coastline. The land was rugged here, steep, craggy cliffs rising above the pounding surf. Hundreds of acres of old-growth timber. Hidden coves that the Pacific had carved at the shoreline.

Lots of places to hide.

And, more importantly, that was where *she* was.

As they traveled, he sensed the change . . . the slight shifting of the world . . . the moment when he slid inside himself and let his senses take over, the slipping of this outer skin to open to his true self.

*There are many of them. So many.*

*"You cannot kill them all," the old woman warned me, and I nearly strangled the life from her right then for not believing in me!*

*"I can. I will," I told her.*

*"God will save them. . . ."*

*But they do not listen to God. Their master is from the dark realm of hell. Satan is their soul mate. Their lover. Father to their children. Father to them!*

*I cannot wait to do God's bidding and fulfill my mission in this world.*

*First, there are those outside of the walls. One is nearby . . . and near to the old woman as well, who has survived against all odds. It is my duty to end her torment. Dear, dear, mother.*

"Hey, man." Cosmo's voice sounded liquid and wavy. From a long distance away.

Justice opened his eyes and saw lights ahead as they approached the town of Tillamook. He felt the uneven roll of the Vanagon's wheels, smelled the familiar scent of cattle from the surrounding dairy farms. Located on the south end of Tillamook Bay, the town was actually inland from the ocean. Still, he was closer, felt more alive, his nerve endings snapping.

"You took a nap, but like with your eyes open. Creepy." Cosmo glanced his way and grinned.

Justice was glad for the dope, which had obviously slowed down Cosmo's perception.

"We made it," Cosmo added. "But I think the tire's really shot now. I'm gonna have to hit some kind of service station. God, maybe I should call the old lady. It's kind of a pisser."

"Don't call her."

Cosmo turned the Vanagon south onto Highway 101, the road that ran straight through Tillamook's gut. Though Justice wanted to head north, he wasn't quite ready yet.

"Man, are you giving me relationship advice?" Cosmo turned his way again, his Lennon glasses winking in the streetlights.

Justice thought a moment, his skin tingling as he mentally slipped it back on over his naked soul. His camouflage. He already knew he was going to have to kill Cosmo and hide the body so that when his van was discovered, there would be no trace to Justice. Mentally, he ran over what he'd touched. The pump. The left rear tire. The passenger door handle, the toolbox, the hammer . . .

"Keep going," Justice said as Cosmo glanced toward a service station that looked half-deserted on the south end of town. Its bank of fluorescent lights flickered, and the red stripe painted on the extension over the pumps had dulled and chipped away.

"We ain't gonna make it much further," Cosmo said, ignoring him.

They pulled into the service station, and Cosmo rolled down his window under the weird, unsteady lights. After what seemed a millennium the teenager who seemed like the only one on duty stepped out of the office to look at them. "You gettin' gas?" he yelled, his face screwing up as if he couldn't see well.

"Gotta patch a tire," Cosmo yelled back.

"Can't help ya unless you want gas."

"Shit."

"Go on down the road," Justice said quietly, though his nerves were jumping. "I'll pump it up again."

"Might as well get out and pump it up now."

"No."

"What's up, man?" Cosmo gave him a searching look.

Justice wondered if maybe he wasn't quite as stoned as he'd made out. Either way, it sealed his fate. "Go on down the road," he said again, and after a moment, and with a shrug, Cosmo pulled onto Highway 101 south and the dark road that cut through the farmland. There were plenty of little nothing roads both east and west of the main highway, lanes really, that wound through fields and brush and the Coast Range foothills, scarcely traveled byways where a vehicle could be hidden indefinitely.

Perfect.

"Just keep driving." Almost reverently, he fingered the box cutter he'd slipped into his pocket.

"It's your funeral," Cosmo said, unaware of the irony in his words.

# CHAPTER 5

Harrison drove into the parking lot of Ocean Park Hospital with a sinking heart. The Channel Seven van was parked outside, and Pauline Kirby and her gophers were already setting up for a report on the escapee. He had remembered the psycho's name—Justice Turnbull—on the drive over and had double-checked with Geena Cho to make sure he was right and she'd reluctantly confirmed.

"You didn't hear it from me," she'd said over the wireless connection, "but now you owe me two."

Bingo. Justice Turnbull was the lunatic who had escaped.

The wind had kicked up and Pauline's perfectly coiffed hair was trying desperately to escape, but under the security lights for the parking lot a hairstylist was spraying something at her head that worked like industrial glue, as the dark tresses were slicked to her scalp and stayed there.

Harrison had no interest in dealing with Pauline. He wasn't sure she would recognize him. He would have been safe except for the brouhaha that had developed after he accused Manny's business partner of being involved in his death. Then the news vultures had descended on one of their own. Him. And Pauline had been in the forefront.

Microphones had been thrust at him, and he could recall the way her lips pulled back from her perfectly capped snow-white teeth and the sneer that seemed a brush away from the smile.

Did anyone like her? he wondered as he got out of the Chevy. Maybe you didn't have to be liked as long as you got ratings. She sure as hell was anywhere there was any kind of story, and she usurped the competition by virtue of being overbearing, in his biased opinion.

The warmth he'd felt earlier at the café table had disappeared completely. He hadn't bothered with a coat, a mistake at the coast, and now he shivered as he walked, head bent, eyes on the asphalt in front of him as he skirted her entourage.

Her bright eyes spotted him. He could feel it rather than see it. He hoped he looked like a visitor to the hospital, but it was getting later by the minute. Visiting hours were long over.

"Hey," she called.

Harrison picked up his pace. If he could get inside, he could escape. She didn't want him for this assignment, anyway. He wasn't part of it.

But she had a nose for a story, and she was sniffing at him. He might not be part of the Justice Turnbull saga yet, but Pauline wasn't one to let anything get by her.

She actually took a couple of steps his way as he passed; he could see her in his peripheral vision. But then he was walking through the opening sliding glass doors that led into Ocean Park's reception area and continuing blindly straight ahead as if he knew where he was going. Normally he wasn't quite so seat of the pants, but he did *not* want to deal with Pauline Kirby, who could splash his face across the eleven o'clock news and destroy current and future investigations. He was sick to the back teeth of his own notoriety.

He found himself in a hospital hallway like a thousand

other hospital hallways: shining linoleum beneath his feet, fluorescent lighting, a chemical scent that hinted at procedures and pharmaceuticals that left a sense of disquiet in his gut. He didn't have a clue whom to talk with, who might be in charge. Ocean Park wasn't a huge hospital; it was only three floors, though its size could be deceptive as it ambled over several acres.

Harrison abruptly turned on his heel and headed back the way he'd come as he realized he'd turned the wrong direction from the ER, which was bound to be where the hub of the action took place. He passed by reception once more, shot a quick glance through the sliding doors just in time to see Pauline moving to just outside, camera lights glaring as she started talking into the mic.

In the ER he encountered a number of people waiting for help: a whimpering child with a slack arm, tight in his mother's embrace; an older man who was almost tipping out of his wheelchair; a stoic woman who was holding her bleeding right hand in her left, a huge gash offering Harrison a quick glance down to the sinews and muscle that appeared to be barely holding onto her thumb.

He caught up with a nurse who, after directing the woman with the thumb injury to another nurse, had lifted her head to look around. He grabbed her attention. "I'm Harrison Frost with the *Seaside Breeze*. Is there someone I can talk to about the victims brought from Halo Valley, Ms. Solano?" he asked, reading her name tag.

She was about to tell him to get lost; he could tell. But then her dark eyes sized him up and down, and she seemed less ready to blow him off. "You're not with Channel Seven?"

He shook his head. "Is that good or bad?"

"Good." She smiled thinly. "They're a pain in the gluteus maximus."

"I even know what that is."

"We're kinda busy here," she said, looking around.

"I won't be in the way."

"That's probably a lie, but c'mon. And, please, whatever you write, keep my name out of it, okay?"

"Sure." He followed after her as she directed others in the waiting room to where they needed to go or, conversely, assured them they would be seen by a doctor soon. Then she crooked her finger toward Harrison as she moved to a spot just inside the emergency room doors. From this angle they could see the long drive the ambulances took from the highway to the ER.

"What do you want to know? I can't give out much."

"What time was it when the ambulance from Halo Valley arrived?"

She hesitated.

"It'll be on the logs; the nine-one-one call."

"Okay. It was around eight. Eight thirty maybe?"

"And there were two victims, the van driver and one of the doctors."

"The van driver was actually one of our security guards. He was assigned to go pick up a patient from Halo Valley and drive him here in the van."

"But he was attacked at Halo Valley."

"Yeah." She seemed to consider that a moment.

"What happened to the van?"

"I don't know. Probably still there. Conrad sure wasn't driving it."

"Conrad?"

"I told you, I can't give you names," she backtracked quickly, throwing him a pleading look.

"I imagine Pauline Kirby's got most of this already," Harrison reminded. "Her team went to Halo Valley first. She's bound to have interviewed hospital staff and the sheriff's department."

"I guess."

"I just want to know some other details for my story," he admitted. "I'm not trying to get you in trouble."

She shot him a look from under her lashes. "Okay . . ."

"I've been told the victims were attacked by one of HV's inmates. This is the same guy who went on a rampage in this area a couple of years ago, killed some people, some women, actually. Went after his own mother and—"

"*Him?*" Her face lost all color.

"You remember him?"

"Who doesn't? He terrorized everybody!" Visibly shaken, she added, "And you newspeople said at the time that he had a thing for the cult women!"

"The cult women," Harrison repeated, remembering. Yeah, there had been something about that. He needed to get to a computer and log on to the Internet, refresh his mind about what had happened a few years back.

"I know he killed some of 'em." She paused, frowning and biting the edge of her mouth as she remembered. Now she didn't seem so worried about speaking with him. "Well, he killed a bunch of people, and they caught him at that motel that's still boarded up."

"You recall the name of that motel?"

"It's . . . I don't know. They took the sign down. It's the one that's boarded up just outside Deception Bay. On the cliff above the water. It was a wreck then, and it's been closed and boarded up ever since. Like the lighthouse. You know, the one where that psycho lived!"

"Ahh, right. The lighthouse." Harrison nodded, some of the story coming back to him.

"It's boarded up, too. Ever since they caught him, it's been totally off-limits, not that it wasn't before. But to think he escaped . . ." Fear shined in her eyes. "He's nuttier than a fruitcake, you know. A real scary dude."

That much Harrison did remember. "So, how extensive are the injuries to the two men he attacked?"

"Extensive enough. He beat Conrad's head in, and the doctor got stabbed in the throat with a pen."

"Was this his doctor? The one he attacked?"

"I don't know."

"Are they in surgery now?"

"Recovery." She moved away from the wall. "Are you going to quote me?" she asked, torn between excitement and trepidation. Fifteen minutes of fame or the loss of her job. "Remember, I said I didn't want you to use my name."

With a quick nod, Harrison said, "How about if I just say 'a source at the hospital'?"

"Yeah, fine—"

The other nurse came back, and spying Nurse Solano, she beelined toward them with her mouth a grim line. "Carlita," she snapped.

With a last beseeching glance his way, Nurse Solano shifted away.

The new nurse demanded, "Can I help you?"

He read her name tag: Nurse Nina Perez. "I'm Harrison Frost—"

"With Channel Seven?" she interrupted.

"No."

"I recognize you," she snapped back, as if he'd lied to her.

"Not from Channel Seven, you don't."

"But I—"

Before she could go on any further, a doctor strode from the ER in their direction. In scrubs, his hair rumpled, as if he'd just ripped off his surgical cap, he was tall and lanky, his expression sour. His authoritative manner stopped Nina Perez in mid-syllable. She snapped her jaw shut and turned to him carefully.

"Where's Laura?" he demanded, running a hand over his hair, trying to tame it.

Nurse Perez visibly bristled. "She left. Her shift was over."

"Well, get her back here. We're under siege from the damn media, and we've got another ambulance coming in. My shift is over."

"You're leaving?"

He didn't argue.

"Who's on duty in the ER?" she asked, alarmed.

"Somebody else." He was weary and self-important, as if he just didn't give a damn. With an I-don't-have-to-answer-to-you look of superiority, he headed through the doors.

"Jackass," Perez breathed, her words barely audible.

"A surgeon?" Harrison guessed idly after the self-important asshole had gone.

He'd memorized his name: Dr. Byron Adderley.

"Orthopedic," she said, lips flattening. Then, as if she understood she was saying more than she intended, added, "He's very good at what he does."

*And lets everyone know it,* Harrison silently added. "He's heading toward the front, where Pauline Kirby lies in wait."

"I think he knows that," she said tartly, then turned away.

Harrison, deciding the story had just moved, sauntered back toward the front doors to see what was about to take place.


Laura had missed dinner, so she made herself a sandwich. Sliced hard-boiled eggs, pickles, a dab of mayonnaise on wheat bread. She had taken exactly two bites when her cell phone rang. Frowning, she picked it up and saw it was Byron. She didn't want to answer, but he would just keep calling. The more she ignored him, the more he kept after her. "Yes?" she answered carefully.

"Get back here. What are you doing? All hell's broken out."

"I'm eating dinner."

"There are reporters here. I'm about to talk to Pauline Kirby. Another ambulance is coming. Two-car head-on collision."

"If the hospital needs me, they'll call."

"Damn it, Laura, check in with your radar thing. Don't wait!" He hung up.

Laura's "radar thing" was her uncanny ability to have a sense of danger. It was really an internal alarm that went off when someone was trying to hammer at her brain from the inside. Sometimes it wasn't *him*. Sometimes it was another person's panic that somehow breached her defenses for a millisecond.

She hesitated for a moment, then climbed to her feet, wrapped up her sandwich in plastic wrap, and headed to her car. The hospital called as she turned onto Highway 101.

Dr. Byron Adderley was holding court with Pauline Kirby outside the front doors of Ocean Park Hospital, and it was love/hate at first sight. Harrison went from mild interest to out-and-out enjoyment as Adderley's responses to Pauline's questions grew shorter and shorter. He stayed just inside the hospital reception area and watched through the glass front doors.

"We've learned that the patient who escaped Halo Valley Security Hospital is Justice Turnbull, from right around these parts." Pauline moved her handheld mic in an arc to include the area as she looked into the camera, even though she was speaking to Adderley. "Halo Valley *Security* Hospital," she repeated. "How do you think that happened?"

"I'm an orthopedic surgeon at Ocean Park Hospital," Adderley said tightly.

"But surely you have some thoughts on that—as a doctor yourself, who treats the public at large. It must be disconcerting to see how easily one can be 'taken in' by someone like Mr. Turnbull."

"I wouldn't know."

"I understand that Justice Turnbull was supposed to be on his way here to see one of your internists, but he attacked one of your drivers and stole the Ocean Park van, which has still not been recovered at this time. That victim, the driver, underwent surgery earlier this evening, as did one of Halo Valley's most prominent doctors, who was Justice Turnbull's primary physician at Halo Valley, correct?"

"I can't speak for Halo Valley." Adderley's lips were practically turned in on themselves. However he'd thought the interview with Piranha Pauline would go, he wasn't prepared for reality.

"Can you speak for Ocean Park?" Her smile was meant to appear benign, but nothing about the woman was safe.

"I've been with the hospital a little more than a year. It's an excellent institution."

"Meaning?"

"That . . . the care here is first rate," he stumbled.

"Dr. Adderley, the truth is, if Justice Turnbull had made it to your hospital earlier today, it doesn't matter whether the hospital's first rate or not. You would have ended up with a determined killer inside your walls." She turned from him and regarded the camera lens with a serious expression. "That's what we're all wondering here. Are we safe? *Can* we be safe? It wasn't that long ago that Justice Turnbull went on a killing rampage in this area of our fair state, and the Tillamook County Sheriff's Department chose to keep silent about it until it was over. And now, forewarned, what can we do to prevent the same terrifying situation from arising? How can we keep ourselves safe?" She turned back to Adderley, who was trying to sidle away. "Will the hospital be taking extra precautions tonight?"

"I can't speak for the administration."

With a quick movement of her hand under camera range, she cut the taping. "Didn't you just tell me you could speak for Ocean Park?" she demanded, glaring at Adderley.

"How was I to know you would make this a circus sideshow?" he spit back. "You call this reporting? It's inflammatory and pointless!"

"Why do I get the feeling you wanted to see your pretty mug on camera until the tough questions started, *Doctor?*"

Adderley marched away, and Harrison strolled outside and past Pauline's decamping group. She saw him again and frowned. This time, he let her get a good look.

"You're the scourge of the *Portland Ledger,*" she said with a snap of her fingers. "Frost."

"Kirby," he responded.

"What are you doing here? Sniffing for another story? You could just make one up again."

"You're doing fine on your own in that regard," he said with a half smile.

"Yeah. Well." She shrugged. "The real story was at Halo Valley. We're just following up, and that asshole acted like he was the boss. What I'd really like is someone with a soul who might look good on camera, and who could offer up some real information, or at the very least, an opinion."

Pauline's cameraman suddenly stepped forward and leaned toward her ear. "Wanna grab her?" he suggested.

Harrison turned, and they both noticed the slim, dark-haired woman in the uniform who had just locked her vehicle and was heading toward them through the pools of radiance from the sodium-vapor lights, her steps slowing as she saw the TV crew. She seemed undecided.

"She's gonna boge out and go toward the ER," the cameraman said.

"Not if I can help it!" Pauline was already on the hunt again, her mic held in front of her like an AK-47. "Turn your goddamn camera back on, Darrell!"

# CHAPTER 6

Laura's thoughts were filled with chaotic visions of her future. What would she do with a baby? What did that mean for her relationship with Byron?

*How can I save my baby? How can I save her from Justice?*

Okay, maybe the baby wasn't a girl, but in Laura's family lineage and history, female births outdistanced male births by a ratio of eight to two. And, for some inexplicable reason—or maybe just part of her family's odd and twisted past—the male children who survived birth tended to die before they reached adulthood.

So, in Laura's mind this child, the one she'd learned of only a few hours earlier, was a girl.

She parked her green Outback, locked the doors, and stepped into the night air, the wind grabbing at her with chilly fingers, just as an ambulance screamed into the drive that led to the ER. She turned from the sound and focused in on the news crew, their collective heads following the ambulance. She had seen them as she drove up but hadn't really thought that they might approach her. But as they turned from the ambulance's trajectory, they looked her way.

*Damn.*

She thought of Justice . . . and the news cameras . . . and her own face on television screens across the region . . . and the chill that ran through her was bone deep. No. Way.

"Excuse me!" Pauline Kirby herself was walking so fast Laura's way, it was almost a run.

It was all Laura could do to stifle her own urge to race away. She held her ground and watched in trepidation as Pauline pushed her microphone in front of her nose and the cameraman's lights blinded her. Turning her face away, she said, "I can't answer your questions."

"I'm just looking for information on the unfortunate victims of Justice Turnbull's horrifying rage, your security guard, Conrad Weiser, and Dr. Maurice Zellman."

Out of the corner of her eye, Laura saw a figure, shadowed by the cameras, move forward toward her. "Information on any patient at Ocean Park Hospital is confidential." She shifted away. With any luck, they would have no reason to put her on television.

"But they were brought here by ambulance, and they've been through surgery."

"I'm sorry. I can't talk about any of our patients. I have to go." She was already giving them her back and walking away.

"We just want an update on their conditions!" Pauline called. "Justice Turnbull is still at large. Do you think he'll come after them again?"

"No," a male voice answered, ringing with authority.

Laura kept moving but saw the newcomer, Dr. Dolph Loman, white-haired, in his mideighties, the osteopath who was semiretired and whom Byron had basically replaced, step into camera range. He was an imposing man with bright blue eyes and a ramrod straight back, a source of pride to him, though occasionally, just recently, she'd seen him use a cane.

She didn't like him one bit.

But she was thrilled and relieved that he'd taken the spotlight from her and she could hurry to the beckoning ER doors, where the ambulance was just jerking to a stop, lights flashing, sirens winding down.

Behind her, she heard Pauline ask Loman, "Can you speak for the patients?"

"I'm Dr. Loman," he introduced, his voice fading as Laura put distance between herself and the news staff. "I've been at Ocean Park for nearly fifty years. Nurse Adderley is correct. Patients' medical conditions are privileged and not for mindless television consumption."

"Adderley?" Pauline's voice was tinny and faraway. Laura doubled her pace. "We spoke with Dr. Byron Adderley earlier."

"Ocean Park Hospital is an outstanding institution . . ." Loman's voice became a mumble behind her. It was too much information. Too much data. The thought of Pauline broadcasting any part of it made Laura's scalp crawl.

A second ambulance, still unseen, was approaching, its siren wailing. It turned into the drive as Laura swept through the ER's sliding doors. Red and white flashing lights strobed the area as Laura headed toward the ER check-in. As a nurse, she helped out wherever she was needed, and tonight, with the injury accident, it was probably going to be the ER.

A man appeared at her elbow, a tall man, hovering in a way that made her glance up at him.

"Hi." His light brown hair was long and slightly shaggy; a five o'clock shadow darkened a strong, intensely male jaw. His eyes were hazel; his smile friendly. Too friendly, she decided instantly. He looked a little familiar and that made her wary.

He wasn't Justice, but maybe somebody she knew. . . .

"I'm Harrison Frost," he introduced, sticking out a hand.

She ignored the gesture, instantly didn't trust him, though she didn't yet understand why.

He let his hand drop. "You handled Pauline like a pro." Again the smile, a flash of white teeth, humor in his eyes. "You often skirt interviews?"

"Who are you?"

"Harrison—"

"I got your name," she cut in. "I mean, what are you here for?"

"A story," he said without hesitation.

"Ahh . . ." She bent her head and would've pushed past him but he stepped in front of her. "You and the rest of the crew need to find someone other than me to interview."

"I'm not with Channel Seven. Pauline Kirby doesn't care who she interviews or what they say as long as it looks good on TV. You looked good on TV."

"They won't put me on, though," she said quickly. "I didn't say anything."

"They might."

"No." Laura was adamant.

"You looked vulnerable. And pretty."

"Please . . . don't try the flattery angle. Okay?" When he didn't respond, she added, "Just so we're clear."

"Okay." He nodded, sizing her up. "Before Herr Loman showed up, Pauline would have given you your fifteen minutes of fame and then some. Wouldn't have mattered what you said. You can thank the good doctor for rescuing you, because it seems like that's what you wanted." He peered at her closely, fishing.

"Who are you with?"

"The *Seaside Breeze.*"

Now Laura gave him a second, searching look. "The *Breeze*?"

He nodded.

"You're here for the local paper?" She didn't bother hiding her skepticism.

"Homicidal maniac Justice Turnbull escapes the mental hospital, injuring two innocent victims, one of them his own psychiatrist. That's a story. And the local paper wants the story, too."

"The local paper is written by . . . well . . . locals." Her eyes narrowed thoughtfully. "You're something else. And I've seen you before."

"Yeah, probably," he conceded. "You're just starting your shift here? Could we meet afterward?"

"No."

"No, you're not starting your shift?"

"No, I'm not meeting you afterward. Please . . ." She held up her hands, asking, make that demanding, a little personal space. It had been a helluva day already, and she didn't need this guy—this *reporter*—with his sexy good looks, practiced charm, and endless questions to make the hours any longer than they already were. "Go away," she suggested, irritation tinging her words. "We're short-staffed, and I've been called in to help. That's all."

"So, you're not working a full shift."

"Mr. Frost . . ."

"Maybe I could talk to your husband? I saw him answering Pauline's questions earlier."

Byron. Great. This just got better and better. Laura didn't bother to respond again. She was as done with the media as she was with her ex-husband. Nurse Perez came through the double doors and, seeing Laura, motioned her forward.

She didn't need any more invitation.


Harrison watched Laura Adderley practically leap away from him, zeroing in on the older nurse, as if she were bolting from the gates of hell. He was used to being brushed off; it went with the job. He wasn't exactly sure why he'd targeted the nurse except that he liked the way she looked.

Fresh and somewhat serious, and yes, vulnerable. He'd seen it all when she'd been caught in Pauline's cameras, and he'd been impressed by the way she'd adroitly avoided dealing with the news crew. Score one for Laura Adderley.

Except if Byron Adderley was her husband, she'd sure picked a super prick, by the looks of it. Maybe he was her brother. Or their names were merely a coincidence.

Oh, yeah right. He'd noticed her tense when he'd brought up Adderley's name. They were involved. Somehow.

Now he watched her round a corner, her slim curves hidden by her scrubs and a jacket, her dark ponytail curling slightly and bouncing between her shoulder blades. He'd seen the crackle of intelligence in her wide blue eyes, noticed a few tiny freckles bridging her straight nose as she'd glared up at him.

Could she really be married to that pompous ass of an orthopedic surgeon?

He followed. More from curiosity about her than the story.

Now, the ER was a flurry of activity. Gurneys rattled inside, carrying human bodies. Blood and oxygen masks and IVs and nurses and doctors, Laura Adderley being one of them, rushed by in a steady stream. There was moaning, too. And one lady emitted a gurgling scream that made the hairs on his arms lift and a couple sitting and waiting clamp closer to each other.

Harrison had never liked hospitals, especially emergency rooms. The last time he'd been in one was when Manny lay dying on a stretcher and Kirsten was touching his hairline and whispering to him, over and over, "It's okay. It's okay. You're going to be fine. It's okay. It's okay. . . ."

But it wasn't going to be okay. It hadn't been okay. And though Kirsten and Didi had forged on, moving to the coast and buying a two-bedroom cottage with a peekaboo view of blue water, and Kirsten had taken a job at a local tea shop, her income supplemented by the life insurance, and Didi had found friends at a local preschool, and everything was just going along peachy, what with macramé and alfalfa sprouts and green tea, a whole new life—Harrison couldn't move on. In the beginning, he'd even tried to stop Kirsten from leaving before following her to the coast himself.

But there had been a period when he'd kept on digging relentlessly regardless of the damage it did to his career. His persistence and obsession had put him on a collision course with other newshounds, and he'd found himself in front of Channel Seven's cameras, where Pauline asked him the hard questions.

*Why was he so sure it was murder?*

*Hadn't the shooter just started shooting? In a line outside the nightclub?*

*Why was Frost so certain it was a conspiracy?*

*Weren't Bill Koontz and Manuel Rojas good friends?*

*Wasn't Bill Koontz good friends with a number of Portland politicos?*

*Could it be that he, Harrison Frost, simply couldn't let it go, and being an investigative journalist, he was digging for a story that wasn't there?*

*Wasn't he being punitive, rather than a journalist?*

Well . . . no . . . there was a story there, all right. But it was one of those things he was going to have to let percolate for a bit. The focus had shifted to him and his so-called vendetta, and Harrison needed time to pass, and a new game plan, before he searched into the truth surrounding what had really happened. He'd been like a bull in a china shop at the time, uncaring of finesse, and it was only when Kirsten herself asked him to stop that he ceased his attack on Bill Koontz. They could fire him and worry about libel, and wring their collective hands, but they couldn't completely stop him. When the time was right, he was going to ferret out the truth. And to hell with them all.

But for now, he had the entitled teenaged thieves and the escape of psycho Justice Turnbull.

Glancing at his watch, he saw it was closing in on eleven.

*Where are you, Justice?* Harrison wondered. *What's your game plan?*

Detective Langdon Stone of the Tillamook County Sheriff's Department looked around at the patrol cars still parked in front of Halo Valley Security Hospital's double doors to Side A, as it was called by the staff and patients, the half of the hospital housing the noncriminal inmates of the hospital. It was not his favorite place. Never had been. Never would be. But the fact that the woman he loved was a doctor here helped him put his own personal demons about the place in perspective.

They'd been here for hours, the night falling around them. Half the personnel from the TCSD had raced out to Halo Valley Security Hospital, about thirty minutes from downtown Tillamook, forty-five from the town of Deception Bay, where Justice Turnbull had once lived and which was still home to the lodge where the Colony women resided. Half of the officers on duty were now gathered in the parking lot that ran on the back side of the building, Side B, which housed the real sickos, the criminals, not the mentally challenged from Side A, who were mostly benign. The other half of his department was back on the highway, most turned toward the coast, as no one really believed Justice was heading inland to Salem and the Willamette Valley.

Two patrol cars other than his Jeep were still here, and Detective Langdon Stone, who had his own aversions to Halo Valley, though he was still working on getting past them, stood outside in the now cold June air along with his partner, Fred Clausen, and an auburn-haired woman in the TCSD's uniform, Savannah "Savvy" Dunbar, who had worked her way up to detective. A couple of other deputies were there as well, Burghsmith and Delaney.

Lang muttered, for the fifth time, "Who the hell thought Justice Turnbull could be moved with *one* security guard?"

"His primary physician," Savvy answered neutrally, for the fifth time.

Lang growled, "Zellman has a God complex."

"And it got him a surgery and stay at Ocean Park," Burghsmith pointed out.

"I'm gonna talk to him, as soon as he can talk," Lang said.

"Whenever that will be," Clausen responded.

Lang glanced toward the front doors of Side A. His fiancée, Dr. Claire Norris, a Side A psychiatrist, had met them earlier, along with a number of other doctors, orderlies, and nurses from Side B. Everyone was alarmed. Justice Turnbull was no minor problem. But there wasn't much more to do here. The bird had flown, so to speak.

"Back to HQ?" Delaney suggested.

"We should all be off duty by now," Lang said, looking up at the dark sky.

"I'm not leaving," Clausen said, and was met by a chorus of other voices, none of whom had any intention of waiting till morning to go after their quarry.

Lang said without much conviction, "Maybe we'll run across him on the way back to Tillamook."

"He can't be that hard to find," Savvy said. "He's in a hospital van in hospital garb."

"Where is that van?" Lang muttered.

"Bet we find it within the hour," said Burghsmith.

Clausen harrumphed. "Neither of you were around last time. The guy's a gold-plated, class A psycho. He wasn't ever easy to find. Even if we find him, catching him will be a trick. He's wily. And weird."

*And deadly,* Lang thought, but he kept that to himself.

They all knew it, anyway.

# CHAPTER 7

The sun was rising in the east, its ascent reflecting upon the western horizon in pinks and golds. The dawning colors made it almost appear like it was rising in the west, a blazing orb about to burst into the skies above the Pacific. It was a lie, a trick, a phenomenon Justice had missed for over two years, and now he stared at it hungrily. The sea . . . the Pacific Ocean, which stretched to forever . . . reached into his heart and pulled. It had always been this way.

And now a memory stirred, crept up on him like a thief. He'd been odd as a child. Everyone told him so. *She'd* dragged him to the cult time and again, but they wouldn't even look at him. *She'd* shoved him in front of that black-hearted bitch with the blond hair and smug smile who had declared, "Changeling," in disgust when she'd laid her witch's gaze upon him. He hadn't known what it meant, but *she'd* started babbling away, swearing it wasn't so, sweeping an arm to include all the little blond girls the black-hearted bitch had birthed and who were accepted into the inner circle while he was kept outside, thrust from the heart of their group, scorned. The bitch had smiled at him meanly from her side of the gates and told *her* to take him far, far away.

"He has no soul," she'd decreed solemnly, crystal blue eyes staring through the iron bars of the gate. Then, with one final disparaging look cast in Justice's direction, the bitch had swept away from the gate back to the lodge, where her precious brood of blond angels were waiting. Giggling. Laughing at him. Secure in their huge lodge with its tall fence.

While he'd been left with *her*.

He hated the bitch with the knowing blue eyes.

But not as much as he hated *her*—the sobbing, babbling puddle of a woman who'd brought him to be judged by them in their high and mighty fortress hidden in the trees.

*Her.*

*His mother.*

*She'd* dragged him from their lodge, swearing, crying that they would accept him. He was no changeling. He was one of them. Couldn't they see?

It was all so pathetic and futile.

Back in his bedroom at the time, he'd hidden from *her* and looked up the word surreptitiously. *She* hadn't suspected he'd had the means. A fine specimen of a fortune-teller, one who couldn't keep track of her only child. While she'd still been wailing at the unfairness of it all, he'd been pulling a nail from the floorboard of the rough-hewn planks that made up his bedroom floor and taking out one of the books he'd stolen over the years and made his own. The one he needed was merely a dictionary.

Heart pounding in dread, he'd rifled through the pages until he found the word he'd sought:

*Changeling: idiot; a being of subnormal intelligence; a human child exchanged for another being in infancy.*

*Another being . . . something* not *human . . .*

At first he'd been repelled; he'd wanted to scream at the world, rage at the black-hearted witch behind the gates that she was wrong about him! He was their cousin. All those twittering, nasty blue-eyed girls. He was of them! He belonged!

Of course, he'd been invited back, and as time had passed, he began to realize that the blue-eyed guardian of the gates was right, in her way. He *was* different than they were. Better. Further along the path chosen by their Maker. God.

*He* was God's choice.

Over time his mission became clear, and as *she*, the embarrassment, the charlatan, *the fortune-teller*, scratched out a living by accepting coins from the tourists, he chronicled the blond angels, learning their names, their habits, their special abilities.

The first one he'd killed had been easy.

Too easy, as it turned out, because he'd been filled with a sense of self-importance and overconfidence, which had tipped off the blond angels, who were much wilier and clever than he'd first imagined.

He'd been blinded by success and he'd lost track of the ones outside the gates, only reconnecting when they were pregnant, when he could smell them again.

And when it had all been coming together again, when he was about to send another of them into the raging fires from whence they'd come, he'd been tricked! Fooled. Cheated by them. Captured and incarcerated.

Laughed at . . .

He'd been patient.

But now he was free.

His lips twisted at the thought that he'd fooled them all again. Including the weakling who had borne him.

He watched the western horizon turn an eye-hurting shade of pink and smelled the dank scents of the sea. A huge whip of kelp, a bladder attached to one end, its way of floating and capturing air, lay twisted on the sand in front of where he stood.

It was in the shape of an *m*.

*Mother.*

God's sign. He was being guided by a divine hand.

Once again he felt himself going to his special place, his outer shell dissolving, revealing his true person, his beauty. But there was work to be done, and he reluctantly fought it off. He couldn't succumb as he had in the past, letting his true self rule, because in this outside world he could stumble and be captured again.

*No . . . no . . . !*

With an effort he held his eyes open wide, refusing to see and feel anything but what was right in front of him: the beach littered with debris; the rising swirl and plaintive caws of the seagulls, scrounging at the tide's edge; the brilliant refraction of light burning in his eyes; the restless, beckoning water in shades of gray and green.

Now he spurned his true self and almost wanted to cry out. It was his only refuge. His sanctuary.

But God had a plan, and he couldn't tarry.

Turning away from the beach, he climbed up a row of sand-dusted stone steps to the parking lot above, where the Vanagon awaited in all its colorful, floral splendor. Anyone who saw it would remember it, but no one had witnessed him driving into this turnout with its view of the ocean.

He walked past the Vanagon without so much as a sideways glance. Cosmo wasn't going to need it anymore, and he couldn't be seen with it.

He was several miles south of a small hamlet called Sandbar, which was south of Tillamook, which was farther south from Deception Bay, his ultimate destination. He had Cosmo's driver's license and his clothes, which fit in length but were too big around. Not a problem for beachwear along the Oregon coast. June's weather was unpredictable, and winds and rain could beat down at any time; the dress code was whatever worked.

He also had Cosmo's backpack, hiking boots which fit okay, and a watch cap he'd discovered beneath the baby gear. He was growing a beard. He had thirty dollars, courtesy of Cosmo, who was really James Cosmo Danielson. He liked the name.

He hiked up the road until he'd passed the jutting rocks that divided this section of beach from the one where he'd left the Vanagon. Now he clambered down a sharp cliff of stones where rubble shifted under his feet and bounced down to the beach thirty feet below. Reaching the sand, he walked to the water's edge and kept meandering northward. Fingers of wind snatched at his jacket, flapping it open. It was colder than it looked, and he passed several people: a couple strolling along, bundled up, their heads tucked together; a woman jogging; a man with a golden Lab, throwing a stick.

No one paid him the least bit of attention, which was just what he expected. He'd grown up in these parts, and he knew this section of coastline better than anyone. No one knew him except the ocean. It whispered to him, God's voice trapped inside its swells and troughs.

A finger of land jutted out to the sea and then took a sharp turn northward, creating a natural bay, dividing the Pacific from a small protected area of smoother water. Justice climbed up and over the jutting, rocky spit, moving closer to the road rather than the ocean. At the eastern bay's edge stood a bait shop, a rickety wooden hovel, part of a dilapidated structure that had once been a cannery; the cannery, in turn, being all that was left of a once thriving industry that had all but vanished over the last decades. Blackened, barnacle-clad posts stood in broken rows along the waterfront, revealing where docks, long rotted, had once stood.

As a seagull cawed, he climbed up a clattery wooden ramp to the back deck of the bait shop, glancing toward the bay before reaching for the door handle. He'd seen the faded FOR RENT sign when he'd driven by earlier, and he'd disposed of the Vanagon at the particular beach parking lot where he'd left it with the express purpose of heading back to this place. If, and when, the search for Cosmo began, it would fan out from the van, and Justice could be vulnerable to detection, except for the fact that he knew this area and he knew exactly what kind of person the bait shop's owner, old man Carter, was: an ex-con with a healthy disregard of police in general, and the Tillamook County Sheriff's Department in particular.

That was, if he was still alive. And still around.

As Justice walked in, a jingly bell above the door announced his arrival. Carter, a few pounds heavier than he remembered, his hair a little grayer, was standing behind the bait shop counter. Though Justice knew of Preston Carter, the man didn't really know him; and anyway, he was half blind and older than dirt.

"Yeah?" Carter barked in greeting, lifting his head. His eyes were bluish, rheumy, above a grizzled beard that sported a bit of oatmeal from the morning's breakfast.

"The room," Justice said.

"You want the room?" Carter repeated loudly. Undoubtedly, he was hard of hearing, too.

"I only have thirty dollars."

"Thirty?" He seemed to consider. "Okay. We can start with that. Ya got any ID?" he shouted.

Justice slipped Cosmo's driver's license from his wallet, and Carter squinted at it. He didn't write anything down, just slid the license back across the scarred Formica counter to him. "What's your name, son?"

"Dan," Justice said, handing him the money.

Carter fingered the bills. "I'm gonna have my girl, Carrie, check to make sure these are tens," he warned. "I don't see as well as I could."

"Go ahead."

He nodded in satisfaction. "All righty. But I guess meanwhiles I can give ya a key. You know, there's a toilet? Back over there by the clamming sinks." He waved an arm to encompass the other dilapidated buildings. "That's all we got."

Justice glanced toward the next building, with its rusted corrugated roof, where a row of sinks and clamming and crabbing paraphernalia, shovels, nets, and the like, stood beneath a listing roof that was streaked with seagull crap.

Justice made a sound of acceptance. He'd certainly seen worse. And despite the building's dilapidated state, he was free. Away from that hellhole of Halo Valley Hospital.

"Good." Carter turned to a coffee can on a shelf behind him, dug inside, and fished out a key. He handed it over to Justice and the deed was done. Justice determined he would stay in the room above the bait shop as long as he needed. Days . . . weeks . . . months . . . But he would be vigilant. If the sheriff's department came looking for him, he would know it.

Climbing the outside stairway, the steps teetering a little, he let himself into a one-room space filled with cobwebs and worn linoleum flooring whose scarred and blackened surface looked like a permanent stain. He thought longingly of the sleeping bag in Cosmo's van, but he'd sensed that people would remember him more later on if he were seen as a hiker of some sort, the guy with the sleeping bag. . . . No, that wouldn't do. So he'd left the bag.

No matter. Justice was an accomplished thief, and he could gather things as needed. He was no good with conversation. No good dealing with people. He was too odd. Said too little. He caused people to remember him without even trying.

But he was a wraith. *She* had once said that about him. "You're in the shadows. A listener. A plotter. A wraith."

It had not been a compliment, but it had been accurate.

Dropping Cosmo's backpack in the center of the room, he unzipped it and rooted through it. The hippie had a few interesting items, one of them being a jackknife. To go along with the box cutter. Moving the knife to his pocket, Justice also pulled out a pack of beef jerky, a picture of a woman holding a baby and the hand of another child, and two joints. He stuck a piece of jerky in his mouth and chewed slowly. The joints he transferred to an inner pocket of his coat. Nothing he planned to use himself, but they might be collateral. The picture of the woman and kids he tore into tiny pieces and shoved the pieces in the pocket of his pants. Later, he would scatter them to the wind.

He left other items in the backpack, planning to examine them more closely later. For now, he needed to sleep, and he lay down on the floor and put his head on the backpack, staring toward the cobwebbed joists above his head. Soon, he would have to get rid of all the rest of the evidence he'd taken from James Cosmo Danielson, deceased.

Then she came to him again, her heavy, vile scent wafting through this dingy room in thin, but distinct waves.

*Sissstterr . . . I can smell you. . . .*

His nerve endings jangled again. His eyes opened more widely.

She was close. Within a ten-mile radius. Maybe she was even with them at their lodge.

He smiled as he sent the message: *The scent of your devil's spawn is a beacon. . . . I'm coming for you. . . .*

Saturday morning Laura stood motionless under the spray of her shower, her face turned upward into the hot needles, eyes squeezed shut, his words branding across her mind as she slammed the door to him once again.

He could really smell that she was pregnant?

Could that be true?

When she herself barely knew.

It was surreal and disturbing, and as she caught the fury and hatred in his message, her entire body quivered, not just with fear, but a building rage. The only person who knew she was pregnant besides herself was this deadly and strange psychotic who was bent on destruction!

*Not on your life, bastard,* she thought, twisting off the taps, then grabbing her towel and drying off. She was dead on her feet, having gotten home at dawn, but she dared not sleep and allow even the small chance that somehow he would find her.

She didn't doubt he would; she'd grown up understanding that like herself and some of her sisters, Justice had his own special "gift," what she considered a curse. While others, people who had grown up outside the walls of Siren Song, would find his heightened senses, his ability to communicate his raging thoughts, outrageous and unbelievable, she knew in the darkest part of her heart that he was hunting her down with the guile and patience of a bloodthirsty predator. That he was communicating with her was a gift. Yes, he did it to terrorize her, and it did. Man, oh, man, she was scared to death. But it also gave her a heads-up, made her aware, gave her a chance to be ready for him, time to thwart him.

"Just try it, you bastard," she muttered under her breath as she wiped the condensation from the medicine cabinet mirror over the sink and saw rage in her own eyes. Before she'd known she was pregnant, she might have felt more bone-numbing terror, but now it wasn't just she who was in danger. It was the tiny bit of life growing within her. Small as it was, she would protect it.

Justice Turnbull be damned. She slung her towel over the shower door and made her way to her bedroom.

After slipping into jeans and a sweater, she tossed on a Windbreaker, then slipped her feet into socks and sneakers. At the bureau mirror, she combed her hair straight down, seeing the thin line of light blondish brown at her center part, her grow-out. Dyeing her hair had become almost an obsession. As soon as she'd learned she and Byron were leaving Portland for the area around Deception Bay, she'd panicked inside, felt she had to do something, anything to hide her identity. She'd left the coast years before, to forge a new life but also to distance herself from her family in order to keep them all safe. Justice was a real threat, though not the only one, but he was definitely the most dangerous, the most immediate, the most determined. She'd tried to disguise herself physically in an effort to stay under the radar, but now she saw she'd underestimated his methods of finding her.

She walked into the kitchen, undecided about what her next move was, and snagged her keys from a hook near the back door. She was off work until the following evening. She thought of her family. The locals called them the Colony, and their lodge Siren Song. She had lived with them until her teens and had taken a job at a local market for a while, one foot in each world as she determined what she wanted. Two of her sisters had been adopted out when they were children. Another had simply wandered away. Most were still at the lodge, younger than Laura, under Catherine's able, vigilant, and near paranoid care.

*Maybe not so paranoid,* she thought now.

When Justice had gone on his rampage a few years back, the gates, which had already been closed to the outside world, were locked shut. Laura was on her own and with Byron by then. She had sent Catherine a letter, asking if she needed her to come back and batten down the hatches, and had received a note in return that simply said: *Stay away.*

Then Justice had been caught, and Byron, never suspecting his wife had been in any kind of danger or that her roots were centered here, on the Oregon coast, had taken the position at Ocean Park. At first Laura had wondered if there was some connection that had drawn him here, if he'd somehow understood that she was from this part of the world, but she'd come to realize it was just a twist of fate.

And though she'd resisted with all her might, driven by fear for her family, a part of her had been seduced by the idea. She'd spun a fantasy to herself whereby she could be part of her family and live a life with Byron outside Siren Song as well. Why couldn't she have that? she asked herself. It wasn't even a difficult request. Most everyone detached from their nuclear family to create their own, and yet the new family kept in contact with the old.

But "most everyone" wasn't her family. They didn't share her secrets and history.

They weren't *gifted*.

Now she gritted her teeth and headed for the door and her Outback. Gifted. What a joke. Right now she would do a lot to rid herself of this gift.

Except it might be all that stood between her family and total destruction.

# CHAPTER 8

Harrison awoke with a start and wondered where the hell he was in the moment before true wakefulness occurred. Then he saw that he was in his sleeping bag. On the floor of his new apartment. And it was damn cold. Jesus. June could be winter on the Oregon coast. Worse than Portland.

Staggering to his feet, he stumbled into the shower, letting the hot spray rain over his head. He didn't know how long he stood there. Long enough to make water conservationists shudder the world over, he supposed.

From the shower he threw on some gray sweatpants and a black long-sleeved T-shirt, then padded barefoot to the kitchen, where he stumbled rotely through the steps of making coffee. He was so lost in thought, he was almost surprised when the coffeemaker beeped at him that it was finished brewing.

After pouring himself a cup, he opened the refrigerator, hoping for cream or milk, knowing there was neither. He drank the coffee black and in between gulps took several deep breaths. After ten minutes he felt almost human, and he switched on his television with its DVR—his one indulgence that was critical to his job—and played back Channel Seven's eleven o'clock news. He had glanced at it when he'd returned the night before, spent a little time on the Internet, researching the escape of Justice Turnbull, then, exhaustion catching up with him, had slid into the sleeping bag. Now he watched the segment that dealt with Justice Turnbull's escape in more detail, taking mental notes.

First there was a bit with Pauline earlier in the evening, in front of the redwood and brick facade of Halo Valley Security Hospital. Patrol cars were parked every which way, some with their lights flashing. Pauline was explaining about the two sides of the hospital, Side B being the section that housed the criminally insane. In voice overlay she explained where Justice Turnbull had escaped, and the camera caught the portico outside of Side B, which was on the back side of the building, the eastern side, and mirrored Side A, which faced west. More sheriff's department vehicles stood in attendance. It looked like they'd sent the whole damn force, and maybe they had.

Questions were asked of law enforcement and the Halo Valley staff. The camera zoomed in on Detective Langdon Stone with the Tillamook County Sheriff's Department. Harrison gave him a hard look as he seemed to be the officer in charge. If he was going to dig into this story, he would undoubtedly butt heads with Stone at some future point, and it was unlikely to be an easy friendship.

Stone wore a black leather jacket, jeans, and cowboy boots, and his brown hair was tossed by an errant breeze. He said, "No comment," enough times to make it sound like a rap song. Pauline clearly knew him, or thought she did, and her usual brisk, probing tone held a kittenish note of wheedling. Clearly Stone found her excruciating, and when one of the doctors from the hospital, Dr. Claire Norris, stepped into the fray, Harrison didn't miss the way Stone gazed at her with an unflinching, yet somehow self-conscious, stare. *Something going on between them,* he deduced.

Dr. Norris couldn't shed much light on Turnbull's escape; she was on Side A, not B. Pauline abruptly switched from them to Side B's portico, where she interviewed another woman doctor, Dr. Jean Dayton, who was serious, cautious, and clearly freaked out that Justice was gone. Mention was then made of the Ocean Park security guard who'd been injured, Conrad Weiser, and Justice's primary physician, Dr. Maurice Zellman, whose condition was listed as stable. Conrad was still in the "serious" category. He'd suffered a head injury that had required surgery. Zellman had been through minor surgery as well, for the damage to his throat and voice box, but he was responsive and alert.

There was a brief moment with Dr. Byron Adderley, who just managed to look pissed off; then the camera's eye turned to Nurse Laura Adderley, her face in profile, before Dr. Dolph Loman's icy blue eyes and white hair filled the screen with a lot of hyperbole about how great Ocean Park Hospital was.

Pauline cut him off quick, then gave a short history of Justice Turnbull's previous crimes, primarily leveled against women, and without saying the word *cult,* brought in mention of Siren Song and even offered a view of tall wrought-iron gates hidden in the thick old-growth timber.

Harrison found his small notebook and jotted down the names of the victims and the hospital personnel listed on the television screen along with nurses Nina Perez and Carlita Solano. He also added Detective Langdon Stone with the TCSD, and Dr. Claire Norris from Halo Valley, Side A.

He stared down at his scribbled notes and had a piercing moment of insight. The real story wasn't about Justice's escape, or the victims at the moment of his escape. The real story was about the past and future victims of his murderous passion.

The cult.

That was where he should start.

Rinsing out his coffee cup, he ran a hand through his drying hair. God, he needed a haircut. Then he changed from his sweats to jeans, T-shirt, and plaid overshirt, his "look" for the teenagers, though he wasn't planning on following that story until later in the day. This one was a helluva lot more interesting and just heating up.

Throwing a glance around his apartment, he fervently wished he had a bed, a few sticks of decent furniture, and maybe twenty thousand or so in the bank.

He headed downstairs to his Impala, examining the bald tires with a rueful eye. He had to get these stories written and turned in so he could be paid. Was desiring some cold hard cash such a bad thing?

As he turned from his Seaside apartment south, it occurred to him that he'd just encountered the sixth deadly sin: greed.


Lang shared a squad room desk with Detective Savannah Dunbar, who sat in a chair against the wall used for collared perps. She was balancing a laptop on her knees and stared at it in concentration. Lang had tried to tell her he didn't care if he had a desk; the reason for sharing was a matter of space rather than budget. But Savvy just waved him off. She was a young, attractive, serious woman who listened more than talked. She'd risen to detective with the speed of a comet, coming from the Gresham Police Department, a large urban city that butted up to Portland's east side, having made a name for herself by her deep dedication and willingness to work the hours and then some. She'd come to the TCSD on the heels of Lang himself, although there was really no place for her on their roster. Lang had wondered about Sheriff O'Halloran's decision until one of the good old boys at the TCSD who'd outlived their usefulness was gently eased out of the department. Then Savvy's hiring made sense.

Feeling his gaze on her, Savvy looked up. Her eyes were a crystal blue, her hair a lush auburn shade, though it was currently scraped back into a ponytail.

"It's Saturday," he said.

"And?"

"What are we both doing here?"

She smiled faintly. "It's a shame criminals don't have regular hours."

Lang grinned and ran a hand around the stubble on his unshaven jaw. He just couldn't find the energy to shave this morning. "Find anything on Justice?"

"Nothing we don't already know. He grew up around Deception Bay. His mother's name is Madeline Turnbull. She's known around these parts as Mad Maddie. She made her living managing a fleabag of a motel and as some kind of fortune-teller." Savvy looked up at him with serious eyes. "I don't go in for all that mumbo jumbo, but some people swear she was uncannily accurate in her forecasts. Two years ago Justice nearly killed her, though it's uncertain whether that was by accident or design. She may have just gotten in the way when he was targeting Rebecca Sutcliff. Detective Sam 'Mac' McNally was lead on the case from the Laurelton Police Department, and Clausen and Kirkpatrick were on it from the TCSD."

Lang had taken Kirkpatrick's place when she'd taken a different job. "Clausen was involved in the capture," Lang mused. "Maybe I should talk to McNally, catch his thoughts."

"I've got the Laurelton PD's number." She rattled it off to him, and Lang wrote it down. "McNally's retired now," she added.

"Okay." At that moment Clausen and Burghsmith clambered into the room, looking dead tired. They shook their heads in unison at his lifted brows.

"Nothing," Clausen said. "The guy's in the ether." He let out a sigh. "Goddamned ghost."

"Psychotic ghost," Savvy muttered.

"Maybe he went toward the valley," Burghsmith suggested but showed no enthusiasm for that theory.

"Nah, he's coming to the coast." Clausen gave the other deputy an annoyed look that said they'd been over this and over it.

"So, where's the hospital van?" Lang said, almost a mantra for him now. "Someone would have seen it."

Clausen lifted a shoulder. "He either ditched it, or he snuck through and nobody saw him."

"Unlikely that he snuck through," Savvy said.

"So, then, where'd he ditch it?" Lang asked. "And does that leave him on foot?"

"Maybe he had someone waiting for him," Burghsmith suggested and yanked at his suddenly tight collar.

"He's not that kind of guy." Clausen frowned as he sat down at another community desk. "He's too weird."

"Even weirdos have friends." Burghsmith was not going to concede.

Clausen was adamant. "Not this weirdo."

"Okay, then, he's on foot, or he found some other means of transportation," Lang said.

Savvy suggested, "Maybe he flagged down another motorist."

Clausen harrumphed, a sound he made frequently. "It was all over the news about his escape. You think anybody missed that? And just decided to give some hitchhiker a lift?" He slammed open the top drawer and searched around for some gum, pulling out a pack and holding it up in silent query. Everyone shook their head to his offer.

"Somebody mighta missed it," Lang said.

"Well, then he could be anywhere." Burghsmith shrugged.

"We've been trolling up and down the coast, but so far no-body remembers him."

Lang said, "If we don't get a clue soon, we'll have to go to the lodge and talk to Catherine. Warn her."

"And what about Rebecca Sutcliff?" Savvy asked. "She still lives in Laurelton, as far as we know. She escaped him once, but if he's as single-minded and on a mission as everyone seems to think, she should be warned."

"He's on a mission, all right," Clausen said. "That's just who the bastard is."

"This Sutcliff woman probably saw it on the news, too," Lang said. "I'll give her a call, too."

"In case he heads inland," Burghsmith said again.

Clausen sent him a dark look. "No way. It's the god-damned sea that's in his blood. Like some of the fishermen around here. He's got a thing for it." When Lang looked up at him, Clausen added, "It's in some of the original reports. Trust me, if Turnbull's heading anywhere, it's closer to the ocean. Bet a month's salary on it."

No one took him up on the bet.

They discussed the extensive search that had taken place up and down the highway to the valley and also their traversing of Highway 101. It had been over twelve hours since Justice's disappearance.

"Where's his mom now?" Lang asked Savvy.

"Madeline Turnbull is a patient at Seagull Pointe. It's both assisted living and a nursing home. She's on Medic-aid."

"State funding," Lang agreed. "She's in the nursing home, out of touch with reality," he said, repeating some-thing they all knew.

Savvy nodded, her auburn hair gleaming under the un-forgiving overhead lights. "I'll stop by and see if I can in-terview her in some way."

"Good." Lang pushed away from the desk. "I'll bring O'Halloran up to date," he said, "and then make a few phone calls."

"I got some more traversing of 101 to do," Clausen said. He didn't even bother looking at Burghsmith, who shrugged and said, "I'm dead on my feet, man."

"We all need more sleep," Lang agreed. "Let's meet back here at noon. With any luck, we'll have a lead."

# CHAPTER 9

A s fog began to creep in from the sea, sending long fingers of mist inland through the old-growth firs with their drooping, moss-laden boughs, Laura nosed her Outback onto the lane winding through the forest to Siren Song. Twin ruts cut through the stands of fir and pine, while the clumps of shiny-leaved salal grew to the height of trees.

Branches scraped the sides of her car, and the rising mist caused Laura's imagination to run wild. At every turn she expected Justice to leap from the shrubbery, a knife in his hand, the expression of a rabid maniac twisting his features. Her heart was hammering, her fingers sweaty on the steering wheel, as the Subaru bounced and shuddered over hidden rocks and potholes.

Around a final curve, the massive gates of Siren Song loomed. The hair on Laura's nape rose and her throat was dry. This was dangerous. Exactly what she'd tried to avoid at all costs when Byron announced they were moving to the coast.

But Justice was loose, and there was no believing in safety any longer. He could be here now, lurking in the shadows, lying in wait for her.

*Sssssisssterr . . .*

She could almost hear his sibilant warning, but it was a trick of her mind, a memory. She cut the engine, listening to it cool and tick, hearing mournful cries of seagulls, their lonely songs underscored by the distant roar of the sea.

*Don't freak yourself out,* she said as she climbed out of the car and locked it. The thick, damp air was cold and pressed against her face, and memories slipped unbidden through her mind, memories of braided hair and dresses whose hems brushed the plank floors of the old, rough-hewn lodge.

*Home,* she thought, though long ago she'd rejected Siren Song and everyone in it.

Fighting off a shiver, she crossed the damp ground where ferns and nettles abounded and wrapped her hands around the wrought-iron bars of the front gate, where she could see the lodge, dark windows winking in the weird half-light of the shrouded woods.

There was no good way to contact the residents of Siren Song. They didn't have phones. There was no cable television, Internet, anything electronic. Electricity was through a generator and only on the main floor. The women inside the lodge were living in another century, a decision that was consciously made by Laura's aunt, Catherine Rutledge, who had made the decree in the late '80s, when Laura herself had been just a girl. Laura had rebelled against the restrictions and had caused Catherine no end of grief. It was only after she got her way and was allowed into society outside the gates that she came to appreciate the simplicity of their way of life, and even more so, the careful isolation that had been built to keep them all safe.

She called out, "Hello! Catherine?" but her voice seemed to fade. There was no buzzer, so she rattled the gate, but that sound, like ghosts rattling chains, sent another shiver down her spine, and she realized she was on a fool's mission. What did she hope to accomplish by coming here? Did she intend to warn her family? Or was this lodge a place she ran to as a sanctuary?

If so, it was the first time she'd come here in years. She'd learned to fight her battles outside the gates of Siren Song.

But that was before Justice.

She was about to give up and get back in her car when she caught a glimpse of movement through the branches of the trees, the front door of the lodge swinging open. A woman about her same age stepped onto the broad front porch. For a moment Laura didn't remember the slim thirty-something—it had been so long—but then she recognized Isadora's somewhat aristocratic features and Laura's heart leapt. "Isadora," she whispered.

Isadora was the oldest of her sisters at the lodge, and she'd remained frozen in Laura's mind as a younger, more modern woman. Now, however, Isadora's blond hair was twisted into a single long braid, and the dress she wore was a blue print dress that reached floor length to a pair of sensible shoes.

As if sensing someone watching her, Isadora turned toward the gate. Her eyes were still cerulean blue and welcoming, yet there was a quiet, cautious, almost furtive demeanor to her.

"Isadora!" Laura called, grinning widely. God, she'd missed her! Until right this moment, she hadn't realized just how much.

"Laura? Really?" Isadora's face broke into a smooth smile, showing even teeth. Quickly she crossed the stone steps, avoiding the wet mud, the hem of her long dress swaying as she walked to meet Laura.

When she was within easy earshot, Laura said, "God, Isadora. It's . . . it's amazing to see you again." She blinked against a silly rush of tears that choked her throat.

"Your hair . . ."

"I know. I dyed it." She didn't say why, didn't have to.

"What're you doing here?" Isadora asked, her fingers linking with Laura's on the bars. With her free hand, she dug into a deep pocket in her dress.

"I need to see Catherine."

"She'll be glad you're here," Isadora said, glancing past Laura as she pulled out a ring of jangling keys from her voluminous skirts. "It's so great to see you." She unlocked the gate with a metal *screech* that scraped Laura's nerves. "Earl, our regular handyman, has been ill, and we've been a little more tethered here," she said by way of explanation, and then the gate was open and they fell into each other's arms. Laura fought an onslaught of emotions and blinked against the stupid tears as she clung to her sister.

*Was this really home?*

Or was she just stressed? Her hormones out of whack?

"It's good to see you, too," she said, finally releasing Isadora and looking at her.

"What do you want to see Catherine about?" Isadora asked. "Why now?" Those knowing blue eyes were suddenly sober. Worried. She glanced toward the road, as if she were expecting someone else.

So they knew. "You're afraid he's coming here, aren't you?" she asked, not mentioning Justice's name.

Isadora's gaze slammed back to Laura's. She nodded, as if unwilling even to speak the thought aloud. "Let's go inside." As Laura stepped through, Isadora was careful to re-lock the gate.

Laura fell in step beside her, resisting the urge to look over her shoulder as well. *Hurry, hurry, hurry,* she thought. Justice hadn't mentally spoken to her for several hours, but she could sense his weighty presence, as if he were walking beside them.

The rough-hewn oak door to the lodge swung inward as soon as they reached it, and Catherine, tall, austere, with her graying blond hair scraped into a tight bun at her nape, gazed at Laura through blue eyes that were faintly misty.

She wasn't known for emotion, quite the opposite. But after Laura's teen rebellion subsided, they'd been close, almost like mother and daughter.

Almost.

"Lorelei," Catherine greeted her, and after only a moment's hesitation, Laura swept into the older woman's embrace, her throat hot. Catherine gave her one firm hug, and then Laura released her.

And when she looked around, she saw all her sisters. Over half a dozen of them. Blue-eyed. Blond hair ranging from a dark ash color to nearly platinum. Wearing look-alike calico-printed dresses, about which Byron, finding the only dress Laura had saved from her youth and holding it away from his body, had disparagingly said, "Hey, Ma. Hey, Pa. Let's go on a hayride!"

Laura hadn't explained. She'd merely shrugged and smiled, as if it were some kind of costume.

In a way it was.

Now Catherine shepherded her charges and Laura past the staircase that wound upward to a second story and toward the huge table, an oak plank that was large enough to seat them all in the dining room. A fire, embers glowing bloodred, burned with a quiet hiss in the huge stone grate and tinged the air with the smell of smoke. Overhead, suspended from the tall ceiling, a dimly lit fixture gave off a soft glow as the girls stood silently, their eyes burning with unspoken questions, their fear almost palpable. They all knew, each and every one, about the danger that Justice Turnbull posed, and she had a horrid sensation that she might have innocently brought the madman closer to all of them.

"You've all grown up," she said as the last bench was scooted closer to the table where they'd had family meals and meetings for dozens of years.

"It happens." Ravinia ran a hand down her long blond tresses, combing the unbraided locks. She was fifteen and full of herself. Even Catherine's icy stare didn't get her down. Laura recognized the signs of trouble; she knew them firsthand. She also knew if the rules weren't abided by, strange and terrible things could befall them.

Cassandra leaned forward. Her hair was the darkest, almost a light brown. "I saw him," she said on a soft breath. "Justice."

Laura didn't have to be reminded that Cassandra hadn't really seen Justice with her eyes. She'd seen him in some kind of mental picture or dream, her own special gift, but she had seen him.

"You know that he escaped Halo Valley Security Hospital?" Laura looked to Catherine.

The older woman nodded solemnly, the lines on her face more apparent than Laura remembered. "From Cassandra," Catherine explained.

It was their form of knowing what was going on beyond their gates, and it was narrow . . . and surprisingly accurate. Laura looked to Cassandra, who'd been christened Margaret, but then, when her precognitive skills were realized, their mother simply changed her name to Cassandra, after the Greek goddess who could predict the future but was never believed. Laura had been named Lorelei after the German myth where Lorelei lured sailors to their death by her singing, a take on the Greeks' Sirens who called to Odysseus and his crew. That myth was how their lodge became named Siren Song, a derogatory gift from the locals who believed the women who lived within the lodge's walls were capable of bewitching the men and stealing them from their wives, among other things. When she was younger, Laura had deeply resented the way they were treated as outcasts, but she also knew that her family suffered from, or was blessed with, depending on how you looked at it, inexplicable abilities that ranged from precognition to mind reading. Now, for ease and without the intended malice, even she thought of the lodge as Siren Song.

"You predicted I would be pregnant by the end of the year," Laura said softly to Cassandra, who was only a year younger than Isadora.

Cassie swept in a breath. "It came true!" Her eyes danced and a smile lit her face. "I knew it!"

Laura nodded and Catherine murmured, "Oh, no . . ." She closed her eyes and bowed her graying head for a second, as if the weight of the world was just too much for her.

"He wants your baby," Cassandra said on a gulp.

Catherine's head snapped up. "He wants destruction!" she corrected, eyes blazing, jaw set. "Of all of us!"

"He's been in my consciousness," Laura said.

They all turned to her, and Catherine, after a long moment, rose to her feet. "I need to have some privacy here with Laura," she said. "Cassandra, you and Isadora stay, too." She shooed the rest of Laura's siblings from the room. Ravinia rolled her eyes at what she perceived as favoritism, and Lillibeth, from her wheelchair, sent Catherine a pleading glance, desperately begging to stay.

The older woman was implacable. "Please. Just . . . go to your room, just for a little while," she told Lillibeth quietly, to which Lillibeth wheeled reluctantly away, her chair gliding over the old wood floors.

Once the others were out of earshot, Catherine shook her head angrily. "He wants every girl child, every woman, all of us. I can't see him like Cassandra does, or sense him like you do." She was completely aware of Laura's own ability, of all their abilities. "But I've known him since boyhood." She glanced out the window warily. "Mary . . . she was not kind to him." She was shaking her head. "I was afraid it would come to this," she whispered, her voice like dried leaves rustling in an ill-fated wind.

Her skin crawling, Laura thought back to her childhood and tried to remember Justice or, for that matter, Mary, her own mother, who gave birth to all of them and then just disappeared one day.

It had been odd. Disturbing. But then everything Mary had done could be placed in the "odd and disturbing" file.

Never a giving soul, Mary had been hard on Justice in a way Laura had never fully understood, though she remembered the taunts:

*"Cretin."*

*"Moron."*

*"Idiot!"*

*"Changeling."*

All said with a sublimely malevolent relish that had, at the time, turned Laura's blood to ice. They were issued with such vile superiority that Laura, even as a girl, had known no person with an ounce of goodness in her soul would ever speak as Mary had to Justice's face and especially behind his back.

Vaguely Laura could recall Justice's mother, Madeline Turnbull, as a younger woman. However, those faded memories had all but disappeared over the years, and now Laura remembered Justice's mother from the lurid news reports after Justice was caught and Madeline was nearly killed. Madeline had also had extra abilities, and she'd used them for profit. The locals had unkindly dubbed her Mad Maddie. A cousin to Mary and Catherine, Madeline shared some of the same genetic history, but she'd lived outside of Siren Song, which had been built by Mary's great-grandfather.

"He tried to kill Madeline," Laura said.

"He's an aberration," Catherine stated firmly, her lips flattening in hatred. "But we've had plenty of those over the years."

Laura didn't know how to respond to that. Though she knew Catherine was right, Justice was in a class by himself. A man on a mission to kill them all.

"He calls me Sister," she said, though she knew he was a cousin, generations removed. They shared Nathaniel and Abigail Abernathy as great-great-grandparents, and yet he referred to her as "sssissterrr," tried to make her think they were close. . . .

"Slam the door on him, Lorelei!" Catherine insisted. "He can't hurt you, if you keep him out."

"I'm worried about my baby girl." Laura swallowed hard.

"You want to keep her?" Catherine asked.

"Oh, yes!" she said automatically, a little surprised by her own vehemence. Yesterday at this time she hadn't even known she was pregnant.

No one questioned her belief that it was a female. In their family, girl children were the norm, and if by chance a male child was born, there was generally something wrong, some affliction that severely impaired them in some way. Her flesh pimpled as she remembered her brother. Nathaniel was a case in point, though his death had been hastened by human hands, not disease. She had two other brothers, who were gone now as well.

And then, of course, there was Justice . . . a surviving male child, the monster.

"Have you told your husband?" Catherine asked.

Laura looked at her, thinking hard, but the message leapt from her mind to both Catherine's and Cassandra's, because they both gazed at her with a mixture of surprise and worry. "You've left him," Catherine said.

"I divorced him," Laura said. "I'm pregnant because I was trying to make it work when the marriage was already dead." She felt cold all over again. "It . . . it was a mistake."

"So you're going to raise this child on your own?" Catherine was skeptical.

*Yes!* Laura spread her hands, not even knowing how to explain her mixed emotions, her attachment to this new being growing inside her. "Look, right now I just want to keep her safe from Justice."

Cassandra stared past them. Laura slid her a look and

felt the hair on her arms lift. From her childhood she remembered that stillness, that frozen mask when Cassandra saw something, the way her breathing was so shallow as to have nearly stopped. What Cassandra saw wasn't a vision, per se, but flickering images that were somewhere in the future. Random pieces that might not fit together. But the pieces themselves were telling.

"You need him," Cassandra said, her voice distant.

"What? Who?" Laura asked, trying to understand. "Oh, God . . . Justice?" Laura swallowed back a feeling of horror.

"No. The truth seeker," Cassandra said in that far-off voice that caused Laura's scalp to crinkle in apprehension.

"Who's that?" Laura asked.

Catherine said, "Don't listen to this. You know how she gets sometimes."

Laura did. And it scared her. "Cassie? Who are you talking about?"

Cassandra slowly shook her head from side to side, and her eyes were focused to the middle distance, a world of her own. "He's waiting for you."

"I don't know who you're talking about." She placed a hand on Cassandra's arm, and the girl didn't so much as react. Frustrated, Laura said, "Cassandra, come on . . ."

But there was no response. It was nerve-rattling, the way Cassandra received information, as if she were getting bits and pieces, scraps of important messages. Laura had witnessed it before, years ago, when Cassie had warned of a deadly storm on a clear day. That night, she, Laura, had nearly been killed when the wind had picked up, gaining strength to hurricane force while she was working. The electricity in the store had gone out, and she'd tried to make her way home, through the rain and the dark, a car nearly running her down as the driver lost control. . . . She'd survived; the driver, a boy of nineteen, hadn't been so lucky.

And then there was her pregnancy.

She hadn't been here, to the lodge, in years. She'd barely known her younger sisters because she'd made a point to distance herself during her teen years. Catherine had told her of Cassandra's pregnancy prediction in one of Laura's intermittent communications with her aunt, yet the girl had been spot on.

"I'll look for him," she said, worrying about the prediction, wondering what in the world it meant. A truth seeker? Really?

"And keep Justice locked out," Catherine warned again. Her brow was knit; her hands were worrying each other.

"You should stay with us," Cassandra said, blinking, her blue eyes finding Laura's again. She was back from whatever disjointed future she'd seen, but there was trepidation in her voice. "At least until he's caught."

"No." Laura was adamant. She had a life and it was one outside these walls. As for the others . . . her sisters . . . "Don't worry. I'll be okay." And somehow she would make that so. "But Isadora said you don't have a handyman." She turned to Isadora. "Who's picking up supplies?"

"We have a driver," Isadora said. "He's a Foothiller, and he's been taking Catherine to the market once a week."

"Don't leave the lodge," Laura said urgently. "Any of you. It's not safe."

"It's dangerous for you, too!" Cassandra's face was animated again, her pretty features etched with worry.

Laura tried to allay her fears a bit. "I know. It's not safe for any of us, but I live on the outside. I have a job. A life on the other side of the gates. I'll be okay." She said it as if she meant it, with renewed conviction.

"Then why did you come?" Catherine wanted to know.

"To make sure you were all right."

"We're fine," the older woman assured and smiled, though her eyes remained somber and a dark, shifting blue. "He can't get to us."

They all knew that was false hope.

With a shiver, Laura said, "Check the fence line. Make sure there's no easy way in."

"Oh, we have." Catherine was light-years ahead of her. "And we'll know if and when he's coming, anyway."

They all looked to Cassandra, who nodded solemnly. "Yes, I'll probably see him, but . . ." Her eyebrows slammed together and her features pinched as she thought hard. Then, she sighed, as if finally understanding she was totally helpless. "It's you who's the most vulnerable, Lorelei," she said as Laura looked out the window to the surrounding gloom of the forest and the shifting morning fog.

"I know," she whispered.

# CHAPTER 10

Harrison strolled into the Sands of Thyme Bakery a little after eight o'clock. It had been about a forty-minute drive to Deception Bay from his apartment in Seaside, and he yawned as he approached the counter. Two women were working the front of the shop, one of them being a girl whose name tag read Cory; the other being his sister, Kirsten, who placed a hand over her heart when she saw him.

"You're up before noon? Stop the presses."

"I get up before noon lots of times," Harrison told her as the warm scent of fresh-baked bread mingled with the aromas of coffee and cinnamon. "It's all related to what time I go to bed."

"Exactly. And when was the last time you went to bed before midnight?" She raised a skeptical brow.

"Two nights ago," he said. The truth was he was a bit of an insomniac, a condition that had worsened since Manny's death.

"Why?"

"I was . . . watching a DVD of a movie I'd seen a few times and passed out before it was over."

"What time was that? Eleven fifty-nine p.m.?" She smiled, a crooked smile that was an echo of Harrison's own.

He smiled back. "And fifty-five seconds."

"Can I get you something?" she asked, flipping a towel at him.

"Coffee. Black. Lots of caffeine."

"What are you doing here so early, really?" she asked, grabbing a paper cup and handing it to him as the other girl yelled, "Low-fat vanilla latte," toward a group of three women who'd clustered around a newspaper strewn at one of the glossy tables.

"Oh, that's mine!" A woman in rain gear scooted back her chair and approached the girl holding out a steaming cup with a frothy top of foam.

Harrison wandered over to the self-serve area and pulled the lever on a hot pot, shooting a stream of steaming brown liquid into his cup. He didn't bother with a lid, which caused Kirsten to come around the counter and grab one for him, pressing it into his hand. "We make it hot here," she said. "Don't spill in the car."

"I'm not leaving yet."

"Yeah? You're even too early for this date with destiny, whatever it is?"

"Very funny," he said sarcastically, then eyed the glass display case where baskets of cinnamon rolls, scones, bagels, and coffee cake were visible. "What about those scones over there?" He waved a hand at the case. "Got any with cranberries?"

"Didi's favorite," she said, returning to her spot behind the counter.

Cory was helping another customer, a girl who'd just walked in, so Harrison stepped out of the way as she, after handing the teenager a paper coffee cup, pointed to the hot pots he was crowding. The newcomer looked as if she'd just rolled out of bed and was still wearing her pajamas. She stumbled as if in a fog toward the coffee thermoses.

Kirsten picked up a cranberry scone with tongs, put it on a plate, looked at Harrison quizzically. "You want this heated?"

"Nah."

She handed him the plate as the teenager nearly staggered into him. He was grateful the girl had the sense to put a lid on her coffee as she wasn't exactly the picture of grace and stability. He sat down at a table and did the same, pressing the lid over the cup before picking up his scone and taking a sample bite. It was good, and he wolfed down the rest, then pressed his thumb on the crumbs, transferring them to his mouth.

The teenager sipped her coffee for several moments, and it was almost like Harrison could watch the caffeine do its job. Brighter-eyed, she headed outside to a newer model BMW. The vanity plate read BRITT88.

He watched her wheel out of the lot and head north with a screech of tires. Idly he wondered if he'd just met Britt Berman and she was heading back toward West Coast High. There were still a few days of school left before summer break.

Glancing over, he saw Kirsten watching him closely. "She's a high school student," she hissed in a stage whisper.

"I'm not looking for a date," Harrison assured her flatly. "I just thought she seemed familiar, but the girl I'm thinking of lives in Seaside, not Deception Bay."

"I think her father lives around here. She's come in with him a few times, called him Dad. She pulls in from the south, picks up coffee, then drives north. Maybe she goes to her mother's before school."

"It's Saturday," the other girl at the counter said as she grabbed some ceramic cups and squeezed past Kirsten to the coffeemaker.

"Maybe she's just heading home," Harrison mused. "She always wear her pajamas?"

"Pretty much," Kirsten said.

"You know her name?"

Kirsten shook her head. "Her license plate says Britt."

Harrison nodded. A couple came through the door at that moment, and he subsided into silence. The girl's appearance had reminded him of the other story he was working on, which he sensed was on the verge of taking a turn. He needed to balance that story with Justice Turnbull's escape. It was an embarrassment of riches when just a few weeks ago he'd been working on nothing more exciting than the coming Fourth of July parade.

Getting to his feet, he walked to the counter so he wouldn't have to shout. "You know where the lodge for the cult is?" he asked Kirsten.

Before she could answer, Cory, who'd filled two ceramic mugs for the people who'd just entered and taken them to a table, walked around the back of the counter and said, "The Colony? It's just up Highway 101. Looks over toward the ocean. Sometimes it's kind of hard to see if your eyes are on the road 'cause of all the bushes and stuff on either side of it. But it's amazing."

"Just up the highway?" Harrison jerked a finger toward the north.

"Uh-huh. But you can't go see 'em, or anything, you know. They don't come out anymore."

"Anymore," Harrison repeated.

"Well, I guess they used to. But they're like weird, you know."

Kirsten said, "How do they get their groceries?"

Another man entered and asked for a sixteen-ounce cup. Cory handed it to him, popped open the cash drawer, dropped in his money, and made change. She then slammed the register drawer shut with her abdomen. The man slid a look between Harrison and Kirsten as he stuffed the bills in his wallet and headed for the coffee thermoses.

"I don't know." Cory shrugged. "Somebody gets it for 'em, I guess."

Finishing up his coffee, Harrison tossed the cup in the trash, checked his cell phone for the time, then took a step toward the door.

"I would've given you a regular mug if I'd known you were going to stick around," Kirsten said.

"I didn't know it myself."

"Are you taking Chico out anytime soon?" Kirsten called after him.

"God, I hope not. I'll let you know."

The door slammed shut behind him. Outside he inhaled a lungful of briny air thick with moisture as he unlocked the Impala's doors with a remote button. He had to click it several times and recognized he needed new batteries. Sliding into the driver's side, he fired up the engine. Morning light was dimming with the arrival of a bank of gray clouds. More typical June weather at the coast. Looked like they might descend into a blanket of fog. Peachy.

As he was pulling out of the lot, he saw a middle-aged couple climbing from their pickup truck, both wearing T-shirts that said CLEAN UP THE BEACH! He remembered that today was the annual event whereby people from all over the state combed the beaches for trash.

A noble pursuit, but he had other plans on this day. It was still early, but what the hell. He wanted to get a look at the cult's lodge up close and personal.

As he drove northward, he thought about the thieving teens, the Deadly Sinners. He suspected it would be afternoon before they started gathering; that was like the teen credo. But he bet his bottom dollar they would be gathering. Their robberies had all been on weekend nights, thus far. Saturdays, mostly. It just felt like tonight would be a great night for them.

Maybe he would forget Chico today and instead go for some other look. Maybe actually follow one of them home. Surveillance was where he was on that story. Follow them around. See who their friends were. Catch them in the act of their next bad behavior. Tonight, maybe . . .

But first.

He missed the turnoff to the lodge the first time he went by. Drove right past it, which was easy to do as it wasn't much of a road and what there was of it was disguised with laurel and Scotch broom and thick grasses waving in a stiff, brisk breeze. The lodge itself was down a side road that was basically two water-filled ruts that led to a wrought-iron gate and the imposing building beyond, a two-story structure of wood shingles and rock and a flagstone walk leading to the front door.

There was a car parked outside the gate. *Theirs?* he wondered, pulling up next to it. A green Outback with mud splashed up its sides from the rear tires. Huh. Just didn't seem to jibe with the whole isolated cult thing, but then, who knew?

He was considering getting out of his car when two women stepped outside into the morning light; he could see them through the right side window of his Impala. They were saying good-bye to each other. An older woman and a younger one. It was a tad awkward, like they didn't know whether to hug or shake hands or just get the hell out.

They both noticed his car at the same time and froze as if touched by a magic wand.

Harrison whispered on a surprised breath, "Laura friggin' Adderley."

What the hell was she doing here? he thought the half second before her resemblance to the older woman slammed into his brain like a meteor.

*Mother and daughter?* Apart from hair color, they bore a strong resemblance.

They finally became animated again, whispering to each other urgently. Then Laura seemed to draw a deep breath and set her jaw. Her eyes narrowed upon him as she started marching across the flagstones to the gate. The older woman followed, and Harrison saw the heavy keys in her hands. She opened the gate for Laura, then locked it distinctly behind her as she threw Harrison a dark glance that told him in no uncertain terms that he wasn't welcome.

No surprise there.

Laura walked straight for the driver's side of the Outback, and Harrison, whose engine was still running, pushed the button that lowered his passenger side window, where her lower back was perfectly framed as she hit a button on her remote door lock.

"So . . . you're a cult member," he said loud enough to be heard over the distant roar of the surf and a few birds calling, unseen in the thick forest.

She stiffened as if hit with a hot prod. After a brief moment, she turned and leaned into the open passenger window. He was surprised at how blue her eyes were, how mesmerized he was by the darker striations fanning from the pupil, how smooth the skin was on her cheeks.

"What are you doing here?" she demanded without the barest trace of a smile.

He asked, "Why do you dye your hair?"

Neither of them answered the other.

Laura seemed to think that over hard; then she abruptly turned away.

"You want me to write up something about you being a cult member? Or, maybe we could catch breakfast together and you could tell me all about it?"

"I'm leaving." She opened her car door.

"How about I follow you?"

"How about I call the police?" she snapped angrily.

"Somehow I don't think that'd be your first move," he said, watching her. She was beautiful in her own way, near-perfect features with a little bit of mystery surrounding her. *And married to that prick Adderley,* he reminded himself. He knew now they weren't brother and sister. "You're related to them, aren't you?" Harrison asked, hooking his thumb toward the gate and lodge beyond. "Is that why you dye your hair? To hide your resemblance to them?"

"I don't owe you an explanation."

"Are they afraid Justice is coming back for them? What about you? Are you afraid?"

She was slamming into her car, so Harrison climbed quickly out of the Impala and skirted her front bumper to end up at her driver's window. She gazed at him stiffly through the glass.

"Let me buy you breakfast," he suggested. "I'd like to talk to you. Off the record, of course."

She rolled down her window reluctantly. "Of course," she mocked, distrust twisting her features. "*For* the record, I don't believe anything's really *off* the record."

He couldn't help but smile. So she did have a sense of humor.

"I wasn't trying to be funny," she said.

"Okay, okay. So if you want it that way, it will be. I promise. But I am going to write an article about the cult, with or without your help."

"The 'cult,'" she repeated, with a shake of her head. "Great. That would be without my help," she assured him. She jabbed her key into the ignition and, before she twisted her wrist, glared up at him. "And they're not a cult. They're a family."

"Your family."

She said something unintelligible under her breath. "What 'they' are is people who just want to be left alone," she said, picking her words carefully.

Time to get to the point. "Justice Turnbull isn't going to leave them alone. What does he want with them? Why are they his targets?"

"You're jumping to conclusions." But she visibly paled.

"No, I'm not. He went after them before. One was dead from over twenty years ago, and he went after another one. And then there was that reporter woman. And his mother . . .

the one in the rest home. And you're one of them." He motioned again toward the lodge. "So, he's related to you and bound to be a threat?"

She hesitated half a second, then shook her head. "I'm not talking to you."

"Why not?"

"Because you're all like this! Digging for a story. Avidly searching for that angle, that spin, that *something* that will make your story stand out! You don't give a damn about anything but making money. You're as bad as the paparazzi. Just chasing people down, no matter what the cost!"

"What is that cost?" he asked.

"Everything! You said it yourself. He's after us. He wants to kill us, Mr. Frost." Whatever cool demeanor she had left cracked completely, and he saw a gamut of emotions skitter across her features. Fear. Rage. Uncertainty.

For a few seconds, they stared at each other, and the darkness of the surrounding forest seemed like a shroud. He found himself wanting to reach in and comfort her. Rub her back. Stroke her hair. Touch her. It was way out of line, and she probably would scream assault if he even tried.

"I've said enough." She twisted on the ignition and the car sparked to life.

"One breakfast, and I'll leave you alone," he promised and wondered why it mattered so much that he talk with her. "Pick the place."

She closed her eyes. He had the impression she wanted to bang her forehead on the steering wheel in frustration or do anything to make him leave her alone. "Okay. The Sands of Thyme Bakery."

"Not that place."

Opening her eyes, she frowned at him. "You just said—"

"I know. My sister works there. You don't want to go there with me. How about Davy Jones's Locker?"

"The bar?" she asked with disdain.

"They also serve breakfast. It's pretty good."

"It's a dive bar," she reiterated and looked at him as if he'd lost his mind or never had one to begin with.

"Hey . . ." He shrugged his shoulders and spread his hands. He was trying hard to be his most charming.

Her fingers squeezed the steering wheel. "I . . . can't."

"Why not?"

"Because I'm very careful not to do crazy things."

"Who says this is crazy? It's not crazy."

"Your definition of crazy is clearly different than mine." She gave him a sideways look as she slid her car into gear and said reluctantly, "But if you promise this is our one and only meeting, that I'm off the record, and that after this you'll leave me and my family alone forever, I'll do it."

"Deal. Except I reserve the right to change your mind." He grinned.

"You won't."

"Maybe if you get to know me you'll like me. I'm not all bad. Yeah, I'm after a story, but I'm not Pauline Kirby. I want facts. The real deal."

"You're still a reporter."

"I'm a truth seeker, Mrs. Adderley. That's all."

He didn't quite understand what he'd said that caused her face to lose all color. "What's wrong?" he asked quickly.

She shook her head. "Nothing. I'm—" She hesitated on a half laugh. "I'm not . . . It's Ms. Adderley, actually. I'm not married."

"Not married. As in not married to Dr. Byron Adderley?"

"That's correct."

He grinned. "Well, that's a plus."

"I'll see you at Davy Jones's, Mr. Frost," she said, and he noticed her hands were trembling over her steering wheel. "One breakfast. And that's all."

"Whatever you want," he assured her.

"Off the record."

"They have really good huevos rancheros there."

"Off the record," she insisted.

"Off the record," he agreed, stepping away from her car as she backed around and turned the Outback's nose toward the main road. "Unless you change your mind, of course . . ."

# CHAPTER II

Laura pulled into the parking lot at Davy Jones's Locker. The once red, now sort of pink shingled building looked decrepit with a sagging roof and scarred wood plank steps and porch. She'd never actually stepped foot in the place. When she was younger, it hadn't held one iota of interest for her. Since she'd been back to the coast, she'd never had occasion to even think about the place, but now here she was.

She had a moment in her car while she watched Harrison Frost's brown Chevrolet nose into the lot and slide into an empty space at the far end from her car. Her heart was pounding a strong, fast beat. A truth seeker. Could that really be said of a reporter? Could that be said of Harrison Frost? He seemed so . . . blunt . . . and yet . . . friendly. Or was that just a ruse to get information from her?

Could he possibly be whom Cassandra meant?

The skin on her forearms prickled. A warning. She told herself to tread carefully; who knew Frost's true intentions?

She climbed from her car and locked it, then watched as he skirted puddles that had formed in the gravel lot. He wore jeans, a black T-shirt, and some kind of thin jacket with a hood. He looked like half the teenagers in the area, she thought, as he approached, but then nobody dressed up at the coast unless they absolutely had to. Harrison Frost seemed to be taking dressing casual to a new level.

He shoved a hank of brown hair from his eyes as he reached her, but the wind gleefully grabbed at it. His eyes were hazel with dark specks, and the smile on his lips was meant to disarm her. He had the trace of dimples, and Laura found herself comparing him to Byron, whose countenance was stern and direct and whose eyes were laserlike; she'd often felt pinned beneath their glare.

This guy was much more approachable.

Or so he'd like her to think.

She reminded herself to keep her guard up.

"Thanks," he said as a means of greeting as he reached her. "For the record, I'm buying."

She almost laughed.

"I wasn't kidding when I said they have the best huevos rancheros along the whole damned coast."

"I was thinking more of a fruit plate," she said, smothering a smile as they walked between a couple of pickups both sporting toolboxes in their beds.

He gave her a sharp look and those hazel eyes glinted. "That was a joke, right?" he said, gesturing to the dilapidated building they were about to enter. Then, showing more dimple, added, "You're funny."

It *had* been a joke, because Laura was pretty sure Davy Jones's Locker was the kind of establishment whose menu was scarce on fresh fruit; it looked like it catered to fried food and plenty of it. She was honestly surprised at herself; joking wasn't her style, as a rule. She was too . . . cautious . . . to engage in that kind of repartee, that kind of flirting.

Flirting . . . Was that what she was doing? She almost winced. *Don't be taken in by his charm. Do* not *trust him.*

They headed up the broad worn steps together, and Harrison pushed through the door with its porthole window. Inside were wooden tables and benches and booths with red faux-leather seats lining the room on three sides. The fourth side was the bar, which, though its reddish laminate had a few chips and scars, looked surprisingly clean. Or, maybe that was just her impression since the bartender was wiping it down with a white cloth as they entered.

"Sit anywhere," the barkeep said, and Harrison led her to one of the booths.

Surprisingly there were a number of people in the place, eating breakfast. It looked like a haven for construction workers of all kinds, and there was a lively conversation going on two booths over about the residential work, or lack thereof, in the area.

"I'm not going to say anything about my family," she said after hanging her jacket on a peg located on the edge of the booth's back. She slid into the seat across from him. "I'm not really sure why I agreed to this. I'm . . . I'll figure that out later. But I'm not going to give you a story."

"I think you need some breakfast. Two huevos?" he asked her.

She considered her stomach, decided it wasn't rebelling at the thought, and nodded. "If they're really that good."

"They are."

"Okay. So remember, anything I say is strictly off the record," she warned again.

The handsome bartender, whose dark skin suggested a Hispanic or Native American ancestry and who doubled as a waiter, apparently, came their way. Harrison held up two fingers and said, "Huevos. Coffee. Two?"

"Sure," Laura said. "With cream."

"That'll be it, then," Harrison told the bartender. "Unless you have a fruit plate."

"I got orange juice and other mixers."

"Thanks, but no," Laura said with a faint smile.

He nodded and headed back to fill their order. As soon

as he was out of earshot, she asked Harrison, "Did you hear what I said?"

"I heard that you want to talk to me," he responded, which made her lips part.

"I said anything I say is off the record!"

He leaned closer, and she felt herself automatically pull back. There was something too attractive about him, some facet of his personality that she suspected he knew about and was exploiting. "Let me tell you a few things. The media is going to be all over this story until Justice Turnbull is caught. Television, newspapers, the Internet . . . A psycho on the loose is big news. Right now reporters are digging through old reports on what took place a couple of years ago. Justice is part of your family. All of that's going to be dredged up. Your family can't escape it. Maybe you can, because you're on the outside and no one seems to know about you, but the rest of 'em . . ." He slowly wagged his head from side to side. "That lodge isn't a safe haven. It's a target with a big red bull's-eye on it. He's after them, and that's where they are."

"He can't get them there," Laura said.

"Why not? Because they have a *gate?*"

"He won't attack them straight on. It's not his game plan."

"You think you know his game plan?"

Laura hesitated, then said firmly, "Yes."

"Well, maybe you oughta tell the police then, so they can find him and put him back in the mental hospital."

"They wouldn't believe anything I said, and if I told them how I know, they'd think I was a psycho, too."

"Okay, I'll bite. How do you know?"

"This is off the record, right?"

He nodded wearily.

The bartender brought them two white mugs and an insulated pot of coffee. He poured them each a cup and left a bowl of sugar packets and a small pitcher of cream. Laura gratefully used up the time it took her to pour her coffee and add a bit of cream to think about what she was going to say.

Stirring the cream slowly, concentrating on it, she finally said, "Everyone thinks we're a cult. We're not."

"You've already pointed out we have different definitions for the same thing," he rejoined. "But I don't care about semantics, anyway."

"We're just women who live together. In my case lived, past tense. We're sisters," she said, though the word felt alien on her tongue. Thanks to Justice Turnbull.

"Are you sisters? Real sisters, by blood?"

"Yes. Well, technically, I guess, some are half sisters. I, uh, I'm not really sure."

He stared at her as if she were making it up.

"Seriously," she said, then reminded him, "You asked."

"And you live, lived with your aunt? That was the woman I saw at the lodge."

She nodded, thinking back to the lodge, how safe she had felt there while growing up, but that had been a false sense of security. "My younger sisters live there now, well . . . some of them." She took an experimental sip of her coffee. It was hot and chased away the chill that had been with her since leaving Siren Song.

"No brothers?" he asked.

"I had a brother who died, and another two . . . who left. . . ."

"Just left, never to be heard from again?"

She shrugged. How could she explain that she didn't know, that there were many secrets held in Siren Song, secrets she, herself, couldn't begin to understand? There was just no way this man would ever comprehend the complexities of life within the gated walls.

*And maybe he shouldn't. Maybe that was better.*

"What about your mom and dad?" Harrison persisted. He offered a smile, then sipped from his mug.

"Mom and Dad," she repeated, realizing how weird this was going to sound. "We never knew our fathers," she said carefully.

"Fathers. Plural?"

"Off the record," she said again.

"Yes, damn it!" he said with a shake of his head. "You might not claim to be a cult, but you're sure as hell paranoid about the outside world learning about you."

She sighed, wondered how much, if anything, she should confide. Probably nothing, but here she was. At Davy Jones's frickin' Locker. With a reporter. "Okay, listen, it's . . . hard, okay? My mother . . ." How could she explain about a woman she barely knew herself, a mother who was distant, secretive, and dark? "I guess the easiest way to say it was that she was mentally unstable." Laura rubbed at a stain on the table with her fingertips. "Mother—Mary—she took lovers fairly indiscriminately, or so my aunt has alluded. I remember a little bit of this, but mostly I pieced it together over the years. My mother had a lot of children, one after the other. Some of the first were adopted out, I think, and then something happened and that stopped."

"What happened?"

"I don't know exactly. Catherine, my aunt, was ill for about a year and my mom was in charge and that didn't go so well." Laura shuddered, the interior of the restaurant easing to the edges of her vision as memories of the lodge surfaced again. She recalled a white-faced, angry Mary standing at the window on the upper floor, looking out toward the sea, tears running from her eyes and blood staining her long gown. . . . Laura had been on the shadowed stairs and, while her mother cried, she'd stayed mute, slipping silently downward, knowing that if she said a word, disturbed her mother, a terrible fury would be unleashed.

Now, with the smells of the deep-fat fryer reaching her nostrils and some laughter from a booth near the video poker machines jarring her, she blinked and found herself staring into the disbelieving eyes of Harrison Frost. Incredible, intelligent eyes. Sexy, even. But skeptical.

She cleared her throat, stuffed the unwanted memories back into a dark corner of her mind where they belonged.

"You don't know what happened to Mary," he prodded, seemingly intrigued.

She glanced away, couldn't stare into his inquisitive, oh-so-male eyes. "The last time my mother was pregnant, she miscarried, and then she was attended to by a doctor, and then . . . not long after she was gone."

"Gone?"

She was nodding, remembering the wind whispering through the old lodge, like the sinister chatter of ghosts slipping under the eaves. She was suddenly cold as a bitter arctic wind.

"Like dead?"

"Yes." She cradled her coffee in her hands, her elbows on the table, as she tried to gain warmth through the ceramic mug.

"What happened?"

"I don't know. I don't think any of us, the sisters, do. At least no one's said anything to me."

"But someone does. Catherine," he suggested.

"If she does, she's kept it to herself."

"But you're sure?"

"Hey, I'm not certain of anything," she snapped, because that was the God's honest truth. "But there's a graveyard on the property and Mary's there."

"In a private cemetery," he clarified.

"Yes. It was all kind of secret at the time. My aunt was afraid of scaring us, but then she showed us the grave. After my mother, Mary, was gone, Catherine changed everything. The adoptions had stopped long before, and then Catherine locked the gates and the outside world from getting in. I was one of the oldest of my siblings, at least of the ones still at the lodge, and I didn't like it much. I kept trying to run away, so Catherine bargained with me and I worked in Deception Bay, at a grocery store, for a while, and then I wanted to go to nursing school and I left when I was eighteen."

"And you were the last one out?"

"Yes . . . I, well . . . yes. As far as I know, and Catherine would have let me know if things had changed. We write letters. Snail mail. They're not exactly electronic there."

Harrison nodded as he pulled out a tiny digital recorder from the pocket of his jacket.

"Hey, no." She shook her head. "We made a deal, remember? No recording."

He hesitated, then slipped it back into his pocket.

"It's not on, is it?" she asked, about to march out of this dive. "You didn't turn it on and leave it running like in the movies?"

"Oh, for crying out loud!" He retrieved the tiny device again and set it on the table. Its record light was dark, but to prove his point, he turned it over, opened the back, and removed the batteries. "Satisfied?" he asked.

"I guess."

"Good, but I would like to take a few notes." He dropped the disabled recorder into his pocket again and pulled out a notebook and pen. When she was about to protest again, he leaned across the table. "Look, we had a deal and I'm holding to it, okay? I'm not planning to blast your story all over the place, but I'd like to remember some points for a story about Justice when they catch him."

Laura didn't like it. "You're making me regret talking to you."

To her shock, he reached across the table and grabbed one of her hands. "Trust me," he said, and his fingers were incredibly strong and warm. She felt an unlikely current of electricity slide through her veins and quickly retrieved her hand. His smile seemed as sincere as it was engaging. "I won't do or print anything you don't want me to. I promise. Unless it'll help catch the bastard."

There was the dilemma, the real reason she'd agreed to the interview. If Frost could help put Justice behind bars, then she'd do anything she could to help him and that included allowing him some insight into Siren Song. Once more, he was staring at her with his damned eyes.

Practiced charm. Again.

"But you'll let me know first? Right? Before you do anything?" This wasn't going exactly the way she planned. Not at all.

"Yes."

She stared at him, wondering, really, if she could believe him.

No way, not with him scribbling notes. But there it was; he already had clicked his pen and flipped open his notepad.

"Back to your mother. Mary. Give me some background content. What was she like?"

"I don't really know, honestly. She was a bit of a mystery to all of us. Catherine says that she and my mom fought about us all the time. Different philosophies about raising us. Catherine wanted austerity and my mother wanted free love."

"How old were you when your mom died?"

"Ten, almost eleven, I think. I don't really know. I was just a child, and it was kind of a taboo subject."

He made a note, then said, "And that's about the time Catherine locked the gates."

"I think so, yeah."

He shook his head. "That's wild."

More than wild, she thought as she took another sip from her cooling coffee, it had been necessary.

To keep the demons at bay.

# CHAPTER 12

Justice awoke with a jerk that nearly lifted him off the makeshift bed he'd constructed of Cosmo's heavy overcoat and his own Halo Valley uniform scrunched up and used as a pillow. The old oak floorboards beneath were hard as metal. His heart pounded harshly against his ribs as he sat up. Light filtered in gloomily through cracks in the siding and the one, dirty, cobweb-shrouded window on the western side of the building.

He needed transportation . . . he could—

The smell of sick perfidy filled his nose.

One of them was nearby!

The pregnant one.

His lips curled of their own accord.

The stench of her was calling to him to send her and her growing monster into the black abyss from where they sprang.

He felt his pulse jump, his heart begin to pound, and he began to sweat, though it was still the cool of the morning, the single window showing a foggy morning shroud through its dirty panes. All drowsiness left him, and he had a sudden sizzling vision of the thick and twisting evil that ran through the roots of their family tree. A snake that bored into them and poisoned their blood. It had been there for years. Generations. And it had found a home in the female heart and womb, sent straight from hell to do Satan's bidding.

His flesh crawled. He'd seen it in the woman who'd given birth to him. Smelled it in the flesh of his sisters. Whores every one. Hiding like snakes under rocks . . . except the scent of this one was too strong. She was nearby.

He let the excitement build. He'd spent years in a fogged and frozen state, impotent, unable to do what needed to be done. Then there had been Jezebel. Outside the gates of their evil manse, he'd tracked her. Until she'd been allowed inside. Welcomed. Into the very heart of Siren Song, the vile spot from which he'd been tossed out like garbage. Along with the bitch who'd birthed him. He'd been forced to live through her subsequent pregnancy and the twisted mass of human flesh she'd borne. His sisters. The ones who had been closest to him by blood, much closer than the women who lived in the lodge now, who, he knew, were cousins of his, connected through the ancestors who had built the lodge . . .

*Sisters* . . .

He shuddered, thinking of them all. He'd been uncertain and inadequate until he'd caught up with and stabbed Jezebel. Then he'd known. His path was clear. But the mother bitch had descended into madness and was laughed at in the town. Reading palms and cards for money. Lying to feed herself. Wishing she could be back with *them*.

Though he'd never been told the truth—oh, no, it had been that witch of a mother's intention to keep him forever in the dark, but he'd learned. She, that whore who'd borne him, had been cast out because she had lain with one of the black-hearted bitch's men. He hated her as much as the rest of them. He'd almost killed her once. Now he had been given a second chance to get the job done.

It was God's will.

He heard the scrape of talons on the roof, and then a solitary raven's call. He blinked, rubbed a hand over the stubble on his jaw. He needed transportation. He was no more than a man himself, no matter what names they called him. Psycho. Schizo. Homicidal maniac. Nutcase. It scarcely penetrated any longer, though once upon a time it had hurt like they were driving nails into his eyes and ears every time one of his *sisters* rained their epithets down on him.

*Bastard.*

*Stupid.*

*Retard.*

*Sicko.*

They were no better. In fact, far worse.

He was more than willing to perform God's will. His mission. He embraced the duty of killing them all. Each and every one, so the sickness that twined through them was banished forever.

He could count on no one else, he thought as he stood, feeling his full bladder and rotating his neck until it cracked. Justice was the only male in the family who'd lived to adulthood. The sisters had managed to kill them all. Every last male child. Aside from him.

Anger slid through his bloodstream and his teeth clenched at the unfairness of it all. His fists clenched until his veins showed in his wrists.

He was determined to avenge his brothers' deaths.

And he was determined to be the last member of their cursed tribe left on earth.

Savvy pushed through the glass doors of Seagull Pointe and walked across a strip of industrial-grade blue carpeting to the front desk. She wasn't in uniform, as she wasn't exactly a deputy. She'd been a detective in Gresham, and she was a detective at the TCSD, and she didn't like the conspicuous nature of the tan uniform. But she did have her badge, and she held it in front of the girl at the counter that separated the office area from the reception foyer. The lingering scents of coffee and bacon, leftover odors from a recently served breakfast, hung in the air, and a few of the residents still sat at tables in the dining area, a large room that jutted off the back of the main entrance. The receptionist stared at Savvy's card as if she had no idea what to do.

"Detective Savannah Dunbar with the Tillamook County Sheriff's Department," Savvy said. "I'd like to see one of your patients, Madeline Turnbull."

"Oh . . . uh . . ." She looked over her shoulder, as if hoping someone with more authority would appear, then, realizing that she was on her own, glanced at the clock mounted near the door. "Uh . . . let me call the director." The receptionist, who looked all of eighteen and whose name tag read KERI, punched a button and waited. For nearly two minutes. "Uh . . . He must not be in." She licked her lips nervously; talking to anyone official obviously worried her. She was off her stool and said, "Just a sec. I'll get Inga for you."

Whoever the hell Inga was, Savvy thought. She waited a few minutes and eyed all the plaques of excellence displayed proudly near the sign in/out sheet and a vase of silk flowers—roses and carnations.

Keri reappeared with Inga, presumably, and without bothering with introductions, slunk back to her stool.

"I'm Inga Anderssen," the newcomer said. A middle-aged woman with blond hair going to gray, Inga was trim and direct and eyed Savvy carefully. "Our director, Darius Morrow, is unavailable. How can I help you?"

Savvy explained again about her mission, and Inga simply shook her head. "I'm afraid that's impossible. Madeline can't answer any questions for you. For the most part, she's unaware of her surroundings."

"I would like to meet her, all the same."

"The media has already tried." Inga's voice held a certain amount of satisfaction. Clearly, the press had failed and she had prevailed.

"I understand why you would want to keep the media out, but I'm here in an official capacity."

"And I told you, she's unavailable."

While Keri shuffled papers on the other side of the desk and an elderly couple pushed matching walkers down a hallway snaking off the central reception area, Savvy and Inga sized each other up. Savvy was very aware that her youth and looks worked against her more times than not in her job. "Are you going to make me get a court order?" she said with a smile, though her voice brooked no argument.

Inga looked her up one side and down the other. She wanted to battle. She really, really did. But it was clear to both of them that in the end, Savvy had the law on her side. With a pressing of her lips, followed by an indifferent shrug, she said, "Fine. This way," then led Savvy down a hallway to the right, which in turn led to the nursing home part of the establishment. The assisted-living rooms were in the opposite direction, according to the signs posted on the walls.

Inga slowed at one of the rooms, then entered, leaving Savvy to follow.

Madeline "Mad Maddie" Turnbull lay in a hospital bed, her skin gray against white linens. The room was bare, not a personal item to be seen. No pictures in frames, no bouquets, no knickknacks from her previous life. A chair with a toilet seat and receptacle was parked beside the bed and a tray table angled toward her with a glass half filled with water and a straw. Even the window shade was drawn, and the room seemed cloying and dark, almost tomblike, the smells of urine and antiseptic unmistakable.

Madeline's eyes were open and staring straight toward the ceiling tiles. Savannah had seen a similar look on her father's face as he entered a twilight world of unreality that just preceded his death. She didn't know anything about this woman, but she would bet it was a matter of weeks or days before she was gone, not much longer.

"I'm Detective Savannah Dunbar," she said, introducing herself to the silent woman. "Until yesterday your son, Justice, was a patient at Halo Valley Security Hospital. He escaped last night and is still missing."

Madeline lay quietly, her chest barely rising and falling. No reaction to the news.

"He may try to see you." Savvy waited, but nothing happened. The closeness of the room started to press upon her, and she experienced a roll of nausea. She was surprised to feel a physical reaction because she hadn't believed she could be so susceptible to atmosphere; she prided herself on her professionalism, in fact, and had always been the one with the strong stomach. But now the feel of imminent death and the smells of chlorine and sweat and something sweet she couldn't identify made her head swim a bit.

Hearing a soft beep behind her, Savvy looked to Inga Anderssen, who examined a small pager she had pulled from an inner pocket. "Are you almost done?"

"Yes."

"I'll take this outside," the older woman warned, then swept out. Savannah heard her make a cell phone call to someone and begin instantly berating them for their care of another patient.

She blocked out the sound and turned back to Maddie. "We're alerting the staff here, and they'll make sure you and the other patients are safe. If, for any reason, he should manage to contact you, press your call button. Let us know immediately."

She waited, counting off the seconds in her head until it would be safe and prudent to leave without seeming to rush from the room. She heard Inga Anderssen winding up her call in the outside hallway and half turned toward the door herself.

"It's a boy," the woman in the bed said.

"Pardon?" Savvy glanced back, her heart nearly stopping. She'd thought the woman was almost comatose, but her words were clear. Maddie's eyes had rolled to the side, pinning her in a way that was almost eerie. A ripple of unease rolled across Savvy's arms.

"Do you want to know your future?" the older woman asked.

"Detective?" Inga's voice from the hallway caused Savannah to jump as if goosed.

The nurse had pushed open the door farther and was frowning at her, her expression fierce. "Are you finished?"

Savvy glanced back at Madeline, whose eyes were gently closing, as if her efforts had exhausted her. She stared at the near-dead woman a long moment, before turning back to Inga. "She just spoke to me."

One of Inga's eyebrows quirked. "What? No."

"She doesn't speak?"

"Not a word."

"Well, she did to me."

"Must be your winning ways," Inga said, disbelieving. "Hear that, Maddie? The officer thinks you spoke with her."

The woman on the bed was barely breathing.

"Yeah, right. She's a regular Chatty Cathy. What'd she do? Want to read your fortune?" Inga was chuckling, and Savvy, seeing that Mad Maddie had once again slipped into that twilight world between life and death, left, walking past the brittle nurse and into the hall. She skirted around an old guy in a wheelchair and walked swiftly toward the outside doors. The cold of the morning slapped her hard in the face, but she kept going, refusing to give in to the urge to run. So Mad Maddie had slipped out of her coma and said a few words. So what?

"Jesus, get hold of yourself."

She was across the parking lot and had just reached her

department-issued Jeep when her cell buzzed. Expelling a pent-up breath she hadn't known she'd been holding, she answered, "Dunbar."

"Burghsmith and Clausen found the van," Lang stated curtly. "The one from Halo Valley that was transferring Turnbull."

"Good. And what about him?"

"No sign of the escapee yet, but it looks like we guessed right. He's heading to the coast. The van was found miles west of Halo Valley."

Savvy glanced over her shoulder and around the near-empty parking lot, as if expecting Justice Turnbull to leap from the shrubbery. Of course he didn't.

Lang asked, "How'd it go with Mad Maddie?"

Frowning, Savvy glanced back to Seagull Pointe's front doors. "She's bedridden. Not really aware. I told her about Justice, but I don't know how much went in."

"She respond?"

"I thought she said something to me, but . . ." *No, you know she said something!* ". . . The nursing staff says she's not responding at all."

"Get on back here, and we'll go to the site where they found the van together. The way it looks, I guess, is that Turnbull drove it up the mountain a ways and pushed it down a ravine. So he musta caught a ride with someone. I suppose he could've headed back to the valley at that point, but he woulda had to drive right past Halo Valley and all our people. And, anyway, we know he has unfinished business here. Think he'll try to see his mother?"

"Maybe." Again that ripple of unease slid over her, which was ridiculous. She was a cop, for God's sake, nerves of steel and all that.

"He tried to kill her once before," Lang reminded, sounding like he was talking more to himself than Savannah.

"The staff's on alert, and they're very protective of

Madeline. They tried to stop me from seeing her. She should be okay."

"What did you think of her?"

"Like I said, she's not really aware."

"I've asked people around town about her. She was apparently a pretty accurate psychic in her day."

*It's a boy!* Maddie's words skittered across her brain.

Lang went on. "Some people are still scared of her, though I guess she was more a nuisance in her last years, before Justice came after her. We're patrolling the area around her boarded-up motel, but nothing's happening."

"And the lighthouse?"

"One way in. One way out. He hasn't tried to go there. We'll keep watching Mad Maddie, her motel and the lighthouse, and Siren Song, and wait for him to show. But he's in the wind, could be anywhere and too smart to go back to his usual haunts." Lang's frustration echoed over the wireless connection. "Anyway, get on back here and let's go."

"Wait! Did you get hold of McNally?" she asked, referring to the retired detective from the Laurelton PD.

"Haven't connected yet. Found out he's on a camping trip with his son this weekend. Out of cell range apparently. But I talked to Becca Sutcliff Walker. She and her husband, Hudson Walker, are definitely on pins and needles since Justice has been loose. I told two of 'em I would call them first, as soon as we've got him in custody again."

"I hope that's soon," Savvy said with feeling.

"You and me both."

Savvy hung up, closed her eyes, and tilted her face toward the sky. The air was heavy with moisture. Fog had crept down the mountains and covered the beach, darkening the morning, making everything seem less distinct.

Climbing into her Jeep, she caught the time and realized the entire ordeal with Inga, Maddie, and now the phone call with Lang, had lasted less than thirty minutes. God, it was going to be a long day! She gazed in her rearview at the building as she drove from the lot. She knew Justice Turnbull was a killer. An obsessive psychotic with a one-track mind. But if he was half as creepy as his mother, he was something more than those labels. Something as yet unnamed.

*Do you want to know your future?*

She shook her head and switched on the ignition.

Hell, no.

# CHAPTER 13

Laura's stomach began to growl.

After what seemed an eternity, their plates of huevos rancheros were delivered with an apology. "Mix-up in the kitchen. Sorry," the barkeep said, as they'd ordered over half an hour earlier. Laura cautiously tried the food. Harrison's gaze was on her, and she admitted with surprise after the first bite, "It is really good."

"Told ya," he said with satisfaction. "Worth the wait."

"I don't know about that."

They tucked into their food for a few moments, and then Laura ventured cautiously, "You're a little too easy to talk to."

"I get it, you don't trust me."

"Should I?"

He laughed. "You tell me."

"Not an answer, Frost." She jabbed a fork in his direction. "I'm guessing this—the meal, the laid-back attitude, the easygoing smile—is all part of your own interviewing technique."

"If it's working, call it what you will." The corners of his eyes crinkled.

"I know. You're not into semantics."

He found a bottle of hot sauce and sprinkled some over the remainder of his meal. "Tell me," he wondered aloud, "why would the police think you're a psycho if you told them you knew about Justice's game plan?"

"Wouldn't you?"

"Maybe." He took a bite and washed it down with coffee. "By the way, what is it?"

"His game plan?" Laura gazed into his hazel eyes, found herself slightly mesmerized. Scary. "I guess only he could really answer that." Harrison poured them each more coffee from the pot, and she added a little more cream, watching the clouds come to the surface of her mug. "Do you believe in psychic phenomena?" she asked cautiously as she stirred and the cream dissipated. She knew she was treading on dangerous water here. He was a journalist, into the facts, things he could touch, taste, hear, and smell. He wouldn't be into "feelings" or "sensations."

"Not really."

"Didn't think so."

He scooped a forkful of beans, tortilla, and ranchero sauce into his mouth. "Why?" he asked after he'd swallowed.

"The police don't either."

"You're saying you're a psychic?"

"Not really," she said, purposely echoing his words. "But my family has experienced . . ."

"Experienced?" he repeated when she faded out.

"We have . . . we all have . . ."

"Yeah?"

She wondered, really wondered, if she was really going to admit this. Her heart started pounding hard.

"Something woo-woo?" he suggested.

"I knew you'd make fun."

"I'm not making fun," he said so sincerely and she almost believed him. Almost. "I'm just trying to see where you're going." When she remained silent, he suggested, "Are you saying you have some kind of ESP, or something?"

"Wow, I'm sorry I started this," she said, meaning it. "I knew I would be."

"Look, I might have trouble swallowing all the psychic stuff, but I'm not completely closed-minded."

"Aren't you?" she challenged.

He smiled, offering up that sexy grin she found ridiculously fascinating. She looked down at her plate, resisting his charm, his winning ways. "I'll prove it. Why don't you give me an example of what you're talking about?"

She said, "I'm a nurse. I'm a good nurse, and I believe in science and healing through medicine. If you repeat what I'm about to tell you, I'll deny it. I'll flat out lie, because I'm good at my job and I don't want my patients thinking I'm a nutcase."

"Fair enough."

She smiled back at him, disbelieving.

"Look, making judgment calls isn't conducive to interviewing people," Harrison pointed out. "I gotta say, you've got me on the edge of my seat."

"I have a sister who is precognitive," Laura stated. "She sees things in the future."

"Such as?"

"She knew Justice had escaped before I told her."

"Well, it was on the news. . . ."

"Uh-uh." Laura shook her head. "No television. No outside information. They didn't know anything but what Cassandra had told them."

"Cassandra?"

"Don't write that down!" she stated quickly as Harrison reached for his small tablet as the door to the restaurant opened and a group of three men entered to take a seat at a nearby table. She lowered her voice. "I'm serious."

He lifted his hands. "I know. I get it. I was just going to

ask you what all their names were. From the sound of it, there are enough of you that I'll need to write them down."

"I'm not giving you their names. Don't make me sorry I told you about Cassandra."

"Okay," he said.

"Okay." She was firm.

"What about you, then? What's your special ability?"

She glanced at her half-eaten food and gently pushed her plate aside. She'd never told anyone. Had known not to.

*You need the truth seeker.*

"Ms. Adderley?"

"It's Laura . . . Lorelei, actually."

"Lorelei. Like in the myth?"

She stared at him, surprised. So few knew. Fewer still made any connection.

"I majored in journalism with an English minor," he explained.

She didn't know what to say. He kept surprising her, which made her question whether she was the one who had the prejudices. No, no. She wasn't going to second-guess herself. If she'd learned anything from her marriage to the God of all know-it-alls, Byron Adderley, it was that she did know her own mind. She took in a calming breath, then said, "Okay, here it is. I sometimes know what's wrong with a patient, physically. I can guess the diagnosis."

"Is that so weird . . . for someone in the medical field?"

"Maybe not." She pressed her lips together. She knew her ability was something special, but if he wasn't interested in believing, she wasn't about to push the issue. But she also wanted help in finding Justice, and so far, he was her best candidate. "But the thing is . . . the real psychic ability that I guess I want you to know . . . is . . ."

"Is?" he prodded.

She almost laughed. What good was this admission going to do for her? "Okay, it's that I can hear Justice."

"Hear him? How do you mean?"

*Oh, God, here goes nothing.* If anything would convince Frost that she was off her nut, this would. "What I mean is that I can hear his voice scraping at my brain. He talks to me."

Harrison Frost was trying really, really hard to keep his face from giving him away. Laura could sense the effort he was putting into his act of believing her. "Well, then, what does he say?" he asked carefully.

"I knew it. You're humoring me."

"What does he say?" he repeated.

"He says, '*Sssisssterrr,*'" she rasped. "He says it with a menace so strong, it actually scratches across my brain and I know he's coming for me." Harrison was staring at her intently, but there wasn't disbelief in his expression. "I've sensed him all my life. He's sent messages off and on for years, although I didn't really get what they were about until I was older. I only really fully understood the last when he was on his mission."

Harrison's face was sober now, his eyes darkening gravely, his jaw rock hard, not a hint of a smile on his lips. "His mission of killing people? A few years back? That's what you're talking about?"

She nodded. "Justice is after my family. I don't know why exactly. He wants to kill us all."

"And he's sending you messages to that effect?"

"Yes." Then, "I know what it sounds like." She rubbed her face hard, wishing she hadn't started this, knowing there was no backing out now. Besides, she needed someone to know that she had contact with Justice, though she supposed trusting a reporter like Harrison Frost wasn't the best idea. "His voice is really strong right now. He knows where I am. I'm on his radar."

"You think he wants to kill you."

*And my baby.* "Oh, yeah." Of this she was certain.

"What's he got against all of you?"

"Good question. Catherine says Mary was cruel to him

when he was young. What that means, I don't really know. People can be unkind, even brutal, or cruelty can be imagined. Even so, to the victim, it's real."

He clicked his pen as he frowned thoughtfully. "What about Justice's own mother?"

"Madeline," she said, remembering. "I—I don't know. He tried to kill her before, though. He's never sent me any kind of message about that, and when . . . when he reaches toward me, I block him out."

"You mean mentally?"

"Yes. Absolutely."

"So, he's got this ability, too."

She nodded. "Yeah, I guess so."

Harrison's gaze narrowed. "So, how does it work, exactly?"

"I raise up a wall inside my mind, and he's blocked out. I mentally visualize the wall, build it strong and tall, and it cuts him off."

"But didn't you say his voice is stronger now?"

"Since he escaped. Yes." She nodded, felt the hair on her nape rise when she thought of Justice's hideous sibilant messages. "Oh, God, this is horrible."

Harrison stared at her a moment, then said softly, "I think I've got enough. No more questions for now."

"Good." The truth was, she was drained; dredging up all the old memories and concentrating on Justice's malevolence was exhausting.

Harrison leaned back, caught the bartender's attention, and signaled for the check. Within seconds, the bartender brought over the tab. Harrison left several bills on the table as she shrugged into her jacket. Together they wended their way through tables and past the bar, where, despite the early hour, the barkeep was drawing beers and making Bloody Marys.

Laura felt Harrison's hand in the small of her back once,

guiding her around two newcomers who were talking and taking up more than their share of personal space in the aisle.

At the door, Harrison leaned closer and said, "I want to get this guy. I mean I *really* want to get him."

"Me, too," Laura responded with feeling. She wouldn't rest easy until he was behind bars. Or dead.

"If you can help me, I'm all for that, no matter how you do it," he said, shouldering open the door to the gray day beyond. "If he calls to you, let me know."

"I will." And she would, though what good it would do, she didn't know. Standing on the front steps and looking toward the ocean, she noticed a fog bank crawling closer to the shore. Eventually, it would obscure the beach completely, making it difficult for the beach cleaners, volunteers who had come to the coast, to pick up the garbage, to do their job.

He thought for a moment as they started down the wide stairs, disturbing a seagull that was scavenging near the walkway. "Wait a minute. Does it work both ways? Can you call to him?"

Laura had never tried. Didn't want to. "I don't know. Maybe." Anything was possible.

"Maybe the question should be, would you consider calling to him? You know, to draw him out?"

She paused on the bottom step and glared at him. "Let me get this straight. You want me to place myself in danger. He's a psychopath, you know. If . . . if I let him in, he'll know where I am."

Harrison frowned, squinting against the fractured sunlight slipping through the thickening fog. "And he'll come for you. That's what you think?"

"Yes!"

"You're certain?"

"Pretty much—yeah."

His scowl deepened. "Okay. That's not good."

"Not good at all." She felt the cold dampness of the morning caressing her skin, chilling her bones again.

"Does he know where you work?"

"He doesn't know anything about me but my name. At least I hope he doesn't," she said with a catch in her heart as they crossed the pockmarked parking lot, their shoes crunching on loose gravel.

"Does he know what you look like?" he asked.

Laura touched her dyed hair before she could stop herself, and she saw his eyes follow the gesture. "If he got anywhere near me, he'd know me, I think."

"That why you didn't want to be on camera last night?"

"I didn't want to be on camera for a lot of reasons, but yes," she admitted, "that was the biggie."

"So when was it that you last heard from him?" he asked.

"This morning, when I was in the shower." She remembered his hiss over the shower's pulsing spray, and she felt Justice's malevolence all over again . . . so close . . . so damned close. "He told me he was coming for me."

"In those words?"

"No . . . I don't know." Laura felt embarrassed now. Her secrets bared. The way Harrison was looking at her and struggling to understand was excruciating.

"Let me get this straight. Since he escaped, you think you've been getting stronger messages," he reiterated.

"I know I have. It's possible his messages might have been blocked while he was at Halo Valley. I hadn't heard from him at all while he was incarcerated." Harrison nodded slowly, and she said, "I know what this sounds like. The lady is loony, one step away from a room at Halo Valley herself."

"Nah." He shook his head, and she noticed his hair was darkening with the damp air. "I've heard a lot of weird stuff over the years. Maybe you've got some ability. Maybe you don't. Maybe this is just insight. Maybe it's something more. I don't really care." He seemed sincere. She didn't dare look too closely into his eyes, though, because she was afraid she might get lost in them and start believing everything he said, and that, she knew, would be foolish. He was saying, "But I'm willing to go with it and see where it leads. You obviously believe it, and if it helps find the bastard, fine. But it sounds like you think you haven't heard from him for a while because he was locked away."

"Yeah . . . it might be the distance, but . . . I have the feeling that it could be because he was on some kind of meds, drugs that inhibited his ability somehow. But that's just a guess. I don't really know."

"Doesn't matter. The thing is he wasn't able to reach you until he escaped. But now he's coming in loud and clear."

"Right," she said, knowing it was, at least partially, a lie.

*The pregnancy. That's why he's so close. He found me because I'm pregnant.* It wasn't just because he'd been incarcerated.

"What?" Harrison asked, his gaze searching her face, as if reading her thoughts.

*I need to save my baby.*

She nearly stumbled at a pothole, and Harrison caught her arm. "Hey, you okay?"

*No, I'm not. I'll never be as long as Justice is free, maybe not until he's dead.* Trying to get a grip on her runaway emotions, she closed her eyes and faced the ocean, feeling the heavy air, pent up with rain, calm her racing mind, while his strong hand held the crook of her elbow steady.

"Look, I'm going after him," he said with conviction. "He's a killer. Maybe the police will find him. Maybe I'll find him first."

"For your story?" She heard the bite in her words as they reached her Subaru.

"For the good of humanity." He offered her a smile and dropped her arm. "And yeah, it'll be a helluva story."

A question hung between them—unspoken and blurry, like fog—yet she guessed what was on his mind. "You want me to help you find him, don't you?" Of course he did. That was what this interview was really about.

"Yes." He was honest. "But that decision's yours. Meanwhile, I'll do some investigating. Maybe his mother knows something. Or maybe one of your sisters or your aunt? Any chance I could talk to them?"

"No," she stated quickly. "You're a reporter. And a man."

"Hmmm . . . okay. Well, Justice lived around here. Your family's here. He's going to come back this way to get to you all. The police aren't idiots. They know that, too, and it's merely a matter of time before he's caught."

"But you want to find him first," she guessed, fishing in her purse for her keys.

"That's the plan."

"A crazy plan."

He shrugged.

"And 'the cult' will make a big story."

"Not bigger than the recapture of a psychotic killer. Maybe a nice side story," he admitted, unabashed. "But I'm off the record until you give me the green light."

She had to believe him. Trust him. She'd just bared her damned soul . . . well, almost. She hadn't mentioned the baby or the fact that being pregnant made her more vulnerable, more easily found by Justice. "So, what are you going to do now?" she asked as she unlocked her car.

"Right now? For starters, stick close to you. If he's sending you messages, I want to be around when you receive the next one." Harrison slid her a look. "And if you change your mind and decide to call him first, I want to be on that party line."

"Why do I feel I'm being used?"

"Not at all."

*So much for the "good of humanity" line.*

"I don't think you should count on me dialing up the psycho," Laura said, opening the Outback's driver side door. "It's the old self-preservation thing, you know."

"I wouldn't put you in danger."

She sent him a look that said more sarcastically than words, "Sure."

"Seriously, I'll be with you every step of the way."

"Oh, yeah, right. Save that for some idiotic romantic, B-rated movie."

He touched her arm again. Long fingers curling over her jacket's sleeve. "I'm not kidding. But this is your call."

"You've got that right."

"If you change your mind, if you want to catch him soon, let me know."

"Don't hold your breath!" She pulled her arm back, grateful to break any touch with him. What had she been thinking? That he cared? For the love of God, she barely knew him! "There's the sheriff's department. They'll handle it."

"They're doing their best, I'm sure," he agreed.

But the unspoken end of that sentence was, "They just don't have your unique resource to pinpoint his location."

"Will you call me? The next time you 'hear' from him?" He handed her a card and scratched a number on it. "My cell," he said, and she, telling herself this was crazy, the damned reporter was on a fool's mission, slipped the card into a pocket of her purse. Foolish, foolish woman!

"I'll think about it. Thanks for breakfast. You were right. The huevos were worth it."

"You're welcome, Lorelei." He gave her a quick grin, and he headed for his Impala, jogging across the asphalt and gravel, his back straight, his legs striding in an easy, athletic lope.

She dragged her gaze away and climbed into her car.

Pulling out of the lot, she checked her rearview mirror

and saw him slide into the interior of his beat-up Chevy. A sexy man. A very sexy man with a mission. Just exactly what she didn't need in her life right now.

Still, she watched him nose the Impala out of the lot and wondered what the hell she'd gotten herself into.

# CHAPTER 14

D r. Maurice Zellman sat in a room on the second floor of the hospital. As Lang strode across the threshold, he noted the white gauzy bandage around the man's neck and the sharp lines of pain that bracketed his mouth. Zellman's eyes, however, were bright with anger, and as soon as he saw Lang's TCSD uniform, he lifted a hand and motioned him forward.

"Dr. Zellman, I'm Langdon Stone with the Tillamook County Sheriff's Department," he introduced as he took a few steps toward the bed.

Zellman motioned more furiously, and Lang moved next to the bed, to where he was gazing down at the man with the trim beard and grimly set mouth. Zellman touched his bandaged throat, then pointed to his quivering lips and shook his head slightly.

"You can't talk." Lang nodded. "You've had surgery. How about I ask a couple of yes or no questions and you let me know what the answer is by nodding or shaking your head?"

A curt nod.

"I just want to clarify some facts. Your patient, Justice Turnbull, stabbed you in the throat with your own pen."

Zellman pressed his lips together and nodded again as the sound of a rattling medication cart slid through the door Lang had left ajar.

"He wasn't wearing handcuffs. Was that your decision?"

The doctor gazed at him with burning eyes and didn't respond.

"He attacked the security guard, Conrad Weiser, and took off in the hospital van. Thinking back, do you remember anything, anything at all, that now seems significant? Something that could lead us to him now? Something small, maybe, but that on reflection, could have been a clue that he had plans to escape?"

Zellman just stared at him. Lang could feel the man's fury rolling off him in waves. Anger and embarrassment, perhaps. The doctor's lax standards had directly led to Justice's ability to escape. And he knew it.

Lang said, "If something comes to you, maybe you could write it down. Or, if you remember something that may have come from your therapy sessions, something that could help . . ." Lang knew he was treading down that super sacrosanct road of patient/doctor confidentiality, but hey, the psycho had stabbed Zellman in the throat and that had to count for something in Lang's book.

Zellman, pursing his lips, motioned imperiously for a pen and paper, and Lang stepped into the hall and grabbed the attention of a junior nurse, who scurried to get him what he needed, returning quick enough for Lang to flash her a smile of gratitude that made her blush.

He handed the small pad and pen to Zellman, who looked long and hard at the pen itself for long seconds before writing: *The lighthouse. His mother's motel. Seagull Pointe?*

"Seagull Pointe is where his mother resides," Lang said for confirmation.

Zellman nodded once more, and his shoulders seemed to sag a bit, some of the starch leaving him.

"We're checking those places, but so far, he hasn't shown up at any of them. Anywhere else?"

Zellman considered, his eyes narrowing. After a few moments, he wrote: *He wants to watch the sea. He spoke of it with reverence. He would face west. Even being locked up*.

Lang thought about that and considered. There was a lot of seashore along the Pacific Ocean. "You think he'll stay around Deception Bay?"

Once again, Zellman inclined his head sharply.

"And will he go after the women at Siren Song again?"

At this, Zellman frowned and wrote: *They are his obsession*. He paused, then scribbled: *But anyone in his way will be at risk*.

"He never directly attacked the lodge last time," Lang said. "Think he would launch a full-scale attack now?"

Zellman's mouth compressed. *He'll take them one by one. They are too strong in numbers. He is smart. Calculating. Capable*.

There was almost admiration in the words. Had the good doctor let himself be taken in by Justice? Or was he trying to explain his ridiculous lapse in judgment in allowing Turnbull to get the better of him?

"If you think of anything else . . . ," Lang said, glancing at the notebook he was leaving in Zellman's care.

The doctor nodded grimly, then gazed straight ahead, his brows a black line of fury and resolve. Lang figured Zellman detested being bested, being played for a fool, and good old homicidal Justice had done just that.

Zellman's eyes blazed a quiet, smoldering anger.

Maybe he'd been taken in, but he sure as hell wasn't happy about it.


The June day was gray and gloomy and cold, and fog was creeping from inland, obscuring surrounding dunes, houses, commercial buildings, and the Coast Range. Justice stood on the socked-in beach, able to see little but the frothy waves that rushed toward his booted feet.

Even with the fog, there were people everywhere, and it had taken him by surprise. Normally, on a day with this weather, Oregon beaches would be practically empty. He was so involved with his internal world and the urgency of his mission that he'd nearly run into two separate individuals in the short distance from the parking lot of the clam shack and the beach itself.

Now he heard, before he saw, a group of maybe seven people wandering his way, talking together in bright tones, wearing coats, hats, gloves, and boots, their heads turning this way and that, arms stretched out and fingers pointing. He turned away as they approached and then saw the baseball cap that one sported with bright red letters that said, CLEAN UP THE BEACH!!

A beach cleaning day with volunteers. He felt instantly protective and selfish of this stretch of sand. *Get away,* he thought. *Damned do-gooders. Leave me and this place alone.*

His fingers curled inside Cosmo's gloves. He looked just like them, he realized. It was a perfect cover. God's next gift to him. Cosmo's boots, jacket, and pants, which were belted tight as Justice was thinner than the hippie by at least twenty pounds.

The group moved on, a vanishing knot in the low-lying mist, and Justice let out a pent-up breath. He stood quietly, his face to the sea, and thought about the crowds that were bound to be scouring the sand all day. Crowds hidden in the fog.

But maybe that could help him.

Where there were people on the beach, there was bound to be vehicles left in the various lots and turnouts near the dunes.

He was good with vehicles.

Energized, Justice walked northward and toward the road, pretending to be bending down and searching through the beach grass for litter as he put distance between himself and his temporary abode. It was still miles to Deception Bay, but he didn't plan to walk the whole way. He could take a car or truck or SUV and keep it for hours, maybe days, if he planned it just right.

About a mile from where he'd started, he trudged through the dry sand of the dunes toward the beachfront houses beyond, then followed a short, two-block road that teed into a meandering lane that eventually found its way to Highway 101, which began an upward rise along this stretch, allowing for a wide parking area with a view of the ocean, at least on clear days. Normally, this lot held about three or four cars, but today they were crammed in every which way, with even more vehicles jammed in behind them and fog wisping between the tightly packed bumpers. About three rows back from the beach was a silver compact, its rear end dangerously close to the highway. It was nose in to the viewpoint, but there was really no room for it. Its driver was a young woman on a cell phone who was half in, half out of the opened driver's door and was practically spitting into the receiver.

"No! Hell! I can't park anywhere. *Anywhere!* This volunteer stuff is crap, Kay. God, no. I haven't seen Derek at all, and if he's not here, then fuck this. I'm outta here." She listened for a few seconds, then said, "Just tell him I was here, okay? I'm going home and sleeping off this damn headache. I'll call when I get to Portland."

She snapped the phone shut and suddenly felt Justice's attention. Without turning his way, she demanded, "What are you staring at, freak?"

He felt a familiar coldness spread through his insides. Freak. Changeling.

There was no one around. Fog had settled over them, making the farthest cars seem like some indistinct humps in a lot that time forgot. He leaned forward and said, "You're going to get your tail hit."

"Fuck you." She grabbed for the door handle, but Justice was between them. "Get lost, *loser!*" she screamed.

He backhanded her so hard that her head made a popping sound.

"Wha—what?" she cried, trying to stand up from the driver's seat, but Justice grabbed her head with both hands, stared into her wide, blue, terrified eyes, then twisted with all his strength. She fought him hard, scratching his arm, which only excited him more, convinced him that she was vile. With renewed energy and a thrill running through his soul, he wrapped his hands around her throat and squeezed until she gasped what sounded like a last breath.

She was no one. She had to die.

"*Sisssterrr,*" he whispered aloud, sending a message to the others like her. This one didn't matter, but they would know what he'd done and their black souls would shiver.

Shoving her limp body into the passenger seat, he leaned her head back against the headrest. Her eyes were wide open; her tongue protruding a bit. Closing her eyes with his fingers, he gave her a quick consideration. She looked dead. He buckled her in, then carefully turned her face toward him, arranging it so that it looked as if she were nodding forward in sleep.

Then he adjusted the driver's seat to give himself some legroom and backed carefully onto the highway, heading into the fog-shrouded day.

*Sissstterrr . . .*

The message sizzled beneath Laura's skin, and she straightened with a jerk from where she'd laid her head on the table and fallen asleep.

She blinked several times, coming back to the moment with difficulty. She was home. Dozing in a chair. Memories crashed through her brain. In the parking lot at Davy Jones's Locker she'd managed to convince Harrison Frost that she would contact him immediately should Justice contact her, and so they'd parted ways. And now this—Justice's mental assault.

Fully awake, she mentally castigated herself for talking so freely to Frost, wondering what it was about him that had made her want to trust him so much, envelop him, drag him into her world. And him, being a reporter, no less.

This dozing . . . this lapse in concentration had cost her. She'd inadvertently released her grip on her mental wall, and Justice had slipped his message inside.

*Sissterrr* . . . His hiss curled through her brain.

Her heart shuddered. Oh, God, no!

Though Laura had almost instantly slammed her wall against him, she'd received a backwash of information that left her quivering with fear.

*He's killed someone. A woman. Someone in his way.*
*An innocent!*

Climbing unsteadily to her feet, she walked to the window and stared out the panes, her fingers trailing on the sill. She realized Justice *wanted* her to know. Wanted them all to know. She wasn't even sure what he'd thrown out to the mental airwaves was true, but he certainly wanted her to think so. To terrify her.

"Bastard!" she muttered.

She shouldn't have let Harrison go, she thought now, grabbing for her purse and digging for his card and her cell phone. With shaking hands she first inputted his cell number into her call log. Then she held her thumb over the green button, ready to place the call.

But . . . was this the right thing to do? He wanted her to signal Justice herself, and she wasn't certain she could.

But what if Justice really had killed someone? Should she call the police? Someone?

Pressing her hand to her mouth, she counted her heart-beats and sank into one of the living room chairs by the small fireplace. Justice wanted her to believe the woman was dead. If she was, then she was no longer in danger; Justice had taken care of that. And if it were an untruth, then if she called the police or Harrison, for that matter, they would want to know where she'd gotten her information and it would all be a mess for nothing.

Harrison would believe her more than the authorities, but it was risky to alert him, too.

But what else could she do? What should she do?

Staring down at the phone, she let her poised thumb descend to the green call button and dial through to his cell.

Saturday afternoon, with threatening fog like a gray fur coat hanging on the mountains and down the beach to the south, but not yet covering the city of Seaside. Harrison was seated at the table outside the coffee and ice cream shop, this time without Chico's company, thank God.

He'd ordered a coffee, which he'd left untouched. His mind was full of his morning with Laura—make that Lorelei—Adderley. Ex–Mrs. Byron Adderley. A member of the cult itself and a onetime resident at Siren Song.

That, in itself, was a story. Not one she was willing to broadcast, yet, but a story worth cultivating.

However, it was only a part of the Justice Turnbull saga, he thought as he watched the pedestrians and motorists cruise slowly down the long stretch of Broadway and felt the cool breath of sea air against the back of his neck.

He hadn't wanted to leave her, yet he couldn't just demand to be her bodyguard. She wouldn't stand for it, and anyway, he had things to take care of, too. He didn't much believe her ability to "talk" to Justice, but it didn't matter in the least. She was connected to the cult. A card-carrying member. And if by some strange kink in reality, she could sense where the psycho was, well, okay, he'd go with that. All the better.

Didn't matter. One way or the other, the whole thing was a reporter's dream. He took a long gulp from his cooling coffee.

"Hey, mister," a cold female voice said behind his left ear.

It took an effort not to jump at the sound, but Harrison covered up a momentary lapse by stretching and yawning and saying, "Yeah, what?" in a bored tone.

She came around into his view. It was not the girl he'd spoken with the day before. This was the one who worked at the gelato store. The hair at her crown was braided, the rest of her dark tresses falling over her shoulders. A tattoo of some kind of heart shape peeked out of the neckline of her uniform, while several woven bracelets surrounded her left wrist.

And she was pissed, but good.

"What are you doing?" she demanded. "Hanging around here, trying to pick up jailbait? I should call the cops."

She was pretty, in a kind of pinched way. Suspicion made her seem older than her probably sixteen or seventeen years; it also made her seem harder.

"Can't a guy just be jobless and aimless without being a pervert?" he snapped back at her. "I've got an old lady, okay? She's about all I can handle, and she's at least old enough to have some brains!"

She bristled. Surprised. Then quickly armed for a new attack. "What are you saying, mister? That I'm stupid?"

"I'm just sitting here, okay?"

"Like you've been for days and days."

"Hey, I buy coffee. It's a free country. Go be miserable around somebody else." He waved his hand, shooing her away.

"I saw you talking to Lana. Asking all kinds of questions that are none of your business!"

He gave her a hard stare, like he was totally annoyed at her for getting in his space. "Well, Jenny, I don't know any Lana," he snarled. "So, why don't you just go back to your job and leave me alone?"

Her eyes widened a bit, and then she clapped her hand over the built-in name tag on her red-and-white-striped uniform top.

"You . . . stay away from us!" she sputtered and then stalked back to the flip-up counter that was her entry to her side of the shop.

"Gladly," he muttered, stretching out in the chair and throwing her a dark look of pure disgust.

Inside, he was jubilant. He'd already known Jenny's name from reading it on her name tag, but he hadn't known Lana's. Now he had two of the seven members of the Deadly Sinners, and Lana had alluded to N.V., which made three. And these kids weren't exactly hiding their exploits and staying under the radar. They were entitled and angry and looking for attention. It wouldn't be hard to figure out the whole lot of them.

Idly, he wondered when Jenny got off work. He thought it would be a simple matter to trail her. He'd bet she and Lana would get together and meet the others. Down on the beach. With all these damn cleanup people swarming across the sand, they would be just another group among many.

And it was Saturday. To date, their burglaries had all been on Saturday nights.

His cell phone rang and he didn't recognize the number. *Second time in two days,* he thought, annoyed. "Frost."

"Hi, it's Laura Adderley. I . . . I'm calling you . . . because . . ." She trailed off on an intake of breath.

He was surprised. Pleasantly surprised. The way she'd

shut down this morning, after their huevos, hadn't boded well for her calling him with information anytime soon. As it stood, she'd phoned within a matter of a couple hours. "Because?" he coaxed.

"I think Justice may have killed someone."

# CHAPTER 15

Harrison was stunned.

Had he heard right? Justice Turnbull had killed someone, and Laura knew about it? All his attention was now on the conversation, the sounds of Seaside in June fading.

"You're sure about this?" he said into his cell.

"Yes. No. Maybe. But . . . yeah, I'm sure," she said, and he heard the tremor in Laura's voice. "It's a woman. Not one of my family, I'm pretty sure. Someone else." He heard the panic rising in her voice.

"Hey, slow down. Are you okay?"

"No. I'm definitely not okay. Oh, God."

Frowning, thinking hard, he kicked out his chair, climbed to his feet. "How do you know?"

"You know how I know. I explained."

He glanced over at Jenny, who was standing behind the counter, her arms crossed under her breasts as she glared suspiciously at him. Giving her his shoulder, he asked, "He called you? Telepathically?"

A pause. "Well . . . yes."

"And . . . ?"

"He wanted me to know . . . he'd killed someone. Oh,

God I . . . I don't know who. I know I sound like a freak
but—"

"You don't. Not to me." He tried to cut her off before she
really lost it.

"This has never happened before."

"Try to calm down."

"Are you nuts? Calm down? Did you hear me? He just
murdered someone!"

"Okay," he said, pulling out one hand and splaying his
fingers as if she could see him.

"Hey, buddy! Watch it." A woman jogging past nearly
ran into his arm. He ignored her.

"Okay. Where are you?"

"At my house."

"Where's that?"

She hesitated.

He couldn't blame her. He was virtually a stranger.

"I want to help." He didn't remind her that she had
called him.

She let out a long breath, then, with a "What does it matter, anyway?" rattled off her address. Quickly. As if the
longer the words stayed in her throat, they might choke her.

"Got it. I'll see you in about half an hour," he told her,
calculating the drive without traffic and fog. Inaccurate for
a Saturday afternoon on any day in June, worse today because of the fog that was between Seaside and Deception
Bay, and the extra cars driven over to the coast for the
beach cleanup, but he didn't want her to think it would take
him as long as it really would. She might regret everything
and try to back out of seeing him.

Glancing back once to Jenny, he saw she was helping a
customer, her attention on scooping up some pink-tinged
ice cream into a waffle cone, while the woman counted out
bills from her wallet and a toddler clung to her leg. He
knew that he was leaving the robbery story at a critical

time, that Jenny might just lead him to the rest of the teen criminals, but he didn't care.

But Justice Turnbull was *the* story of the moment.

And Laura might be in danger. Alone. Vulnerable to whatever Turnbull wanted to set into motion. And you were instrumental in this, weren't you? Encouraged her to "communicate" with a homicidal maniac.

He felt more than a little pang of guilt, but then he hadn't really bought into the telepathy, or whatever she called it. . . . The lodge, dead mother, creepy aunt, mental communication, and walls she built in her mind all sounded a little paranoid.

Except that Justice Turnbull was on the loose again.

That thought spurred him on.

He hurried to his Chevrolet, jumped in, and drove with repressed urgency, one hand on the horn at the lollygagging weekenders, who were all over the place for the Clean Up The Beach!! event. The miles rolled slowly under the Impala's wheels, and Harrison was a bundle of nerves, alternately standing on the brakes and willing himself not to pound on his horn at the slow-moving traffic. Vans, SUVs, sedans, pickups . . . a line of summer traffic that stretched along 101.

Swearing under his breath, he finally reached the turnoff to her house, a humble cottage with loads of deferred maintenance. It had been over an hour since her call.

"Damn."

Jumping from the car, he snatched up his laptop from the backseat, then set it back down again, leaving it with his digital recorder. After locking the Impala, he patted his back pocket for the small notebook that always resided there. He didn't want her to think he was setting up shop, though that was what his half-baked plan was. At least partially.

There were creaky wooden steps that led to an equally creaky front porch, all painted gray, worn through on the treads, listing slightly. He pounded on the door, peering through one of the three diamond window inserts that ran in a diagonal across the top. He watched through the tiny pane as she hurried to answer him, appearing from the back of the house, her darkened hair tucked behind her ears.

When she opened the door, all he saw were her eyes, greenish blue, serious, careful, full of secrets. And scared to death.

For an instant, he wanted to yank her forward and fold her into his arms, to tell her that it would be all right. To even brush his lips over her hair and comfort her.

Holey moley!

He slammed on the mental brakes before he did something stupid and was shocked by his reaction. His arm actually reached out before he caught himself, and he ended up gesturing lamely to cover the lapse. What the hell was wrong with him?

"You okay?" he asked, and she, too, appeared to want to rush into his arms, but she didn't, just hung onto the side of the door and let out her breath.

"Yeah. I mean, I have to be." She managed a weak, unhappy smile and nervously peered over his shoulder. "Come on in." Ushering him inside, she shut the door and shoved the dead bolt into place. Then they stood in the foyer, with the gray light emanating through the three diamond panes. She chewed on a corner of her lip and shook her head. "He's toying with us," she said softly. "He wanted me to know what he'd done. That he'd murdered someone." Her eyes thinned thoughtfully. "He wanted to crow about it."

"He told you his motives?" Though it still seemed ludicrous, the whole telepathy thing, he let that go. For her, at the very least, it was real.

"I just . . . Oh, God, sometimes it's like I understand him." She shivered. "Sick, huh?"

"No judgment calls here," he said. "So who's this woman you think he killed?"

She shook her head. "I don't know."

"Did you . . . see . . . her?"

"No."

"Well, what happened? What did he say to you?"

"You sound impatient," she said suddenly.

"I am impatient," Harrison responded right back. "If he's killed someone, you bet I'm impatient!"

Her blue eyes assessed him, charged him with lying. "You don't believe me. Not really. You just want information and you think I'm an idiot!"

When she turned, he grabbed her arm, and she jerked back as if he'd burned her. "You called me," he reminded her.

"And I thought you'd be a better choice than the police. Am I wrong?"

She was half turned away and gave him only her face in profile. He noticed her lips and chin and the curve of her cheek. The downy softness of the hairs at her temple. The wing of her brow, many shades lighter than her hair color.

"I don't know what I'm doing," she said to the room at large, as if it were an awakening. She walked through an archway.

"You've got a killer after you," he stated bluntly, following her into the living room with its rock fireplace and furniture that had seen better days. "That, I believe, is fact. I don't know about all your communication with him and your family, but I don't really care. You're not safe. A lot of people aren't, like maybe this woman he let you know about."

She shrugged and shook her head, her arms wrapped around her torso, as she stared through the window facing the street and driveway. His Impala, parked in the drive, was visible, as was a house, a similar bungalow, across the street.

"If you had something more concrete, I'd tell you to call the cops."

"I don't want to talk to the authorities," she stated quickly.

"I know. And I get why you don't. Hey, I've had my own problems with them, and sometimes they're just too damn difficult to deal with. Take Detective Fred Clausen, for instance, at the TCSD. I was looking into some unsavory behavior on the part of the deputies there, and he barely contained himself from physically throwing me into the street." She didn't seem to hear him, but he soldiered on. "'Course, I was . . . inferring . . . that the guy had looked the other way when his brother had sex with an underage high school student, and that didn't go over so well."

"Inferring?"

"Okay, accusing. I wasn't wrong about the bastard, but nobody wanted to hear it, especially Clausen. I ran the piece anyway, though my editor was quivering in his boots."

"What happened?" she asked, turning slightly so he could see her profile again. There was something sinuous in her movements that she was completely unaware of.

"Guy got fired from his coaching position at the school for some 'other' reason," he said. "Then the girl turned eighteen and they took off together. Everybody was pissed at me, even her parents. They didn't like the affair, but they didn't like publicity even more. No charges were filed. But the story was true. It happened when I first got to the *Breeze* and I was getting over a few image problems of my own at the time."

"Such as?" Now she turned all the way to face him.

In for a penny, in for a pound. He didn't like talking about what had happened to Manny, but she'd opened up to him. Now it was his turn. Tit, as they say, for tat. "I accused my brother-in-law's business partner of setting up his murder and making it look like an accident."

Recognition lit her eyes. "Now I remember you. I saw

you on television in conjunction with that shooting outside the nightclub. You thought there was more to it."

Harrison snorted. "I'm a conspiracy theorist, if you believe Bill Koontz's lawyers and the implication of Pauline Kirby and her news crew."

"Koontz was your brother-in-law's business partner?" she clarified, her eyebrows pulling together as she pieced together what she'd heard.

He nodded. "He's sole proprietor of Boozehound now. Manny's dead. And my sister and niece got next to nothing."

"You believe Koontz set up your brother-in-law to be murdered."

"You got it. I can't prove it. Yet. But I will." He added, "I lost my job at the *Portland Ledger* over the way I handled the story, but again, I wasn't wrong."

She thought that over. Opened her mouth several times to say something, then closed it again. Finally, she said carefully, "If you stay ahead of the police on this story . . . if you could find Justice first, or a lead to him . . . that would go a long ways to reestablishing your credibility, wouldn't it?"

"Well. Yes. Of course." He gazed at her seriously.

"Okay," she said and inhaled a long, shivery breath as she dropped onto the couch.

"Okay?"

"I want you to help me. Really help me, and my family. I want you to keep us safe from Justice, and in return I'll try to lead you to him, or, more accurately, allow him to be led to me." She shivered as she spoke, as if she felt she were treading on the graves of the undead.

"Okay," he repeated.

They looked at each other.

After a moment, Harrison asked, "So, how exactly do you call Justice?"

"If I drop the wall down for a moment, he'll sense me."

She glanced away, as if embarrassed at how silly it sounded.

"So . . ." He lifted his palms, silently asking what she wanted to do next.

"I don't . . . I just can't do it yet. I'm afraid," she admitted.

He nodded, watching her. "Got any kind of timeline on that?"

She half laughed but still worried her hands. "No. I've just got to work up my courage. It's . . . it's not that easy."

"Okay. Yeah. I see. I'll wait till you're ready." And in truth, he wasn't too thrilled about the prospects of her communicating with Turnbull. If there were another way, if he could hunt down the bastard personally, or find a way to sic the police onto him, that would be better. But, for now, there weren't any other options.

She gazed at him through wide, soulful eyes. "Thanks. I'm just . . . I need . . . to know that my sisters are all going to be safe. I don't want to make things worse." She closed her eyes for a second, buried her face in her hands. "If I did anything to hurt any one of them, I don't think I could live with myself."

"I'm not going to let him hurt you," he said, meaning it.

"Us," she said softly.

"All of you," he said. "Catherine. Your sisters. But no one's safe while he's on the loose. Trust me, Lorelei, I just want to get him."

"And write about it." She lifted her head and smiled then, without a trace of humor. He felt a small twinge of conscience at using her for his own purposes, but he meant to keep her safe. He'd promised himself.

"And write about it," he admitted.

# CHAPTER 16

The hospital's van was winched from the gully by its back axle. Once at the top of the mesa, it was given a cursory examination by the detectives before being loaded onto a flatbed and hauled to the department for forensic scrutiny.

Langdon Stone walked to his Jeep and waited for Savvy Dunbar, who'd accompanied him after she'd gotten back from visiting Mad Maddie at Seagull Pointe. Savvy wasn't known for idle chitchat, but she'd been dead quiet the whole trip. "What's eating you?" he asked as Savvy approached.

"I was thinking about whom he found to give him a ride."

Lang nodded. The thought had been circling his mind as well. "Whoever it is, if they're still alive, they're in danger."

"Big-time," she said, staring at the road where the tow truck with its cargo of a mangled hospital van had disappeared. "What time do you think they picked him up?"

"You mean, they probably weren't listening to the news and/or hadn't had time to talk to anyone to be warned about Justice."

Nodding thoughtfully, she tucked an errant strand of

reddish-brown hair behind her ear. She was too pretty to be a cop, in Lang's opinion, not that he hadn't seen his share of lookers on the force, but for one reason or another they seemed to move on quickly. He expected Savvy to last another six months at the most.

"He drove off from Halo Valley around six or six thirty," Lang said, going through the timeline. "Headed west. Got to the turnoff and drove through the chain around sevenish? Had ditched the van by seven fifteen or seven thirty. Walked back to the road and waited. Somebody came along and he flagged them down."

"He would have been in his inmate clothes," Savvy said.

"A woman wouldn't have stopped for him, most likely."

"Not a man, either. Not dressed the way he was."

Lang thought that over. "If he was on foot, we'd have found him by now."

"Is there anyone he could have contacted to help him?"

"Not that we know of." Lang grimaced. "The man had no friends, and he tried to kill all his relatives. Even his mother."

Savvy opened the passenger door to Lang's Jeep and climbed inside. Lang slid into the driver's seat and gave her a sideways look. "There something you're not telling me about her?"

"I hope we find him soon," was her only answer.

Laura felt almost ill with worry. Promising was one thing; following through was quite another. She'd said she would let down her guard. Allow Justice into her thoughts. She'd promised; then she'd backed off.

But it wasn't just herself she was thinking of: it was her baby, too. Justice wanted to harm them both. And that was how he'd found her. Something to do with the baby she didn't really understand, but that was why she was in his crosshairs now.

Harrison, after convincing her that he was really on her side, had then brought his laptop into her house and was currently balanced on one of her kitchen café chairs, typing across the keyboard with surprising alacrity. When she'd started waffling about "calling" Justice, he'd simply made himself comfortable and mumbled something about catching up on his notes.

Laura had tried not to pace. She'd tried not to think too much about the baby growing inside her and the fate of Catherine and her sisters should Justice actually get past their defenses. She knew she was the most vulnerable, because she seemed to be the one he'd most zeroed in on. Because she was outside the gates? Because she was pregnant? Maybe both?

Maybe she should go to the police. Lay it all out and take her chances with them. But the explanations would be so messy, and she knew she would be believed even less by them than Harrison Frost.

Could she really count on Harrison to be her ally? It seemed kind of unlikely except that he had something to gain, too. And so far he was the only one who knew she was related to the women at Siren Song.

And, well, she liked him.

Laura ran her hands through her hair, closed her eyes, shook her head at herself. She dragged her gaze from Harrison's shoulders as he bent over the laptop and concentrated instead on her own relationship with the man who wanted to take her life, Justice Turnbull.

When she was younger, she had sensed Justice but hadn't been fully aware of what his voice was trying to say, what he was planning. Her gift hadn't been as refined then, and she'd only been interested in the messages that crossed her mind in a mild eavesdropping way. She hadn't understood that he was a killer until he began his rampage two years earlier, and then, just as his voice had crystallized in her consciousness, he'd been captured and incarcerated, his sibilant, hissing tones disappearing with him inside the walls of Halo Valley Security Hospital.

Thank God.

But then, yesterday . . . was it just yesterday? . . . his voice had suddenly blasted into her head again. Louder. Persistent. Boiling over with his hateful need to hurt them all!

She'd slammed the door down but good, and still he managed to penetrate if she wasn't completely vigilant.

And now she was thinking of cracking open that door?

She looked over at Harrison again. He was raring to go, ready to contact Justice through Laura, find out where he was, and go after him. Was that the way to handle this? Would she help capture him again, or would playing a game of cat and mouse only do worse harm?

As she watched, Harrison ran his hands through his hair, much as she just had, but then he pulled on the longish strands at his nape. His gaze was glued to the words on the laptop, but she sensed his sideways interest. It was a kind of radar reserved for people who knew each other well. She'd seen it in people in love. Had experienced it a bit with Byron, though he'd been one of those people hard to understand at any real level. It was a silent communication that spoke volumes. Harrison was tuned in to her, but she was currently shuttered, powered down.

She was afraid.

"Wanna talk about the Colony?" he asked casually, his gaze still on his laptop.

"No." She'd already told him more than she'd intended.

"Maybe some of the past history, long before you and your sisters?"

"There's a book with the Deception Bay Historical Society that lists my ancestors," she told him. "It was written by a doctor who attended us when we were younger, I think, and Catherine considers it a violation of ethics and our privacy."

"She might be right. Where's this doctor?"

"Dead. Fell off the jetty into the Pacific a long time ago."

"Is that so? You know, a lot of people associated with the Colony wind up dead."

"Every living thing dies, eventually, Harrison," she said.

"I know. But some of the people at Siren Song seem to have died before their time." He set the laptop aside and looked up at her as she stood near the sink. "Take Mary, your mother, for example. I found no record of her, no birth or death certificates. Kinda odd, don't you think?"

"I don't know what to think anymore," she admitted. And that was true. No matter how hard she tried to gain some "normalcy" in her life, it never happened. Her youth had been centered at the lodge, and yeah, the people within, her relatives, were strange by anyone's standards. She'd escaped and gone on to nursing school, but even there she had been isolated, hadn't made many friends, and then there had been Byron . . . and now she was pregnant by a man from whom she was divorced. "A lot of what goes on at the lodge is 'odd,'" she said, making finger quotes.

"So, you're telling me I should look up this book if I want to know about your family?"

"It's like a family tree, I understand." She thought a moment, then added, "I just worry that something might end up in print that I never meant to broadcast. If you check the history, that's all available information. I don't want my family to think I'm a traitor."

"I don't want to hurt you," he said seriously, his gaze touching hers through the wire-rimmed glasses he wore while working on the computer. Oh, God, how she wanted to believe him, to trust him, but he really didn't understand about Justice's sense of injustice, his need for revenge, how deep the seeds of evil had been planted in his heart.

She licked her lips nervously and walked to the small

pantry near the back door, to search for tea . . . to do something, anything to keep busy.

"I told you I won't write anything you don't want me to." He turned all the way around in the chair and looked at her with such honesty that she believed him. Sort of.

"Thanks."

"Can you tell me a little more how Justice fits in, though?"

She snagged a bag of herbal tea, something called Calm, and closed the cupboard door. "All I know is that Madeline Turnbull is a cousin to my aunt and mother. So Justice is some kind of distant cousin to me."

"But you've met him? He was part of your . . . clan?"

She tried to roll back the years, the memories that for so long she'd kept at bay. "Yeah, I've met him. When I was a kid. He used to come to the lodge when he was younger, I think." She found a cup and filled it with water.

"You were how old then?"

"Six, maybe?" In reality she wasn't completely certain. There were secrets within secrets between Catherine and Mary, and Catherine never felt compelled to bring them to the light of day unless it was absolutely necessary, even to Laura and her sisters.

"Around Justice's age?"

"I guess." She placed the cup in the microwave and set the timer before hitting the START button. "You want some tea . . . or coffee or . . . ?"

He shook his head, intent on his questions. "And your mom died when you were around ten?"

"That's what I said," Laura said stiffly. He'd hit a nerve again. Because she just didn't know, and really, she should. But the details around her mother's death were hazy, and Laura was almost embarrassed that she knew so little.

"And she's buried in the graveyard on the property?"

"I think I already told you that."

He took off his glasses and set them on the table. Lacing

his fingers on the crown of his head, he looked over at her. "What happened to her? I mean, what killed her?"

"Catherine said she died of a broken heart. I know that sounds . . . unreal." The microwave bell dinged and she grabbed the cup, then dunked the tea bag into the steaming water.

Harrison skewered her with a look. "What does that mean, exactly? 'Died of a broken heart'? People say that all the time, but what does it really mean? She wasted away after being rejected by her lover?"

Laura shrugged and shook her head. "I think there wasn't any one particular cause. She just died." She hesitated, stared at the darkening blossom of water from the bag, then added, "She had a number of lovers, apparently."

"You all have different fathers."

"Yes . . ."

"It must have been before they closed and locked the gates."

"Not funny."

"A little funny," he argued, one side of his mouth lifting. "I was just trying to lighten things up."

"Sure."

"Really. I'm sorry," he said, but the glimmer in his eyes told her otherwise. "So, how many sisters do you have?"

Back to business. Of course. "There are seven living at the lodge," Laura admitted.

"How much do you remember of your mother?"

"Not much." There were a few memories, of course. Mary smiling rarely at her daughter, even laughing on a rare occasion. She'd spent hours braiding her daughters' hair, or looking wistfully in a mirror at her own image. Laura remembered Mary taking long walks, toward the sea, always alone, never letting any of her children tag after her. They'd followed, of course, and found her standing upon a cliff, staring down at the crashing waves far below. In those moments, she'd seemed lost to Laura and her sisters. As they stood under the canopy of shivering firs, rain plopping along the forest floor, Mary had seemed unconscious of the weather.

She blinked, chasing away the blurry images and finding Harrison Frost sitting in her cozy, if worn little kitchen, staring up at her so intently, her heart kick-started. "It's Catherine who's forefront in my mind. She was the one who was with us. She might have been my aunt, but she was available . . . she was there . . . when my real mother wasn't."

"Where was Mary?"

"Oh, she was around." Laura set the wet tea bag on a saucer near the faucet. "Just living her own life. I remember different men coming from her wing of the house, where we weren't allowed," Laura admitted uncomfortably. "And then they stopped coming, and for a while we didn't realize she was gone, until Catherine showed us the headstone."

Harrison got to his feet and leaned back against the table, his fingers curling over its edge. "That's some story. It's strangely fable-like."

"This is still off the record, right?" She blew across the hot, fragrant water.

He lifted a hand of surrender. "Until you give me a signal, I'm just gathering information."

She wouldn't meet his eyes, felt slightly panicky. She had set this in motion but still wanted to put on the brakes. She buried her nose in her teacup and took a long swallow of a blend of jasmine and spice, trying to calm herself. She was a jangle of nerves, as much from Harrison Frost as Justice. Maybe it was because her hormones were out of whack from the pregnancy, or maybe it was the race of adrenaline through her blood at the thought of Justice free and stalking her, but she found it difficult to stay calm. Despite the name of the damned tea.

"Your mother named you?"

"Yes."

"You know, Lorelei had an unfaithful lover and threw herself to her death into the Rhine River. Sailors were lured by her voice from the large rock where she drowned and to their own death. There is a real voice-like sound that spawned the fable, apparently, an auditory trick of nature around that area that's been smothered now by the sounds of modern urbanization."

"You have a good memory," she said.

He smiled and threw a glance at the computer. "I have the Internet." He pointed to the device sticking out from the side of his laptop; his wireless connection enabled him to pick up the Internet anywhere.

"Ahh . . ."

"Have you ever wanted to find out more? About your father, for instance?" he asked curiously.

"Mostly I've tried to blank it all out. It's always seemed . . . safer. I didn't want to move back here at all. That was my ex's idea."

"But now you're divorced, and still you've stayed."

She nodded slowly.

"And you're not leaving, even though Justice is out there, because you want to help protect your family?" he guessed, having been around her enough, she supposed, to read her.

"Yes." She looked past him, then said, "What if I call him and it just spurs him to come after us? Speeds up the timetable."

"That's a risk."

"I don't know if I can do it," she admitted.

Harrison looked at her. Really looked at her. As a man eyes a woman. She felt a blush start beneath her skin. Embarrassed, she turned away. What was wrong with her? Good Lord. She'd met him yesterday, the day she'd learned she was pregnant, and she was thinking these kinds of thoughts?

It wasn't right. It was downright wrong.

There was an awkward silence between them. Then he said, "Tell you what. Let's take five. I've got another story I'm working on. One that's popping. You want to help me with that one tonight?"

"What story?"

"It's a project I've been working on for a couple of weeks. In Seaside. My Deadly Sinners."

"Your what?"

"Get your coat. I'll tell you on the way."

"So now you're cryptic."

"So now I think we need to get going." Glancing outside, he added, "This damn fog's making everything hazy and cold, but it's perfect for their purposes. It's probably reached Seaside."

She looked at him, mystified.

"Come on. It'll get you away from Deception Bay for a few hours," he went on. "Give you some time to think about what to do about Justice. Grab your hoodie. It's bound to get colder tonight."

"Okay," she said uncertainly.

"You help me, and I'll help you," he said. "Maybe all the stars will align and we'll get my Deadly Sinners tonight, and Justice Turnbull tomorrow."

She snagged her coat from a hook by the back door. "Dreamer!"

"Always," he said, his gaze searching her, and ridiculously, Laura's heart did another little flip.

She walked to the back door and told herself that Harrison Frost was trouble.

Right now she had more than enough.

The last thing she needed was this reporter with his strong jaw, knowing eyes, and quick wit. But like it or not, for the rest of the day, it seemed, she was stuck with him.

The problem was, she did like it. She liked it far more than she should.

# CHAPTER 17

It was like she'd been transported from one life to another, Laura thought as the miles spun beneath the tires of Harrison's brown Impala while they traveled north to Seaside. Yesterday morning she'd been a nurse at Ocean Park Hospital just getting over a divorce; today she was a source, companion, and possible sidekick to an investigative reporter who was bent on dragging a story from her. A *pregnant* source, companion, and possible sidekick to an investigative reporter who was bent on dragging a story from her. And she was a willing participant in his plan. More than that, she was half counting on him to keep her safe from a killer focused on a mission of evil.

Less than twenty-four hours earlier she hadn't known him. Hadn't known that she was pregnant. Hadn't known Justice had escaped and had her and her family in his sights again.

Now, as she cracked open the side window, she closed her eyes, turning her face to the rushing wind that swept inside. She was worried about Catherine and her sisters, though she knew they were probably as safe as they could be behind their locked gates and with the sheriff's department—the whole damn state—alerted to Justice's escape. It was certainly no secret whom he was targeting. There was nothing to do to help them. She was the one in the most danger.

So, it was with a feeling of relief that Harrison was taking her away from Deception Bay. She hadn't wanted to come back to the town, anyway, and now her fears had been proved right. She shouldn't have listened to Byron. Ever.

But she couldn't leave now. She had to see this thing through and do what she could to protect herself, her family, and her baby from Justice.

She wondered if she should tell Harrison Frost that she was pregnant. Was it germane to anything they were dealing with? Only in the fact that Justice was doubly focused on her because she was carrying a child, one of their kind, and he was determined to send them all to their doom. She knew that much. She'd heard it in his mental ravings, and it scared her to the bone.

Sliding a look Harrison's way, she examined his profile and felt a flutter of interest, a quickening of her own breath.

Good. God.

*"Clean up the beach!"* he muttered as they encountered vehicles parked in every view point, turnout, and parking lot all along the way and everywhere as they entered Seaside's outskirts. Harrison drove through the clogged town, his frustration mounting as he tried and failed to find a parking spot to save his soul. After a few slow trips down crowded side streets clogged with pedestrians, bikers, and trams, as well as the usual cars and trucks, he finally got lucky and nosed into a lot behind a Space Age gas station, just as an older couple in a Buick pulled out.

Laura, lost in thought, wondered if the intensity of the situation was sending her nerve endings into overdrive and she was ascribing something more, some deeper emotion and desire, to the man she was currently with because of fear. Out of desperation? Was her own susceptibility in this cat and mouse game with Justice making her think she wanted Harrison?

She was in a strange, strange place, all right. A thrum of fear ran beneath her skin, and it was jangling up her thought process, turning random emotions into desire.

Or was it something more?

After switching off the ignition, Harrison yanked out a tin of breath mints from the glove box, opened it, popped one in his mouth, then offered the tin to her. Her stomach twisted in minor revolt at the thought, and she shook her head.

"You okay?" he asked, glancing over at her.

"Yeah. Why?"

"You keep making little sounds."

"I do? What kind of sounds?"

He let out his breath in a weary sigh a couple of times, and Laura faintly smiled. "I'm . . . thinking," she said.

"*Overthinking*. Try to forget about Justice for a while." He grabbed her hand, gave it a squeeze.

"Oh, yeah. That's going to happen."

"No more messages today?"

She shook her head as he let go of her hand. "I think he has the ability to block me out, too. At least he does now."

"You think he knows you're outside of Siren Song?"

"Oh, yeah. He knows it," she stated positively. "But okay, I'll try to put him aside. Tell me what's on your mind for the Deadly Sinners."

On the ride to Seaside Harrison had explained to Laura about the group of teens burglarizing their wealthy classmates' homes, had related his subsequent conversations with Lana and Jenny, and had explained about their leader being N.V., like Envy. Now he added, "I want to catch them in the act, maybe tonight."

"Why tonight?"

"It's a Saturday. They seem to be escalating. They like

what they're doing and feel smarter than everyone else. Then there's the fog," he said, gesturing to the thick mist hovering through the streets, like an ethereal curtain. "It makes it harder for them to be seen. I figure they're not going to let an opportunity go by."

"Don't the police have any idea?"

"Oh, yeah. The Seaside police know about the burglaries and have been patrolling some of the nicer residential communities around, but they can't be everywhere, and summer weekends in Seaside have their own problems. Brawls. Public drunkenness. Domestic disputes. Other theft. You name it."

"So, are you going back to the ice cream shop?"

"Only if Jenny's still on duty. More likely I'll find one of them along the main street and follow after them."

"But they know what you look like."

"I'll have to be careful."

"If they see you, the jig'll be up, so to speak."

"I'll wear a hat. Big overcoat." He shrugged. "I've got clothes in the back." He gestured with his thumb to the rear seat, where she had also tossed her own hoodie.

"Let me follow them," Laura said. "You point them out, and I'll go."

He looked at her as if she'd lost her mind. "No way."

"They don't know who I am, and I'm a woman. Less likely for anyone to worry about if I get too close to them."

"Forget it."

"Why?"

"It's . . ." He trailed off, but Laura knew what he'd been about to say.

"Dangerous? More dangerous than calling Justice Turnbull, a psychotic killer, to me?" She almost laughed. "Give me a break!"

"Well, no. I'm just not letting you do it."

She felt her hackles rise. "I see. You don't believe I can call Justice, so that doesn't count. But this . . ."

"I can't have you be the collateral damage to my story," he stated flatly.

"I'm choosing to do it," she informed him coolly.

"No."

She went on. "If you find one of them, I'll just meander around after them and see if they lead me anywhere."

"They'll meet on the beach," he said. "In this fog, I'll be invisible."

"Not if you need to get close enough to hear them."

"No eavesdropping," he declared. "Too risky. All I want is a head count."

"So, that's a yes?" she asked and saw him shake his head.

"No."

She sensed this was going against everything he believed in. Every male fiber of his being. But she wanted to help. Needed to think about something other than Justice Turnbull and his deadly obsession with her and her unborn child. "Listen, you can be a few feet behind me in your disguise."

"No . . ."

"In this beach-cleaning crowd, in the fog, nobody's going to be looking at either one of us."

"You're a nurse. Not Mata Hari."

"I'm a young woman in jeans and a hoodie who's ridding the beach of debris and garbage, so bent on my task that I might just stumble over a group of teenagers by mistake in the fog. I'm just trampling around in a zealous quest to make the world a better place. The worst thing that'll happen is they'll glare at me and go quiet until I disappear."

"Jesus . . ."

She grabbed the aforementioned hoodie from where she'd tossed it into the backseat and put it on. "Now I look like everyone else."

He reached in the back next and grabbed his coat and a

baseball cap, jamming the cap on his head. "I don't want you to do this."

He was so serious that Laura found the whole thing strangely funny. "This doesn't scare me," she assured him. "This is . . . therapy."

It was the truth. For the last twenty-four hours she'd lived in gut-shaking fear, and the thought that she could be proactive on something else, something that might actually do good for someone else, made her feel as if she were on a head-spinning high.

He frowned. "I don't like it."

"This is child's play in comparison to calling Justice," she said soberly.

"Just because these guys are kids doesn't mean they're not dangerous. They're thieves, but they're one bad situation from being something worse. You corner them, they'll come out fighting."

"You say they'll meet on the beach?"

"You're not listening, Lorelei. There's no script, but there is danger."

"Look, if I can do this, I can contact Justice. How's that? One for the other." She threw open the door, and he was forced to scramble from his side of the car to keep up with her.

"I'm not bargaining with you!"

"Oh, come on. Seriously, let me help." She pulled the hoodie over her head and smiled at him.

"Damn it."

She laughed at the way he looked so helpless, surprising them both. She couldn't remember the last time she'd laughed. "I'm half-hysterical," she admitted.

"Fully hysterical," he rejoined.

Laura stepped away from him into the June gloom. She'd taken two steps when she felt him by her side. "If they see you with me, this will all be a big waste of time."

"So be it," he muttered, but he didn't try to stop her, or send her back to the car, and Laura saw that as a win.

They walked down Broadway together, passing people who were coming from the beach, moving toward them like gray ghosts who disappeared into the gloom behind them. CLEAN UP THE BEACH!! T-shirts peeked from jackets and overshirts and hoodies like Laura's own.

In an uneasy partnership Harrison pointed out the ice cream shop, which Laura gazed at with interest. She started to cross the street toward it, then felt his hand clasp down hard on her shoulder, stopping her forward progress. Leaning into her ear, he whispered through his teeth, "Okay, look. There are rules. Don't get too close. Don't do anything. Just recon. You got that?"

She nodded.

"That's Lana standing in front. The first girl I talked to. Jenny's not behind the counter, but—" He cut himself off, then swore softly. "There she is. Coming from around the back. She must be just getting off work. What time is it?"

Laura pulled back her sleeve and checked her watch. "Four thirty."

"Okay. C'mere." He swiveled her toward him beneath a hard grip until her gaze was leveled on the three-day stubble of his chin, which was apparently part of his look. "I'm going to kiss you," he said. "Try to be into it."

She opened her mouth to protest, but his lips crashed suddenly on hers. Warm. Supple. Moving gently. A slight wintergreen taste lingering from his earlier breath mint. Her knees, stupidly, wanted to buckle. She tried to speak, but he held her a little tighter, and she slid him a look from the corner of her eyes and saw that while he kissed her, his eyes were open and staring across at the ice cream shop.

The kiss went on, but once she knew he was detached, that this was all a damned act, she felt both relieved and a little deflated. And embarrassed. Still, it gave her a long moment to assess her situation, and she felt a shiver of anticipation mixed with fear. She was pregnant. She was kissing a man she found attractive. She was running from a man who wanted to kill her. She—

*Sisssterrr . . . ! With your filthy incubus growing inside you . . .*

Laura jerked in shock, causing Harrison to break the kiss and gaze down at her with a frown. She slammed the door in her brain shut with finality.

"What is it?" Harrison asked.

"Nothing. Nerves." Her teeth were chattering.

"They're on the move," he said, glancing across the street. "In this fog I can follow them without them recognizing me."

"No. I want to do it." She pulled herself from his embrace, immediately regretting the loss of heat.

"Are you sure?"

"Yes!"

"Then I'll follow after you in thirty seconds. I'll be at the end of the turnaround. Don't approach them. Just hang around, if you can."

She held up a hand in goodbye and headed toward the beach, in the direction the two girls had gone.

# CHAPTER 18

Harrison tried counting to twenty but stopped at nine. It was all he could stand before he moved in the same direction. West. Where a watery sun could be barely discerned through the layers of smoky gray.

He sensed he was making a lot of mistakes. A lot of mistakes. He sensed there was something going on here with Lorelei that was more than just pumping a source for information. Something even more than roping in an accomplice, something he almost never did, yet here he was, doing it.

*What the hell are you doing?* he asked himself.

Getting a story.

He made a sound of disgust directed solely at himself. Oh, sure. That was all this was. Immediately, he sought to interview himself. A trick he used to make certain he wasn't fooling himself about anything.

*She's pretty,* his mind pointed out.

Yes.

*She's serious but has a sense of humor.*

Yes, again.

*She's adventurous, even though she believes she isn't.*

Right-tee-o.

*You like her way more than you should. You have bad luck in relationships. You should keep this on a professional level, or else someone gets hurt. I'm not telling you anything you don't already know.*

"Bingo," he said quietly.

*And she can kiss with a passion that sets your mind reeling and your damned cock to start rising to attention.*

Oh, hell. He pushed the unexpected, runaway thoughts aside.

For now.

He couldn't see more than six feet in front of him, though he could hear the surf, a buzzing roar with the occasional crash of a wave breaking on the rocks. People's voices sounded like dull mews in the soft, fuzzy light. The whole world was surreal.

*Be careful,* he thought with a strange twist of his heart.


Laura stopped to grab a black garbage bag from a table where two middle-aged women in CLEAN UP THE BEACH!! baseball caps and oversized sweatshirts collected donations and passed out information. She nodded to the women, then followed a safe distance behind the girls, who walked ever closer to each other as they neared the sand. Harrison had been right; they went straight to the beach.

She found her thoughts divided between the task at hand and the kiss that still lingered on her lips. Justice was locked into another room in her mind entirely, and she was happy to leave him there for now. More than happy. She wanted to live in the moment.

The kiss had been knee-weak spectacular, and Harrison Frost hadn't been affected in the least. This would have sent her into paroxysms of self-flagellation if she hadn't been able to keep her own cool, at least in front of him. As it was, she found herself in a kind of mild shock, wondering at herself.

The girls reached the beach and slogged through the softer sand near the road, turning right rather than toward the packed beach and dull, roaring surf. They were trudging purposely northward, avoiding the crowd closer to the water. Laura drifted along behind them, sometimes closing the gap when the fog swallowed them up, sometimes shifting to the right or left to give the illusion that though they were traveling in the same direction, they weren't going to the same place. They met other beachcombers, parents with toddlers, dog walkers, and cleanup people along the way, but no one stopped to talk.

The girls were in their own world. They never looked at Laura. About a half mile from the turnaround they started slowing down and looking around. They were arguing with each other, and Laura had to pull closer, bending down to pick up an imaginary something in the sand, to hear them.

"We went too far!" Lana complained.

Jenny snapped, "No, we didn't. They're around here. Noah!" she called. "*Noah!*"

"Shut up," Lana responded. "Jesus. You want to just call the cops while you're at it?"

Jenny stomped forward, and a figure materialized from the fog. A male. He grabbed Jenny's arm and pulled her down toward the sand and farther away from Laura. Lana followed with a snort of disgust. "Well, geez, leave me out, why don't you?"

"Shut the fuck up." The disembodied male voice filtered toward Laura, who had stopped short and stood still and quiet in a cocoon of gray. She couldn't see anything, but she was close enough to hear. She bent down again, this time actually finding an old soda bottle, which she tossed into the garbage bag, but her ears were trained on the ongoing conversation.

"Noah," a female voice said.

"It's Envy," he hissed back.

Another male voice hacked out a short laugh, which

caused Noah/Envy to snarl, "Stupid fucks. Pay attention. We're going back for seconds."

"What do you mean?" the unidentified female voice asked.

"I'm gonna change your name from Pride to Dumbass," he barked. "Anybody else got a stupid question?"

"We're going to hit one of the places we already did?" Jenny guessed.

"Yeah, baby. Lana's favorite."

"Lust!" Lana hissed. "My name is Lust. You called Ellie Pride, so call me Lust!"

"Give it a rest," Ellie/Pride said. "Ian doesn't even like his name," she added tauntingly.

"Who gives a shit?" Noah demanded. "Did you hear what I said? Don't you want to know *who?*"

"I'm losing weight!" another male voice protested. "Jesus! I don't want any stupid name!"

"Ummm . . . ? My favorite?" Lana questioned. "I don't know what you mean, Noah . . . Envy."

He snapped back, "Both names start with a *B*, moron. Know who now?"

"Oh . . . you mean . . . Britt . . . Berman?" she asked, unsure, and there was a flurry of scuffling as Noah/Envy must have clapped his hand over her mouth and gotten them all to go quiet. Laura was afraid to move yet worried maybe Noah/Envy might materialize in front of her. Time to leave.

Carefully she took a step backward, heart pounding, then a second step, then a third toward the surf. She wanted to run but she forced herself to move slowly, though her ears were practically buzzing with fear.

"Hey!" Noah/Envy's voice was suddenly right in front of her. "You. What are you doing?"

Laura couldn't see through the fog, and then an angular boy of about seventeen materialized. He wore a dark scowl and his mouth was a snarl. He looked dangerous and determined and deadly, and she couldn't help the zip of a chill that ran through her. "What?" she asked. "Are you talking to me?" She looked around.

"Yeah, bitch. I'm talking to you. What are you doing here?"

"Cleaning up the beach!" she said, holding up her bag and ignoring a tiny niggle of fear in her brain. "And my name isn't bitch. You got that?"

He stepped closer, menacingly. "You listening in on something you shouldn't?" he demanded.

She forced herself not to back up. "I said I was cleaning up the beach, the *public* beach, with my family," she lied, hoping he'd think she was with a group. "Isn't that why you're here?"

"Don't be stupid!"

"Don't be insulting." She wasn't going to let this teenaged punk push her around.

"Shit!" He grabbed her arm and shook it once, hard. She saw the group of them then, moving toward her, a dense wall of youth that was definitely frightening in that mob way. There were seven of them, all right. Three girls and four boys, all scowling at her.

She stared hard at the leader. "Let go of me," she said with the same calm, determined voice she used on unruly patients and tried to yank her arm back. His fingers only tightened.

One of the guys glanced around, uncomfortable. "Oh, come on. We don't need to scare people," he said.

"There are a ton of people around," Ellie, the third girl, reminded.

Noah/Envy was having none of it. He moved closer, glaring into Laura's eyes with pure fury. His hand held her arm fast.

She caught a whiff of something minty and earthy. "Chewing tobacco causes mouth, tongue, and throat cancer," she said rotely. "You should be careful."

"What the fuck do you care?"

"Hey, man," the worried guy said as voices approached from behind her. A child's laughter and a man's deeper baritone.

Noah/Envy dropped her arm reluctantly.

She heard, "Lorelei? You there?" in a disguised, almost unrecognizable voice that she nevertheless knew to be Harrison's. She turned toward the sound and melted into the fog, blindly moving in his direction. Relief washed over her as he materialized, and she slid easily into his arms, as if he were, indeed, her disgruntled husband. The kids were swallowed up behind drifting wisps of gray smoke. She half turned, expecting Noah/Envy to keep coming for her, but they were gone in an instant, invisible behind the shifting curtain of fog.

Silently, Harrison pulled her away from them. She was half lost, aware only of the sound of the surf, which kept her oriented enough to know they were walking south, quickly, back toward the turnaround. They reached it in silence and then were among the other beachgoers and cleanup volunteers, walking up the street in the direction of his car. She dropped off her small, nearly forgotten bag of garbage at a collection site, where a woman offered her a starfish sticker that said I CLEANED UP THE BEACH.

Not really. But she wasn't going to quibble.

Harrison shepherded her along the promenade that ran the length of the beach in Seaside, then opened the door of a small deli, where he guided her to a two-person table toward the back of the room, away from the door. He seated them both with their backs to the windows before he said a word.

"I heard him," Harrison told her grimly, his lips flattened over his teeth, his jaw clenched. "I was going to jump out and kill him if he threatened you further."

"That's a little over the top."

"They're dangerous."

"So am I," she said, then flashed a bit of a smile. "I deal

with belligerent patients all the time, and then there's that communicating with a killer thing."

"Yeah, that," he said but seemed to lighten up a bit.

"They're kids."

"JDs."

"Even so, a few punk kids don't scare me . . . well, not much."

"They should."

"Maybe." She leaned closer to him but had to wait until a bored-looking girl popping her gum walked through the tables to take their order.

"What can I getcha?" she asked.

Laura glanced at the menu, a huge blackboard that hung over a counter. "Turkey sandwich, with the cream cheese and cranberry sauce," she said, spying the first thing that looked good.

"Clam chowder and a hot tuna melt," Harrison said.

"Anything to drink?" the girl asked on a sigh.

"Coke," Harrison said and glanced at Laura.

"Water's fine."

The girl turned and wandered to another table, where a young mother was struggling to keep her three-year-old in a booster chair. Once the waitress was out of earshot, Laura kept her voice low and said, "So, from what I could tell, there were seven of them. His name's Noah and he calls himself Envy. They didn't say his last name. Lana is Lust. Ellie is Pride. There was another guy, who was obviously Gluttony, though he didn't like it much. Ian. I don't know Jenny's 'sin' name, but they've got Greed, Wrath, and Sloth left. They're planning to re-hit the Bermans' house."

His brows shot skyward. "You heard that for sure?"

"He said they were going for seconds at Lana's friend's house. He gave her one guess and said it was two *B*s. She came up with Britt Berman before he stopped her from saying more."

Harrison made a sound of disbelief, or wonder, or something; Laura couldn't be sure. "Sometimes, things just happen," was all he eventually said. Grabbing his cell from his pocket, he looked at it for a moment, his mind calculating. Then he stuffed it away and said, "C'mon," and he grabbed her hand. "I'm gonna write a story," he said. "Then we're going to see the Bermans and give them a little heads-up." He paused at the counter. "Our order," he said to the girl, "we'll take it to go."

Hours later, sunk low in the passenger seat of Harrison's Impala, her butt numb from inaction, Laura watched as the Deadly Sinners appeared like a dark horde and spread out around the Bermans' house like a plague. Harrison, seated behind the wheel, slid the binoculars to his eyes and smiled. "Just like clockwork. If only *Envy* realized how predictable he was, he might be dangerous."

Thirty seconds later an alarm sounded. Not the Bermans' house, whose alarm had been smashed in the previous burglary and hadn't yet been replaced. The next door neighbors' alarm was the one blaring through the melting fog, the same neighbors where the Berman family had since taken refuge after Harrison had alerted the Seaside police about the pending target.

Harrison loved it. He waited, observing for a while, then stepped out of the car to confer with one of the officers. Laura found herself feeling detached and oddly content. Spending all day with him had given her insight to the man. Observing him in action, whether interviewing her, chasing down the Seven Deadly Sinners, writing his story, or sitting with her on the stakeout, she'd learned far more about the man than she'd expected.

Trouble was, she was starting to feel like she'd known him for years, which was ludicrous. Studying him now, as he stood under the lamplight, his shoulders broad, his waist and hips slim, his hair dark in the fog, she felt it strange to think a few days ago they hadn't met.

He turned, as if he felt her gaze on him, and started jogging through the wisps of fog to the car. Moments later he slammed back into the Chevy. "His name's John Mills," he said, referring to the young officer. "I've talked with him before. Some of the cops are hard-asses, but Mills talks to me, so he's the one I called about this."

"Uh-huh."

"I'm writing up the story so far, and then I'm gonna talk to him tomorrow, see if I can learn anything else."

"Where are we going now?" she asked, intrigued with how animated he was just talking about his work.

"My apartment. I've got the notes and most of the story on my laptop. Just need to write it down and send it off. It'll be front page of the *Breeze* tomorrow."

"Let's go," she said, still intrigued as he jammed the car into gear and did a three-point turn.

They drove to his bare second-story apartment, where she found a single director's chair and sat. "Still working out the details of the interior design," he joked as she took in the lack of furnishings.

"Easier to keep clean."

"Hmmm." He barely noticed as he was so into his story. He snapped open his laptop, pulled up the file, then added a few final words about the capture of the Seven Deadly Sinners. "No names," he said. "They're all underage." Then he e-mailed the changes to his editor and said, "Good copy," as he closed the lid on his laptop. "Wanna get a dinner? We can drive back and get some chicken strips and fries at Davy Jones's. Then I'll tuck you in."

"I'll take the drive back, but I'll skip the bar food," she said, wrinkling her nose. "Davy Jones's twice in one day might be more than I can handle."

"You don't like fried food?"

"I like fried food as much as the next woman."

"No woman likes fried food. Or admits to it. It's all about salads and nutrition and weight loss. There's no fun to it. The fun level is directly related to oil/fat consumption, and you're not going there," he teased.

"I had huevos rancheros this morning," she reminded. "With you."

"That's baked, I think. Minimal fat content."

"Maybe." She smiled. "But I'll take a rain check on dinner, thanks." She'd spent way too many hours with him already, she determined, and yet she wanted to be with him longer, and though she could tell herself it was because she was nervous about Justice, that Harrison Frost made her more comfortable, less anxious, it was something more.

Something she couldn't even consider right now.

"You have to eat, don't you?" he pressed.

"I've got stuff in the fridge."

"How much stuff?"

"You wangling for an invitation?"

"Maybe. What have you got in the fridge?" When she didn't immediately respond, he added, "Salad?"

"And other things."

"Other healthy things."

"Don't you eat healthy things?"

He half smiled. "If you invite me to, I will."

He was blasting her with a kind of irrepressible charm that she sensed could be a real pain in the ass. "Okay," she said, relenting not only to him but to her own secret desires as well. "Take me home and I'll dig up something for us to eat. But you're not tucking me in."

He offered her a lazy, self-deprecating smile. "What if I just stay at your house, say, on the living room couch?"

"What if I say no?"

"Might not work," and he was serious again. She knew that their time ignoring the real threat that menaced her was over. The exhilaration of being instrumental in catching the

Deadly Sinners was fading. She couldn't escape her own problems forever, though she'd done an admirable job of it today.

"The couch has saggy cushions."

"You're a nurse, right? Maybe you can fix me if I . . . need help."

"Maybe." She ignored the tiny voice inside her head that nagged at her. *What do you think you're doing, Lorelei? This is crazy. Nuts!* But it was a little thrilling to think of him spending the night.

He locked the front door, and they headed down the outside stairs to his car. The scent of the sea reached her nostrils, and the night was cold. Raw. Deep. As they climbed inside the Impala, Harrison said, "Hey, I heard you diagnose Noah with future mouth cancer. That one of your woo-woo predictions?"

"No." Laura almost laughed. "I was just trying to distract him. I could tell he'd been chewing. And it doesn't really work that way, anyway."

"Can you tell if there's something wrong with me?" He turned toward her, eyeing her with amusement, his hand on the keys in the ignition, the gloom outside the car thick.

"No."

"How does it work? Do you see my aura, or something?" God, his eyes were dark, sexy in the night.

"There you go, making fun of me again." She tried to be annoyed. She wanted to be annoyed. Instead, she was amused and managed to break his gaze. Instead, she stared out the front windshield, willing herself not to look at him, her fingers curling over the armrest.

"Well, how does it work?" he insisted.

"I don't really know."

"You must have some idea."

"Well," she said reluctantly. "It's better if I touch you. Maybe I could see something, then."

"Bullshit."

"Total truth." She turned back toward him, smiling.

"Okay." He left the keys dangling in the ignition and held out his hand, clasping her fingers. He gazed at her penetratingly, and she found herself mesmerized by the warmth of his skin.

After a moment she frowned and ripped her hand away.

"What?"

"I don't really want to say."

"Oh, come on!"

"All right." She shook her head. "You're on the way to serious digestive problems. The kind with . . . unpleasant surgeries."

"Is there a pleasant surgery?"

"But this problem is just a small possibility. Not a reality, yet. I think you might be able to avoid it, given some changes." She rubbed her hand where he'd touched her. He stared at her hard, and she could tell he was wondering if, just maybe, she was really, just possibly, for real. "I'm sorry to say, Mr. Frost, but you need to give up fried food."

"Oh, hell!" His fingers twisted the keys, and the Impala's engine roared to life. "Like I said. Bullshit."

"Total truth," she rejoined; then they both started laughing.

Forty minutes later they'd pulled into her driveway, their jovial mood disappearing with each mile that passed beneath the tires of Harrison's car. She thought of the maniac who was related to her and his thirst for blood. Her blood. Her sisters' blood. Her unborn child's blood.

Could she do it?

Call to the maniac?

Dance with the devil?

She stared out the window into the inky night, over the cliffs to where she knew the ocean rolled in restless waves. She closed her eyes and remembered him as a child. Small. Blond. Blue-eyed. And filled with hate. He was pale and lean, and the few times she'd seen him, there had been a weirdness evident. Even then his intense gaze curdled her blood, but now . . . with his vicious hissing voice, she couldn't imagine facing him.

But she would . . . if she had to.

She didn't even realize they'd reached her home until she heard the crunch of the Chevy's tires on gravel, saw the arc of its headlights wash up against the siding of her little house.

It was now or never.

Harrison, alone with his own thoughts, switched off the ignition and turned to her, ready to ask her what was next. Before he could open his mouth, she said, "Let's do it. I'm ready."

"Call Justice . . . in your way?" he asked, a bit surprised by her sudden capitulation after the seesawing indecision that had plagued her throughout the day.

She swallowed hard, then pushed open the passenger door and felt the cold, damp night press against her face. She slid out, slammed the door behind her, and said over her shoulder, "That's right, Frost. And you'd better damn well be ready to take this investigation to the next level, because I guarantee you, he's going to be pissed."

# CHAPTER 19

*T*he sea calls to me.
  The lighthouse is my sanctuary in God's mansion of many rooms.

I belong at the lighthouse, and my soul flies there even when I am not able. But now it is guarded closely by the robotic members of the sheriff's department. Guarded against me. Yet, it is my place to stand at the edge of the world. My place on the small island where the lighthouse stands, an island accessed only by boat or the arched pedestrian bridge available at low tide whose braces and beams have been worm-eaten and waterworn, condemning it for public use.

This has always worked in my favor, but even I cannot reach it now.

Until I find a way to shake loose those who would capture me. Evade them. Misdirect them. Send them away.

My mission cannot fail this time. I will get them all. All those blond, vile witches with their taunting, smirking lips and their condescending blue eyes. Fling their black souls into the dark pit where there is no escape. Leave them forever. I smile when I contemplate their misery.

"Well deserved," I whisper and realize I've been caught

*in my own fantasy. Driving by rote. With a start, I drive by the entrance to the lighthouse, a worn track that is weed-choked down the middle. I can see the dark hump of the patrol car. A man is smoking inside. He is bored. Waiting. Cursing this detail that has forced him to sit while others frantically seek me like dogs chasing their own tails. Another one sits beside him, hat down low over his eyes. Or is it a woman? I can't tell, but I mustn't slow down and stare.*

*If I must, I will kill the deputies inside the vehicle, but I will need to lure them away first.*

*First . . .*

*I glance at the dead woman beside me. She is a nuisance, but I need her vehicle.*

*I have people to meet.*

*Her head lolls forward, and I push her cheek to the passenger side window. She looks asleep.*

*Justice . . .*

*My name hurtles through the atmosphere.*

*What! I gasp.* Justice. *The sound rings in my ears, deafening, stunning.*

*She is calling me?*

*No . . . never! But there it is again.* Jusssstice! *shivers through the air, a hissing sibilant sound, as if she is mocking me.*

*"Bitch!" I yell, jerking on the wheel, my view out of the windshield lost as her face fills my mind. I nearly drive into the oncoming lane.*

*"Satan's whore!" I shout aloud, wrenching the wheel.*

Come and get me, you bastard.

*Abruptly I pull to the side of the road, wrenching the wheel, spraying gravel as the vehicle slides into the shoulder. A horn blasts behind me, and the driver of a pickup with monster wheels, the cab jacked to the sky, throws up a middle finger.*

*My companion keels forward and nearly slides to the*

*floor, but I hold her in place with a hand that fills me with rage when I see it quiver.*

*With fear?*

*Never!*

*Just a seething, burning rage. Oh, this one who's called me is destined for the flames of hell!*

*Lorelei. Her face comes to me again as the car shudders to a stop and the mist rises in the surrounding forest. How she needs to be tortured. Burned.*

*But then they all must be destroyed, I think again. All of them, burned . . . burned.*

*"I will rip your black heart from your chest, bitch!" I say it aloud as I toss it into the airwaves, forcing it into her mind.*

*No sound. No ripple. No word.*

*She is afraid now. I feel myself smile in the gloom of the obscuring fog. She is pregnant, and the last one outside.*

*The easiest to smell.*

*The easiest to find.*

*The easiest to kill.*

*A new surge of adrenaline races through my bloodstream. Soon . . . I will find her soon. . . . New confidence fills my soul.*

*"Lorelei," I say again, sending the message through the dark corridor that reaches into her mind. "I am coming."*


Laura's face was white as chalk as she sat at her kitchen table, across from Harrison, her eyes focused somewhere in the middle distance.

Jesus, what had he done to her? Suggesting she call a madman.

"Laura!" He reached across the tabletop for her hand.

Her fingers were cold as ice.

Hell!

"Laura!"

She didn't respond. She was there in the room, but her mind, maybe even her soul, was definitely somewhere else. He'd half laughed at her insistence that she and Justice could communicate, but now he had a glimmer of something he didn't understand, thought there was something to her claims.

This wasn't right.

"Lorelei," he said, squeezing lifeless fingers with his own. "Okay, you win. You're scaring me."

Nothing.

"Laura!" He was on his feet now, rounding the table.

She came back with a sharp gasping inhale of breath, tears filling her eyes. "Oh, God . . ."

"You okay?" he asked, not liking the fear that was inching up his spine. What the hell had just happened? "Jesus. You really had me going."

"After today . . . I . . . I almost forgot how evil Justice is." Her shoulders sagged and she closed her eyes tightly, only to blink them open.

"After today?" He frowned.

"Being with you in Seaside was . . ." She stopped herself for a moment, then let out a long breath. Finally, her eyes were clear again, warmth returning to her fingers. "Being in your world, even with its own dangers, was . . . I don't know . . . a relief." Her eyes searched his as she looked up at him. "It was . . . normal, I guess, in its way. Teenagers seeking a thrill, or revenge, high drama, whatever, but this . . . it's really vile."

"So, you . . . reached him?" Harrison asked, dropping her hand but still standing over her. She made a sound of acquiescence that was almost a sob. She was having trouble talking to him, and though Harrison understood she was emotionally wrenched, he needed to know what had happened in those few moments when she was staring blankly into space. "And?"

"I challenged him," she said in a small voice. "I told him to come and get me."

"Oh, for the love of God."

"Isn't that what you wanted?"

"I want us, make that me and the police, to find him. I didn't want to put you in harm's way."

"I'm already there," she admitted. "You had nothing to do with it. Calling to him might have forced the issue, but trust me, it was already there." Her lips twisted wryly. "At least it gave him a little of his own back."

"So he responded?"

"Oh, yeah. He responded." Her smile fell away. "He said . . . and I quote"—her voice lowered—"'I will rip your black heart from your chest, bitch.'"

Christ!

Harrison nearly recoiled. Her voice wasn't her own. It sounded nothing like Laura herself, and he could almost be swept up in this strange scenario where Laura and her ilk apparently talked to each other without speaking.

When she looked up at him almost coyly, he wondered if he was seeing Lorelei or one of the others, even Justice himself.

He'd pretended to believe. Hell, he kinda wanted to. He liked Lorelei. A lot. He could imagine sleeping with her, being with her, maybe even loving her a little.

But he couldn't quite make that leap into believing in this communication. Yes, she feared Justice and she had reason to, since she was part of the cult family, but really? Mental communication? Couldn't it just be more a form of fear and suggestion?

*I will rip your black heart from your chest, bitch.*

No, this was real. At least to her.

"I just shut myself off then," she said, unaware of Harrison's inner dialogue, her face relaxing into that of the woman he found so fascinating. "But it's clear he got the message, and now . . . he's going to come straight for me."

She said it with surprising calm, as if she were finally ready for the showdown she'd expected all her life.

"He has to find you first," Harrison reminded firmly.

"He knows where I am. He can sense me."

"Sensing someone and really knowing where they are, are two separate things, right?"

"Not with Justice."

"Well, I'm not leaving you alone, in any case," he stated positively, even though a rational part of him, the journalist in his soul, still said this was some weird, dark fantasy brought on by Justice Turnbull's escape. Nonetheless, Laura believed it. "Look, I'll be your bodyguard, for better or worse. I can't believe I'm going to say this, but maybe we should call the sheriff's department and talk to them."

Laura looked at the clock, and Harrison noted it was going on eleven. "I've got work tomorrow," she said, practical again. "I don't want to call the police and make this night any longer."

"You have work in the afternoon," he reminded her. "See. I listen."

"I'm not calling them tonight and trying to explain this thing I've got with Justice. They'd talk to me for hours, then chalk me up as just one more of the . . . Let's see, the kind word for it would be 'eccentric' women of Siren Song. Not a lot of people know I'm from there, and I'd like to keep it that way for as long as I can."

"That's going to be impossible."

"I know, but I'm dead on my feet. Really. No police. Not tonight."

Her face had regained most of its color, and he recognized the stubborn set of her chin. She had a faint resemblance to his niece, Didi, at that moment, and he felt a stab of protectiveness meant for both of them.

"Okay," he said.

Laura got up from the table and seemed lost on how to

proceed. After a moment, she stuck out her hand. "Well, then, good night . . . Mr. Frost."

"Mr. Frost. Really?"

She looked away, and he could almost swear she almost smiled. "Harrison," she said, scraping her chair back and getting to her feet.

"Good night, Lorelei."

"You know, no one calls me that except my family."

As she stood in profile, her hair sweeping her shoulders, her full lips curving into a shadow of a smile, he was reminded of their kiss. Oh, he knew she'd looked at him, and he suspected she wondered if he wasn't affected somewhat. The truth was, yes.

And he wanted to kiss her again. Right now.

"I like Lorelei," he said, both of them aware of the double meaning.

He half reached for her again, but she was already moving away, toward the bedroom. "There are blankets and a pillow on the couch," she said, her voice drifting toward him. "Help yourself."

He took one step after her, toward the bedroom, then thought better of it. What the hell had he gotten himself into?


Justice pulled into the parking lot of the nursing home, gazing at all the blank windows that faced into the night. Most of the lights were off. It was after 10:00 p.m. and the patients, those he thought of as inmates, were asleep.

He sat in the car for long minutes, still reeling a bit from the challenge that slithery bitch had sent him. Lorelei . . . oh, he knew her well. She could block him at will, but he could always find a way back in. She was the one he could communicate with the easiest, for reasons he didn't fully understand or care about. It just was.

And now that she had the filth growing inside her, he could smell her. Over the damp scent of the surrounding forest and a hint of wood smoke.

His sense of smell was refined.

His nostrils twitched. He could almost pinpoint her. Somewhere to his south. Close to the sea.

Nearby.

But first . . .

He flexed his gloved hands on the wheel, then started to slide from the car. Suddenly he felt eyes on him. Prying, searching eyes! He froze, his gaze delving into the darker shadows along the building's perimeter. Something by the north side? Something crouching? Something *human?*

He waited, senses heightened.

No one.

Nothing.

The bitch had really gotten to him, and it was a new, and unpleasant, experience. Pushing the driver's door open, he glanced back and got a distinct shock. His companion's eyes were open, and she was staring straight at him!

*Alive?*

A strange terror welled inside him. He stayed frozen, stock-still, rooted in place.

A slight rise and fall to her chest.

*How had he missed it?*

Moisture glinted in her eyes from the illumination off the security lights.

Justice stared at her until his own eyeballs were dry and burning, yet she didn't move, didn't so much as blink as much as he did.

Alive, but not by much.

He calmed down immediately; she could not hurt him. She was mere breaths from oblivion. Still, she represented a problem.

As he considered throwing her body into the bushes that

ran from tended to wild as they fanned out from the sides of the building, an answer presented itself. An older model Ford Taurus wobbled up the drive and slid to a stop beneath the portico that was the front of Seagull Pointe. A gentleman wearing a gray fedora and overcoat climbed out and walked heavily toward the doors. There he punched out a code onto the keypad. His efforts failed him, and after a moment he pushed the bell beside the pad several times in a row, stabbing at the thing in frustration. Finally, a heavy-set woman in purple stretch pants and a printed top came to the doors. She pressed a button on the inside, which slid the doors open.

"What's that code?" he growled, standing outside, refusing to enter.

"You can come in, Gerald," she invited.

"What's that damn code?"

"Two-one two-one. We changed it last month, remember?"

Instead of entering, he jammed his finger at the button again, which closed the doors, leaving her on the inside and him on the out. With a huge sigh that Justice could see, she pressed the button one more time and the doors reopened. Only then did the older man deign to walk inside.

Just within the double doors sat several wheelchairs. Justice noted them as Gerald and the woman moved from the glass-fronted reception area and out of sight. A moment later he climbed from the car, then strode, head bent, toward the entry doors, sliding a look around the building. There were no security cameras, as far as he could tell. Seagull Pointe looked as if it had been built fifty years earlier and hadn't done much in the way of upgrading. It was a low, cinder-brick building, painted white, with jutting wings that had probably been added on as need be.

Touching in the code, Justice waited impatiently as the doors slid open again. He quickly grabbed one of the wheelchairs, then raced it outside to his Nissan compact. Opening the passenger door, he lifted his companion's lax body into his arms; her head lolled toward him, and she glared at him with that fixed stare.

He barely noticed. What had bothered him earlier no longer did. Situating her in the wheelchair, he then pushed her back toward the building, feeling as if unseen eyes were watching him. Shaking that off, he punched in the code once again and entered with no fanfare. He could hear faint noise emanating from down one hallway, a television, and he avoided that direction, turning to the right.

To his happy surprise the rooms had not only numbers but names listed on plaques outside their doors. It took less than three minutes to find Madeline Turnbull, and he wheeled his companion's chair into the darkened room, letting his eyes adjust to the dim light.

The old hag herself lay in the bed, eyes pointed toward the ceiling, as if she were praying to the Lord himself.

"Mother," he snarled.

The eyes blinked but didn't stop their staring upward.

He wanted to gouge them out! Was consumed with the thought. His fingers flexed. But then his sensitive nose caught the whiff of death. She was almost gone, too.

Almost of their own volition, his gloved hands moved upward and he stepped toward her. His hands were claws but they aimed for her throat, not her eyes. Suddenly those eyes opened and snapped sideways. Gleaming in the light from the window. She cackled, a noise that rattled in her chest and shook her frame. "You are doomed," she whispered on an exhale of breath.

"Shut up, whore!" he hissed.

"*You* are the true devil's spawn."

"*Shut up!*"

"You know it. He's inside you," she said with relish. "You . . ."

His hands clamped lightly on her throat. He wanted a knife. Needed a knife. Needed to *cut her dead!* Or burn her. Watch her flesh turn black and melt!

"Burn in hell!" he cried softly.

"Are . . . doomed . . ." The words were more mouthed than spoken, but he heard them as if they echoed and echoed through a canyon of granite, bouncing off ridges, gaining strength, resounding, blasting his eardrums.

His hands shook, clamped lightly. He wanted to squeeze with all his might. Tight. Tighter. *Squeeze!*

But no . . . he couldn't. Didn't want his handprints on her throat. He needed time . . . a way to make them think her death had occurred naturally . . . at least for him to make his escape.

Yanking the pillow from beneath her head, he placed it over her face and pressed down. Garbled noises sounded. She thrashed around, one clawlike hand scrabbling at his arm just where the other woman had scratched him. He pressed harder. *Harder!*

Minutes later . . . she fought him with more strength than he'd believed possible. Her thin body humping upward, faint mewling noises sounding.

Slowly he surfaced. It felt like eons had passed. There was pain in his cramped fingers from the grip of the pillowcase crushed between his hands. Releasing his clutched fingers was a superhuman effort.

He turned, breathing hard.

His companion in the wheelchair was staring at him from her lopsided head. Was she *smiling?*

He raised his arm to backhand her with all his strength just as her head dropped forward to her chest and she exhaled a last breath. Staring at her a moment, he waited, but this time she was truly gone.

He went back to the bed, removed the pillow from the old hag's face, and placed it under her head once more.

His mother. Gone. Finally gone.

For good.

Closing his eyes, he reached into the netherworld, where thoughts moved like rivers.

*I'm coming for you, bitch.*

*You . . .*

*Lorelei.*

# CHAPTER 20

Laura opened her eyes with a jolt.

A shadow chased across the wall.

*Justice?*

She nearly screamed, then realized it was a branch swaying outside her bedroom window. *Her* bedroom. She was safe. . . . For the moment.

And Harrison Frost was probably on her couch.

It was just growing light, a gray dawn casting shadows as the events of the past day and a half flooded back to her. Justice crowded to the forefront of her mind, and she pushed him back, pulling an image of Harrison Frost into the place where his darkness had been. She drew a long breath and exhaled it, feeling her pulse start to slow its rocketing cadence little by little.

Throwing back the covers, she climbed from her bed, tossed on a lightweight robe over her cotton nightgown, and padded down the hall to the bathroom. She could see only an edge of the couch from her angle and caught sight of one bare masculine foot protruding from a blanket. The sight made her feel safe and relieved.

Emotions she'd rarely, if ever, felt with Byron.

In the bathroom she gazed at her reflection.

And a wave of nausea rolled over her.

Stumbling quickly, she ran for the toilet, heaving up the remains of the makeshift meal of leftovers she'd put together for them the night before, just before she'd reached out to Justice.

Pregnancy.

She waited for her jittery stomach to calm down, then flushed the toilet with shaking hands. Turning her face under the faucet, she ran cold water over her cheeks, chin, and mouth. Next, she brushed her teeth for all she was worth and then stood with her hands on the edge of the sink, balancing herself while her whole body quivered.

Was she out of her mind to tweak Justice's tail? Undoubtedly. But the other option was to just wait and hope the authorities caught him, and that didn't seem like an option at all.

Maybe the best thing to do was her first inclination: run away. Go back to Portland. Get the hell out of here!

But she'd thought that before the baby was a reality. And before she'd met with Catherine and her sisters.

And before she'd met Harrison Frost.

And before she'd determined she would help get Justice herself.

Now . . . she didn't know what the right thing to do was. Justice was evil and determined, and she was dancing a very deadly dance with him.

*Knock, knock.*

She jumped at the sound and stared at the bathroom door panels, a hand to her chest.

"You okay?" Harrison's muffled voice sounded.

"Oh . . . yeah."

"It didn't sound okay."

She was embarrassed that he'd heard her throwing up. "Just . . . a reaction to everything, you know," she said lamely. "I—I'm going to take a shower now."

"Okay."

She strained her ears and heard his footsteps recede, then stripped off her clothes and jumped beneath a spray of hot water. Ten minutes later, feeling decidedly more human, she returned to her bedroom, exchanging her robe for her uniform. Her hair was wet, and she brushed it in front of her dresser mirror, seeing the edge of her light brown hair peeking out at the middle part on her scalp. She realized she was through dyeing it. It wasn't much of a disguise in the first place. Certainly not against someone who could reach her by simply using his mind.

And then there was the baby to consider.

*Her* baby.

Hers and Byron's.

Oh, Lord.

She couldn't go there. Not today.

Harrison was rubbing his growth of beard as she entered the kitchen. Spying her outfit, he said, "Thought you weren't on duty till later."

"I'm not but we're shorthanded. I'm going to go to the hospital and see if they need me."

"If I didn't know better, I might get a complex. Sounds like you're trying to get away from me."

"No, I'm just . . ."

He waited for her to finish, but she didn't know where she was going. Her stomach was jumping around as if it were full of grasshoppers. The image almost sent her back to the bathroom, and she swallowed hard.

"I don't want to leave you," he said, watching her.

"I'll be okay at the hospital."

"Yeah? How do you know that? You said you reached Justice last night. That he was coming for you. And he was pretty graphic. You were freaked."

"Yeah. Really freaked. I . . . I know." She frowned. Justice wasn't going to send her scurrying for cover, and in the light of day she felt more secure. "Look, there are a lot of people at the hospital. I know everyone. Safety in numbers."

"I could help."

"Don't you have to follow up on your story, anyway?" When he didn't quickly argue, she added, "So you might as well get to it. I don't want to make you wait around here with me all day."

"I can do my work from here," he pointed out.

"No, really. This'll be okay. I'll see you . . . later?"

"You said Justice was going to be pissed. You said you challenged him. I—"

"Please. Harrison."

He gazed at her in frustration. "I thought we were on the same page about him and what to do." He took a step toward her and Laura shrank back. Her rejection stopped him short.

"You've got a big story to finish up," she reminded him again.

"The Deadly Sinners? Justice is a bigger story. And he's dangerous to you." His expression was grim.

"Follow me to the hospital, then. I really feel like I should go there. I need to work and keep busy." When he hesitated, she laid a hand over his. "Trust me on this, okay?"

"I don't like it."

She grinned then, impulsively brushed her lips across his cheek. "I know."

It clearly went against everything Harrison wanted, but he reluctantly let her have her way.

An hour later Laura was at Ocean Park, asking for extra hours, while Harrison drove back to Seaside. Laura ran into a wrangle with administration over the amount of overtime the hospital was prepared to pay and ended up heading to the staff room to sit down heavily at a table while they worked it out.

After a few moments, she contemplated what, if anything, she could have for breakfast from the vending machines. Her stomach was still sending out ripples of unease, the aftershocks from her bout at the toilet this morning, yet she knew she needed to eat something.

At least she felt safe, for the moment, within the walls of the hospital. She picked at her yogurt, scanned the newspaper scattered across the table, and half listened to the news, the top local story being the burning of an old sawmill, a fire that had kept emergency crews working through the night.

Ten minutes passed, and then Byron strode into the staff room. Spying her sitting alone at the table, he draped himself in a chair opposite her. "What's going on with you?" he asked.

"What do you mean?"

"You look like death warmed over, and why did you come in early?"

"I thought we were short-staffed, but I haven't been granted the overtime."

"So, why are you still here?"

He saw too much. She didn't want to deal with Byron, and she certainly didn't want to explain herself.

"I left some things in my locker and decided to just sit down a minute or two," she lied. "You don't have to give me the third degree."

"Don't I? What was all that mumbo jumbo with Mrs. Shields and her pancreas? You're making me look bad when you start diagnosing with your laying on of hands, or whatever the hell you do."

Laura's interest sharpened. "You found something?"

"Gave her a new blood test just to check. Not a lot of insulin being produced. She was in the lower range before, but nothing to be overly concerned about. But now . . . looks like there's something going on. Some kind of pancreatic tumor developing, possibly, or not. We'll check. But you sure as hell got all the little tongues wagging around this place."

She saw that she'd made him seem a little less godlike in others' eyes and he didn't like it one bit. "Her blood levels changed. It's not your fault."

"Tell that to her," he muttered, his jaw tight. "What the fuck, Laura? Where do you get this stuff?"

"I just asked if cancer ran in her family."

"Bullshit. I know you." He leaned toward her.

Laura stared back at him. *No, you don't. You never have.*

And then her stomach revolted again, and she jumped up, fighting the heaves. She ran from the room to the bathroom, wishing for all she was worth that she could control this.

Ten minutes later she emerged and found Byron staring at her with his laser look. "You're pregnant!" he accused.

"Dr. Adderley?"

They both looked up toward the young nurse hovering down the hallway, a nervous smile flitting across her lips. Her eyes were all over Byron.

"You're way off base," Laura told him in an intense whisper.

"Am I?"

"Yes." She met his gaze and lied for all she was worth.

With a last, dark look at her, he turned to the nurse, his broad hand splaying across her lower back as he leaned down to her and guided her toward the ER.

Her stomach momentarily under control, Laura headed for the cafeteria and the faintly appealing thought of dry toast.

Harrison drove to the *Seaside Breeze* offices, which were housed in a flat-roofed, glass-fronted concrete-block building with a stationery/gift store on one side and a place to buy team trophies on the other. Pulling into the front lot, he climbed from the Impala, stretched, ran a hand through his hair, and determined that as soon as he was finished with the follow-up on last night's story, it was time for a shower. Heading inside, he picked up one of the morning papers, scanned the front page, and smiled.

SEVEN DEADLY SINNERS NABBED FOR BURGLARY: LOCAL TEENS CAUGHT IN POLICE STING

"You sure were Johnny-on-the-spot with your story," said Buddy, one of the paper's stringers who wrote local-color pieces in the hope of becoming a full-fledged reporter. Harrison could have told him there was no money in the business, but Buddy was as eager as Harrison had once been, and money and job security weren't really what either of them was after. "How'd you get your byline out so fast?" Buddy demanded.

"Experience and talent," Harrison said.

Buddy snorted.

"Is he still here?" Harrison asked.

"Went home. Be back around noon."

"Okay."

*He* was Vic Connelly, the paper's owner and editor, a garrulous guy with wild white hair à la Albert Einstein and a gruff attitude. Harrison had hoped to catch him and talk about the follow-up articles he planned to put together and also tell him that he next intended to put all his energies into going after the Justice Turnbull story.

After checking in with Buddy and his office voice mail and e-mail, then dinking around with his follow-up story for half an hour, he left the offices, heading to his apartment to run through the shower and make himself feel human again. Keeping to Lorelei's side was all fine and good, but her couch, as she'd said, left something to be desired.

When he was dressed, he pulled the piece of paper John Mills had given him from his wallet and yanked out his cell phone. Written on the scrap was the young officer's direct cell number. As he placed the call, Harrison examined his beard growth in the mirror, scowling at his reflection. He looked like he'd just come from a weeklong bender.

Maybe it was time to spiff up a bit. Get rid of the down-and-out look he'd cultivated for the Deadly Sinners. He didn't need to pretend he was anyone but who he was any longer, now that his deception with them was over. Not that his usual look was much more than what he'd been projecting; he wasn't exactly the Brooks Brothers type. But now he thought about Geena Cho and the Tillamook County Sheriff Department's staff. If he expected even the least modicum of information from them, it was best to look a little more tended, somewhere in between his own scruffiness and Pauline Kirby's camera-ready slickness.

"Mills," a serious voice answered.

"Officer Mills, it's Harrison Frost of the *Seaside Breeze.* You suggested I call today? That you might have some information for me?"

"Oh yeah . . ." A pause. A hesitation. Then, as if Mills had finally connected the dots, he said quickly, "Bryce Vernon is a developer with property up and down the northern Oregon coastline. His son Noah is turning eighteen the day after tomorrow."

*Click.*

Harrison hung up thoughtfully. Bryce Vernon was Noah Vernon's father and Noah Vernon—N.V.—was turning eighteen the day after tomorrow. In a very few days he would no longer be a juvenile, and then all kinds of things could happen. He might be tried as an adult. He could go to jail. He might want to talk to a reporter about how misunderstood he was by his parents and how persecuted by the local police. He might lawyer up, and then again, he might have a helluva lot to say.

Faintly smiling, Harrison grabbed up his razor and went to work on his stubborn beard.

\* \* \*

Detective Savannah Dunbar entered the sliding doors to Seagull Pointe and said to the woman at the desk, "The sheriff's department got a call from your director, Darius Morrow?" She flashed her badge.

The receptionist nodded. "Oh. Oh, yes. Let me page him."

Savvy twisted the kinks from her neck. She'd been up half the night with the damned fire at the old Tyler Sawmill. The blaze had exhausted all the county emergency crews, and both the fire and sheriff's departments were stretched thin. She, herself, had already worked a full shift, and it looked like she wouldn't be going home any time soon.

A few moments later a man and a woman met Savannah in the reception area. The woman was Inga Anderssen, whom Savvy had met before, but the man was someone new. Darius Morrow, no doubt. Inga looked disappointed upon recognizing Savvy, as she said brusquely, "Madeline Turnbull died sometime yesterday evening."

"Oh." Savvy was a little surprised since she'd just seen Madeline the day before. "You called because you think it could be the result of foul play?"

"I'm the director of Seagull Pointe," the man broke in, holding out his hand. "Darius Morrow." He had a horse-shoe of dyed black hair around a bald pate and wore a worried expression that looked perpetual. "We called because when we checked on Ms. Turnbull, there was, ah, another woman in her room. Unconscious. Seated in a wheelchair."

Savvy asked, "Who's the woman?"

"We don't know," Inga responded, her voice tight, her lips even tighter. "She's not a patient here."

"Where is she now?"

"We moved her to a bed in an empty room. She was about to fall out of the chair."

"Still unconscious?"

"Yes. The doctor on staff isn't in today, so we called nine-one-one. They're sending an ambulance."

"She's alive, then?" Savannah asked. The vibe here was all wrong.

"The ambulance should be here any second." He seemed nervous.

"What about Madeline Turnbull's?" she asked. "Her death was expected," Savvy said, touching all the bases. "Natural causes. Right?"

"The medical examiner will determine that," Morrow said.

"You think there's a chance of foul play?" Good God, what had she stepped into when she'd taken the call? Neither Morrow nor Anderssen answered immediately, and they seemed to be a tad too careful in not looking at each other.

"Foul play? No," Morrow said after some consideration. Then, tellingly, "We don't see how."

"Excuse me for a moment." Savvy took a few steps away and called dispatch, confirming what Darius Morrow had said, that an ambulance was due to arrive within minutes and that the ME was on his way. "Send another unit here," she added. "I just don't like the feel of this." She snapped off the phone and said back to them, "I need to take a look at the Jane Doe."

"Of course . . ." The director was beginning to sweat as he and Nurse Anderssen led the way to a small room down the end of one long hallway. At the door Morrow hemmed and hawed and finally left Savvy with Inga. He racewalked away, either to another situation that needed immediate attention or from the issue at hand. Inga entered the room first, with Savannah coming up behind her. The woman lying in the bed had been hooked to an oxygen supply; her breathing was labored.

What struck Savvy the most was how young she was;

she'd expected someone much older. The atmosphere of the nursing home/assisted-living facility, she supposed.

"She's been strangled," Savvy said, seeing the bruise marks forming on the woman's throat.

"What?" Inga seemed surprised.

"Didn't anyone examine her?"

"Yes, yes, but we were just concerned about her breathing. . . ."

"What about Madeline Turnbull?" Savvy had no time for excuses. "Was she strangled as well?"

"Maddie? No . . . I don't think . . ." The older woman's face was full of consternation, and Savvy realized no one had examined the dead woman that closely; they'd been overtaken by the more immediate problem of their new, unexpected patient. By bringing up the staff's lack of response to Madeline Turnbull's death, Savvy had inadvertently embarrassed Inga Anderssen in a way that wouldn't do any good in her public relations with the woman.

"How did she get here?" Savvy asked aloud, though it was more a rhetorical question than anything else, as she motioned to the woman lying on the bed.

Inga Anderssen pursed her lips and folded her arms across her chest. "We aren't certain."

"Who found her?"

"I think the morning nurse's aide, but I'm not sure," Inga hedged.

Savvy turned and pinned the woman with her gaze. "Find out who it was, and send her to talk to me. I'll need a conference room, a list of anyone who visited Madeline Turnbull or had access to her room and this one as well. I want this facility sealed off and any tapes from your cameras inside these walls, as well as the film from the parking lot."

"But . . . but . . . I don't think we have cameras or . . ."

"Then tell the director what I need. But first, take me to

Madeline Turnbull's room." She thought for a moment that Inga would refuse her, but Savannah was the law. Inga turned on her heel and, stiff-backed, led Savvy through a maze of hallways to the room where Justice Turnbull's mother had died.

There were no obvious strangulation marks on Madeline Turnbull; her neck did not display the same bruising. But Savvy bent down and looked closely into the woman's eyes and thought she saw the telltale signs of petechial hemorrhaging that signified constriction of airflow. She glanced at the pillow, then back at Madeline Turnbull.

Inga bustled up and bent over the woman's body, staring into her eyes as well.

*Smothered,* Savvy concluded and thought Inga knew it as well.

"I'll need that private room," Savvy said. "Where the hell is your boss?"

"I'll get Mr. Morrow."

"Do that," Savvy said, unable to hide her irritation with the incompetence of the nursing home staff in general as she waited for the medical examiner to arrive.

# CHAPTER 21

It was one o'clock when Laura stopped by Conrad Weiser's room in intensive care. She didn't know the security guard all that well but felt oddly responsible for his injuries because of her connection to Justice. She wished she could have warned him somehow of the coming danger, even though she knew that was unreasonable.

Nina Perez was waiting for her as she left the ICU and said, "No change," less a question than a statement of fact, and Laura nodded.

"Dr. Zellman is being released soon," the nurse then told Laura. "He still isn't talking."

"Have they determined whether it's definitely physical damage to the voice box or emotional trauma?"

"I'd say a little of both, but I'm not his doctor." She looked troubled. "You think the police are any closer to catching Turnbull?"

"I hope so," Laura said, wondering if even now Justice was on his way to find her. A shiver skated down her spine. She was having second thoughts about calling to Justice. Despite her earlier bravado, she knew that taunting him was dangerous, even deadly.

As she was walking back to the nurses' station, she happened to see Zellman being released into the care of his wife. The trim woman had wheeled her husband to the door of the hospital, per hospital policy, but the injured doctor practically jumped out of the chair as soon as he was outside the front doors, nearly kicking the offending chair into the surrounding shrubbery. On his feet, he started striding across the parking lot, bristling with outrage or anger or something, his wife half jogging along behind him.

Laura watched them for a long moment. The rumor was that Justice hadn't been handcuffed when he'd been escorted by Zellman to the van, and that his escape was mostly Zellman's fault. Underestimating Justice was something Catherine had said everyone at Siren Song had been guilty of, once upon a time. Laura didn't plan on being a victim to it again.

Or had she already by tweaking his tail last night?

Staring through the hospital's front doors, seeing her own watery reflection, a strange feeling creeping across her skin, she backed away from the glass panes automatically, her heart slamming into her ribs in a hard, systematic beat.

He was out there.

Somewhere.

Waiting.

And it felt like he was right outside. . . .


Justice stared, unblinking, through the windshield of the woman's compact. He was in a different world. A world that swirled with emotion and half dreams and urgency that racked his body with pain. Colors blended and shapes shifted, as if he were underwater. He closed his eyes, and his mission pounded through his brain. He needed to take them. All of them. *Soon!*

They were miserable creatures, and their old taunts ricocheted through his brain, reminding him of why they were all doomed, why he had to defeat them. He felt the one that was outside the gates like a living snake within him, twisting his insides, curling around his guts, tightening and writhing, sickening him. His skin crawled at the smell of her; that nauseating scent filled his nostrils.

She was close. So close.

Then he knew.

She was inside the walls of this hospital. *This* hospital.

Ocean Park.

Inside, tucked away, thinking she was safe behind a curtain of fog and the concrete and steel walls. And she was laughing at him.

Shaking with the effort to fight the bile in his throat, he yanked himself to the present and gazed hard at the front of the hospital. He was parked in the side lot with a narrow, angled view to the front doors. She was in there. Just inside the vestibule. Invisible with the fog.

But she felt him. This he knew. He heard the pounding of her heart, sensed the blood pumping furiously through her veins . . . hers and that nasty little incubus within her. He smiled as he sensed her fear.

Good.

Let her terror rot her from the inside out. She, who dared summon him!

*I'm here, witch. Just like you wanted!*

He thought about the car he was driving, a silver Nissan. How long was he safe with it? He'd left its driver almost dead at Seagull Pointe, but they would learn who she was and come looking for her vehicle. He'd switched plates with old man Gerald's Taurus, which would buy him some time, but he was doomed to find another car.

A frisson disturbed the murky air.

Suddenly he jerked to attention, squinting toward Ocean Park's entrance. Exiting the hospital at that moment were Dr. Maurice Zellman and the woman whom Justice guessed to be his wife. Justice's gaze narrowed on her. Holding on to her hair to keep it in place, she was hurrying to catch up to the doctor's longer strides to no avail. Zellman's large large steps and ramrod straight back ate up the distance to a black Lexus that crouched near a security lamp. Wifey barely managed to scramble into the passenger seat and was still closing the door when Zellman backed out in a tight turn, his tires giving a little *broop* against the pavement as he hit the gas and the sedan leapt forward, narrowly missing a green minivan parked in the next space.

Zellman half turned Justice's way as he passed, and Justice smiled coldly, wondering if the doctor could feel him as he purposely sent the man a warning. But Zellman seemed as oblivious as ever, glowering through the Lexus's windshield. The doctor had no ability to sense Justice at all.

From the interior of the Nissan, Justice watched Zellman's departing car with a sort of detached interest, not the urgency the women of the lodge inspired, but a kind of clinical curiosity. The doctor had counted himself as Justice's savior. This meaningless cockroach, this self-congratulating piece of dirt, deigned to believe he knew something—anything—about him!

And then Justice caught an overwhelming whiff of Lorelei's pungent aroma.

He swiveled his head so hard the vertebrae in his neck cracked. He barely noticed. His nostrils flared and his lips curled at her noxious odor.

Pregnant whore!

*I'm coming for you,* he told her, but the wall she'd erected was tall between them, one he couldn't scale.

*I'm coming for you!,* he screamed. *Sick witch! You can't hold me out forever!*

She was inside the hospital. *Right there.* All he had to do was slip inside . . . !

Blinded with need, he slammed out of the car and moved to the side door of the hospital, stopping just short of the security camera, shaking with a desire to kill so intense it stole his common sense. The middle of the day was no time to attack her, but he didn't care. He wanted her. *Now.*

With a frustrated scream caught in his throat, he dug at his scalp, ripping at his hair. He needed the sea . . . a cold Pacific breeze . . . the lighthouse. . . .

He took a step forward, into the camera's range, then pulled back. Ducking his head, he returned to his vehicle, slid inside, and slouched in his seat. Flexing his fingers on the steering wheel, he attempted to regain control. He couldn't, wouldn't, let the bitch win.

He wanted her badly. Could almost feel his hands clenching over her soft throat as he felt the life seep out of her. He imagined watching her naked whore's body burn in a foul and malodorous stench that would rise to the heavens in thick black smoke as her body was condemned to hell.

Lorelei.

Above all else, he needed to snuff out her life and that of the life she'd spawned.

Could he charge inside and just take her? *Could he?*

Zellman's Lexus was stopped at the end of the parking lot. He and the wife were arguing, apparently, and the vehicle was stalled while they yelled at each other. Then it jumped forward again, and Justice watched Zellman drive to the end of the lot and turn onto the main, tree-lined drive that accessed the hospital from Highway 101.

Glancing back, Justice stared at the hospital until it felt like his eyes were burning in his skull. Then, grinding his teeth with impotent fury, he shoved his car into gear and hit the gas. He'd follow the doctor.


"You all right?" an impatient voice demanded in Laura's ear.

She'd dropped into a chair in the front reception area, her legs practically collapsing beneath her. That feeling . . . that recognition . . . Though she'd had her mental wall held high, she'd sensed Justice on the other side, his malevolence nearly smothering her.

It was Dr. Loman who'd questioned her, his blue eyes cold ice as he glared down at her.

Of course she would run into him. A brush with the older doctor was even worse than one with her own ex-husband. Loman was imperious and arrogant and dictatorial.

What was it with the doctors here at Ocean Park? Most of them seemed to be egomaniacs, well, except for calm Dr. Hanson and funny Dr. Charles, one of the few women surgeons on staff. But the docs at the top. Imperious, self-inflated jerks.

"I'm fine," she said to Loman.

"You're not fine if you're sitting down on the job," he pointed out, frowning darkly.

Oh, great. Of course.

"Just catching my breath." Laura got to her feet and bit her tongue to keep from saying something sarcastic as she sidestepped the man.

He followed after her, soft-soled shoes squeaking on the tile. "I know who you are," he said, surprising her. The hairs on the back of her neck lifted. "You're one of them, and I *know* them."

Laura glanced over her shoulder to catch a glimpse at him. He seemed like he was on the verge of exploding, as if something she'd done had sent him over the edge.

She knew what he meant. Dr. Dolph Loman and his now deceased brother, Dr. Parnell Loman, had been the doctors who'd attended Laura and her sisters when they were children. Laura recalled Dolph, though Parnell was a distant memory. She half recalled something salacious and unpleasant in regard to Parnell and her mother, or maybe it had been Dolph, or maybe it was all faulty memories, a fabrication she'd concocted from the lore she'd garnered about her promiscuous mother. All this time she'd worked at Ocean Park, she'd hoped Dolph hadn't recognized her. Now she knew that hope had been in vain.

"So, you're diagnosing patients now?" he said with a faintly disguised sneer.

"Was there something specific you wanted, Dr. Loman?" she asked him coolly.

"Mind yourself," he snapped. "You're a nurse here, not a doctor. That's all I'm saying."

"Is it?" She reveled in his look of surprise. "Seems to me you're saying a lot more."

"We both know about your family," he said, recovering quickly. "Soothsayers and nuts and quacks."

"Quacks," she repeated, eyeing him hard. "Is that a new medical term?"

He flushed, the barb hitting home. "My reputation is impeccable."

"I remember your brother," Laura said, though it was nothing short of a lie.

That left the old man speechless. He opened his mouth and shut it twice before saying quickly, "My brother was an excellent surgeon! His death was a tragedy."

He seemed to want to say more, but he was definitely flummoxed by Laura's decision to confront him right back. He strode off, muttering about her rudeness, and she wondered what exactly had gone on between her mother and Dr. Parnell Loman and/or Dr. Dolph Loman. Would Catherine tell her, if she asked? Would she even really know?

Laura headed back to her rounds, feeling a bit overwhelmed by the events of the past few days, but since there was no way to explain, and because she wasn't about to blame her weakness on her pregnancy, she drew several deep breaths and soldiered on.

She was beginning to wish she'd listened more to Harrison. She'd been so sure she'd be safe at the hospital, but now she longed to be with him, safe within his protection.

Grabbing her cell from her locker, she placed a call to his and wound up with his voice mail. She hesitated, frustrated, but instead of leaving a message, she replaced the phone and determined she could get through the rest of her shift without talking to him. It was just a case of mind over matter.

# CHAPTER 22

"**D**etective."

Lang strode through the front doors of the department instead of the back because he'd parked his Jeep on the street rather than in the rear parking lot, which was currently full of potholes as deep as the Grand Canyon. May Johnson, the unsmiling, heavyset black woman who manned the front desk, spoke the single word like a cannon shot. She didn't much like Lang, and he didn't much like her. He thought she was arrogant and uncompromising, and she'd disliked him on first sight as well, seeming to regard him as too loose on rules, too entitled, too, maybe, male. She definitely considered him a cowboy in both dress and spirit, and now, looking down at his dusty boots—definitely not department issue—Lang allowed that yes, that part was probably true.

He reluctantly slowed his steps and gazed at her expectantly. He'd just come from the scene at Seagull Pointe, and he wanted to report to Sheriff O'Halloran before he headed back out. "Yeah."

"Sam McNally returned your call."

Lang lifted his brows. Geena Cho was dispatch, and to

date Johnson had let her deliver all Lang's messages rather than go out of her way to make sure he was informed.

"Thanks."

She nodded curtly, then nearly bowled him over by asking, "How's the adoption going?"

Johnson's icy facade was at a full-blown thaw. Lang could scarcely credit the change. "It's going. Slowly."

Lang's fiancée, Dr. Claire Norris, was trying to adopt a baby girl whom she'd grown extremely close to. Lang, too, hoped it would happen soon and had been mulling over dragging his beloved to the altar to finalize that step and hopefully give that process a jump start when Turnbull's escape completely screwed up his timetable.

As if embarrassed by her familiarity, Johnson turned abruptly away, and Lang walked along the counter that stretched the length of the reception area, ending at the back door, then turned down a hallway that led toward the main part of the building and the jumble of offices therein.

The smell of old coffee crept through the hallways from the lunchroom, and phones jangled. A couple of deputies who'd pulled all-night duty at the Tyler Mill fire still smelled of soot as they walked by.

Sheriff Sean O'Halloran was in his office, at his desk, looking troubled. His normally smoothed gray and white hair was in disarray, and his blue eyes, usually bright with inner humor, looked dull and tired. "Goddamn Turnbull," he said.

"Goddamn Turnbull," Lang agreed. "Looks like he smothered his mother and strangled this other woman, whom we're trying to identify."

"She still alive?"

"Just."

"Nobody knows her?"

"Nobody at Seagull Pointe," Lang said. "Savvy and I checked with everyone on staff and the patients who could be of help. We did a turn around the parking lot, checking for extra vehicles. No other cars than those that belong to residents. Also, no security cameras, although the director was quick to point out that they planned on getting some soon. Lot of good that does us. The upshot is we don't know who she is or how she got there. She's young. The theory is, she ran into Justice somehow and he strangled her and killed his mother."

"Any chance—any chance at all—it wasn't him?"

Lang hesitated. "That a rhetorical question?"

The sheriff sighed heavily.

"You want us to work some other angle?" Lang asked.

O'Halloran shook his head. "Nah. Not until we count out Justice Turnbull completely." The two men discussed the case at length, then, after they'd exhausted all the new information and Lang turned to go, the sheriff added, "Got a call in from a farm east of Garibaldi. Seagulls and buzzards circling something, which turned out to be a dead body. Male. Sent Delaney down there. The guy's been dead a couple days."

Garibaldi was south of the city of Tillamook, but still in Tillamook County. "Any missing person reports?"

"We'd checked the tags on this hippie van that's been parked overnight in that day lot viewpoint north of town for two nights. Called 'em up to tell them it was going to be towed, and this woman just started screaming that her husband was missing. So, we think our body could be this guy. Actually, he's her significant other. They haven't officially tied the knot. But the van's in both their names, and he left their happy home in Salem in a huff a couple days ago and hasn't been heard of since."

"Maybe he's just cooling off?"

"According to her, they fight, he leaves, and he always comes right back within twenty-four hours. It's just their way."

"Sounds like the body's him," Lang agreed.

"Could very well be. Description matches. Got his picture from the DMV."

O'Halloran seemed to be holding back something, something important. Lang thought a moment, then said, "Exactly when did this guy take off?"

"About six o'clock Friday night."

"And he drove right past Halo Valley Security Hospital on his way to the coast from Salem. That puts him right in harm's way."

"It's a theory," O'Halloran allowed.

"God damn it. He was Justice's ride!" Lang was running with it. "How was he killed?"

"Blunt force trauma to the head. Talk to Delaney."

"I will," Lang said with meaning. He was already ahead of himself, putting the pieces together of Justice Turnbull's escape. "So, Turnbull took the van, then dumped it right away. Why?"

O'Halloran snorted. "You wouldn't have to ask if you saw it. Damn thing's painted all over with flowers and leaves and shit. Hippie stuff. He'd need something a little less conspicuous."

Lang thought a moment, his mind spinning with different scenarios, then settled to the only conclusion that made sense. "The woman strangled at the nursing home. Justice found a way to take her car after he unloaded the van."

The sheriff sighed. "You think he picked up her car at the same viewpoint?"

"Or close by." Lang shook his head. "Why not just kill her and leave her?"

"She would have been found sooner. Let's just hope she wakes up and can ID the bastard."

"Hell," Lang muttered, rubbing the back of his neck. The woman was near death when he'd left her, the EMTs refusing to give any prognosis as they tried to transfer her to a hospital. "We've got to find out who she is. Someone must be missing her. I'll get a picture on the news. Who is this woman? If you recognize her, call the TCSD. Something like that."

"Do it," O'Halloran said.

Lang strode out of the sheriff's office and nearly ran over Savannah Dunbar, who was looking a little white-faced. "What?" he asked.

"She . . . died." Savannah exhaled heavily. "The Jane Doe at Seagull Pointe. About twenty minutes ago." She let out a long breath. "The EMTs thought they'd save her, but . . ." She shook her head. "She was DOA at Ocean Park."

"Damn!" He thought of the comatose woman he'd seen at Seagull Pointe, how young she was, and he wondered about her family. If she didn't have kids of her own or a husband, she was someone's daughter, maybe someone's sister.

"They might have saved her if the caregivers at the nursing home hadn't been so incompetent," she whispered harshly.

"There'll be an investigation into their practices."

"And hopefully charges leveled!" She was seething. Upset.

"Why do I think you'll see to it?"

"'Cuz you can read me like a damned book."

Lang nodded. "This is all the more reason to find out who Jane Doe is. I was going to put her picture on the news."

"Crime scene techs took photos of the scene. They got Madeline Turnbull and Jane Doe, while she was still alive." She was shaking her head.

"There may be one of her we could post."

"Maybe," she said and met his gaze with her own troubled eyes.

"This isn't your fault," he said.

"No, it's not." Her lips tightened. "Seagull Pointe's staff missed the obvious signs, and they know it. The nurse and director were busy covering their asses."

"If you're right, there will be an investigation."

"Damned straight." Her smile held no mirth. "I'll see to it." She was already walking toward her desk. "I'm going to write up a report."

That should take care of any flaws with Seagull Pointe. Savvy wouldn't let their incompetence go unnoticed. He passed several deputies in the hallway, one who nearly ran into him, sloshed her coffee, and sent him a pissy glance.

"Hey, watch where you're going!" she said, then muttered something under her breath about stupid jerks.

Lang ignored her bad mood and thought about going to his own desk to call retired homicide detective Sam "Mac" McNally, who Johnson had said had finally gotten back to him. The next second he changed his mind, choosing his cell instead as he headed back outside to his Jeep, giving Johnson a hand lift of good-bye, to which she managed a nod. Placing the call, he was frustrated when he got McNally's voice mail yet again, but this time he asked him to phone his cell instead of the department. McNally had been the lead investigator out of the Laurelton Police Department, the city where Justice's last rampage had begun. McNally knew Justice Turnbull as well as anyone, and he'd worked with both Fred Clausen and Clausen's ex-partner, Kirkpatrick, who'd since moved on, leaving a position open at the TCSD, the position that Lang now owned.

Clausen had told Lang that McNally was an "okay guy," high praise from the terse and generally gloomy detective. Lang had wondered if Clausen might be feeling a bit overlooked since O'Halloran clearly expected Lang to be the lead dog in this investigation, instead of the more senior Clausen. Clausen, however, didn't seem to mind. He'd told Lang to call McNally, and Lang had, only to learn that Mac was now retired and on a weekend camping trip with his

son. The Laurelton PD had given Lang McNally's cell
number, and he'd phoned and left a message on the man's
voice mail. Mac had apparently picked up that message
sometime during the camping trip and had called back, but
now it was Lang's turn to keep up with their telephone tag.
And all the while Justice Turnbull was at large.

As he pocketed his phone, he caught a glimpse of
Clausen behind the steering wheel of his vehicle as he
drove into the back lot. Lang circled the outside of the
building on foot to meet with the older man. Clausen was
just climbing from his department-issue Jeep, a twin to the
one Lang drove, when Lang reached him.

"Hey," Fred said, stepping out and into a deep puddle up
to his ankle. He swore for a full minute, and Lang said
mildly, "Not to be an ass, but that's why I park out front."

"Yeah. Well." He stepped gingerly around the monstrous
puddle, which had also dampened his pant leg. "You are an
ass. Just for the record."

Lang grinned.

"You seen the *Breeze?*"

"Glanced at it," Lang said.

Clausen snorted. Shook his foot. Swore again, then said,
"Harrison Frost is playing big shot reporter again. Seaside
PD busted this ring of high school students that were invad-
ing and burglarizing houses, but Frost took credit for giving them the tip. Whole article's about the kids calling
themselves the Deadly Sinners, or something. Seven of 'em.
Frost got to know 'em, apparently."

"This the same Harrison Frost who was with the *Portland
Ledger?*" Lang asked. He knew enough about the man
from when Lang was with the Portland PD. Frost had gotten into hot water over the shooting outside a Portland club
called Boozehound. "He was related to one of the owners
of Boozehound and practically accused the other one of in-
stigating the homicide of his partner."

"Ye-up. Same guy. Works for the *Seaside Breeze* now

but can't stop stirring up these *big* stories. He'll be dogging us before you know it." Clausen slid Lang a glance as he walked toward the building, his shoe still making a sloshing noise. "Turnbull's escape is just the kind of news he wants to report."

"He's left us alone so far."

" 'Cuz of these kids." Clausen snorted. "Damn West Coast High teens. My stepson knows one of the Bermans. Britt Berman. Her dad lives in Tillamook, and she's at some of our games. Bermans kinda think they're better than everyone down here."

"She one of the seven Deadly Sinners?"

"No." Clausen waved a hand at him as he pushed open the door. "Could be, though, I guess. She fits the profile. But she's the victim, in this case." He sounded almost disappointed, and Lang figured his stepson had been snubbed by the girl, or something like it, to elicit this response from Clausen.

"You're not a fan of Frost," Lang observed. "Any particular reason?"

"The guy just wants to make mountains out of molehills." Clausen seemed about to say more, then changed his mind. "But he's right about the West Coast High kids. That place is a breeding ground for entitled, selfish, ungrateful kids."

"Sharp as serpent's teeth," Lang said.

"Huh?"

"Shakespeare. 'How sharper than a serpent's tooth it is to have a thankless child.' "

Clausen looked at him as if he'd sprouted alien antennae. "Sure," he said but obviously didn't get it.

"Learned that one from my mother," Lang said lamely. "I think I was a bit of a thankless child."

Clausen did not know what to do with that. "Kids, huh," he said and brushed past Lang as he headed toward the restroom.

Lang half smiled to himself and circled back to the front of the building and his own Jeep in search of Deputy Delaney and the dead body found outside Garibaldi.

Harrison checked the time on his cell phone as he returned to the *Breeze* with his follow-up article. Three thirty p.m. He hoped he could catch up with Vic this time, and was about to ask about the paper's publisher when Buddy pointed at the phone on Harrison's desk and said, "Channel Seven on one."

"What?"

"That's what they said." He shrugged. "Look, I don't have time to screen your calls, okay? I've got a story to write. The Tyler Mill fire. No one knows for sure, but it could be arson." He appeared thrilled at the thought as he turned to his computer.

Punching line one, Harrison picked up the receiver. "Frost."

"Mr. Frost," a smooth, young female voice said. "Channel Seven is following up on the Deadly Sinners story. Are you available to answer a few questions?"

Harrison realized Pauline Kirby's production team had found the story and was running with it. He wondered if she had any boundaries whatsoever. He was both flattered that it had caught their eye and irked because Pauline would usurp the whole damn thing if she could and take all the credit. "I'm around."

"Is there a better number to reach you?"

"Nah. Call here. The paper'll find me."

He hung up and Buddy grinned at him. "Putting yourself on the map again with this story, aren't you?"

Harrison said dryly, "Rich kids burglarizing other rich kids' homes. Pauline Kirby loves that stuff."

"And so do our readers and her viewers." He watched as

Harrison, who'd been shrugging out of his jacket, thrust his arms back inside the sleeves. "Leaving so soon?"

"Tell Vic I want to talk to him, when you see him. I just want to check in."

"Sure. You following up on these kids some more?"

Thinking of Justice, he said, "That and other things."

"If the entourage shows up from Channel Seven . . . ?"

"You've got my cell number. Call me. Just don't give them the number. I'll call 'em back later."

"You're a little nuts about giving out your cell number," Buddy pointed out. "You know that, right?"

"Yeah, I know."

It came from being hounded after his brother-in-law's death and the debacle that followed. Giving Buddy a short wave good-bye, Harrison stepped back outside and into the fingers of fog that hadn't quite dissipated from yesterday's deep shroud.

# CHAPTER 23

The dry toast Laura consumed in the late morning had carried her through lunchtime, but she still felt distinctly off and ended up taking an early dinner break, where she was able to handle a bowl of chicken soup, French bread, and a small green salad from the cafeteria. Still, she felt a little dizzy with the thoughts that plagued her throughout her rounds. She was pregnant and Byron suspected the truth. She'd thrown out a challenge to Justice Turnbull, and the psychotic killer was planning to attack her. She was feeling her way through a new and unexpected acquaintanceship with Harrison Frost that felt like it could turn into something more.

Where did that ridiculous thought spring from? A single kiss—two, counting the buzz she'd brushed across his cheek—did not a relationship make! She barely knew the guy, had met him just the other day, at the start of all this madness.

Oh, Lord, then why did it seem like an eternity?

Her world had been turned upside down since Justice's escape on Friday night, and it was only Sunday.

Conversation buzzed, the ice dispenser clunked, and bored-looking cafeteria people waited while the staff and visitors hemmed and hawed over their choices. The smells of garlic and marinara sauce and day-old clam chowder reached her nostrils. Conversation flowed around her, but she barely noticed. She was stacking her lunch tray and turning to leave when Carlita Solano entered with one of the orderlies and headed toward the soda stand. As she passed, Laura heard Carlita say, "I'm not making this up! I know one of the nurses at Seagull Pointe. The police are trying to keep it under wraps, like they always do until every last living relative is contacted, but Jessica said they think that psycho killed his equally psycho mother! It'll be on the news soon enough!"

The psycho could be only one person. Laura's heart began beating a wild, adrenaline-fueled tattoo. She had to force her hands to remain steady as she set her tray down.

"Seriously?" the orderly said. "Wow." He added dryly, "Great care over there, huh?"

Laura couldn't stand it. "I'm sorry," she said. "I couldn't help but overhear. Are you talking about Justice Turnbull? And his mother?" In her mind's eye she caught a quick image of Madeline as a younger woman . . . pretty and unsure, in a floral dress, standing near a shabby row of rooms in an old motel, her hair windblown, the hem of the dress floating around her calves as the sea, far below the motel perched on the cliff, roared and crashed on the rocky shore. She had sad eyes, Laura remembered, eyes that were dark with secrets. . . .

"That's right." Carlita turned in Laura's direction. She looked happy that someone was finally listening to her with the right amount of interest. "And there's some other woman, too," she said eagerly. "He smothered them both. Or strangled them. Anyway, they're both dead now."

"They'd better beef up security over there. It just doesn't look good when patients are murdered." The orderly's attempt at humor fell flat as he finished at the soda machine and the cola hissed and foamed over the ice in his cup.

"Who's the other woman?" Laura asked through a dry throat. Oh, God, not one of her sisters! Surely Catherine wouldn't let any of them out of the gates. . . . *But there are ways to escape the walls of Siren Song. You know this. So do the others.* Her sisters' faces came to mind: Isadora or Cassandra or Lillibeth or—

"Probably some relative," Carlita said with a dismissive "who cares?" shrug. "Isn't that who he tried to kill before? I think I saw that on the news when he went nuts before and targeted those women at Siren Song."

*Because you called him. That's why he went on his rampage! You should never have listened to Harrison. . . .*

She caught herself up short. She couldn't blame Harrison. She was the one who had mentally challenged Justice, dared him, sent him into a rage. If there was anyone to blame, it was she.

Her insides turned to water.

Had she made a mistake?

One that had cost two women their lives?

Hadn't Harrison told her to go to the police?

But with what? A telepathic message?

She imagined how the detectives would have shared a look when she'd tried to explain about her connection, her mental conversation with the escaped mental patient.

"You okay?" Carlita asked and Laura snapped out of it.

"Yeah," she said, trying not to sound uncertain, even though "okay" was far from how she was feeling.

Carlita's friend had grabbed a lid and straw and had moved farther into the cafeteria, so Carlita hurried to catch up to him. Laura's heart twisted. Guilt burrowed deep into her soul, and she gently touched her abdomen, reminding herself of the baby growing within her.

Oh, Lord, what a mess.

She left the cafeteria on leaden feet as she walked back toward the first floor nurses' station. Who was the unknown woman? Someone she knew? Again, she thought of her sisters; they were the most likely victims. Hadn't he said he would kill them all?

She paused in the hallway and concentrated.

No, she told herself. It wasn't someone from Siren Song. She would know. If not from instinct, then someone from the Colony would have tracked her down and delivered the news. Catherine would know if any of her charges had gone missing.

Still, two people were dead. At Justice's hand.

Maddie and someone else . . . an unknown victim.

"Bastard," she growled under her breath as she thought of him. "Murdering, soulless bastard."

"Hey? You talkin' to me?" a patient pushing an IV stand demanded. Balding, his hospital gown draping off one shoulder, he glared at her as he passed.

"Sorry. No." Her head began to pound. She was still on break, so she turned toward the staff room and, once inside, blindly navigated to an isolated table at the back of the room. Lost in thought, she barely noticed two nurses huddled together over a crossword puzzle, and another watching the news while dunking her tea bag into a steaming cup. Laura stared at the screen as the facade of Seagull Pointe came into view and a reporter gave a few more details than Carlita had of the tragedy.

Did Harrison know what had happened at the nursing home . . . ? Surely he did. He worked at a newspaper, for crying out loud. Funny how her thoughts kept running to him.

When the story on the television flipped to a fire at an old sawmill, she'd had enough. Pushing back her chair, she walked out of the room and hurried to the bank of lockers where the staff kept their personal belongings. Twisting open her combination lock, she grabbed her cell and dialed Harrison's number, without hesitation this time, aware how much she'd come to depend on him in such a short period of time.

He didn't answer and she was instantly deflated. She planned to just hang up, but then changed her mind and left a message. "Hey, it's me. You probably heard what happened at Seagull Pointe. I think Justice may have killed Madeline. Maybe another woman, too." She paused, filled with emotion suddenly. Fear. Need. Anger. "Call me," she said, hoping she didn't sound as desperate as she felt.

The Sands of Thyme Bakery wasn't doing much of a business in the late afternoon, though the smells of cinnamon and coffee lingered and the glass cases held a few loaves of bread and overlooked muffins, left after the morning and noon rush. Only a few customers were scattered amongst the small tables, each nursing a cup and picking at the crumbs on their plates.

Harrison found his sister leaning on her elbows at the counter and reading the morning paper.

"You've been busy," she said, looking up from his article in the *Breeze*.

"The *Breeze* isn't the *Ledger*."

"Yeah, well, it's not really about the paper. It's about the story," she said, quoting him. "This Deadly Sinners story is the kind of thing that gets picked up. A bunch of privileged teens burglarizing their friends' homes." When he didn't immediately respond, she gave him a long look. "Aha. I get it. Someone's already trying to yank this story from you, maybe steal a little of your thunder."

She was needling him, one eyebrow lifting. "Who? Not that jerk who was always breathing down your neck."

"That guy was at the *Ledger*. No, it's Channel Seven."

"Pauline Kirby?" Kirstin guessed, sounding appalled. "Lord, she's a witch with a capital *B*."

"Down, tiger," Harrison warned, though he knew how she felt. Channel Seven's reporting on Manny's death had not been a warm and fuzzy experience for any of them. In fact Pauline's team had shone their camera lights directly on Kirsten's face and captured the glittering track of her tears for all to see. The other stations weren't much better, but Kirsten had a real thing against Pauline, which Harrison appreciated.

"She's not my favorite, either," he said now.

His sister's eyes slit, and he guessed she was remembering how callously she was treated by the press. "They're all the same."

"Reporters?"

"Yes," she shot back. Then, after a moment, her lips twisted wryly. "You're just as bad as the rest of them."

He smiled back, fleetingly; then his tone changed. "I should've been there more for you after it happened. I was too . . . single-minded."

She waved that aside with a brisk snap of her hand. "You wanted to prove Manny had been murdered. I wanted you to, too. But it's all water under the bridge now."

She sounded so final, it surprised him a bit. "You think it was just a case of his being in the wrong place at the wrong time now?"

"Oh, I don't know." Kirstin glanced toward the door as two of the patrons left their table and made their way outside, the bell over the door tinkling. "I don't know if I'll ever know. What I do know is it's over and I have to move on." She touched the back of Harrison's hand. "Sad, I know, but true." Then she let out a long sigh and retrieved her fingers while a customer ordered a coffee to go. With a smile, Kirsten took his money, gave him a smile and a cup, and pointed him in the direction of the freestanding thermoses.

Harrison gazed at his sister, realizing for the first time how he was the only one still hanging on to Manny's death, the only one who couldn't let go.

As if reading his mind, she said, "I've got Didi to think about. All this dwelling on the past isn't good for her. I don't want this dark cloud of suspicion hanging around us all the time. I've got a new life with my daughter and our dog. And we're happy to have you in it, too, of course," she added, again reaching a hand across the counter to catch his. "It's just . . . every time you and I are together, one way or another, we're either talking about or thinking about Manny's death. I'm not saying I want to forget him. Lord, no. I want to *remember* him. Like he was. Like it was between us before all the really bad stuff started."

"You want me to give up the investigation completely?" he asked, surprised.

"That's not what I'm saying. Do what you have to do. Just . . . let's . . . not make it all that you and I are about anymore, okay?"

"I didn't know I was doing that."

"*We* were doing that. Both of us. Even when it seemed like we weren't." She stared at him with eyes far older than her age.

Harrison took it in, realized she was right. He'd been too immersed in his own need for revenge to really pay attention to what Kirsten was thinking. But then, he still believed in Koontz's duplicity. "I'm not going to give up unless you tell me to."

"I wouldn't want you to. Let's just not have a post-mortem on everything, okay?"

"Okay."

"That said, I think *this* story could launch you back into the bigger pond again." She retrieved her hand and, with one finger, tapped on the paper with his article.

"You think the *Ledger* will have me back?" he asked dryly as one of the customers placed his empty cup and plate in a tub before flipping up the hood of his jacket and stepping outside.

She cocked her head. "I'm pretty sure you're done with them. But yeah. They'll want you back. Especially if you follow up the Deadly Sinners with the Justice Turnbull story."

"Did I say I was on that story?"

"Oh, please. Of course you are."

The bell over the door jingled again as a new customer entered the shop. Harrison held up a hand in good-bye to his sister and headed out. His cell phone beeped at him as he was crossing to his car, and he realized he'd missed a call somehow. Before he could ring back his voice mail, however, the phone buzzed in his hand. Glancing at the caller ID, he saw it was the *Breeze*. Buddy. "Yeah?" he growled as soon as he'd snapped it on.

"I didn't give them the number," Buddy stated before Harrison could say anything else. "I promise. But they're right here. And they're planning to film in front of West Coast High and they'd like to see you."

"They're right there in front of you, at the paper?"

"You got it."

"Is Pauline there, or is it just production?"

"Production."

"I'm not anywhere near you. I'm in Deception Bay. Don't tell them that. Tell Pauline to call me and I'll . . . I don't know . . . give her a quote, or something. Better yet, have her call the public information officer at the sheriff's office. That's what she's paid for."

"But—"

"Oh, hell. Give her my cell number. Give 'em all my number." Clicking off, he climbed into the Impala, irked. He was going to have to hand out his digits to every Tom, Dick, and Harry, because Kirsten was right: his days of being banished to a small town were nearing an end. He was headed for the big game, which had been his plan all along, right? And if he was going there, he needed people to be able to reach him.

And then, as if already knowing he was changing his protocol, his cell phone buzzed at him again.

Without looking at the caller ID, he answered, "Frost."

"Hi, there," Geena Cho said. "Got a minute?"

"Geena, for you . . . always."

She snorted at his bullshit, then said, "You know what happened at Seagull Pointe?"

"No."

"Where the hell have you been? Hiding under a rock?"

"Something like that," he hedged, realizing he hadn't been near a television all day.

"And you call yourself a reporter?" she joked. Then, before he could answer, her voice lowered. "So get this. It looks like Justice killed his mama, Mad Maddie. And some other lady, too, who was just found in a wheelchair, apparently, half dead. They transferred her to a bed and she later died. We're putting her picture on the evening news because she's unidentified at this time. They're keeping Maddie's death under wraps as long as they can. Don't want to cause a panic about Justice, but they're pretty sure he's the doer."

Harrison's heart nose-dived. "Where did you say this happened? Seagull Pointe?" he asked, more convinced than ever that somehow Laura had reached him, taunted him, challenged him. His throat tightened at the thought, and he was sick that she, along with the two people already murdered, was in the psycho's sights.

"You got it. And you owe me a drink tonight at Davy Jones's. I'll be there around eight. Don't tell anyone I told you. . . ." And she was gone.

"Son of a bitch," he said into the phone. Switching on the ignition he was about to throw his Chevy into gear when he remembered to check his phone log and the call he'd missed. He recognized the number as Laura's. His heartbeat ramped into overdrive. "Damn." He hadn't expected her to phone him from work, and he listened tensely to her message.

*Justice may have killed Madeline. . . . Call me. . . .*

So, she'd already learned that Justice had possibly murdered his mother. But at least she was alive. Safe. Or had been when she'd called.

Quickly, he pressed in her number, then waited impatiently while the phone rang and rang and rang. Swearing under his breath, he debated on leaving her back a response on voice mail, then instead decided on "Got your message. Call me back."

"Damn it all to hell." He snapped on the radio, finding an all-news station, then revved out of the Sands of Thyme's lot. He considered driving straight to Seagull Pointe, but he would really like to talk to Laura first. Make sure she was all right. He called again as he hit the highway and, like before, was sent directly to her voice mail. Swearing, he hit the gas, pushed the speed limit.

He knew she was working, that she didn't have her cell on her. That was undoubtedly the reason she wasn't picking up.

Still . . . his mind wheeled to unconscionable images— Justice Turnbull, the icy-eyed psychotic with his need to kill, and the victims. His own mother. An unknown woman and the others . . . oh, Jesus! He punched the accelerator and headed straight to Ocean Park, taking the curves on 101 a little too quickly, the cliffs and dark forest racing by on the eastern shoulder of the road, the sea shrouded by fog stretching to the west. The hospital was on his way to Seagull Pointe, and he intended to stop. If only for a few minutes. He needed to see Laura, to witness for himself that she was okay.

Despite getting hung up behind a logging truck mounded with a heavy load of fir, he pulled into the lot at Ocean Park within half an hour. He parked what seemed a mile from the front doors, as the place was full of vehicles. Jogging, he made his way through the vehicles and into the building, where he didn't bother with the reception desk, entering purposely and heading straight for the elevators. Ocean Park was only three stories high, but he wasn't sure which floor Laura worked on and he would rather discover where that was on his own than reveal his intent to the beady-eyed, suspicious woman manning the desk.

In the end he found that Laura worked mainly on the first floor, and he wound his way back to her nurses' station, only to learn that she was busy with a patient. A petite woman with spiked hair and too much mascara asked him if he would care to wait in one of the two molded plastic chairs set against the wall. Unhappily, he planted himself on the edge of the first chair, taking out his phone to check the time. Five p.m. He'd really wanted to get to Seagull Pointe before the dinner hour. He hoped to interview as many people as possible about both Madeline Turnbull's death and the unidentified woman left in a wheelchair. That was headline news in itself. Who was she? Did her condition have anything to do with Justice Turnbull?

"Harrison."

Laura's voice sounded from down the hall, and he looked over to see her walking his way. Her hair was pulled into a ponytail. The earpiece of a stethoscope peeked out of the pocket of her scrubs, and a look of worry darkened the even features of her face.

Relief washed over him and he shot to his feet. God, it was good to see her.

She was near enough not to shout when she said, "What are you doing here?"

"I got your message. Called you back, but you didn't pick up."

"I know. I'm on duty." She glanced around and seemed to notice the teenager slouched in one of the nearby chairs. He appeared to be asleep, his iPhone tethered to his ears as he listened to music. Nonetheless, Laura shepherded Harrison away from the cluster of uncomfortable chairs.

"I knew you were working, but I just didn't know if you . . . needed me. You told me to call you, and when I couldn't get through . . ." He left the thought unfinished, thinking about how she'd challenged Justice. "I just wanted to make sure everything was okay."

"Everything's fine." She glanced around again, very aware of others' listening ears. As if on cue, an older nurse appeared from the south hallway, one Harrison recognized from Friday night. Perez, he remembered as she approached, a frown deepening across her face as her gaze fell on him.

"You're that reporter," she said, her dark eyes moving from him to Laura.

"I'm following up on the victims of Justice Turnbull's attack," Harrison said to shift the spotlight from Laura.

"One of them was released earlier today," Laura answered, giving him a grateful look, which Perez didn't see.

"I'm assuming that would be Dr. Zellman, as he had the less critical injuries?" Harrison asked.

"I really can't give out any patient information," Laura said, and he caught the warning in her eyes.

Nurse Perez jumped in. "Mr . . . . ?"

"Frost," Harrison supplied. "Harrison Frost with the *Seaside Breeze*."

"Frost," she repeated. "If you have questions, there's a protocol. Talking to our nursing staff isn't the way it's done." She shot Laura a warning glance.

Harrison nodded. "All right. I'll check with the front desk and have them connect me with your media liaison."

"Good," Perez said with a bite. She looked Harrison up and down, clearly wondering at his easy capitulation.

He sketched a good-bye to both Nurse Perez and Laura, keeping up appearances, but his jaw was rock hard on his way back to his Chevy. Perez's attitude bugged the hell out of him, but he reminded himself that Laura was healthy and safe. That was all he really cared about here, at Ocean Park. As he was getting into his vehicle, his cell rang and it was Laura.

"I only have a second," she said. "I'm off around eight tonight."

"I've got a meeting with a woman from the TCSD at the same time," he said. "I'll come by your place afterward." He made it a statement, but he was waiting for an answer. "Make sure Nurse Ratchet isn't with you."

"Nurse Rat . . . Oh, I get it. Funny," she muttered, and he thought there might be relief in her tone. "Trust me, Perez slash Ratchet is not invited."

"Good."

"See you."

"Looking forward to it, Lorelei," he said, meaning it.

"Only my family calls me that," she told him again.

"I know."

"Okay," she said after a moment and then hung up.

Lang checked the clock in his Jeep: 5:15 p.m. He was driving back from the crime scene site, where he'd met with Deputy Delaney and viewed the dead male body that had attracted the carrion birds. He and Delaney had ended up hanging around a lot longer than either of them wanted while the CSI team swarmed over the scene and the ME finally arrived and examined the body before it was sent to the morgue.

"Busy day for Gilmore," Delaney had said, referring to the medical examiner. "First the body at the nursing home and now this guy."

Lang had nodded. "I'm going to check in at the department and then call it a day."

"You and me both," Delaney had said, giving a last look around, his nose wrinkling in distaste.

Lang drove straight to the TCSD without encountering too much traffic and caught O'Halloran as the sheriff was getting ready to leave. "The would-be wife's on her way from Salem to see if the body belongs to James Cosmo Danielson, her significant other," O'Halloran informed him as they stood on the worn wood floor of the hallway outside the sheriff's office.

"Did our Jane Doe's picture hit the news?" Lang asked.

"Uh-huh. Got her photo and Turnbull's posted about everywhere we can think of."

"Okay. I've got a little paperwork to finish. Then I'm outta here. Unless there's anything more to do tonight?"

O'Halloran sighed and shook his head. "Nope."

"Nothing from the cars watching the lighthouse or the motel?"

"We're having to move around and answer other calls, you know," the sheriff said, a bit defensively. "We're short staffed already and stretched thin with this Turnbull business and the Tyler Mill fire, along with everything else, but we're still patrolling regularly. Somebody'll find him."

Lang had fallen in step beside the sheriff as the older man headed for the back door. They could see through a window to the back lot and together watched as a beat-up Ford Focus dragging its back fender suddenly careened through the mud puddles of the parking lot and came to an abrupt halt outside the back door.

"Who's this?" O'Halloran muttered.

"Don't know."

A woman jumped out of the Ford, her long brown hair a mass of tangles, a baby in one arm and a toddler stuck to her leg like a burr, holding on to her around a tie-dyed dress of olive green, brown, and burnt orange that looked as if it could use a good cleaning.

"Glad I'm leaving," the sheriff muttered.

"Me, too," Lang said.

As she was obviously headed for the back door, they both retraced their footsteps into the hallway, giving her room. Then she burst inside, her face red and puffy, her eyes wild, still balancing both of her kids. The back door was used almost exclusively by the members of the sheriff's department, and when she entered, May Johnson steamed over to bar her from entering.

"Ma'am, you are not allowed through here," Johnson told her sternly.

"I've got my sister's car!" the woman wailed. "I have to see him! I have to see Cosmo! Oh, God."

"The would-be wife," Lang realized in an aside to O'Halloran. He felt instant sympathy for her. She was frantic and then there were the little kids. . . .

"Ahh." The sheriff nodded.

"Ma'am . . ." Officer Johnson had on her deepest scowl.

Which cut no ice with the newcomer, who screeched hysterically, "Where is he? Where's my man? Oh, God. Oh, please, please, God, where's my beautiful man!" And then she collapsed on the floor along with her children, and for once May Johnson looked perplexed and at a complete loss.

# CHAPTER 24

Harrison was buzzed into the reception area of Seagull Pointe and then was immediately greeted with suspicion by the woman at the desk as soon as he said he was a reporter. This was nothing new; it was a condition of the job, a reporter's bane. After dealing with her, he was ushered swiftly into a small room with a calming decor: gray walls, a jade plant near the window, a seascape mounted over a bookcase that held a few tomes, including the Holy Bible. He took a chair at the round Formica-topped table and faced both the director of the place, Darius Morrow, a man in his late sixties with a pious expression and a way of folding his hands in front of him in a holier-than-thou way that set Harrison's teeth on edge, and his female head nurse/administrator/jailer, Inga Anderssen, who, if you looked in the dictionary, the picture beside her name would read "Battle-ax."

"You need to be a relative to receive information on a patient," Darius informed him as soon as he asked about Madeline Turnbull. The man had a habit of wrinkling his nose, as if there were a bad smell in the room, and with the way he held his hands, he looked as if he were about to pray.

"I understand Madeline died from either smothering or strangulation," Harrison said.

"Confidentiality, Mr. Frost," he was reminded tartly.

"The police are investigating," Harrison pointed out. He was winging it, in a way, but Geena Cho's information was generally golden, so it wasn't that much of a stretch, and he'd seen a cruiser parked outside. "They're going to release her name to the media soon enough. I'm going to start reporting today, one way or another. You can give me facts, or I can go on conjecture."

Inga had leaned close to him, glaring at his audacity, but Darius held up a smooth white palm. "Seagull Pointe is a prime facility with an excellent reputation. Of course we don't want *conjecture*."

Harrison thought he heard a little capitulation in his tone. Just a little. "It sounds like Justice Turnbull came to your facility, found his mother, and killed her."

"That is untrue. He could not get in," Inga snapped as she threw Darius a harsh look that said as well as any words, "Don't buy into his BS." To Harrison, she said aloud, "The doors are locked."

"You need a code," Darius explained and Harrison nodded; he'd been granted entry by the woman at the desk, who clearly watched every newcomer enter with a suspicious eye.

"But if he had the code, he could get in any door, right? He wouldn't have to pass the front desk." Harrison sat back in his chair, growing impatient with the way they carefully thought through every response.

Both Darius and Inga stared straight ahead, as if they were both, independently, trying hard not to give away something on their faces. Harrison reviewed what he'd just said, and it came to him as if their thoughts had materialized in the air in front of him. "The desk isn't manned at night."

"After ten," Darius admitted.

"But he'd still need a code." Harrison was puzzling it out. "Is it a big secret, or just a means to contain the patients with dementia?"

"He's never been here before," Inga stated. "He would not know it."

"Before," Harrison repeated. "So, you do think he did come last night. And it's definitely what the sheriff's department thinks, too." When they didn't respond, he said, "The other woman he killed . . . maybe she gave him the code?"

"She wasn't a patient here," Darius told him. "She is no one we know."

"Maybe she was visiting someone?"

"She was a stranger," Inga said firmly.

"You know everyone who visits everyone?"

Darius dropped his pious look for a brief moment to shrug and spread his hands. "This is a nursing home and an assisted-living facility," he explained. "If a new face comes through, it's noticed. Someone notices. No one knows this woman, and she would not have been able . . ." He let his voice trail off, as if realizing he was giving away more information than necessary.

"Would not have been able . . . to . . . let him in? Because she was already injured before she arrived?" It was like pulling teeth.

"She was not attacked at Seagull Pointe!" Inga declared.

On this, he thought she might be right. She came here with him, Harrison realized. And, on the heels of that thought . . . She was his transportation.

Darius pointedly consulted his watch at the same moment Harrison's phone bleeped at him: a new message. He glanced down and saw it was a Portland number. He was pretty sure it was Pauline Kirby.

"Excuse us," Darius said, and he and Inga turned toward the south hallway. Harrison headed back to the reception area, but tried to keep out of earshot, searching for a modicum of privacy. He found a nook with a fake ficus tree and a window that overlooked the parking lot and punched out the number for his mailbox. Sure enough it was Pauline who had left him a voice mail.

*Phone tag,* he thought. *Pain in the ass.* Punching in his security code, he waited for his voice mail to deliver.

"Hey, there." Pauline's assured tone reached his ears. "You avoiding me, Frost? And just when we found each other again. Give me a call. We're rolling, but I'd like your thoughts. . . ." She rattled off her cell number, which matched the one on his caller ID.

Yeah, right. She'd like his thoughts. She'd like to rip the facts that Harrison had gathered, put her own spin on them, and regurgitate them like they were her own.

*Sure thing, Pauline. Can't wait for it.*

Nevertheless he called her back, once more deflected by her voice mail. Tersely, he told her he would be available most of the afternoon. Hanging up, he gave a mental shrug. What the hell did he really care, anyway? If Pauline wanted to bounce over to the Deadly Sinners story, so be it; he couldn't stop her. Harrison planned to meet with Noah Vernon the next day and hopefully get the boy's skewed perspective on the whole thing, but then he was going to move full speed ahead on the Justice Turnbull investigation.

An older gentleman in a V-necked navy sweater and gray sweatpants came into the reception area from the north side hallway at that moment. He was pushing an empty wheelchair in front of him. Seeing Harrison, he cocked his head. "You the one who was talking to our esteemed director just now? What's his name again?"

"You mean Darius Morrow?"

"Oh, yes." He pursed his lips and rolled his eyes like he'd had more than enough of Morrow.

Having been brushed off by both Morrow and Anderssen, Harrison considered this new source. The receptionist looked like she wanted to say something, but then the desk phone rang and she was forced to answer it. Taking his moment, Harrison crossed to meet the man. He could feel the woman at the desk shooting him daggers. He half expected her to slam down the phone and call security.

"I'm Herm Smythe," the older man greeted him with a handshake. "Mind if I sit down?" He indicated the chair he was pushing.

"Do it," Harrison invited, holding the chair while Herm worked his way around to the other side, sinking heavily into its leather seat, heaving a sigh.

"Who'd you come to see?" Herm asked him and waved toward the hallway, as if he expected Harrison to push his chair.

"Anyone who knows something about Madeline Turnbull's death. I'm a reporter."

"Mad Maddie's dead?" He sounded surprised and upset. "Nobody tells me anything!"

"You knew her?" Harrison proceeded to wheel the chair down the hallway from the direction Herm Smythe had appeared. He probably had five to ten minutes before the forces of Morrow and/or Anderssen descended on him.

"Sure did. I knew all the women like her."

Wondering what that meant, Harrison was nevertheless beginning to think he might have happened upon a gold mine of information. "Which women, Herm?"

"Catherine. Mary. Maddie. I wrote their history, you know," he added proudly.

"The women of Siren Song?" Harrison asked in surprise.

"The Colony," he said, nodding his head with satisfaction. "That's what they're called."

"*You* wrote their history?"

"Don't sound so surprised, mister. Wrote it down in a book," he said proudly. Then, "Where the hell is that thing? Parnell had it last."

"Parnell?"

"Dr. Parnell Loman. I didn't give it to him. He took it. But he's dead now . . . a long time. Killed himself off the jetty. Wait. Whoa, Nellie. Here's my room." He pointed to the door with his name on it.

Harrison processed the information Herm had given him as he turned the chair and wheeled the older man inside. The room was furnished with two orange molded-plastic chairs and little else besides Herm's bed. Herm eased himself from the wheelchair into one of the chairs and waved Harrison to the other one.

Harrison perched himself on its edge, glancing toward the open door.

"Close it," Herm ordered. "Don't need 'em all listening in."

He rose to shut the door, then reseated himself. "There's a Dr. Loman at Ocean Park Hospital," Harrison said. "An osteopath . . ."

"That's Dolph." Herm spat the words. "Parnell's brother. A pompous ass, if there ever was one!"

Harrison silently agreed on that point. "This Parnell did not write the book, but it was in his possession."

"That's right."

"You wrote the book of the Colony's history. The book that's at the Deception Bay Historical Society?"

"Yes, I . . ." Herm considered a moment, concentrating hard. He pressed a finger to his lips, then shook his head in frustration. "Dinah told me something about it. . . . I don't remember. . . . Damn, it's hell getting old!"

"Dinah?" Harrison prompted.

"My daughter." His gray eyes held a secret. "She might be a sister to one of 'em, you know? A half sister, anyway."

"To the women of the Colony?" Harrison felt a little like he was swimming upstream. Every time he made progress, he seemed to slip backward.

"I had my times with Mary." Herm twinkled at Harrison. "I was quite a swordsman in my day, you know."

Another time Harrison would have encouraged Herm Smythe's amusing dialogue, but it just felt like the conversation was seesawing from one side to another without direction on a topic Harrison really wanted to hear. "What did Dinah tell you about the book?"

"Parnell took it," he said. "He wasn't supposed to, but he took it."

Harrison inwardly sighed. "The book at the historical society."

"Yes, the book I wrote. It's a history of the Colony. Did I mention that?"

"You said Dinah told you something about the book," Harrison reminded.

He nodded. "Dinah's my daughter."

"Yes."

"It's all about their history, you know. The Colony. How they came to be what they are. You say the book's at the historical society now?"

"A friend told me that," Harrison agreed. "She thought a doctor wrote it."

He vehemently shook his head. "What friend?"

"Her name's Laura," Harrison said, wondering if he'd tapped the older man out of information.

"Who's Laura? You mean Lorelei?"

Harrison couldn't quite contain his surprise. He hoped it wasn't as obvious to Herm as he sidestepped, "My friend's a nurse at Ocean Park Hospital."

"With that bastard, Dolph." He nodded sagely. "He was always jealous of me. Mary liked me, and Parnell, but she couldn't stomach Dolph." He cackled out a laugh. "Yeah, I wrote the book, but it doesn't really have the good stuff. Mary was a loose woman, you know. Free love. It was the seventies and eighties. We were all into it. But Catherine put the kibosh on everything. She never, ever liked me.

Doesn't matter, 'cause Mary and I had our times, you know." He skewered a look at Harrison with his gray eyes under salt and pepper brows. "That DNA stuff that's all over television? Sometimes I think I should go back there and test some of those girls, find out if one of 'em's mine, you know. Can you do that for me?"

"I don't think so." He wasn't unkind. "When you were with Mary?" Harrison prodded. "What year was that?"

He shrugged, uncaring. "Ask Dinah."

"Do you have a number for her?"

"Sure." He waved a hand over to his bedside table. "Go over there."

Harrison cruised around the bed and found a list of phone numbers written in large black lettering on a paper that was taped to the table. Dinah's number was listed, along with several others that weren't labeled. Harrison scratched them all into his small notebook, just in case they had a meaning that he couldn't quite see yet.

There was a knock on Herm's door, to which he called gaily, "Come on in!" as if he'd completely forgotten his earlier desire for privacy.

One of the staff members stuck her head inside, her eyes darting to Harrison. "Everything okay, Herm?"

"Oh, sure. This is my guest. . . ." He glanced toward Harrison with a faint frown.

"Harrison," he said.

"He's dating my daughter, Dinah."

The woman stepped into the room, standing erect and giving Harrison a long, meaningful look. She was in her thirties, heavyset, with a cold manner that said nobody, but nobody, better mess with her. Her gaze never wavered as she said, "Oh, I don't think so. He doesn't look like Dinah's type."

"I was just leaving," Harrison said, giving her his best smile. He shook Herm Smythe's hand.

"You wanted to know about Mad Maddie," Herm suddenly said. "She's down the hall. The other side."

At the mention of Madeline Turnbull's name, the aide visibly stiffened.

Harrison didn't remind Herm that Mad Maddie was gone. It probably wouldn't stick in the older guy's mind, anyway. "Thanks."

The woman stepped back into the hallway and Harrison followed her out. Her name tag read TONI. Harrison nodded at her, but there was no way she was going to let him go without a postmortem.

"Keri said you were a reporter."

"Keri works at the front desk," Harrison guessed.

"Mr. Smythe isn't a reliable source," she said tightly. "As I'm sure you noticed, he has trouble with his short-term memory."

"But his long term's okay?"

"Whatever you're working on, his word isn't to be taken as fact. He wanders from the past to the present to places of his own fantasy. As for anything about Ms. Turnbull, you'd be better off speaking to the director."

"Already had the pleasure," Harrison said.

They reached the reception area together. Keri glanced over at him balefully, and he responded with a smile, as if they were old friends.

"Can we help you with anything else?" Toni demanded.

The buzzing of his cell phone prevented him from having to answer her. Shaking his head, he moved to the door, waiting for Keri to buzz him out. He clicked on to his cell. "Frost."

"Well, well, well. We finally connect." Pauline Kirby's cool tones made Harrison almost smile. She might be an out-and-out bitch whose narcissism was legendary and whose interview technique was tactless, discomfiting, and altogether annoying, but there was something about her chasing him for a story that definitely warmed the cockles of his heart.

"Pauline," he said, a world of meaning in his tone.

"Look, I don't have a lot of time. I just want a quick few words on what you think of these entitled, pissant teenagers. Are they dangerous, or just poseurs?"

"Both."

"Think their daddies'll get 'em off?"

"Only property crimes, so far. What do you think?"

"The tone of your writing, Mr. Frost, suggests that you would like to see the little darlings have to pay for their mistakes with more than a slap to the wrist."

"I think they should know there are consequences to every choice. Action and reaction. Yin and yang."

"Are you saying they should go to jail?" Pauline asked.

"I'm saying that they need to get the big picture somehow," Harrison responded.

"How do we get them to do that?"

"I don't know," he answered honestly. "What makes a good parent? What makes a responsible child? Who's at fault? Why does this happen? What can we do to prevent our own children from taking the wrong fork in the road?"

"Do you have children, Mr. Frost?" She sounded truly curious, but Harrison knew better.

"No."

"Plan to have them?"

He flashed on Laura, his feelings for her. His amorphous thoughts about a possible future together. "Not if they're going to break into other people's homes just because they can. I gotta go."

"Just one more thing. I get the feeling that you've moved on."

"What makes you say that?"

"Something in your tone. Your impatience, maybe."

"Maybe I'm just impatient with you, Pauline."

"No." She sounded sure of herself, and he figured she'd already guessed what he was working on. "You're on to the

Justice Turnbull story, aren't you? I mean, it's practically in your backyard. Hope you don't mind if I check in with you some more as we go along."

Harrison couldn't decide if he was outraged or amused. He settled on the latter. "It's flattering that you need to follow after me to find your own news, Pauline."

She laughed. "Are you still mad about that whole episode with your brother-in-law? C'mon, Frost. We're all adults here."

He could practically see her sharklike smile. "Are we?" he asked, then clicked off before he lost his sense of humor.

Lang wanted to clap his hands over his ears at the rhythmic moaning filling the offices. He felt like he couldn't just leave, although O'Halloran had no such qualms, and was at his desk, finishing up some work he'd planned to put off till tomorrow. He might have stuck around the department, but he was definitely glad that both Johnson and Geena Cho had been the ones to separate James Cosmo Danielson's significant other from her clinging children so that Savvy Dunbar could escort the hysterical woman to the morgue to identify the body. The woman's ID had been positive—a loud keening wail before flinging herself atop the body, according to Savvy—and now she, who had said her name was Virgin, short for Virginia, according to her ID, was crying softly and rocking her children to and fro. The aforementioned sister had been called to come collect her, and the sister and her husband were on their way to the TCSD together as Virgin had the sister's vehicle. The sister's husband was going to drive the flowered van back home, but there was the impound to pay, and it was that injustice added to Cosmo's death that had sent Virgin into her current chanting, rocking fugue.

Into this distracting noise, Lang's cell phone rang. It was lying on his desk and he snatched it up. He recognized the number displayed on his LCD as Sam McNally's, so he headed out of the squad room to the relative quiet of the sheriff's office, closing the door behind him.

"Detective Stone."

"Sam McNally," he responded in a serious tone. "I understand you've been trying to get hold of me."

"That's right. About Justice Turnbull."

"He escaped from that hospital, huh?"

"Friday night. We think he's driven back here and is somewhere on the coast."

A pause. A soft remark that sounded like "Shit." Then McNally said, "You know he's after those women at the lodge, Siren Song."

"Yeah. And you were the lead investigator the last time he was after them," Lang replied.

"I worked with your department. There's a woman who lives in my county. Rebecca Sutcliff Walker. She was adopted out as a child, but she's one of them. She was tops on his hit list last time but escaped. I'm going to put some protection around her. Otherwise, he'll probably try to get to the ones at the lodge. He's got a total obsession about them."

"He wants to kill them all. . . ." Lang heard the questions in his words, even though he had meant to make a statement.

"He seems to try to pick off the ones outside the gates, but that doesn't guarantee he won't go after the ones inside. He's really a whack job. I mean it, a bona fide psycho."

"I got that," Lang said with feeling.

"Any others on the outside that you know of?"

"I don't think so," Lang said slowly. "I could ask Catherine. She's like the matriarch," he said, for lack of a better term.

"You talk to her?" McNally was bowled over.

"Some. Our sheriff, O'Halloran, has known her for years, and my fiancée is a doctor at Halo Valley. She's talked to Catherine a few times. Has even been inside the lodge," Lang admitted.

"Really." McNally sounded amazed. "That's more than Rebecca ever managed."

"What can you tell me about Justice? Something that might help find him now."

"Nothing you probably don't already know," McNally said. "He squatted in the lighthouse. His mother owned that motel, which I understand has been boarded up ever since. She went to a nursing home, I believe, after he attacked her."

"Seagull Pointe," Lang clarified. "It hasn't been publicized yet, but it looks like Justice got in and smothered her last night or early this morning."

"What? For the love of God!" Then with more urgency, "You gotta keep those women safe, Stone. If you can reach this Catherine, do it. Hell, we don't even know if they're aware he's out."

"Yeah, well, they have interesting ways of getting information," Lang said. "But I'll try to breach the gates, make sure they're all okay. We've been patrolling outside their lodge, and they have to know it, so they must know something's up. Sam, can you update me a little bit on what happened last time? I've got the gist of it, but since you led the case . . . ?"

"Call me Mac. Everyone does." He then went on to explain how Justice had targeted Rebecca Sutcliff and nearly managed to kill her. Sutcliff and her then-boyfriend, now husband, Hudson Walker, had learned that Rebecca was once a member of the Colony but had been adopted out when she was a baby. But Justice, who had a thing against all of them, had found her by a means they didn't fully understand and had gone after her, intent upon killing her, and it wasn't the first time he'd attempted to; it was just the first time Rebecca was aware that she was his target.

Mac went on to explain about a murder over twenty

years earlier that had links to the Colony and how this murder had played into the investigation that had finally led to Justice's capture.

He finished with, "You know, I just got back from a camping trip with my son, Levi, who's thirteen. He met a kid at a soccer tournament last fall. Mike Ferguson. Mike and some buddies and his older brother were at that school that was razed a few years ago, St. Elizabeth's. There was a maze attached to the school and the kids were trying to scare each other and they uncovered a skeleton which had been buried in the middle of the maze, in front of a statue of the Madonna. That's when I got involved with the case. The discovery of those remains kicked off the Turnbull investigation.

"Anyway, this Ferguson kid knew I was Levi's dad and that I headed up that case not long before I retired. He's apparently been following it. Really into it. Wonder what he thinks about Justice's escape."

"Yeah," Lang said, his mind already moving on to a possible meeting with Catherine, Keeper of the Gates. "Kids, huh," he added, echoing Clausen.

"You just never know what they're gonna get up to. . . ." McNally warned.

But Lang was already hanging up. He had a lot of other things to think about.

# CHAPTER 25

Thirteen-year-old Mike Ferguson stretched his neck as far as he could without lifting the heels of his boots off the floor, pushing the top of his head to the ruler placed on his crown. His gaze was glued to the TV set across the bedroom, which was nearly obscured by the baseball jacket he'd tossed across the room that had gotten hung up on the shelf above. One sleeve dangled across a portion of the screen, which was airing the evening news. "How tall?" he demanded, never moving his eyes.

"Five foot six," his brother James said in a bored voice.

"Bullshit." He put his finger to the top of his head and twisted away, holding his place. "Five-eight!" he yelled.

"Whatever, *Mikey*. You're still a dwarf." James was six foot one and growing.

"It's Michael," he said, as he always did when his brother tried to stick him with that same nickname. He'd grown five inches since he'd become a local celebrity a few years ago. No more was he Little Mikey Ferguson. Now, he was thirteen and a half, which was almost fourteen, and his face had lost its baby fat, and girls were starting to act stupid around him, which made his head swell even while he pretended he didn't notice.

Now Mike glanced to the left and the mirror mounted on his chest of drawers and smoothed his hair across his forehead, Justin Bieber style.

"God, you're stupid," James declared, groaning. It felt like he could ralph right here and now—*ralph* being his new favorite word (lots better than puke or upchuck or vomit or the really lame "tossed his cookies"). And because he was nearly three years older than Mikey, James definitely wanted to *ralph* when his mind even brushed on the idea that his little brother might be considered *hot*.

He had a gag reaction just thinking about it, and he made a bunch of disgusting sounds in front of both Mikey and Woofy Larson, James's best bro since his last best bro, Kyle Baskin, and his family had moved to California. But Mikey had moved from absorption in the TV and his own face to his cell phone, where he was texting like mad.

Woofy ran a hand through his mop of red hair and asked, "Who ya texting?"

"It's not a text. It's a tweet. Channel Seven." Mike's thumbs moved rapidly across the tiny keyboard.

James said, "Mikey's a butt-face."

"That would be Michael's a butt-face," Mike said, looking up.

"Fuckin' A," Woofy said, impressed.

"Why are you on Twitter?" James demanded. "Get off that." He made a grab for the phone, which Mike deflected with a sharp turn.

"You sound like Mom." Mike, unfazed, turned back to his phone.

"It's all you do!"

"Yeah, like you don't use your phone twenty-four-seven."

James kicked at a soccer ball that was lying on the bedroom floor and sent it crashing into the wall. It rebounded, hit the shade of Mike's bedside lamp, sent it spinning to the floor, where the bulb promptly made a *fitz* sound and popped, sending shards of glass out like tiny shrapnel.

"Nice," Mike said, too cool to flip out, like James wanted him to, though he certainly felt like it.

And James did want him to explode, that was for sure. Mike witnessed the fury rush to his head and turn his skin a dull red. James wasn't normally so quick to anger but everything just seemed to piss him off. "What the fuck," James muttered, then, after a few tense moments, bent down to pick up the slivers of glass.

Woofy, who was good-natured and easygoing as a rule, made a halfhearted attempt to help him, though he wasn't known for his cleaning skills. He always wore the same rugby-style shirt and jeans, enough to convince half the school he was dirt poor, when in reality he just didn't give a rat's ass.

Mike said after a moment, "I'm just trying to figure out where he went."

"Who?" Woofy asked, but Mike could tell James knew.

"That killer, dude," James said in a long-suffering tone. "Justice Bullshit, or whatever. Mikey's obsessed."

"Justice Turnbull." Mike finally lifted his eyes from his phone, switched it off, stuck it in his pocket.

"Oh, yeah." Woofy screwed up his face in deep thought. "The dude they caught who killed that girl, the one with the hand you found."

"It was sticking out of the ground," Mike reminded. "Skeleton fingers. Turned upward, reaching for help."

"Like a hundred years old!" James said, bugged in a way he couldn't define.

"Twenty years old," Mike corrected.

James snorted. He thought his brother was becoming a real pain in the ass.

"He escaped," Mike said. "You know that, right?"

"Of course, dude." Woofy sounded miffed, but Mike suspected he didn't really know what he was talking about.

"From that high-security hospital," Mike insisted. "Nobody thought he could get out. Nobody. But he did. He's like a ghost. Whispers through the night . . ." He spread his hands out as if he were parting a curtain. "He's kinda . . . ethereal."

"What the fuck does that mean?" Woofy asked.

"Like insubstantial, man," James clued him in.

"I'm gonna find him," Mike said with certainty.

"Bullshit," James shot back.

"I am. He lived in that lighthouse before. He'll go back. For sure! But it's a little ways out. We'll have to go by boat, I think."

James stared at his younger brother as if he were the psycho.

But Mike knew differently. He was one of those guys who just knew what he wanted to do . . . and then went and did it. James, who second-guessed anything and everything, found him a little scary and just short of completely weird.

"Oh, yeah," James mocked. "That's just what we're gonna do, butt-head. Drive to the coast. Rent a boat. Motor to the island and check out the old lighthouse where the psycho used to live!"

"I think we'll have to use a rowboat and oars," Mike explained earnestly. "I don't think anybody would rent a motorboat to us."

James threw up a hand in disgust. "We're not going, shit for brains. You can't even drive."

"But you can," Mike retorted, staring at James through blue eyes. "I'll navigate."

"Jesus, you're serious," Woofy said, blinking in disbelief.

Mike added, "I think a rowboat is the answer."

"I thought we were playing Guitar Hero." James glared at him.

Mike's eyes flicked back to the TV, and he noticed, from the corner of his eye, that James let his gaze wander there, too. That hot, bitchy, dark-haired reporter was coming on.

"Turn it up," Mike demanded.

"I'm not your slave, asshole," James muttered, but Woofy, who was near the remote, hit the volume.

"Call themselves Deadly Sins. Seven privileged teenagers who found a way into other people's homes . . . homes that belonged to the parents of their classmates . . . and who helped themselves to their possessions . . ."

"Shit," Mike muttered. "She's not talking about badass Justice Turnbull! Everybody's forgetting him!"

"They're not forgetting him," James said, long-suffering. "They just can't find him. He's probably in Canada by now."

"Or Mexico," Woofy put in.

Mike turned to James. "Mom and Dad are leaving on Tuesday. They'll call us on our cells. They won't know we're not here. We can head to the lighthouse on Tuesday or Wednesday."

"Fuckin' A," Woofy said again, full of admiration.

"We're not driving to the beach!" James glowered at his brother.

"I bet we could find him. I bet we could be heroes," Mike insisted.

"Hey, moron. The guy's a psycho. Did you forget?" James demanded.

"You get me there. I'll do the rest."

"You're gonna really go out to that lighthouse?" Woofy asked, his eyes wide with anticipation.

"No. He's not." James was repressive.

"Yeah, I am. Just gotta get a rowboat," Michael said.

"Find yourself a kayak, 'cause you're going alone!" James yelled. "God, you are such a 'tard."

"I think you mean nerd."

"Nope."

Mike's attention swung back to the set, where a picture of a woman's face filled the screen. No one could identify her, apparently. Since the news wasn't about Justice, Mike turned back to James. "School's out Tuesday. Mom and Dad'll take off and be gone until the next week. We got nothing but time."

"You're as much of a psycho as he is!" James was sick of the whole mess, especially of Mike. He strode out of his little brother's bedroom and yelled from the hallway, "If you don't want to play Wii, then I'm not gonna hang out. And you're a fuckin' idiot. We're not going to the beach."

Heroes. Ha. This was just another way to get into trouble. Another bad idea. James had no interest in taking his determined little ass of a brother anywhere.

Woofy wandered out to meet him in the garage, where James had picked up a paddle and was shooting a line of table tennis balls over the low net to the other side of the table. Beneath the flickering fluorescent lights, the balls bounced once and then flew off the Ping-Pong table and onto the floor. Some ricocheted into the exposed rafters; another hit the old fridge, where Mom kept extra sodas and beer; another smashed into the workbench. Woofy picked up another paddle, the dropped balls, and served to James. They went at it for all they were worth for twenty minutes; then James slammed a Ping-Pong ball straight into the garage door and flung down his paddle. "He really pisses me off!" he declared.

Woofy grunted. "Yeah?"

"I'm not doing it."

Woofy shrugged. "Didn't say you were."

"He thinks I'm gonna do it."

"Why do you care? You're not gonna." There was a silence, and Woofy, who wasn't known for his perception, nevertheless picked up the vibes radiating from his friend. "Are you?"

"No," James stated.

But a little kernel of interest had been planted. Even while James railed long and loud that he wasn't, wasn't, wasn't going to drive his little brother to the coast so that he could get involved in the search for some sicko, psychotic psycho, a part of him liked the idea of being a hero. James could see himself on the news with that hot bitch reporter, telling the world how he'd captured the guy. . . . It would be so intense . . .

If the fucker didn't kill them.

The dream evaporated in a puff. James valued his life, even if his obsessed little brother didn't.

Woofy left a few minutes later, and as James returned to the house, his cell phone rang. To his disbelief, it was Belinda Mathis. Only the hottest girl in the school! They'd exchanged cell phone numbers one day, though he'd suspected she was just humoring him to be nice. But now she was calling . . . !

"Yeah?" he answered cautiously.

"Oh, my God, I can't believe I'm doing this." It was a breathless little girl's voice. Not Belinda Mathis, for sure. "This is Kara Mathis, Belinda's sister," she explained. "Is this James Ferguson?"

"Uh-huh." He tried not to sound too disappointed.

"I'm using my sister's phone. Your cell phone number was on it. Um . . . I know your brother, Michael? Do you . . . could you . . . give me his cell number?"

The nightmare that never ended.

Closing his eyes, James mentally counted to ten, then rattled the number off to her. Minutes later he heard his brother's cell ringing and Mikey picking up.

James headed to the refrigerator, opened it, hung on the door, and gazed inside unseeingly. He could really use a boost to his own status with the women, that was for sure. He could use a little hero worship of his own.

And well, this psycho Justice dude . . . if he *didn't* kill them, they would definitely be heroes. . . .

*Huh,* James thought.

*That* would be really cool. Even Belinda Mathis would have to take notice. At least she had his number.

# CHAPTER 26

Geena Cho wore skinny black jeans that looked like they'd be impossible to take on and off, a pink, green, and white sleeveless silk top that scooped in folds at her neck, and a pair of diamond studs, one of which winked under the lights as she'd pulled her black, shoulder-length hair away from her left ear.

Harrison slid onto the empty bar stool next to her and said, "You're a little overdressed."

"I'm underdressed for this weather," she contradicted. "Jesus, when is this fog going to lift?"

He looked around at the other occupants of Davy Jones's Locker. Everyone was in parkas and sweaters and boots except for Geena. She looked exotic and attractive, and more than one male eye turned and glared balefully at him. He wanted to let them know he wasn't interested, but the bigger problem was Geena herself. She *was* interested, in him. And it was bound to be a finely choreographed dance for him to get out of this tête-à-tête with the friendship intact. He wasn't really sure he could make it happen.

"Thanks for all your tips," he said.

She waved over the bartender, the same one who'd served him and Laura huevos the day before. He and Harrison made eye contact, a silent awareness, but the man kept his own counsel, a job requirement of all good bartenders.

"You're entirely welcome," Geena said with a smile, showing off a deep dimple. "I could probably be in trouble with my job, consorting with the press."

"You could definitely be in trouble."

"Then here's to living dangerously." She leaned toward the bartender. "I'll have another appletini, and get him what he wants. He's buying."

"A beer. Draft. Whatever," Harrison said.

"Done," the man said.

As he started to move off, Geena called after him, "What's your name, honey?"

"Alonzo," he threw over his shoulder.

"Keep 'em comin', Alonzo!" Geena then turned to Harrison. "I plan to get a little drunk," she warned him with a knowing smile. "I'm off on Mondays."

"You're on your own on that, Geena. I'm staying sober until Justice Turnbull's in custody."

"Damn it, Harry," she said, disappointed. "That could be months. Let's take a little time out now, hmmm?" She pressed her martini to her lips and took a deep gulp. "Like I said, you owe me."

"I do. But I'm not sure our ideas of payment are running along the same lines."

"My God." She set down her drink after draining the rest of it. Alonzo showed up with another appletini and Harrison's beer at that moment. Geena carefully lifted her new drink to her lips and took another long sip. "So, am I wasting my time with you? Is that what you're saying?"

"I'm not really the relationship guy," he deflected.

"Who said anything about a relationship? Jesus. You're getting ahead of yourself, pal. I just wanna get laid." She looked at him over the rim of her glass. "Don't look so worried. And okay, maybe it's the first step toward a relationship. I wouldn't be against that, entirely, you know."

Harrison twisted his beer glass around on its cardboard coaster. "Generally, for me, sex is better suited somewhere past the first date. Nothing good happens when sex comes first. And it's really not where I am, anyway."

She squinted at him. Understanding bloomed. "Oh, my God. You're seeing someone else."

"Now, where'd you get that?" he asked, slightly annoyed.

"No guy talks like that unless he's already hooked into somebody else. Oh, crap. Are we destined to just be friends?" She sounded discouraged. "Alonzo!" she called. "You gotta keep 'em coming faster than this. I just got dumped by this guy before we even made it to first base. Wait a minute. We did share a kiss last time, right?" She frowned at Harrison. "Kinda chaste, if I remember right, but I guess it counts. So, we didn't make it to second base, more's the pity." She rolled her eyes expressively.

"I can help you with that!" a male voice called enthusiastically from a corner of the room. He wore a baseball cap, and brown hair curled out from beneath it while he held up his hand, nearly touching the rather dusty-looking fishing net that was draped from the ceiling, part of the Locker's decor.

Geena gave him a dimple. "Maybe later, pal. I gotta have a few more of these." She turned back to Harrison. "So, why'd you meet me? Trying to pump me, so to speak, and not in the way I was looking for?"

"Jesus."

"Oh, don't be such a prude." She let out a disgusted breath. Irritated, she took another swallow as a Chris Isaak song filtered through speakers hidden somewhere in the dark ceiling.

"You know Dr. Maurice Zellman, one of Justice Turnbull's victims?"

"Uh-huh. The one that got stabbed in the throat. A real prick, I understand. Don't know him personally, but yeah," she said in a voice that sounded just short of "duh." "He lives in that fortress above the beach just south of Tillam-ook. It's the rock cliff above the beach just past Bancroft Bluff? Used to be a bunch of cabins there, and then Zell-man bought the property and built that monstrosity." Harri-son was shaking his head, and Geena gave a deep nod. "Oh, that's right. You're new to the area. It was a big brouhaha at the time. People wanted to save the cabins and all that rah-rah historic shit. They were built in the forties—not much style, anyway. But Zellman got his way. You can't miss it. Stone pillars at the entrance. Used to be a wrought-iron gate across the drive, but his son, or somebody, crashed through it a few months ago and it's open now. I live south and drive by it every day on my way to work."

"I was going to try and interview him."

"Good luck with that. Like I said, Zellman's a real prick."

"Nothing new on the search for Turnbull?" he asked.

"Nah," she said while the warbled notes of "Wicked Game" filtered through the cavernous room. "Sure you don't wanna take this someplace else?" She waggled her sleek little eyebrows at him.

"Honestly, Geena, if things were different, you wouldn't have to ask me twice."

"Damn it, you *are* in a relationship. Alonzo!" She rapped her knuckles on the bar. "Bring on the booze!"


Justice stood in a copse of trees with a good view of the Zellman estate. The house was huge, constructed of a sand-colored stone. Carriage lights lit the front entrance and the four-car garage, which tilted away from the house at an angle. A number of vehicles sat outside the garage—a black Range Rover and white BMW blocked two of the doors, though the Lexus must have disappeared into the garage, as it was nowhere in sight.

It was growing dark, but it was mostly because of the

remnants of the fog, as daylight lasted till nine o'clock or later in June in this part of Oregon. Justice had followed the doctor home with no real plan in mind, had parked his car outside the front gates and to the north about a half mile, in the lot of a small grouping of businesses that sported fresh seafood and local artwork and a variety store called Phil's Phins and More.

Now he stood in the bank of trimmed shrubbery flanking the building. Rhododendrons heavy with dead blossoms, and hydrangeas starting to bloom. Through the fog, he saw a shadow. Froze. Then realized it was only a gray cat slithering behind a trellis.

Earlier, Justice had determined he was going to have to dump the Nissan altogether and soon, and had left it down the road with that intent. But now his mind left thoughts of planning behind and drifted instead to that place where he felt best. He was thinking about them, their golden hair and smoky eyes and smirking smiles. Distantly, he felt himself grow aroused, and normally that would snap him out of his fugue like the slap of an icy wave, but now all he could think about was their hips and butts and mysterious crevices and hot pink nipples. He could see them lying before him in a row, breasts heaving, thighs quivering in anticipation, and he moved to press himself inside each hotbed that awaited him. He would take them, rutting for all he was worth, sweating, groaning, spilling his seed into their waiting urns of molten heat. He would ride them in all his glory, screaming to the heavens as he branded them, one by one, fornicating, spilling his seed, making them sweetly sticky with his unborn souls.

He would take them all. They were his.

Forever.

He awoke as if slapped. Horrified.

He looked down to see he'd ripped open his pants and his hand was still on his cock, stroking furiously, as if by someone else's hand. He dropped himself as if burned, ashamed at the way his member still rose up, pointing hungrily to the night sky, wanting them.

Throwing himself onto his knees, he dug at his hair and face. They were not his to take. They were rotten. Unholy. The devil's playthings.

He had the sense that he was unraveling. Something . . . something . . . wasn't the same.

With an effort he tried to think again of the sea. The sea . . . the lighthouse . . .

*I turn my face to the cool air, the horizon, the molten ocean with its hot, waiting wet mouth. . . .*

Justice snapped to in shock. He couldn't go to his safe harbor! He couldn't go there without thinking of *them* in *that way*.

He needed to start the killing. He needed his mission to be fulfilled.

He needed to begin.

Now.

With that idea sharp in his mind, he thought about transportation. . . .


Laura left the hospital at a quarter to nine o'clock and walked toward her car in the company of another nurse, who was yakking on her cell phone to her boyfriend. Her eyes darted around the lot; she half-expected Justice to appear. She knew what he looked like: blond, like her and her sisters; thin; stony. She knew more because of the picture they'd put on the news, one taken at Halo Valley, than anything from her own recollection.

But there was no Justice anywhere around, and she made it to her Outback safe and secure, waving good-bye to the other nurse, then punching down the button that automatically locked every door in the vehicle.

Her heart still pounding a bit, the car's windshield wipers swiping the moisture from the glass, she drove the curving road to her house. All the while, she wondered how secure she really was. For all her bravado about going to work today, she hadn't completely thought through the coming home part. At night. To an empty house.

She passed by several turnouts and viewpoints cut into the cliffs above the Pacific, then a number of businesses, most closed for the night, including a small sandwich shop in a blue shingled building, where a worker was just shutting its take-out window.

She pulled off the highway to the unnamed access road that led to her driveway without signaling, not wanting anyone to be forewarned. In her drive she clicked off her lights and coasted to a stop by her back porch. Her yard was dark, the shrubbery taking on eerie shapes in the fog-shrouded night. She thought of the two dead women, victims of Justice, and a deep shiver slid through her. There was a chance he was here.

Waiting.

She sat in her car awhile, thinking about the few steps to her door, the moments it would take to unlock it, the millisecond of darkness before she snapped on a light. Why hadn't she left a lamp burning? Right now her place seemed ominously black and uninviting.

Her hand was on her cell phone. Should she call Harrison? Let him know she was home? Or would she interrupt his meeting with the woman from TCSD?

She stared down at the square lighted screen of her phone, then punched in his number. She didn't really give a damn about interrupting him, she saw with a moment of surprising self-realization. She wasn't wild about him having drinks with a woman, no matter what the reason . . . which was saying something she didn't want to examine too closely.

But he didn't pick up, which wasn't surprising, and she clicked off without leaving a message. She thought about testing her mind, seeing if she could reach Justice, find out if her fears were founded or if he was in some distant place, but her courage fled before she could even muster it.

Why hadn't she listened to herself, taken her own advice? Hadn't she told Catherine to increase her wariness and get a dog? Laura could use a German shepherd or a Rottweiler or even a damned pug about now, any animal that would raise a ruckus if trouble ensued.

Like now.

She sat for ten minutes, willing herself to be calm, then cautiously stepped from her car. The fog was gone but the air was dense and cool. Night had fallen slowly, and though it was dark, there appeared to be the dimmest afterglow, which allowed her to make out the shape of trees, her back porch steps, the woodpile at the end of her drive from some previous owner.

Her hands fumbled in her purse for her keys, her fingers closing over them a moment before yanking them free. She hit the remote lock on the Outback and heard its chirp, letting her know she'd successfully locked it up; then she moved quickly to the back porch. With surprisingly unsteady hands she threaded the key in the lock and opened the door, pulling it shut behind her quickly, throwing the dead bolt.

Her house was dark and quiet. She flipped on a switch to the kitchen, and the room lit up with eye-hurting brightness.

She stood motionless except for her eyes, which darted to every darkened corner, every shadowed area. The dishes she'd left this morning were still in the sink; the jacket she'd tossed over the back of a chair, as she'd left it. Nothing looked out of the ordinary.

Yet . . .

Her heart thudded. She could count her heartbeats, hard and fast. Her mind was darting as well. Searching out the row of knives attached by their blades to the magnetic holder nailed to the side of the cabinet, the iron pan in the drawer beneath the oven, the various and sundry items that could wound or maim, like the meat thermometer with its tiny, sharp point.

She stood silently for an eternity of less than a minute before she willed herself to get past this frozen paranoia. He wasn't here. She was alone. It was only her own fear working on her.

Forcing herself, she placed her purse on the table and sank into one of her café chairs, her back to the door at the far end of the kitchen, which opened into the pantry. She thought about that room behind her. Her mind suddenly couldn't focus on anything else. After a half beat, she jumped up and yanked open the door, a scream rising in her throat.

But it was empty. Nothing there but cans of food, her mop and broom, a vacuum cleaner, the hose of which was duct taped against a leak, some odds and ends of paper products and cleaning supplies.

She never uttered the scream. Instead, feeling like she'd run a marathon, she returned to the table, resuming her seat. "Moron," she muttered under her breath and still hoped Harrison would arrive soon. Staring at her purse, she pulled it off the table and sat it on the floor beside her, sliding her fingers into its side pocket, extracting her cell phone. She wanted to call Harrison again. Maybe leave a message this time. Let him know she was home and safe.

Except she had a bad case of the willies.

Something just felt off.

*Hurry back, Harrison,* she thought, sending the message out as if she could contact him mentally, as she did Justice. *Hurry. . . .*

# CHAPTER 27

Geena was growing more kittenish by the minute and had engaged Alonzo, the bartender, in their conversation. Harrison just needed to put in a little more time before he could ease away. If he was lucky, Geena would scarcely notice in her pursuit of the definitely interested bartender or the guy in the back corner, wearing a cap.

Alonzo, though, was ahead in the "get Geena race." He was one of those guys who threw a bar towel over his shoulder and made the move look like a come-on. Geena wasn't immune and turned a cold shoulder to Harrison after she'd decreed him interested in someone else.

Harrison could probably leave now, he reasoned, but a few more minutes wouldn't hurt. He didn't want to lose Geena as a source or a friend; timing was everything.

Alonzo had just learned Geena worked for the Tillamook County Sheriff's Department, however, and it was almost a deal breaker.

"Goddamn sheriff's D arrested me once," he revealed, his amiable expression fleeing as if it had been ordered to leave. "Thought I was in a gang." He shook his head. "Fuckers. That Clausen . . ."

Harrison's ears perked up. "Guy doesn't like me much, either."

"Clausen?" Alonzo shot him a look. "Why? What'd you do?"

"Made the department look bad." Harrison shrugged. "Luckily, Geena doesn't hold it against me."

"Fred Clausen is a one-note act," Geena said, waving a hand in that "let me tell you, even though I'm drunk" kind of way. "He likes who he likes, and he doggedly goes after stuff, I'll give 'im that. But he doesn't really look at every side, y'know?"

"I know," Harrison agreed.

"But to say you were in a gang . . . ?" Geena slowly shook her head from side to side, struggling a bit as she focused on Alonzo.

"I knew guys from the Seaside area," the bartender allowed. "Weren't exactly a gang, but they were trouble. It wasn't even Clausen's case, though. Way outside of Tillamook County, but he knew I knew 'em, and they were involved in some kind of brawl. I ended up getting thrown in the department's jail. Took a while to sort it out."

"I hope you're not gonna hold that against me," Geena said. "I just work there."

"I won't hold it against you."

There was a long look between them, and Harrison, seeing his opening, slid off his bar stool and stretched, just to make it look good. "I think I'd better get going."

"The hell with that," Geena told him.

"You and Alonzo can sort out the world's problems without me." He leaned in to give her a friendly pat on the shoulder, but she grabbed him and pulled him close.

"One more drink," she said.

He laughed. "Gotta go."

"I might need a designator driver . . . *designated* driver."

"You might," he agreed, but he was still determined to split.

"One more," she said. "Then I'm done. I promise."

Harrison glanced at Alonzo, who said, "I can't help you. I'm here till one thirty. I'm off tomorrow, though." He gazed meaningfully at Geena.

But Geena had switched from Alonzo back to Harrison. "Please?"

"Make it a quick one, Geena." With an inward sigh, he perched back on his bar stool.


Laura realized she was being an idiot.

There was no reason to stay in the kitchen, as if she were afraid to go through the rest of the house. It wasn't even that big a place. Two bedrooms and a bath on the main level with the kitchen and living room.

No big deal.

But her skin prickled despite her big talk to herself.

There was a basement to the place, and just thinking of that dark, unfinished area sent a shiver scampering up her spine. Fortunately, the only access to the basement was by an outside stairwell. No way to get in here from the basement unless you went outside first.

She was nuts to be so worried. Why now?

Nervously, she glanced at her cell phone and wished Harrison would call her back. Fingering the keypad, she almost dialed him a second time. Thought better of it.

The old clock mounted over the arch to the living room counted off the seconds.

Maybe she should leave. Just go out for a while. She wasn't due at work until tomorrow afternoon, so there was no reason to stay here. Despite her earlier bravado, the night was getting to her and she felt as if unseen eyes could watch her through the windows.

Telling herself to just get on with her life and quit being

a scared little ninny, she forced herself to walk toward the living room. She hit the lights in the short hallway and flooded the room with illumination. Leaving them on, she walked to the bathroom, then peeked into each bedroom, her pulse accelerating each time.

She thought she heard the softest of sounds. . . . Someone breathing? A stifled sigh? The hairs at the back of her neck lifted. Oh, dear God.

She stared at the closet in her bedroom. Closed tight. The doors latched. She should just open them and . . .

Again she heard an almost inaudible sound. . . . A hiss?

Her heart slammed inside her chest, and she backed up, one hand on the wall, fingers sliding along the textured surface. The creaky floorboard in the hall groaned against her weight, and she nearly jumped out of her skin.

*This is ridiculous!* But she couldn't convince herself to let out her breath.

She needed a weapon.

If only for her own peace of mind.

She stepped back to the kitchen and reached for a knife from the rack but stopped, her hand poised over the hilts.

One knife was missing.

An empty slot in the magnetic holder.

Oh, sweet Jesus.

The blood in her veins froze.

She whipped around, breath coming fast. Ears straining. Muscles poised.

He was here!

Where?

She nearly screamed.

Clamped her jaw shut.

Her phone was still in her hand; she'd taken it with her like a security blanket. Now she gave it a glance. Nine-one-one. She should call 911!

Except . . .

*Was* a knife missing?

Had there been a space on the end of the rack already . . . maybe . . . ?

Her heartbeat out of control, she glanced at the sink, where the dishes were piled. No butcher knife visible. She felt faint. Close to collapse.

What was wrong with her? Was it really all in her head?

The door to the basement was by the back steps, set into a bump-out from the house and facing the steps and driveway at a right angle. She walked to the kitchen back door. Its window was a black square into the night. She peered out cautiously. She could just make out the basement door, about ten feet away. It was closed. Locked. Accessible only by a steep concrete staircase that led to an equally concrete area with posts supporting the back of the house above and very little headroom.

She was safe inside.

Still . . .

In her mind's eye, she saw him, the hatred twisting his handsome features, the carnage of dead bodies, mutilated . . . the joy he found in the slaughter. Oh, dear God, she'd unleashed the monster. No, Laura, you didn't unleash him. He escaped . . . remember?

Oh, she remembered. And she recalled distinctly how she'd taunted him, challenged him.

Just like when they were children.

She pulled a utility knife with a five-inch blade off the rack, then stood silently, counting her racing heartbeats.

*You're doing this to yourself! Pull yourself together, Laura. Don't freak. Do not freak!*

She drew in a long, calming breath, her heart slowing a bit, her skin relaxing over her muscles. After a few moments in the blazingly bright kitchen, her ears registering the silence of the house, she thought very clearly, very condemningly: *Now what? Television? A book? No way.*

Slowly, she sat down once more at the table, the café chair squeaking protestingly beneath her weight. She set

her cell phone onto the tabletop and looked at the knife in
her right hand.

"Get a grip!" she said in a harsh whisper.

She thought about putting the knife back. Almost did.
But didn't.

Couldn't.

A moment passed.

The clock ticked loudly, and in an instant, she *felt* him.
*Heard* him. Warning bells clanged through her mind, and
her gaze jerked to the back window.

Justice Turnbull was standing right outside.

Staring at her through the glass with his damning pale
eyes.

The butcher knife clenched in his right hand.


Harrison gazed down at the illuminated screen of his
phone. Laura had tried to call him. Didn't look like she'd
left a message, but he checked his voice mail, anyway,
thinking about the time. She'd phoned about thirty minutes
earlier, probably when she was getting off work or maybe
even walking through her bungalow's door.

Geena had slowed down on the alcohol, but she was
feeling no pain. "Okay, who is she?" she asked with a the-
atrical sigh. "Come on. You're seeing one some . . . someone . . . or something. . . ." She laughed and shook her
head. "Whew. I'm close to really, really wasted. You could
get lucky, if you tried."

Harrison wondered if he should call Laura back. Was it
urgent? Was she in trouble? More than likely she was just
checking in. They'd gotten to that place in their "relationship" already. But she'd contacted Justice, mentally, if that
was even possible, and he kinda half thought, believed, it
was . . . maybe . . . whatever, the guy was a psycho and he
could be tracking her, 'cause that was what he did.

Alonzo, the bartender, was hanging back, assessing

whether to throw his hat in the ring with Geena or if she was just playing a game and using him as a pawn. Harrison read the guy's mind; he'd been there before. Maybe that was what Laura's thing was with Justice, a kind of understanding rather than actual mind reading, or in her case, mind talking. Maybe it was a whole load of bullshit, but it hardly mattered because Justice was a dangerous threat, and that was what counted.

"I gotta call somebody back," he said.

"It's her, isn't it?" Geena looked over at Alonzo and nodded. "Told ya," she said to the room at large.

Ignoring her, Harrison held the cell phone tight to his ear.

The phone buzzed on the table at the same moment Laura opened her mouth to shriek. The ring caught her attention, and she glanced away for a split second. One nanomoment.

When Laura looked back at the window, Justice had disappeared.

As if she'd conjured him up, as if her fear had created his image.

*Crash!!!*

Glass splintered. Shards flew into the room. Spraying in an earsplitting explosion. She threw her hands up to protect her face and saw his arm snake through the broken pane, fingers scrabbling for the back door handle.

"No!"

Grabbing the knife, she flung herself toward the door. The phone rang on and on, but she couldn't stop. She jabbed the sharp blade into the back of Justice's hand, and he snarled in pain.

*Oh, God, oh, God!* She stabbed his hand for all she was worth, pulling the bloody blade out and slamming it back. She caught the fleshy part beneath his little finger before he yanked it free with a howl of pain and fury. Blood splattered over her, over the floor, into the shimmering glass upon the floor.

She screamed and turned to the phone, flinging herself to the table.

*Bam!*

Wood splintered in the door.

Grabbing her phone, she hit the CALL button, and ran through the house. She tried to dial, but her hand was slippery with blood, *his* blood. She lost the cell in her fumbling grasp as she slid around the corner toward the front door.

"God . . . damn . . . damn!" she cried. She couldn't lose the phone, not now!

*Crrrraaack!*

The back door gave way as she threw herself onto the floor and snatched up the phone again. "My God . . . oh, my God . . ." She scrambled to her feet, heard him tear at the back door as she reached the front. She yanked hard.

It didn't move. Locked tight. "Hell!" Frantically, her heart racing, she turned the lock. Pulled on the knob again.

The door opened, and she flung herself onto the porch.

She ran across the wet boards, only to slip crazily on the wooden steps. Sliding, half falling. Banging her knee, she caught herself on the railing. "Help!" she cried frantically. "Help me!" But she saw no lights shining in neighboring windows, just the sheer darkness of the foggy night. "Oh, God, please!"

*"Sisssterrr . . ."*

His voice. Not in her head this time. His real voice. Slithery. Cold. Scraping her spine.

She screamed and glanced at her phone.

Her finger touched the green button. Harrison was the last call. The top of her menu list. Wildly, she hit his number, sliding down the last step on legs that were water.

She managed to stay on her feet and ran. Jerkily. Along the gravel path at the bottom of the front stairs. It twisted through overgrown shrubbery ahead, disappearing into the gloom. "Help!" she cried.

*Think, Laura, think! Outwit him. Run to a neighbor's!*

He was close behind her. His breathing loud and labored.

"Witch!" he rasped. "You called me! You called me!"

*Oh, no!* He was too close. She ran blindly, her feet slipping, her hands in front of her, one clutching the phone, the other protecting her from the branches and fronds that slapped at her face while berry vines swiped at her ankles. Still she ran. *Answer,* she thought. *For God's sake, Harrison, answer your phone!!!*

"I'm here!" Justice taunted. Too close. She was breathing hard, cutting through the brush, heading for the main road.

She felt his breath. Hot. Fetid.

Oh, God, he was barely a step behind her.

She threw herself forward, stumbling.

One huge hand snagged in her hair.

Snapped her head back.

She screamed. The pad of his finger slid down her nape and spine.

She leapt forward, frantic to get away from him. Scorched by his touch. Branded.

Her stomach lurched and the phone jangled in her hand.

Too late!

She hit a button.

"Lorelei?"

Harrison's voice called to her. Tinny. Distant. From the speaker in her phone.

"He's here!" she shrieked and felt the monster's hand clamp over the back of her neck, only to slide away. "Oh, God!" She stumbled over a root or bump or something unseen in the dark. She pitched forward and the ground shifted, gave way. The end of the property. Where it dropped to the highway.

Behind her. Breathing hard. He was *right there!*

"I will kill you and your filthy incubus!" he roared.

Without a thought to the consequences, Laura leapt from her hands and knees, forward.

Into nothingness.

The phone fell from her fingers.

And she tumbled into darkness.

# CHAPTER 28

"He's here!"

"Where? Where is he? Where are you?" Harrison demanded, jumping to his feet, upending his stool in the process. It clattered to the floor as he yelled into his phone, "Laura! Lorelei! *Laura!*"

Dead zone. No connection.

He turned and was running for the door in one movement.

"Hey!" Geena called behind him.

"Call a cab! On me!" he yelled over his shoulder and then dropped her from his thoughts in the next moment.

He was at his car in less than seven seconds, yanking open the door. He had no illusions about what Laura meant. The bastard was there. Justice Turnbull had found Laura.

"Damn . . . goddammit . . . damn . . ."

With fumbling fingers he tried to call her. No answer. Tossing his cell phone into the passenger seat, he growled in frustration and fear.

He should have stayed with her. He should have listened to his own inner voice, the one that cautioned him. He should have never left her alone. God, why did he leave her alone? What if something happened to her? What if Justice hurt her . . . or . . . what if he . . . ?

Harrison slammed the door shut on his worries. No time for that. He had to get to her. He had to find her. Save her from the maniac and kill that son of a bitch, send the psycho to kingdom come.

His hands flexed on the wheel.

If that bastard hurt her . . . if he hurt one hair on her head . . .

He wondered how he'd been so foolish as to put her into danger. By not believing, thinking her "connection" to Turnbull was all in her head. Guilt bored through his soul and panic kept his foot hard on the accelerator as the night, and oncoming cars, rushed by, headlights muted by the fog, their beams arcing through the night to shimmer on the wet ribbon of asphalt that wound through the cliffs to Laura's cottage.

God be with her.

He floored it around a final corner and drove like a maniac. At the access road that led to her drive, he spun off Highway 101, up the hill, and nearly sideswiped a black SUV in the process. Wrenching the steering wheel, Harrison barely slowed down, bumping and blasting forward. Then, shooting into her driveway, he stood on the brakes, skidding on the wet gravel, his tires whining, tiny rocks spraying wildly as he stopped behind her car, the only vehicle in the driveway.

He threw open his door and jumped out, stumbling a little in his haste. Down on one knee. Staggering. Up again, in control, balanced on the balls of his feet.

Ready.

The lights were blasting inside her house. Illuminating both the back steps and front porch. Darkness crouched behind this bright scene. Quickly he glanced around, then, bending down, reached into the gravel drive, his fingers searching for a larger stone. No luck. But then his hand closed over a laurel branch that felt at least an inch in diameter. Good enough.

Crouched low, he swept around his Impala, then checked Laura's car. No one. He couldn't see her in the house, which was now a fishbowl, yellow light shining from every window. Bright, uncurtained, empty rooms. No sign of any life anywhere.

*Laura . . . Lorelei . . . ,* he thought achingly, fear tearing through him like a brittle cold wind.

Should he go inside? Make his presence known? If Justice was still around, he couldn't have missed his approaching car.

He straightened, listening, the branch clutched in his hand. "Laura!" he said aloud, hearing how sober and serious his tone was. No answer. "Laura!" he yelled louder.

A moan sounded. A mewling sound.

Toward the highway. West.

He turned to it, bent over, scuttling, moving fast. The moan came from somewhere that sounded far away, at the western edge of the property, which faced the highway and, farther out, the ocean. The land at the front of her bungalow sloped slightly downward, then suddenly dropped off. Highway 101 lay about fifteen feet below.

Fingers holding his stick in a death grip, he stole along the gravel path that led from the front door. All his senses were alert. Ready. His muscles flexed, his heart beating a steady, fear-driven beat. If the maniac jumped out at him, the bastard was going to be in for one helluva battle.

"Lorelei," he called softly again, his voice sounding loud in the covering darkness.

The cry that came back to him was of relief. "Harrison?" Her voice was strangled with emotion. "I'm—I'm down here!"

*Thank . . . God . . . !*

He leapt forward and skidded to a stop at the edge of the

short cliff. He could see her form, huddled in the ditch below that ran along the side of the highway. Ten to fifteen feet down. He glanced around quickly. Where was Justice?

"You okay?" he asked, sinking to his knees, grabbing a hanging limb from a shivering laurel, then stepping toward the edge, aware the limb wouldn't hold his weight. At that moment, it snapped and split, but Harrison had only partially given it his weight, and he swung and scrabbled downward into the dirt, half rolling to the ground beside Laura, who was sitting up and quivering.

"Harrison . . . ," she said brokenly. "Harrison."

He pulled her quaking body close. "Lorelei."

"I'm okay," she said through teeth that chattered. "I'm okay."

He didn't believe it for an instant. He kissed her head, squeezed her, fought back his own fear at losing her. He ran his hand down the back of her head, entwining her hair in his fingers, wanting to fuse her to him, feeling her heart beating as the cloaked surf pounded the shore somewhere far below them. "Where is he?" he demanded in a cold voice.

She shook her head. "I don't know. I—I fell and it just went quiet. He was up above and I saw him. I think. It was hard to tell. Too dark and all this fog . . . but I think he looked down at me but couldn't come down, probably for fear of being seen with the headlights from the traffic. I don't know. Anyway, he's gone, I hope . . ." She buried her face in his shoulder. Harrison clutched her as hard as she clutched him, feeling her warmth, the desperation of her grasp.

Harrison glanced back up the short cliff. Justice could still be on the grounds, waiting. Hidden in the shadows.

"Are you hurt?"

"No. Scraped a little. I was scared. I just fell, but it was okay. I heard you on the phone, but I was running and I lost it and . . ." She shuddered.

He squeezed her and whispered into her hair, "Don't move. Stay here. I'm going to check the house—"

"No!" She scrambled to get her legs under her. "I can't stay here. No way. I—I'm going with you!"

"I don't think—"

"And I don't care." She was emphatic, her spine stiffening as he held her.

He sighed. "Anyone ever tell you you're stubborn?"

"You're the first."

"Yeah, right. Okay. C'mon." Clasping her hand, and keeping low against the cliff face, he led her along the ditch until they reached the access road that led east and upward toward her driveway. "You okay?"

"Okay, enough."

Climbing the steep few feet to the top of the ditch together, Harrison held on to her tightly. As one, they crept up the road. He tried to shield her body with his, but in the shadowy, thick night, Turnbull could be hiding anywhere, could leap out from behind the solitary fir tree or the laurel hedge or the car.

Harrison squinted into the darkness. He held on to her fingers with one hand; in the other he still clenched the smooth-barked stick. Approaching her driveway, he spied both their cars and the bright squares of the windows of her bungalow.

He squeezed her hand and they both stopped. For a long moment they stood quietly, eyes and ears straining, hearts pounding rapidly.

Harrison said in an undertone, "My phone's in my car. I should've called nine-one-one."

"No . . . ," she murmured.

"It's time the police were called. Past time."

"I know. But . . . do you think he's here? I don't think he's here anymore. I *knew* he was here before, and it doesn't feel the same now."

"Lorelei, I'd like to trust your instincts, but he came after you this time. Physically. There's a difference."

"I know. But I just want to go inside."

Against his better judgment he gave in and led the way to the back door, which was gaping open, unable to close, because Justice had smashed the lock through the casing. Now Harrison pushed at the door panels with one finger, opening it wider. A knife with a short, bloody blade lay on the floor in the shards of glass.

"I left that," Laura said, her voice slightly unsteady. "That was my weapon, but I wanted the phone." As Harrison bent to pick it up and place it on the table, she said, "He has my butcher knife."

"Jesus." Harrison's gaze scraped the interior of the cottage again.

"He's not here. He's gone." She looked around the room a little wild-eyed.

"You're bleeding," Harrison said neutrally, though seeing the blood soaking through the knee of her uniform's left pant leg was a bit harrowing.

Following his gaze, Laura said, "Oh," then bent down to it, pulling up the pant leg and revealing a long bloody scratch. "It's not deep." Remembering, her fingers then flew to her cheekbone, which was red and sporting a coming bruise. "Got hit by a branch. But he's gone. He's not here."

"Let's make sure."

"Okay," she said.

He grabbed the knife with his right hand and transferred the stick into his left. Carefully, with Laura in tow, he crossed the living room and closed and locked the front door, which had swung open, giving a sweeping glance around the porch first. Then he checked the bedrooms, bathroom, and closets.

"You're right. He's not here," he said, returning to the kitchen.

"He must've run away when he heard you, or after he realized he couldn't get to me. I thought I heard something crashing through some brush."

"Which direction?"

"North, maybe? Or up the hill into the woods?"

"How did he get here?" Harrison asked, more to himself than to her.

"I think he was already here when I got home."

"Well, we're not staying here." Harrison reached for her hand again. "We'll call the police and—"

"No! Not tonight." She let out a weary sigh. "I know I should have called them earlier, and I kicked myself that I didn't, but . . . I just can't face them and all their questions."

"You have to."

"I know. But . . . can it wait? Until morning at least? Please. I just can't."

"He's a murderer. An escapee from a mental hospital."

She nodded and shook her head. "All right. They can check the break-in. Tell them to come over. But I'll talk to them in the morning."

Harrison weighed the options. "Okay, then, we'll go to my sister's. She doesn't live far."

"No . . . I . . . don't . . ."

"You're not staying here," he insisted. "It's not safe. And tomorrow we're going to the authorities," he stated flatly. "Tonight it's either my place, a motel, or my sister's. But wherever it is, I'm not leaving you. Your choice."

She swallowed, glanced down at the knife, then very deliberately picked it up and placed it back on its magnetic holder. "Your sister's?"

"My sister's," he repeated. "Right after I call the police."

She remained silent.

"It'll be okay," he said, hearing her unspoken reluctance. "They'll have a fresh trail. You can talk to them in the morning." His gaze met hers. "We have to."

"Oh, hell . . ." She nodded. "Fine!"

Something was off. There was a strange, pillowy thickness to the air, and Justice felt both lost and intensely furious with Lorelei as he strode, head down, along the edge of the surf, which curled and licked at his boots.

*Lorelei . . .*

Justice ground his teeth together and squeezed his mind hard, seeking to reach inside her evil head. He threw all he had into making a mental connection, but she thwarted him. Oh, she was strong! Stronger than he'd believed. He'd had his hands into her Medusa hair, and now his skin felt on fire.

He was walking along the beach, but inside he was running. How many miles was he from the bait shop? Six? Eight? Maybe ten? He wouldn't be able to walk the entire distance on the beach; there were several rocky cliffs that broke up the sand. Those would be the dangerous places. When he would have to move from the beach to where people could see him. But he wouldn't have to walk along the main highway, either. There were twisting roads and paths between 101 and the ocean. He could find his way.

He would make it.

He fingered the butcher knife in his jacket pocket.

Tomorrow he would finish her.

He knew where she lived.

He knew where she worked.

He knew *her.*

*The baby . . .*

Laura ran a hand lightly across her stomach as Harrison

drove with controlled urgency to a rather dilapidated cottage a little less than ten miles south of her bungalow. As he'd promised, he'd called the police, and they had come to the house. They'd talked to her quickly, the interview was shorter than she expected, but the officers assured her detectives would want to speak to her again in the morning. In the meantime, her house was being cordoned off as a crime scene.

Now, two hours later, she was looking at the home of Harrison's sister. Like hers, it was perched on the uphill/eastern side of Highway 101, facing toward the sea, and also like hers, there were a lot of buildings and foliage on the western side of the highway, which obscured most of the view, though as soon as she stepped from Harrison's car, she could hear the sea's dull roar.

She'd wanted to tell Harrison this was a fool's errand the whole way, but she hadn't the energy. He'd suggested she pack a bag and she had, like an automaton, her thoughts dull and scattered, focused on Justice and the indelible etching in her mind of his features, a cold, lean face with glaring, empty eyes. A nightmare.

She'd forcefully pushed thoughts of him aside, and her next fear had leapt into the space in her brain: *the baby*.

Her fall hadn't been far but it had been jarring. She'd lain out of breath and slightly dazed, adrenaline pumping, fear magnified, as she'd thought he might fling himself over the edge after her. Only the traffic had kept her safe while she huddled in the ditch beside the road, far enough down that she was shielded by debris and Scotch broom from the sight of passersby.

Harrison climbed from the driver's side and around to her. They both skirted a blue Honda Accord parked on the cracked asphalt drive. His sister's, she surmised.

Harrison glanced toward the front window, where a sliver of light escaped through drawn curtains. "Didi's probably asleep, but Kirsten's still up," he said. He gave her a sober look. "You sure you're okay?"

"Yes."

They both knew it was a bald-faced lie. She wondered if she'd ever be "okay" again. He squeezed her hand and her heart turned over. A glance at his face and the beard shadow covering his jaw almost convinced her that she was falling in love with him. Which was ridiculous. Still, the flash of his teeth when he smiled, the slight dimple in his cheek, and his eyes . . . hazel eyes as green-gray as the Pacific . . . She almost laughed at her stupid romantic fantasies.

She didn't know why she'd agreed to come. Maybe because she hadn't wanted to be alone. Maybe because she wanted to be with Harrison. Maybe because she felt he was right and the time for fooling around with Justice was long over.

Maybe because there was no other choice.

She led the way up a short path lined with small white shells that glowed under the faint light from the crack in the blinds and a half-moon that was playing tag with scudding clouds. There were two steps leading to the small cement porch, which was dark beneath a burned-out exterior light.

Harrison knocked on the door, then called, "Kirsten, it's me."

A dog started yapping wildly, and Laura heard Harrison mutter a series of swear words beneath his breath and something that sounded like, "It can't even see me, the little bastard . . . !"

"Are you talking about the dog?" she asked, but then the door opened and a slim woman in gray sweats and a white, collared, fuzzy sweater with a front zipper appeared.

Her gaze swept over them, landing on Harrison. "What are you doing?" she demanded, annoyed. "It's after ten!"

"I've got a small favor to ask," he said.

"Ask it in the morning!"

"I'd like to stay here tonight, with a friend. At least I'd like her to stay and me with her."

That caught her attention and she turned toward Laura, who stood motionless, feeling slightly idiotic. "Okay," she said carefully, waiting for more as her eyes narrowed thoughtfully.

"This is Laura Adderley," he introduced. "Would you just open the door and let us in?"

She stepped back and a small, hairy dog charged forward, barking madly. "Shut up, Chico," she muttered fondly. "Damn it. You'll wake Didi! Harrison, get in here and sit down. Chico!" she hissed through her teeth. To Laura, she said, "Hi. Sorry. The dog and Harry just don't connect."

Chico, ignoring her, kept barking at Harrison, who, once the door was shut behind them and locked, walked to the far end of the living room and a straight-backed chair, his gaze on the dog, who glared fearlessly right back. Chico's barking turned to a low-throated growl.

"Good grief," Kirsten muttered.

Laura saw the resemblance. Kirstin looked like Harrison in a way, the same eyes and mouth, but whereas he seemed to cultivate a scruffy, "I don't care" kind of look, her hair was combed into a sleek ponytail and she seemed more put together.

Kirstin gazed apologetically at Laura. "Umm . . . I've got an air mattress that I could put in the living room? The sheets are in the hall cupboard for it and the vacuum's there to blow it up. Or, I can move Didi into my bed with me, and we can remake up her bed. . . ."

"Don't worry about us. Lorelei can have the blow-up and I'll take the couch."

"The couch will break your back," Kirsten said dryly. "As you well know."

"I'll live."

"So, are you going to tell me what this is all about?" she asked.

"Tomorrow." He shifted in the chair, where Chico stood stiff-legged in front of him. The dog's little black lips quivered and Harrison looked askance at his sister. "Really . . . ?"

"C'mon, Cheeks." Kirsten scooped the dog into her arms, and he wriggled and yapped and tried to keep his gaze on Harrison. Kirsten gave Laura a pitying look before she went down the hall. "You really shouldn't get involved with him, you know. He's nothing but trouble."

"I'm just her bodyguard," he stated before Laura could respond.

"Sure you are." Kirsten disappeared out of view.

As soon as they heard her bedroom door close, Harrison got to his feet and found the vacuum and bedding for Laura and an extra blanket for himself. He blew up the mattress, and then they put the sheets and blankets on the air mattress together, but as Harrison straightened, he saw Laura had taken the extra blanket and snuggled onto the couch.

"Hey," he said.

"It's too short for you," she said. "And I don't want your back to break."

He gave her a studied look. "You could share the mattress with me."

Laura, feeling the effects of a very long day, tried to muster a smile. "I'm going to go change out of these pants and check the scratch on my leg. Make sure I have a pillow when I get back." With that she scooped up her bag and headed to the bathroom. All the while she wondered what she was doing, staying another night with Harrison, this time at his sister's place. As odd as it was, she somehow felt at home. "You're a head case," she told her reflection as she stared into the mirror of the medicine cabinet mounted over the sink, then brushed her teeth and rinsed her mouth. "A bona fide head case."

And, deep down, she feared she was falling in love.

"The least of your problems."

When she was finished with her evening ablutions, she returned to find he'd tossed a pillow onto the couch.

As she settled down, she was unnerved to see he was lying on his back on the air mattress, staring at her.

She stared back, her pulse rising with each silent moment. Feeling a bit breathless, she turned away, wrapping a protective arm around her abdomen, and reminded herself that she was pregnant.

With her ex-husband's child.

# CHAPTER 29

It was barely 8:00 a.m., Lang realized, glancing to the clock on the wall, yet it felt like a year had passed since he'd awoken this morning. As soon as he'd gotten to work, a murder-suicide had been reported by a neighbor from one of the expensive houses along Bankruptcy Bluff, as Bancroft Bluff was euphemistically called, since a number of the homes had fallen off the bluff or been condemned, having been built on a geologically unsound area that had eroded beneath them. Supposedly the problem had been fixed, at least temporarily, but the homes' sales had first languished and then, with the economy's downturn, fallen off altogether, so to speak. The people that owned the houses along the bluff were fighting a bitter battle with the developer and the city, and it was anybody's guess how long it would last and if anyone would come out a winner.

His cell phone rang and he saw it was Fred Clausen, who'd gone out to check the crime scene. "What's it look like?" Lang asked.

"Scratch murder-suicide," Fred said. "Looks like double homicide. The husband and wife were bound and shot. Message spray painted on the walls had to do with Bankruptcy Bluff."

Lang grunted. It wasn't a surprise, really. The situation was a mess, and it waxed and waned in volatility. "What did it say?"

"The message was *blood money*. The victims are Marcus and Chandra Donatella. They were in business with the builder, and some of the other home owners think they paid off the city to get approval for the project."

"This has already been through all the lawsuits," Lang said.

"I know. It's just a total cluster fuck," Clausen agreed. "Nobody was really screwing anybody. It was just a stupid place to build with half-assed geological information. But these people are dead, so somebody's pissed off."

Lang frowned. "Any chance it could be something else, and the Bankruptcy Bluff stuff is just a convenient smoke screen?"

"It's early days. Could be anything."

"Stick with it, then. O'Halloran's backing off the patrols around Justice's habitats and giving you some help."

"Yeah . . . ?" Clausen sounded as unsure as Lang felt.

"We know he was at the home of Laura Adderley last night, but he's in the wind again, probably running scared. We'll know more once we interview her and see what the crime scene guys get. Helluva thing that. We'll just have to patrol as best we can, stretched as thin as we are."

"Okay." Clausen hung up and Lang felt a rising frustration. Where was the bastard? It was Monday. He'd been missing since Friday and leaving a trail of bodies behind. In Lang's estimation, Turnbull was still on the coast, in some hidey-hole they hadn't found yet.

But they would. He only hoped it would be sooner rather than later.

Lang swiveled in his chair, but before he could get up to refill his coffee cup, his desk phone rang again. "Detective Stone," he answered tersely.

"I'm at Dooley's, drinking a longneck. Get down here and I'll get you one."

Lang relaxed back into his chair, grinning in spite of himself. "Yeah, well, I'm about a hundred miles away, so it'll be a while. Hey, Curtis. What's up?"

Trey Curtis was Lang's old partner from the Portland Police Department, where Lang had been employed before coming to the Tillamook County Sheriff's Department. They had a long-standing rule that wherever they met, the first one to spot the other bought the latecomer a beer. Dooley's had been one of their favorite spots in Portland, but Lang had been away a long time.

"I got a call for you, actually. For the department there, anyway. A woman named Kay Drescher thinks she knows that unidentified woman whose picture you've been running."

"Yeah?"

"Says the Jane Doe's name is Stephanie Wyman. Drescher's been trying to reach her by phone and can't raise her. Wyman lives in an apartment in the Pearl."

Lang had straightened up as soon as Curtis started talking. The Pearl was a pricey section of Portland abounding with shops and galleries as well as upscale condos and historic homes. "You got the license number and make of Wyman's car?"

"Check your e-mail. It's been sent your way, along with her driver's license and a secondary photo. She drives a silver two thousand four Nissan Sentra." He rattled off the VIN and license plate numbers.

Lang took note as he clicked on to his department e-mail. "Hasn't been released yet, but the woman—Wyman, if it's really her—died last night of her injuries. Let's see what we've got." He clicked open the e-mail, caught the picture of Stephanie Wyman, and felt a new sense of rage when he looked at her smiling, young face. "Yep. Jane Doe and Stephanie Wyman. One and the same," he said.

"Well, shit." Trey let out a long world-weary sigh. "This Kay Drescher's on her way to the station now, so I'll give her the news. When we're done, I'm heading over to Wyman's apartment. I'll call you when I know more."

"Thanks."

Lang wondered if he should drop everything and head to Portland but decided against it. The homicide had taken place in Tillamook County, and he was pretty damn sure it was related to Justice Turnbull and that this Stephanie Wyman, or whoever she was, was just an unlucky victim of his overall plan to harm the residents of Siren Song. But the trail was still here, not Portland.

Savvy was just coming back to her desk with a full cup of coffee, and Lang looked at it longingly and swept up his own cup. Before heading to the vending area, he brought her up to date on the car information, finishing with, "Let's find that Nissan," to which Savannah nodded and sat at her computer to gather all the pertinent details and get the word out to their officers.

The morning routine at Kirsten Rojas's house was more like a study in controlled chaos. Her daughter, Didi, jumped up at six thirty, which got Chico barking and turning circles, and Kirsten herself started calling orders like a drill sergeant just to keep everybody working toward the same goal: to get Didi to preschool by nine.

Laura found the craziness comforting, a normal family living a normal routine and expecting normal things to happen during their day. She had slept in a pair of sweats and a T-shirt and now stumbled into the bathroom to wash her face, only to promptly throw up the little bit she'd eaten the night before.

Rinsing out her mouth and washing her face, she dried her cheeks on a towel and then ran a hand over her abdomen before heading out of the bathroom.

Pancakes were being poured onto a griddle as she entered the kitchen area, and she smiled wanly at Didi, who'd regarded her earlier with wide-eyed suspicion upon finding a strange woman on the couch. The little girl with the dark pageboy had then ignored Laura and jumped on Harrison, who pretended to be able to sleep through her efforts to wake him up, which included beating on his chest with her small fists and attempting to jump on him, which Kirsten managed to halt before real damage occurred by sweeping Didi away from her uncle, hollering at Harrison to get up, and apologizing to Laura for the noise at the same time.

"Pancakes," Didi announced, dipping a piece in a bowl of maple syrup before popping it into her mouth.

"I see," Laura said.

"Would you like some?" Kirsten asked, her gaze moving past Laura to the living room. "Harrison! Are you up! Get moving!"

"Got any coffee?" he responded, appearing at the arch that separated the kitchen nook from the living room. His hair was a disheveled mess, his jaw darker than ever with his beard shadow. He wore a pair of low-slung, disreputable jeans, but his chest was shirtless.

Laura glanced away, but not before the memory of his lean male chest was burned onto her retinas. She felt oddly light-headed and hoped to hell it had something to do with her pregnancy, knowing, really, that it probably didn't.

Kirsten half smiled. "I work at a coffee shop. What do you think?"

"Is it made?" he questioned, to which she snorted and poured him a cupful into a mug that said LIKE I CARE in bold black letters on a white background.

"Would you like some coffee?" she asked Laura, whose stomach still wasn't sure. But she felt Harrison's look and said, "That would be great."

"Pancakes, too?" Didi demanded, frowning as if she expected Laura to refuse.

"Please." Laura just hoped to hell she could get them down without drawing attention to herself. She was momentarily swept by a feeling of drowning; it was overwhelming, the things that were happening. She hadn't had enough time to process half of what she was feeling and going through.

"After I get Didi to preschool, I've got to stop by the store and pick up some supplies. And then I have a half shift today, so I'm going to work around noon. What about you two?"

"Supplies?" Harrison asked.

"Beads."

"Aha." Harrison turned to Laura. "My sister's into quilting and knitting and, of course, macramé. She has beads and hemp and pots and plants and all kinds of stuff." He waved a hand around the kitchen, where there were a number of potted plants snuggled in knotted, ropelike slings sporting colored beads and hanging from the ceiling. "Macramé," he said again, pointing to the knotted rope. "Really big in the seventies. Kirsten's trying to bring it back."

Kirsten shot him a look of mock fury, then hurried Didi through the rest of her meal, while Laura sipped at her coffee and managed a few bites of her pancakes. Harrison tucked into a stack covered with syrup and two cups of coffee before Kirsten and Didi and Chico, who'd been locked, whining, in Kirsten's bedroom while they ate, appeared at the door.

"We're heading out," Kirsten said, glancing between Harrison and Laura.

"You're taking the dog, right?" Harrison asked.

"What is it with you and Chico?" she asked. "No, I'm not taking the dog. Look. He likes Laura."

Chico had taken up residence at Laura's feet, his beady eyes focused on Harrison, waiting for even the slightest move.

"So, you'll be back in like what? An hour?" Harrison asked.

"Yeah . . ." She glanced at her brother. "Chico's already been outside and done his thing, but it wouldn't kill you to walk him."

"Right."

"You're insufferable," Kirsten said on a sigh.

Harrison managed a smile. "Only when it comes to the dog."

"I've got to get to work," Laura said. "We'll be out of your hair."

"It's not that," Kirsten said. "I just was wondering what was going on, y'know?"

Harrison shared a look with Laura, then said, "Full details later, but it's to do with Justice Turnbull."

Kirsten glanced at Didi, who was looking at the adults with a scowl, sensing she was being left out of the conversation on purpose. "Okay," Kirsten said. "I'll be back later. We'll talk then."

After she left, Harrison picked up Laura's barely touched plate and his own clean one, put them both in the sink. "Thought you had the afternoon shift."

"I just wanted to let your sister know I had somewhere to go."

"I'd rather you stuck around here. You look a little pale," he added. "You sure you're all right?"

"I'm fine. Really. But there's something kind of strange . . ."

"What?"

"When I was running away from Justice, he touched me. He got his hand in my hair and then he raked his finger down my back."

"He scratched you?"

"No . . . not really. He just touched me, but it felt like a burn. I can still kind of feel it."

"Want me to look?" he asked, concerned.

She was still wearing the T-shirt and sweats she'd slept in. Carefully, she turned her back to him and lifted up the hem of the shirt. She felt him staring at her skin, but after a moment all he said was, "There's no mark."

"Good." She yanked down her shirt. "And there's another thing. I think there's something wrong with him," she said slowly. To the ironic lift of Harrison's brow, she added, "I mean physically wrong. He's sick. More than what we think."

"Huh."

"I told you I could sometimes tell things about people by touching them."

"Or them touching you?" he pointed out.

"Yes," she said. Then, more strongly, "Yes!"

He lifted his hands in surrender. "All right."

"With Justice, I got an even stronger hit. There's something really wrong with him. It's going to kill him."

"Good!"

"I don't know when, though." She shook her head, wishing she had more answers. "I don't know. But I'm going to tell Catherine and my sisters. It will go a long way to making them feel better."

"You're going to Siren Song today?"

"Maybe."

"We need to go to the authorities."

"I know. I will. Later," she said. "I am a little tired. But I promise. Later today."

Harrison gave her a sideways look, then glanced at his watch. "I've got some things to finish up, but I'm not leaving you here by yourself. Maybe you should come with me."

"Your sister will be back in an hour."

"Will you stay here with her, then?" he asked.

She hesitated, then nodded. "Until work."

"Then, I'll leave when she gets back."

"What's on your agenda today?" she asked when the conversation stopped cold for a few moments.

"First, I'm going to the Deception Bay Historical Society and read about your people. I met a guy yesterday. An old guy who knows Dr. Loman. Herman Smythe?"

Laura shook her head. "I don't know him."

Harrison gave her a quick recap of his meeting with the man in the wheelchair at Seagull Pointe and then said, "Then I'm going to call his daughter, Dinah, and see what she has to say."

"You're still working on a story about my family?" she asked cautiously.

"Just background, but yeah. I'm not going to report anything you told me that was off the record, but, Lorelei, Justice isn't going away. He's trying to kill you. And your family. And the whole damn thing's going to blow up at some point, and hell yes, I'm going to write the story. And I won't be the only one. But first and foremost, I want you to be safe. That's what I really care about."

She wanted to be upset. She wanted to scream and yell, to rant and rave, to let out all her frustrations. Instead she bit her tongue, unable to refute anything he'd said because it was simple fact.

"You're the truth seeker," she said at length, expelling her breath in a sigh.

"Well . . . yeah . . ." He was clearly lost about the direction her thoughts were turning.

"Okay."

"Okay what?" he asked cautiously.

Laura would have liked to argue with him just for argument's sake, but in truth she didn't want to be alone, either. "Okay, I'm going to trust you," she said, then headed for her overnight bag and a shower.

Kirsten was as good as her word and reappeared just as Laura was finished dressing. Harrison told his sister to take care of Laura, received a growl from Chico when he gave her a short hug, then left, sketching a good-bye with his right hand as he headed out.

Laura watched his dusty Impala back down Kirsten's short driveway.

"All right, he's finally gone. How did you meet?" Kirsten demanded as soon as Harrison was out of sight. She had dropped her bag of beads and rope and various other items on the counter and was now rummaging through it. "Tell me the truth. And don't be embarrassed if it started out as a one-night stand. I know my brother."

Laura stood in silence, unable to think of a reply.

Looking up, Kirsten said in surprise, "Oh, sorry. You haven't slept with him yet. I thought the whole bed/couch thing was just you being private about it."

"Your brother's into one-night stands?" Laura asked.

"Not always," she said, but her face said it was a lie.

"Mostly?"

"How did you meet him again?"

Laura thought about it a moment, then admitted, "Justice Turnbull has me on his short list. I'm related to the women at Siren Song. Many of them are my sisters. Harrison was after a story . . . but he's been trying to protect me."

Kirsten stared at Laura in amazement. "Oh . . . sweet . . . Jesus . . . Sit down. We gotta talk."

# CHAPTER 30

In the afternoon Trey Curtis called Lang back and said that Kay Drescher was driving to the Tillamook County morgue to identify Stephanie Wyman's body because, even though Kay was just a friend, Stephanie was estranged from her only living relative, her father, who lived somewhere on the East Coast, anyway.

"Kay Drescher doesn't believe it's her friend," Curtis warned Lang. "Just won't believe it, but is concerned enough to make the trip. I think she thinks she'll get there and be able to tell you that the body is someone else."

Lang thought of the photo ID, and Drescher was going to be disappointed. The woman in the morgue was Stephanie Wyman or her identical twin. "I'll tell O'Halloran."

"Found her car yet?"

"Not yet. Got a few other things going around here." Lang sketched Curtis in a little about the double homicide at Bancroft Bluff. "Clausen and Delaney are on-site, and I'll probably be heading that way."

"Wow. All we got going around here is a TriMet bus driver in a wrangle with a bicyclist that's turned nutty. Fistfight. Threats on the Internet. Lots of play in the news."

"Is Pauline Kirby on it?" Lang asked with distaste. He'd had a wrangle with her himself not so long ago.

"Of course."

"She's everywhere," Lang said.

"Uh-huh. And she's really milking that story about those entitled teen criminals in Seaside. You got any part of that?"

"No. Different jurisdiction, thank God."

"I saw her on the news last night. She says they broke into their wealthy friends' houses and didn't so much steal as pretend like they lived there. Kind of like the teens that broke into the famous people's homes around Hollywood and just hung out."

"They stole a few things, too. I read Harrison Frost's accounts in the *Breeze,*" Lang said. "And Clausen's stepson knew one of the victims."

"Sheeeit. And then you've got psycho Turnbull, who killed Stephanie Wyman."

"Allegedly. But yeah . . . he did."

"Maybe he's left your area," Curtis posed.

"I hope not," Lang responded grimly. "I want to get him." At that moment Lang's cell phone buzzed, and he picked it up and examined the caller ID to realize it was Savannah. "Got a call coming in. I'll check with you later." Hanging up the desk phone, he pressed the green ON button on his cell. "Hey," he answered.

"Burghsmith found a silver Nissan," she said tersely. "Looks like it was abandoned at that strip mall where Phil's Phins is. He ran the plates, but they belong to a Ford Taurus, not a Nissan compact."

"Turnbull switched plates?"

"Uh-huh. The Taurus belongs to a Gerald Moncrief, who's currently living at Seagull Pointe. Turnbull probably switched 'em out when he dropped off the Jane Doe and smothered his mother."

"So, it's like we thought. Then Turnbull attacked Jane Doe for her car, then left her dying at Seagull Pointe when he came to kill Madeline. Maybe he meant for her to die, maybe not. Either way, she's gone, and now he's abandoned her car. We have a possible on who she is. A woman named Stephanie Wyman from Portland."

"Someone coming to identify the body?"

"A friend," Lang said.

"Man . . . ," Savannah said on a sigh.

"I know."

"We gotta get this guy," she said, shaking off the moment and sounding determined.

"Yep. I'm going to update O'Halloran."

"I'm heading over to the double homicide," she said. "You coming?"

Lang considered, then said, "I think you've got it covered. I'm going to follow up on Turnbull. When you're finished there, come on back and we'll put our heads together and try to figure out what he's driving now."


Harrison pulled into the parking lot at the *Breeze,* climbed from his car, and turned his face toward a watery sun that looked like it could build up some real heat as soon as the marine layer burned off. He had gone to the Deception Bay Historical Society and asked for the history of the Colony and was given a once-over by a middle-aged woman wearing narrow-lensed glasses. She informed him that they possessed an undocumented history, and when he said that was okay, she led him to a bookshelf, where she pulled out a slim volume that was more a manuscript with a laminated cover than a real book.

She then told him that many people seemed to have an interest in the women who lived at the lodge and asked what his particular reason for searching into their background was. He thought about telling her that he knew one of them personally, then decided that was a bad idea. But when he said he was a reporter and was doing background work on a story, he thought she was going to rip the missive from his hands. And then, when he wanted to borrow it for a while outside of the building, she visibly paled, as if the thought of a world outside her control might make her swoon.

Before she could find a way to wrest the book from his grasp, he'd walked over to a chair by a window and sat himself down. She hovered nearby, worried, but he ignored her and concentrated on the book.

There wasn't much to learn. The narrative read more like a family tree than an account of their lives, and it stopped at Catherine Rutledge and Mary Rutledge Beeman, the last descendants of their family. There was a branch that included Madeline Abernathy Turnbull. Maddie's father, Harold Abernathy, was a cousin to Catherine and Mary's grandmother, Grace Fitzhugh Rutledge.

"Apparently, Mary was married to someone named Beeman," Harrison said aloud. "And she and Catherine are distant cousins to Madeline, who married someone named Turnbull." He glanced up at the woman, who had stayed within earshot.

She pressed her lips together, torn between freezing him out and bending an ear to gossip. Gossip won, and she came a few steps closer, taking off her glasses and polishing them. "There are no documented marriages," she said, warming to her story and, he thought, really wanting to let him know how much knowledge she'd accumulated. "Madeline Abernathy's mother was the daughter of a Native American shaman who moved in with Madeline's father, Harold, when she was only fifteen and against her father's wishes. She died giving birth to Madeline. Madeline's father, Harold, who by all accounts was a very strange man indeed, raised Madeline on his own, and she became the town oddball, a kind of idiot savant, actually.

She began reading palms and telling people their futures as a means to make a living. She was in her late forties when she gave birth to Justice in nineteen seventy-five, but this account ends around nineteen seventy. You can see that pages have been ripped out of the back. That's the way it came to us."

"How do you know about Justice Turnbull, then?"

"Oh, I've volunteered here for years. Was told the year of his birth by Dr. Dolph Loman. He's a doctor who's lived around here forever, on the staff at Ocean Park, I think. Anyway, he gave us this account upon the death of his brother, Dr. Parnell Loman, over fifteen years ago."

"Maybe Dolph Loman has the rest of the book," Harrison suggested.

"Or maybe it's been lost." She shrugged.

"So, there's no record of Justice's father or this Beeman whom Mary married?"

"Not here."

Harrison thanked her, and she seemed a little more inclined to trust him after their talk, so she left him and moved back to her desk. Before giving her back the book, Harrison studied it a bit longer. There was definitely some intermingling with the Native American population, and there were several shamans listed, as if the Abernathy-Fitzhugh-Rutledge clan couldn't keep away from them, even though no marriages were listed.

There was also the mention of "dark gifts," which seemed to present themselves mainly in the female descendants of the Abernathy-Fitzhugh-Rutledges. There was even speculation on Loman's part that said female descendants found relationships outside their marriages with said shamans, but there was no written proof of these rumors.

Harrison closed the book thoughtfully, wondering if Lorelei truly possessed some of those "dark gifts" or if she'd been spoon-fed the idea of such a thing and the power of suggestion had taken over from there. Was he being too cynical? But what was the alternative? To believe she and Justice Turnbull shared a mystical bond of communication?

If not a mental, telepathic link, then at least some weird connection Harrison didn't understand.

He handed the slim volume back to the woman at the desk and said, "I met the chronicler of this account, Herman Smythe."

"At Seagull Pointe?"

"Yep. He seems a little foggy now, but he's the one who compiled this information?"

"His name's on the book," she pointed out, again puffing up with her specific knowledge of the area.

He left the historical society building and placed a call to Laura, glad when she answered right away. She was still at his sister's, but getting ready to go to work. From the sound of it, she'd had a wonderful morning with Kirsten, who had gone to work but was planning to take a break from the bakery to drive Laura to the hospital soon. Laura had tried to dissuade her, but Kirsten refused to listen. Harrison remarked that stubbornness was a trademark of his sister's.

"The police," he reminded her, but could tell, before Laura said so, that she was going to refuse him again.

"I have a dinner break. If you still think it's necessary later this afternoon, then I'll go."

"I don't want to talk to them again, either. But yeah, I think it's necessary."

"Okay," she agreed reluctantly, and they made a date for him to pick her up from work at her dinner hour.

Harrison then flirted with the idea of heading to Zellman's house and seeing if the good doctor was up for an interview, but the Deadly Sinners story still required a few final touches, so, though it chafed him, he decided to wait on that till later. Instead, heading for the *Breeze,* he put a call into Dinah, Herm's daughter, his curiosity about the Colony definitely on an upswing. But he reached her voice mail, as ever, and ended up leaving his name and number.

Buddy was coming out of the back when Harrison entered the *Breeze* offices. He signaled that Vic Connelly was in his office, and Harrison walked along a short hallway, then knocked on a frosted glass door and heard Vic's gravelly voice call, "Yeah?"

Harrison stuck his head inside. Vic's wild white hair was especially flyaway today and looked like pale cotton candy. "Just checking in," Harrison told the editor.

"You following up on those teen thieves some more? We're getting a lot of good feedback from that Kirby woman jumping on it. People want to talk to you."

"What people?"

"The ringleader's dad, for one. Bryce Vernon. The land developer? Thought he was gonna blow a gasket. Acted like you'd slandered his little darling. But then the little darling himself called for you."

"What? Noah Vernon called the paper?"

"Sure did," Vic said. "Buddy took the call but wasn't sure you wanted to give out your cell number. What the hell's that all about?"

Swearing, Harrison turned on his heel and strode to where Buddy was seated at a computer. Buddy, smiling, picked up a piece of paper and waved it at Harrison, who snatched it from him.

"I told you to give out my number," Harrison growled.

"Is that a full green light?"

"Don't be a pain in the ass. Yeah. Whatever. What time did Noah Vernon call?"

Buddy glanced at the clock. "About seventeen minutes ago. I knew you were on your way, so I thought I'd wait and give you the message in person."

Harrison was out the door before Buddy finished speaking, pressing the buttons on his cell phone once again, this time with Noah Vernon's number. It rang several times and then Noah himself answered with, "Yo. Who's this?"

"Yo. It's Harrison Frost. You called me."

A moment. Then, "Oh, yeah, the reporter. Well, I'm offering you an exclusive for a little cash."

Harrison laughed. "You don't need the money. What is this?"

"I do need the money. My old man's cutting me off." He sounded offended.

"I've got thirteen dollars and twenty-nine cents on me," Harrison said.

"You know what I mean."

"Noah, I'm not going to pay you for your exclusive. A lot of this tale's been told already. But if you want your voice heard, I'll put it in the paper. That's all I can offer you."

"I'm under eighteen, man," he said, testing.

"Until tomorrow."

"You're dialed in," he said, surprised.

"Do you want to meet?"

"I'm, like, under house arrest by my dad," he admitted with repressed fury. "But he's a dickhead and I could use a smoke. Can you pick me up?"

"What about being under house arrest?"

"My dad's at work. He can bite me, anyway. I don't give a shit. Come by the house." He rattled off the address, though Harrison already had scoped out where the kid lived. "He'll be pissed but that's his problem," Noah added with a certain amount of relish.

"I'll be there in fifteen," Harrison told him, and then made good on his promise by driving ten miles over the speed limit to pull up in front of a beautifully restored turn-of-the-century home on a sidewalk lined by trees on J Street, one of Seaside's alphabet letter blocks.

Noah must have been waiting for him, because he came through the front door as soon as Harrison pulled up to the curb. He wore pants that looked like they would fall off his hips and a long blue T-shirt that stuck out from under a black nylon jacket. A black watch cap was stuck snugly on his head, and if he wasn't careful, he was going to bake beneath the growing heat of the sun.

He slid into the passenger seat of the dusty Impala and said, "Nice car," with a smirk.

"Do you always dress like you took your clothes off a street bum?" Harrison rejoined.

"Yeah." He glared at Harrison through fiery blue eyes.

It was with a bit of surprise that Harrison realized Noah Vernon was an exceptionally handsome young man. It irked him that someone so blessed with looks, money, and an obviously caring family, no matter if Noah thought Dad was a dickhead or not, could thumb his nose at every gift he'd been given.

"I can't wait to hear why you're so messed up," he told the kid. "Really. It looks like life's really knocked you down." He glanced back at the immaculately groomed property.

"Well, fuck you," Noah said.

"Back at 'cha," Harrison replied as they drove out of town. He had sized Noah Vernon up immediately and, almost without thinking, knew how he was going to treat the kid: like the loser dirtbag he'd shown himself to be.

"Where are you taking me?" Noah demanded as soon as they left Seaside's city limits and headed south down 101.

"Don't know yet. Where do you want to go?"

"This is kidnapping!"

Harrison actually laughed. "Really? That's all you've got? Lame, Noah. You know absolutely nothing about anything, yet you think you have all the answers."

"You can't say that to me!" he declared, shocked. "Wow. I thought you were cool. You're a reporter! You're supposed to take down what I say." ·

"I'm not cool with people who threaten someone close to me," Harrison said in a cold voice.

"What are you talking about?"

"Doesn't matter," Harrison said. He had no intention of telling him anything about how he knew the woman Noah had caught eavesdropping. "Just wanted to be clear on how I felt about you."

Noah blinked in disbelief. "How *you* feel about *me?* Seriously?"

Harrison told him, "I don't like you. But I'll write up your story, let others make a judgment on you. Is that what you want? To be heard, *Envy?*"

"I got a right to be heard." His blue eyes were searching out the window, half panicked, as if he truly believed Harrison was taking him somewhere against his will.

"I'm all ears," Harrison said. The little shit had everything going for him, and he was determined to be as ungrateful as he could possibly be. Pauline Kirby was right: he did think Noah should be given more than a slap on the wrist for his exploits.

"Okay," Noah said.

"Then we'll stop at Ecola Park and you can tell me all about it."


Kirsten dropped Laura off at the hospital, and Laura turned and waved her a good-bye, to which Chico wagged his tail wildly in response.

It was strange, but Laura felt like she'd really made a friend of Harrison's sister, who'd been fascinated that she was a member of the "cult." Laura had managed to convince her that they weren't as weird as the locals made them out to be, but equally, Kirsten pointed out that their behavior and chosen way of life set them up to be targets of gossip and innuendo.

But then the conversation had eventually turned from Laura and moved to Kirsten and Didi and the tragic situation that had brought them to the coast. "I miss him," she said, after telling Laura how she'd met Manny Rojas, how he'd made her laugh, how she'd fallen in love in one minute. "I've put the bad stuff behind me, pretty much," she said, her smile faint. "But I wish I had him back."

"I'm sorry," Laura said, meaning it.

Kirsten shrugged, as if shaking off the depression and gloom physically. "So, okay, we've covered your family and mine. Tell me more about you and Harrison. If you tell me there's nothing between you, I won't believe you."

"There's nothing between us."

"I don't believe you."

They both laughed and then Laura said, "I've just gotten a divorce. I'm very far away from a relationship with anyone else for a lot of reasons."

"Like what else?"

For one crazy moment, Laura had wanted to confide in her about the baby. But reason reasserted itself, and in lieu of answering, she said, "Justice is after me and my family. Harrison's helping me. We're going to the authorities later today, and I'm going to tell them that . . . Justice attacked me. That's why we showed up at your house."

"*What?* You didn't say that before!"

So, Laura explained about the events the prior evening that led Harrison to take her to Kirsten's cottage, and Kirsten, now aware completely, insisted they both stay with her again that night. Laura agreed, conditionally, needing Harrison's vote on the decision as well, though it was undoubtedly a slam dunk. She didn't want to go home. Ever. Well, at least until she fixed the door Justice had broken in, and even then she worried she might never feel safe there again.

Now, as she entered the hospital and headed for her locker, the first person she ran into was Byron. He was standing outside the staff room door, as if he was waiting for someone. Her? Or, just anyone to sweep into his trap?

He watched her as she approached, and she couldn't contain the groan that passed her lips. How, *how,* had she ever thought she was in love with him?

"You look even worse than the last time I saw you," he told her, his laserlike gaze raking over her with a surgeon's impassivity.

"Hi to you, too." She turned toward the room, but his hand caught the crook of her arm.

"You are pregnant," he stated flatly. Then, "See, you're not the only one who can diagnose around here. Is it mine?"

"No."

"No?"

"No, I'm not pregnant. I guess I am the only one who can diagnose around here," she challenged, hoping the lie didn't show on her face.

"If it isn't mine, whose is it?" He leaned closer to her.

"Is the issue that you're worried there might be a host of little Byrons incubating around the area? Maybe you ought to check with a current girlfriend or two and leave your ex-wife out of it."

His lips parted in true surprise. "When did you turn into such a witch?"

"I've always been a witch," Laura said with a trace of bitterness. "Ask anyone around town."

She left him with a lost look on his face that was priceless. It made her almost laugh. He didn't know her history, of course, and therefore didn't know she was associated with the "cult" at Siren Song.

But as soon as she'd taken ten steps away, she was seized by a wave of reality-based fear, and she leaned against her locker as she opened it. The truth was, she *was* pregnant. And it *was* his baby. And no amount of wishing and hoping was going to change that fact. Sooner or later, she was going to have to stop shoving the issue aside and face it head-on.

# CHAPTER 31

Ecola State Park was on the outskirts of the town of Cannon Beach, named for the cannon replicas from shipwrecks that were placed in vehicle turnouts located at either end of the entrances to the town. Cannon Beach was a more chichi place than Seaside, full of expensive candy stores and clothing shops and restaurants, in contrast to the Coney Island feel of its northern neighbor. It was the "it" place to go on Oregon's northern coastline, although the affluent were slowly moving to towns south of it as well.

Harrison pulled into the park and inwardly sighed as Noah jumped out of the car almost before it stopped moving, slamming the passenger door hard enough to give the Impala a case of the shakes.

The kid walked to an empty picnic table and threw himself onto the bench. Harrison had shed his jacket earlier, when the sun first threatened to come out from hiding behind the clouds, and now he watched as Noah yanked off the watch cap and ran a hand through his rumpled light brown hair. He next pulled off his black jacket, and without the armor he looked skinny and vulnerable and young.

Grabbing the bench opposite Noah, who was facing the ocean, Harrison made sure he wasn't in the way of the kid's view. Noah stared toward the sea for a few moments, then dragged a crumpled pack of cigarettes from his jacket pocket, throwing Harrison a dark look in the process to see if he was going to stop him. When he got no reaction, he shook out a cigarette, jammed it to his lips, then pulled out a lighter and touched the flame to the end, sucking hard. He had to fight back a minor cough, which made Harrison inwardly sigh; then he blew out a stream of smoke and said, "They think they're so smart, you know. The ones we target. Got all the answers. Well, they don't know jack shit."

"Mind if I make notes?" Harrison asked, pulling out his notebook from his back pants pocket.

"Do what'cha gotta do."

"The ones you target . . . Do you mean your classmates or their parents, or both?"

"Their parents are fucked up, man. That's for sure. So are mine."

Harrison shrugged. "Kind of a common complaint from your age group, isn't it?"

"So what? We *did* something about it. That's what I'm saying." He turned a sharp blue gaze Harrison's way. "We hit their weak spot. Opened up their Pandora's box. Showed 'em they weren't gods."

"You broke into their houses and trespassed and pilfered."

Noah frowned. "Pilfered?"

"Stole," Harrison explained with a straight face.

"Yeah, well, we formed an alliance to fight back," he said with sudden passion. "They treat people like they're nothing! We made them realize that we could enter their world anytime we wanted. Anytime! And take things from them. We're deadly, man. The Seven Deadly Sinners."

Harrison wrote down a few notes and said, "But you're from their same world, economic-wise. How does that translate?"

"What do you mean?" he asked, but he knew.

Still, Harrison would play his game for a while. "Your father is Bryce Vernon. He's a successful land developer who's hung on to his wealth, even throughout this whole recession. Your family might be—and probably is—as well-to-do as the Bermans or any of the other families you hit."

"The Bermans suck!" he said through clenched teeth. He turned away, trying to hide from Harrison's gaze suddenly, but he couldn't quite manage it. Harrison noted how his face grew red with some kind of emotion: anger, frustration, maybe . . . even embarrassment?

*Ping.* Harrison felt the answer resound in his brain. For all Noah's posturing, for all his "leading" of his band of entitled misfits, for all his crowing that he needed to be heard—it wasn't about any of it. This was something to do with the Bermans themselves, and Harrison had a pretty good guess what it was.

"Britt," he said, and the stunned look that crossed Noah's face was all the answer Harrison needed.

"Britt?" Noah repeated carefully.

"That's what set this in motion. Britt Berman. Your imagination did the rest. Your initials . . . your need to make something big and important out of mere jealousy. You turned your rejection and angst into a whole *thing*."

"I don't know what you're talking about."

"Sure you do. This Deadly Sinners alliance. It's all smoke and mirrors. A way to attack those who've wronged you. You. Noah Vernon. And you got your posse to go along with it because they bought into your whole alliance thing. What did she do? Berman. Set you up to watch you fall? Humiliate you? Crush you? Maybe just never even look at you?" He paused, then said, "She doesn't even know you exist."

"Oh, yes, she does."

"No, she doesn't."

"Yes, she does!"

Harrison shook his head.

"She knows me!" he insisted. "Especially now!"

"Now that you've broken into her house and got your Deadly Sinners in the news? And then tomorrow, when you're eighteen, you want me to blast your name across the paper and increase the Myth of Noah Vernon. How am I doing so far?"

"You'd better take me back now, or I'll scream that you kidnapped me. I really will."

"Go ahead. You called the paper and left your number."

"And you'd better not print any of that, either!"

"You don't want to be heard anymore?"

"Not the way you're doing it!"

"By pointing out the truth?"

"You say anything about Britt and I'll sue you for every cent you own!" He spat out his cigarette and stomped the smoldering butt with his heavy boot.

"You and dear old Dad?"

Noah looked trapped. He glanced around, as if searching for somewhere to run. Harrison waited a few moments and could almost see the air seep out of his balloon as his shoulders slumped and his body sank onto the bench.

"Don't worry, badass. Your secret's safe with me," Harrison said. "I don't have to tell the world you're just another lovesick loser. I'll say you're a Deadly Sinner and you're the brains of the group and should be tried as an adult. You want to go to jail for this fiction, be my guest. It's up to the judge, not me and not public opinion. I could put a different spin on it, if you want me to. Write that you were going to extreme lengths to be noticed by a girl and that—"

"No." He was firm. "That's not what it's about."

Noah got to his feet and started heading back to the car. Harrison fell in step beside him.

"If this is just about some cockeyed version of street cred," Harrison said, "it won't be worth the consequences you could face."

"I don't care."

"You sure?"

"Yes!"

Harrison climbed into the car, and Noah flopped into the passenger seat, his face turned away, his shoulders hunched. Harrison almost felt sorry for the kid. Almost. But he definitely felt both relief and frustration that this story was ending and he could jump fully onto the Justice Turnbull one; relief that he could move on without worrying he was leaving something big, and frustration because the damn thing had taken so much energy in the first place. He needed to be with Lorelei.

And then he should be writing her story. And the Colony's. And Turnbull's. They were all interwoven, and it was several serious levels more intense than the Deadly Sinners' teen drama.

Harrison dropped Noah off back at his house. Then he stopped at the *Breeze* and typed up a rather banal account of his meeting with Noah, explaining that Noah Vernon, a boy of privilege who was turning eighteen by the time this story would be published, had been bored and wanted to be something bigger, something important, and he coerced his friends into breaking and entering and robbery and trespassing as their golden ticket into another world, the world of crime.

When he turned in the story, Buddy remarked that he'd pretty much nailed Noah Vernon by naming him, but Harrison just ignored him, heading for the door. Noah's father and a sympathetic judge would foil Noah's plans to be infamous. Chances were the kid would be in college in a year, joining a fraternity, with a clean, or expunged, record.

That was just how it went a lot of times.

Harrison's head was full of thoughts of the Deadly Sinners until he passed by the drive to Ocean Park Hospital on his way into Deception Bay. He almost pulled in, just to see

Lorelei, but forced himself to let her work at her job. He'd told her to keep her phone on her whether it was hospital rules or not, and figured she would call him if there was trouble.

Still, it was with great difficulty that he let the hospital grounds disappear in his rearview mirror. Justice had attacked her the night before. Harrison was going to make damn sure he was with her before nightfall this evening, but for now, he wanted to speak with Zellman, if he could talk the man into an interview.

He'd just passed the access road to Lorelei's house when something caught his attention, and he turned around at the first available empty drive and retraced his route back to her access road. As he drove up it, he saw a vehicle nearly obscured by the brush running riot on either side. A black Range Rover. The one he'd damn near sideswiped the night before.

Now he pulled up beside it and got out, circling the black vehicle. Nobody inside. Empty. He tried the driver's door and was amazed when it opened. The interior light came on. Sliding inside, he popped the glove box and pulled out the registration. He stared at it, perplexed, for almost a full minute.

The Range Rover was registered to a Brandt Zellman.

Zellman?

The Zellman he was on his way to see?

*That* Zellman?

"Huh," Harrison said.

What were the chances that this Brandt Zellman was related to Dr. Maurice Zellman? Like 99.99 percent? Maybe Brandt was the man's son? Harrison was pretty sure he remembered the doctor was married and had one teenaged son.

But what the hell did this have to do with Justice Turnbull? Anything?

Had Justice "borrowed" Zellman's son's car?

Harrison felt a chill roll down his back at the thought of what that meant. Was Zellman even okay? Maybe he should call the authorities and have them send a patrol car to check on the good doctor.

Better yet, he decided, he should check things out for himself first.

# CHAPTER 32

Harrison headed south toward Zellman's house but wheeled into the Ocean Park Hospital drive first, squealing a little as he took the turn at the last moment. He drove fast to the parking lot and practically leapt from his vehicle, checking his watch. About three o'clock. Laura would be on the floor somewhere, and he really needed to see her first.

But he was thwarted almost immediately by a flurry of activity in the ER that had the whole hospital hopping: a three-car pileup just north of Deception Bay. Racing teens, he learned, but that was all he got from them.

He tried phoning Laura's cell, but it went straight to voice mail. He started feeling anxious, berating himself for not hanging closer to her, and had to give himself a stern talking-to. *She's okay. She's at work. Getting panicky isn't going to help anyone, or solve anything.* Besides, the TCSD had called; they were scheduled for another interview later in the day, after the detectives had gone over all the initial information.

Phoning her cell again, this time he left a message confirming that on her dinner break, which she'd said tended to be in the late afternoon, they were going to meet with the authorities.

Hanging up, he wondered if he should have told her about finding Brandt Zellman's Range Rover abandoned near her house. Once more he considered going to the police. Once more he decided to be first on the scene himself.

Feeling superfluous with hospital personnel rushing all around him, as if he were the rock in the middle of the stream, Harrison headed back out to his car. The clouds had fully dissipated, and the beat of the sunshine on his head and shoulders was downright hot. He would go see Zellman now. On his own. Geena had told him where the doctor lived, so there was nothing stopping him.

As he turned out of the hospital drive onto Highway 101, his cell phone rang. Damn. He was going to have to get Bluetooth or risk being pulled over for talking while driving. He answered anyway.

"Frost," he said.

"Hi, this is Dinah Smythe. You left a message on my phone?"

"Yes, I did," Harrison confirmed, his eyes peeled for the law as he drove along. "I met with your father." He sketched out his visit with Herman and finished with, "He told me to call you to confirm everything he said."

"You're writing an article?" she asked carefully.

"Just doing research."

"I'm going to guess this has to do with Justice Turnbull's escape, since you're asking about the women of the Colony."

"Your father . . . intimated . . . that you might be related to them."

"He believes he's at least one of thems father, so maybe. Or maybe not. It's not some burning issue I need to know."

"He says he had sexual relations with Mary Rutledge Beeman, who is the documented mother of the women who live there."

"Ahh . . . you've read his account."

"I was curious," Harrison admitted. He wondered how long it would take to get to Zellman's.

"My father likes to act as if there were a time when free love reigned at Siren Song. Maybe it did. Maybe it didn't. There are definitely a lot of women living at the lodge, so somebody fathered them. It's a lot of hearsay, but my father isn't exactly what I'd call a reliable source anymore."

"He alluded to the fact that I should talk to you about them."

"Because I'm the one who still has an accurate memory," she said dryly. "But if you've read his book, you know about as much as I do."

Harrison talked to Dinah Smythe for a few minutes more, until he saw a TCSD patrol car coming his way and hurriedly hung up. After the cop flew on by him, he pulled the note from his pocket with the other phone numbers from Herman's list. He called the first and learned it was a clinic specializing in gerontology. Herm's doctor, apparently. The second was a pizzeria that delivered.

So much for that.

With a feeling of hitting a dead end, he shoved the Colony aside and concentrated on the road ahead. Here, 101 cut inland for a stretch of miles before jogging out to the coast again. His stomach growled, and he reminded himself that the Subway sandwich he'd bolted down for lunch in Seaside wasn't sticking with him as much as he'd hoped.

He drove through Tillamook, spying the Tillamook County Sheriff's Department, which was located in a building in the strip of land between the northbound and south-bound lanes of the highway, the very spot he and Lorelei would meet with the cops. He knew she was uncomfortable talking about Turnbull and how he was connected to her and Siren Song.

Then again, who wouldn't be?

He glanced at the rearview mirror and caught a glimpse of his reflection. "You really know how to pick 'em," he said to the eyes glowering back at him. Lorelei Adderley was trouble with a capital *T*. Aside from her weird childhood at the Colony, there was her mental connection to a madman, whether real or imagined. Either way, it spelled disaster. Then there was that imperious son of a bitch to whom she'd been recently married, a prick if there ever was one. Yeah, Lorelei came with a lot of baggage, and the worst part of it was, he didn't seem to care. She was charming and smart, clever, and had a wicked sense of humor, and when she kissed him . . . oh, hell, he was lost in the wonder of her.

"Fool," he ground out, knowing he was falling for a woman he hadn't known a week, a woman who seemed to attract the worst kind of trouble.

And as intriguing as hell.

He, a man of fact and science, who had carefully avoided any serious relationships for all of his adult life, was falling for a woman whose beauty and spirit called to him, touched him in a spot he'd kept closed off for years. Just like her damned namesake.

It was a real pisser and there wasn't much he could do about it.

He forced his concentration back to the road, where he was following a flatbed truck that was hauling a load of berries, crates and crates of them strapped to pallets that seemed to shift beneath the tethers that bound them.

He sped past the truck and noticed an SUV follow suit, right on his tail. The minute he tucked into the right lane again, the SUV, with a surfboard atop and what looked like paraphernalia for hang gliding, a sport that was popular on the series of capes that rose above the ocean in this part of the state, along the coastline, flew past.

Yet another idiot, who took the next turn toward the west.

Harrison followed, but the SUV was sprinting and disappeared from sight before he reached the next corner. Once again on the coastline, he drove through a small hamlet, which boasted Carter's Bait Shop and not much else, then on past Bancroft Bluff, where he noticed several sheriff's department vehicles and realized they were still swarming around the double homicide, which had come into the paper earlier and which Buddy was writing up. More investigation to follow.

Zellman was lucky he hadn't built on that unstable section of land; his home was on a rock table, and Harrison slowed down at the sight of the stone pillars that marked the drive and the opened wrought-iron gates. He turned into the long, winding drive, which was asphalt bordered by cut stone, and wound through tortured pine trees and a riotous fifteen-foot-high laurel hedge. The woods thinned out closer to the house, and he suddenly burst into a clearing where an imposing house of sand-colored stone stood, shaped into an obtuse angle, the massive garage one arm, the house the other.

The windows were trimmed in cedar, and there were several flower boxes full of petunias. A few cars were parked along the garage side. Harrison slotted the Impala beside the end one, a dark blue Mercedes. He glanced at it as he headed toward the front door and saw the keys were in the ignition. The car beside it was a white BMW, also with keys in the ignition. A car thief's dream.

Harrison walked along an auxiliary stone pathway that led to the front door, which was protected by a post-and-beam cedar portico. Massive wrought-iron door handles were bolted to the double doors, and as he pressed the doorbell, he saw it, too, was a wrought-iron rectangle with a raised design of what looked like beach grass.

The door opened, and a young man stood in the aperture, gazing at Harrison through worried eyes. He was thin, with wavy dark hair longer than Harrison's own, and he was fighting an attack of acne along his jawline. He gazed at Harrison expectantly.

"Brandt?" Harrison guessed.

The worried look turned to a controlled panic. "Who are you?"

"My name's Harrison Frost. I'm actually looking for your father. Is he home?"

"Oh . . . yeah . . . He can't talk, though. . . ." He glanced over his shoulder to the dim interior of the home. Harrison could see down a long hallway to a burst of light where windows opened onto the back view. "I thought you were . . . I don't know. Like coming to tell me something bad."

"About your car?"

Brandt looked thoroughly confused. "My car? No. Not mine. Matt Ellison was driving a red Blazer."

"Matt Ellison?"

"I think he's at the hospital now. It's senior skip day, and that's why they weren't in school. They're not saying on the news yet."

"The three-car accident," Harrison realized. "No, I don't know anything about that."

Nodding resignedly, Brandt turned and led Harrison into the house and down the hall to a large, domed room with windows that curved to allow a view of 180 degrees of sky and distant sea. Buttery leather armchairs were arranged in conversation groups. A glossy black baby grand sat to one side.

Dr. Maurice Zellman was seated on a chaise, holding a book. A sweating glass of iced tea sat beside him on a coaster on a side table made of cherrywood and wrought-iron detailing. The doctor was small and wiry with a sharp chin, and he gazed at Harrison with piercing eyes. A white bandage was wrapped around his throat beneath a casual blue shirt. He wore tan chinos, and his feet were encased in matching tan socks.

He looked . . . thoroughly angry.

"My name's Harrison Frost. I'm with the *Seaside Breeze.*"

Zellman gestured fiercely in a way that made Harrison understand that the doctor knew who he was. Brandt was standing to one side, and he motioned for Brandt to bring Harrison an iced tea as well. Brandt went to do his bidding without asking if Harrison wanted a drink, but it was more because he was distracted than out of general rudeness.

"I'd like to ask you a few questions," Harrison told the doctor, "but I also wanted to tell you that I found your son's Range Rover. Looks like it was abandoned. I mentioned it to Brandt, but he didn't seem to know what I was talking about."

Zellman swept up a small notebook and pen. He jabbed out a note. *Where?*

"Just north of Deception Bay. On an unnamed residential access road off Highway 101."

Brandt returned with the iced tea and handed it to Harrison. Zellman gestured for Harrison to talk to him, so he reiterated where he'd found the younger man's car.

"My car's in the garage," Brandt denied. "I took the Mercedes to school today 'cause it was out front."

"It had your registration inside. A 2007 black Range Rover."

"It can't be." And then, as the realization hit, he added, "No, wait a minute. I left my car outside. Oh, shit! It shoulda been with the Mercedes and the BMW!"

"Were the keys inside the ignition?" Harrison asked.

"Well . . ." He glanced toward his father, who glared back, agitation visible in his silent gaze. "We just leave the keys in the cars. We always have. Where's my car?" he asked, the worried look back in full.

"If it's been stolen, you need to call it in to the TCSD. You have any idea who might have taken it?"

"No."

Zellman scribbled a note. *Could be any of your juvenile delinquent friends.*

"I gotta call Barry," Brandt muttered, yanking a cell phone from his pocket and heading down a hall toward the bedroom end of the house.

Harrison gazed at the doctor. "Have you heard from Justice Turnbull?" he asked.

Zellman blinked several times and shook his head. *No. Why?*

"I think he may be the one who took your son's car," Harrison said, trying not to sound as angry as he felt. If not for Zellman's incompetence, Justice Turnbull would still be locked away and Lorelei would be safe. Jaw tight, he added, "Turnbull terrorized a woman last night who lives near where it was abandoned. Tried to kill her."

Zellman blinked hard.

"And she's not the first, Doctor. Several people have already lost their lives since he escaped."

Zellman blanched and glanced away.

At that moment a door opened from down the hall, and he heard the small *tap-tap-tap* of a woman's footsteps against the wood floor. Harrison turned as Mrs. Zellman entered the room. Seeing them, she stopped short, then came forward again a bit more cautiously. Harrison saw where Brandt got his perpetual look of worry. She was short and slim and had pretty blue eyes and dark brown hair. She threw an anxious look toward her husband that could have meant anything.

Zellman refused to even look at her.

"What happened?" she asked. "I—I'm Patricia, Dr. Zellman's wife. I saw the accident on the news. They say the kids are going to be okay, but one of them broke his leg pretty badly."

Zellman made a chopping motion with his arm, clearly meant for her to cut herself off. She stopped talking and looked slightly stricken. Harrison introduced himself and brought her up to speed on Brandt's car. When he mentioned Justice Turnbull, she paled.

She turned to Zellman. "Morry, that man . . . ," she said in an imploring voice. Then she turned back to Harrison. "He's always scared me. My husband is his doctor, you know. Maurice has really helped a lot of patients. But that Turnbull person . . . I don't even think God could help him."

Zellman looked ready to explode. His eyes flashed daggers at his wife, who, though not immune, simply turned away from him a bit, as if putting up a wall.

*Like Lorelei claims she does when Justice Turnbull tries to reach her.*

Harrison forced himself to keep his voice level. Angering Zellman wouldn't help anything. "Do you know any reason he might have taken your son's car?" Harrison asked.

She thought for a long moment. "Availability," she said, surprising him with her candor. "They're there and he knows where we live. Everybody practically does. They know this house. I told you we should have fixed the gate!" she tossed out to her husband.

Zellman motioned her out of the room and started writing another missive. She hesitated a moment before doing as bidden, tap-tap-tapping down the hall to the front door. Harrison heard it close behind her.

The doctor held out the note to Harrison with quivering fingers. It said: *My laptop is on the dining room table.*

Harrison looked in the direction the doctor was pointing and passed through the kitchen, all stainless steel, granite, and dark wood cabinetry, and into the dining room, which sported a huge rectangular table painted black and made to look distressed, and crowned above by a heavy iron chandelier with a myriad of hatted lights.

The laptop was slim and sleek. Harrison brought it back

to Zellman, who fired it up, waiting impatiently. As soon as he could, he pulled up a blank page on his word-processing program and began writing.

*My wife does not know Justice Turnbull. He is driven by inner forces. He would not steal a car because of availability. His mind does not work that way. He just moves forward and goes after his goal.*

"Nevertheless, I believe he took your son's car," Harrison told him. "He was chasing a woman who once lived at Siren Song, and he left it there."

*Why would he come to my house?*

"Like your wife said, he knows where it is." Harrison shrugged. "Because you're his doctor? Maybe he came for another reason and just found an available car."

Zellman thought that over for a long time. *You haven't told the police your theories yet?*

"No, but like I said, your son should report the missing vehicle."

*This woman he was chasing . . . she's a member of the Colony?*

"They're her sisters. Or half sisters. She used to live at the lodge but hasn't for quite a while."

*Is she pregnant?*

Harrison read these last words in surprise. "No. What do you mean?"

Zellman started rapidly typing. *In our sessions, Justice revealed himself in bits and pieces. He was cagey. Didn't like to give too much away. One thing that came out was that when he was targeting the women, he went after the ones outside the gate. I think he was afraid of meeting them on their own ground. He can't make himself cross that fence into their territory. But he said, he could smell them when they were pregnant and then he could track them.*

"And you're telling me you believed him?" Harrison asked, trying hard to keep the skepticism out of his voice, barely succeeding.

*I'm telling you what he believed. He targeted Colony women who were pregnant and outside the gates.*

"Well, he's tracking this woman because she says they have a mental connection. Like a GPS, I guess. If she lets him in, he can find her. If she shuts the door, he's out."

Zellman shrugged, as if he wouldn't write that off completely. *Justice is capable of many things we may never understand. His psychosis is deep, somewhat indefinable. We made progress, but his world is a dark place with ironclad rules he must follow. He's been off his meds for three days, and he needs them to keep any semblance of reality. His danger is increasing.*

Harrison couldn't argue with that. "So, you don't think he's the one who took your son's car?"

*It's possible, I suppose. If it helped him achieve his goal. This woman you spoke of, if he's tracking her, she needs to be extremely careful. For her safety, she should go back to Siren Song until he's caught.*

Harrison thought that over. Though he kind of thought Zellman was serving up a whole bowl of crazy, he couldn't quite dismiss it all. "I'm going to leave you my cell number. I know you can't talk, but maybe your wife or son could call if you think of anything else?"

He nodded as Harrison wrote his number on the pad of paper Zellman had been using earlier.

*We will let the sheriff's department know about Brandt's car.*

"Good. Thank you."

They shook hands, and as Harrison left, he met Mrs. Zellman coming back inside, her hands full of car keys.

Nothing like locking the barn door after the horse escapes.

# CHAPTER 33

Justice awoke on the floor of the rough-hewn space he'd rented, lying on his back, his head supported by Cosmo's jacket. The ceiling boards let in light through the cracks, which striped his body; the window offered a warm square of June sunshine from outside.

Still, he was cold. It was the shivering that had awakened him. He'd eaten the last of Cosmo's jerky and energy bars and wondered without much interest where he was going to find his next meal. He wasn't hungry now. Wouldn't be for some time. All he needed was fuel to keep going, and he was sure he could find it when he needed it without raising suspicions.

Transportation was the big issue. He'd ditched the Nissan compact, and he'd switched to Zellman's Range Rover . . . And then he'd lost that car somehow.

Justice blinked, his mind twisting corridors that he could run down but in which he could find no end. He couldn't remember why he'd lost the car. There was nothing there. No answer.

Then *bang*. Memory returned in a flash.

Lorelei. The devil's mistress. He'd found her, but she'd escaped!

Justice sat up straight, his head rushing from the effort. *Something wrong,* he thought. It felt like pieces were loose and floating around inside his skull.

*Lorelei . . . ,* he called to her.

*Lorelei . . . I'm coming for you. . . .*

But there was no answer.


Laura's cell phone vibrated in her pocket. She hadn't been able to pick up the call she'd received earlier; she'd been too busy. But now she snatched the phone from her pocket, saw that it was Harrison calling, and punched the ON button. "Hello? Harrison?"

"Hey, there," he said. "When are you off for dinner?"

"Now, if I want to be. We had three accident victims here earlier, but they've been taken care of or moved to another hospital."

"Kid named Matt Ellison?"

"Oh, God. Are you writing up a story?"

"No. I ran into someone, a classmate of this Matt's. I'll tell you all about it when I get there."

"You're coming here?"

"We're going to the sheriff," he reminded. "Didn't they call you?"

"Yeah . . . I know. How romantic," she quipped, though she wasn't really in the mood for jokes. She thought about the upcoming interrogation and the word *inquisition* slid through her mind. All her secrets would be exposed. Of course, she would tell the police everything; more than anything she wanted Justice behind bars forever, but still . . . sharing all her knowledge of the man, of her upbringing at the Colony, of her sisters . . . She shuddered. She'd told the officers everything that had happened last night, when she was interviewed, but the questions hadn't probed too deep into her personal life. Today, she knew, she wouldn't be so lucky.

"It's gonna be all right," Harrison said.

"Of course it won't be, but I'll be looking for you."

"Twenty minutes," was his response.

She had just enough time to check her reflection in the mirror, add a little blush and lipstick, and wrinkle her nose at the pale color of her cheeks. A greenish tinge showed underneath her skin, she thought, annoyed. Pregnancy? Probably.

*Lorelei* . . .

She blocked her mind, fighting a shiver. Justice had been calling her for the past half hour, but she was bound and determined not to answer. If Harrison were here . . . if she were with him . . . she might consider taking the "call." But alone. No way. The twisted fury on his crazed face hadn't left her inner vision, and her quick shiver turned into a violent shudder at the memory.

It was climbing toward 5:00 p.m. when she walked out of the hospital, her purse strap slung over one shoulder. Harrison's Chevrolet came down the drive, its engine definitely louder than she'd noticed before.

She opened her mouth to say something as she climbed in the passenger door, but he beat her to it.

"The damn thing could just quit on me," he said with a certain amount of regret. "If I have to get rid of this car, it'll hurt."

"How long have you had it?"

"Me? Ten years. Before that, I'm not sure how many lucky owners there were."

She was silent for a while as they headed south toward the Tillamook County Sheriff's Department. Then Laura observed, "Sometimes I think you're living in a different time."

He squinted a look at her. "Wow. Spoken from a woman whose family wears long dresses and their hair in buns."

"Have you met any of my family?"

"Not formally. So, how am I from another time?"

"The old car. The longer hair . . . I don't know. I guess you do have a cell phone," she added with a shrug.

"Yeah, well, I have issues giving out my cell number. Hate being called by anybody at anytime and being expected to pick up."

"Isn't that almost a job requirement in your field?"

"Well . . . yes. Your point?"

She smiled. Good Lord, she was starting to like him. No, it was more than that. Far more than simple affection and it was definitely a problem.

"There's been a strange turn to the Turnbull investigation," he said, and Laura was brought back to the present with a bang.

"What?"

"I think Justice has been driving Dr. Zellman's son's car. That's the one that was on your access road. The black Range Rover."

"*What?*"

Harrison proceeded to tell her about his meeting with the Zellmans and the conclusions he'd come to regarding Justice. He finished with, "I told Brandt to let the authorities know about his car. Maybe Justice still has the first car. If not, how's he getting around now? Maybe he meant to use Brandt's car longer and something happened, or maybe not."

"He chased me into the ditch," Laura said. "If he got back in his car, I would have seen it leave and probably known it was him. And then you came right after that."

"It was probably safer for him to abandon the car and walk away."

"I hope he didn't stop a hitchhiker or grab another woman and take her car."

Harrison made a face. "He's got to have some form of transportation. I guess we'll just have to wait and see." After a moment of them each being in their own thoughts, he went on. "You know how you said you thought he was sick? Physically sick, maybe? Well, Zellman said he's been off his meds for long enough to have some effect. Like his psychosis would get worse."

"He's unraveling," Laura said suddenly, feeling the scratch down her back again, as if he'd physically marked her.

"Worse than he already was. Hard to believe." He shook his head. "Zellman said something else, too. Sort of weird. He said that Justice revealed once that he could find the Colony women easier when they were pregnant. That he could smell them. Do you believe that?"

Laura's heart leapt in her chest. Her blood pulsed in her head. "What?" she whispered.

"That his victims are easier for him to locate when they're pregnant . . . or at least in his twisted mind that's what he thinks. Who knows?"

She swallowed hard. Did Harrison know? Suspect? She grabbed the armrest, her fingers blanching white.

"I told Zellman about you," Harrison was saying against the roar that had started in Laura's ears. "Didn't name names. Just said that there was one of the Colony living outside the gates who Justice was targeting, and just being outside is why you're a target. Not because of pregnancy."

She wanted to die inside. Did he know about her throwing up just this morning? Oh, Lord, what a mess.

"Dumbest thing I ever heard," Harrison went on, "and it doesn't bode well for the doc that he seems to give comments like that some credence. What do you think?"

"I . . . really . . . don't know. . . ." Laura could barely swallow. Nervous sweat was collecting in her palms.

"You all right?" He glanced her way, his gaze searching.

With an effort, she managed to fight back her panic and lie all too easily. "Uh . . . yeah . . ." *I'll never be all right. Oh, God, Harrison, if you only knew. I'm pregnant. Justice knows! He senses!* Tears of fear for her unborn child and for a love unrequited burned behind her eyes. With that thought she froze. *Love? You're "in love" with Harrison? No damned way.* But she couldn't find her voice.

"It's going to be fine. Really." But he appeared concerned, and she had to fight to appear normal, hoping color would return to a face she was sure had been leeched of all blood. "Okay. We're here," he said, glancing ahead to the county offices in the center of the city of Tillamook. He wheeled into a back parking lot full of potholes, slowing down and moving the vehicle gingerly around huge craters filled with water. "Our tax dollars hard at work," he muttered.

Laura dreaded this meeting more than she could say. She didn't want the sheriff's department involved. She didn't want to talk to officers with blank faces who were trying to appear to listen when she knew they would consider her a crackpot of the first order as soon as they heard the way she communicated with Justice.

Still, he had chased her last night. Had touched her. Nearly caught her.

They entered through the back door and up a few stairs. To the left was a hallway that led behind the counter, which blocked access to the main body of the building. Harrison and Laura walked along the counter, which ran the length of the room, toward the front door. On the opposite side, an officer sat at a reception desk. Her name tag said JOHNSON, and though she clearly was the gateway to the inner sanctum, her expression was anything but welcoming.

"May I help you?" she asked, the dark eyes settling on Harrison full of unspoken questions.

"We'd like to speak to the sheriff about the Justice Turnbull case," he said.

"Sheriff O'Halloran has left for the day," was the terse response.

"Is there someone else?" Harrison asked.

She hesitated. "What's your name?"

"Harrison Frost."

Johnson reacted with a nod. "Ah, the reporter. Mr. Frost, when the sheriff has something to reveal about the case, he'll announce it."

"We have an appointment." Harrison met her gaze firmly.

"With Detective Stone," Laura interjected. "I heard he's handling the case."

"The sheriff is a very busy man," the receptionist said. Her face became a glower, but outmaneuvered, she picked up the phone and pressed a button. When it was answered on the other end, she said, "Harrison Frost, the reporter, is here with information about the Turnbull investigation," in a tone that suggested she didn't really believe he knew anything of worth.

She listened, then said curtly, gesturing back the way they'd come, "You may go around the counter and down the hall. Apparently Detective Stone is expecting you."

"Thanks," Harrison said.

Under her breath Johnson muttered, "Last to know again."

Harrison cupped Laura's elbow, and she felt a moment of electricity, a kind of awareness that she rarely, if ever, felt.

They had just turned the corner at the end of the counter and were heading down the hall to the rooms beyond when a man in cowboy boots, jeans, and a shirt with the sleeves rolled up came their way. He had dark hair and blue eyes that seemed to see a lot more than they gave away.

"Detective Stone," he introduced himself. "Mr. Frost?" He shook Harrison's hand, and the two men sized each other up; then he glanced to Laura and nearly did a double take.

"Laura Adderley," she introduced herself, sticking out her hand as well.

The detective seemed to think that over as they shook hands. "Come on down to my office."

They followed after him and learned his office was a large squad room with a number of desks arranged front to front in twos. An attractive woman officer with auburn hair and blue eyes acknowledged them with a quick smile as she brought another two chairs to Stone's desk. Laura and Harrison sat down as the officer seated herself at the desk that butted up to Stone's.

"Detective Dunbar." Stone indicated the female officer, who gave them an interested look. "This is Harrison Frost and Laura Adderley. Frost is a reporter with the *Seaside Breeze* and Ms. Adderley is—"

"A nurse at Ocean Park Hospital," Laura finished for him.

Stone swung around to face Laura directly. "You remind me of someone, Ms. Adderley."

Her mouth formed the word *who* but she didn't utter it. She almost already knew.

"Do you know the group of women who live in the lodge called Siren Song up the road? People around here refer to them as the Colony," said Stone.

Harrison's brows lifted. "Where are you going with this?"

Laura said, "He thinks I look like them."

Stone gave them a small smile of acknowledgment. "You do. Your hair's darker, but there's a similarity. I've met their gatekeeper, Catherine. And I've seen pictures of some of the younger women."

"Pictures," Harrison said. "How?"

"Justice's first victims. And others . . ." He frowned, as if deciding how much to tell, how far to go.

"My hair's dyed," Laura admitted in a soft voice. "You've met Catherine?"

"A time or two," he said. "She's never let me in, though. Me being a guy and all. It's a . . . developing relationship," he added dryly. "So, tell me. What have you got for me on Turnbull?"

"I think Justice stole one of Dr. Zellman's cars from his house—his son's car, a Range Rover—and he left it outside Laura's last night," Harrison said.

Stone's eyes narrowed thoughtfully, and Laura said, "I know you have reports of what happened at my house. We spoke with the officers last night. What I didn't tell them was that I'm sure Justice Turnbull tried to kill me last night." Stone opened his mouth to comment, but Laura soldiered on quickly. "He came to my house and he stole one of my knives. Then waited for me. Once I returned home and was inside, he broke down the door and came after me. I escaped. Barely. I called Mr. Frost for help, and then I ran."

"He chased you?" Stone asked. "After he broke into the house?"

"Yes. He chased me outside and I ran to the road and there's a drop-off at the edge of the yard and I kind of tumbled over. That's where Harrison found me."

Stone seemed to pick up on the way she said Harrison's first name, as he gave him a look. It irked Laura a little.

"Detective Stone," she said tautly. "He'll come back for me. Justice will come back for me."

"Why?"

Stone sounded like he really wanted to know, but it was a question Laura couldn't answer. "It's just what he does," she said simply.

# CHAPTER 34

Laura was exhausted after two hours of intense questioning by detectives Stone and Dunbar at the sheriff's department. People had come and gone throughout the evening; she'd seen two men in handcuffs led toward the back door; and phones had continued to ring, while computers hummed and keyboards clicked. There had been a break in the questions, which just gave her long enough to call the hospital and explain that she wouldn't be returning for the remainder of her shift. Her supervisor, a real by-the-rules manager, wasn't happy and let her know it, but Laura had already called someone else to fill in, so it wasn't that big of a deal. At least she hoped not. She couldn't afford to lose her job.

Stone seemed to know more about the Colony and Laura's sisters than she would have imagined and had even asked her about working outside Siren Song at the Drift In Market in Deception Bay. "So, you're that Laura," he said, surprising her. "I looked for you once when I was trying to figure out the Colony women, and I heard one of them worked at the market."

She had admitted she was "that Laura" and then went on to answer his questions as honestly as she could. She spent a great deal of time explaining that she'd known Justice Turnbull as a child, though he'd never been allowed to live within the gates of Siren Song. Nor had his mother.

After another series of questions about the Colony, Stone leaned back in his chair and eyed Harrison speculatively.

"So what's your connection? Other than working on the story, I mean?"

Laura felt her muscles tense. Over the detectives' protests, she'd insisted that Harrison be with her for the interview, and Harrison had promised to check with the sheriff's department before he published anything, but obviously Stone was skeptical.

"We're . . . friends," Harrison said, sliding a glance toward Laura.

"Known each other long?" This from Detective Dunbar. She, too, was suspicious.

"No," Harrison admitted and Laura felt her own head shaking. "We kinda met during this whole mess."

"Tell me," Stone encouraged, and Harrison explained about meeting Laura at Ocean Park, trying to get information for his story on Justice Turnbull's escape as the victims of Turnbull's attack had been sent by ambulance to the hospital.

"And from that you became good enough friends that she doesn't want to speak with us without you," Stone said.

"He saved me," Laura said. "If Har . . . Mr. Frost hadn't shown up when he did, Justice might have found me."

"So you owe him your life?" Savannah Dunbar suggested.

Laura opened her mouth to defend Harrison but caught his warning glance, and instead of praising him for saving her life, she said only, "I just wanted him with me."

Dunbar shrugged and Laura knew what they were thinking, that Harrison was playing her for a story; that they had known each other less than a week and could hardly be considered friends, as they were barely acquaintances. She didn't dare say anything more, that she thought she was falling in love with him while she was pregnant with her ex-husband's child. How could she explain to the cynical cops that she felt as connected to him as if they'd known each other for most of their lives? It was silly, really. Maybe a case of her hormones being out of whack.

Stone asked a few more questions, back to the Colony, as Justice Turnbull's sadistic and deadly intentions were focused on the women within; the police obviously thought his other victims had merely gotten in his way. Which summed up Laura's thoughts exactly, though it seemed Justice was more out of control than ever, really off the rails of sanity. She didn't confide about the way she communicated with Justice, because she was certain, they, like Harrison, wouldn't believe her. And she didn't really blame them. Fortunately, Harrison hadn't brought it up.

Though there were no more questions about the relationship between Laura and Harrison, she felt the detectives' unspoken skepticism as Stone jotted notes. She didn't tell them about her pregnancy; that was too personal, something she'd told no one. Not even Harrison. Especially not Harrison. Guilt nibbled at her conscience a bit, but she ignored it. They weren't *that* close, even if she was having some fantasies about the man.

Again . . . her hormones.

Right?

Eventually, Stone turned to his partner. "That's all I have for now. What about you?"

Dunbar said, "Can't think of anything else."

"Good." Detective Stone got to his feet. "We'll call you if we have more questions, and if you think of anything else, phone me." He pulled his wallet from the back pocket of his slacks and withdrew a card. Hesitating, he found a pen and scribbled a number across the back. "My cell." His face was sincere, almost kind. Laura wanted to trust him, to believe that this man would find a way to catch Justice before he could hurt anyone else, but deep in her heart, she knew it was impossible. As long as Justice was alive, he would be a threat. To her. To everyone associated with Siren Song. To her child.

"I'd like one of those, too," Harrison said, and after giving him a questioning look, Stone repeated the procedure of adding his cell phone to the card, then sliding it across his desk. Harrison tucked the card into his wallet.

"Is it okay for me to go home now?" Laura asked, her throat thick as she thought of the tiny being inside her.

"I wouldn't," Stone said. "We'll be running patrols by the place, but since Turnbull knows where you live, you might want to go somewhere safer until he's caught."

If *he's caught,* she thought but didn't say it.

"We've thoroughly checked, and the Range Rover that was abandoned there has been ID'd." He exchanged glances with his partner again, then added, "It belongs to Doctor Zellman. Once our lab has gone over it, someone from the family will pick it up. But I think you know that already."

Harrison nodded.

"Zellman. The same guy who inadvertently helped Turnbull escape," Dunbar added with a disgusted frown.

Laura couldn't help wondering if Maurice Zellman had been a target, though it seemed unlikely as she was certain Justice had zeroed in on her and her sisters. But maybe there was something else about Zellman. Maybe Justice's primary physician had information on him the madman didn't want exposed.

Stone continued, "But your house is secure. We boarded up the broken door and we're done with our investigation, so you can go back inside, but you should be careful." He was dead serious. "I don't think you should spend much time there."

"Will you have someone watching the place? Watching Laura? She's obviously a target," Harrison said.

Stone met Laura's gaze. "We're short staffed, but yes, we'll be watching your house and you. However, we can't assign a deputy to be your bodyguard. We just don't have the manpower."

"I'm fine," she said, though Harrison wanted to argue. She sent him a look indicating she wanted to leave, then slipped Detective Stone's card into her purse. She felt drained as she walked with Harrison through the offices to the exterior, where the night was clear and cool, the lights of the town stringing along the side streets as well as this stretch of 101, Pacific Coast Highway, that cut inland through Tillamook.

"For the record, I agree with the detective. You're not staying in the house tonight," Harrison said once they were on the road again, heading toward Laura's little bungalow. She groaned inwardly, hadn't thought about calling her landlord and explaining about why the place was trashed. But she'd better do it before he got wind of it from someone else.

"So now you're the boss?" she asked.

He smiled faintly. "Something tells me no one can boss you around. Not even a psychotic maniac like Justice Turnbull."

"Yeah, well, he tries," she said and looked out the window. They'd left the town behind, and beyond the Impala's windshield, she saw the starry night stretch out above them. Wide and clear, millions of stars winking.

As if everything in the world were perfectly fine.

"My car's at the hospital," she reminded Harrison, then slid him a glance. "But I can pick it up tomorrow."

He was nodding. "I'd better call Kirsten and tell her we'll stay with her again. Who knows if Justice has made a connection between you and me? He could have figured out where I live."

"You think he may be waiting for us—me—there?"

"Probably not, at least not yet, but let's not push it. Until we have a plan of action or the police have nailed the son of a bitch, we should try to stay off his radar." Hands on the wheel, he slid her a glance. "So has he tried to contact you?"

She shook her head. "Not since the attack last night."

"I wonder where he's holed up," Harrison mused as the turnoff to Deception Bay appeared and, after waiting for a passing car, he pulled off the main highway.

It had been a long day. Too long.

Stone looked at the notes and files scattered over his desk as he rubbed the kinks from the back of his neck. Goddamn that Turnbull. And goddamn that stupid psychiatrist for not taking the necessary precautions. But then, Zellman was a sanctimonious jerk. Stone had figured that much out a long time ago. He just hadn't counted on Zellman being so careless. No, that wasn't it. What had happened hadn't been carelessness on Zellman's part so much as an utter disdain for the rules when they applied to him. He had enough of a God complex to think he was really smarter than anyone else.

And it had nearly cost him his life.

Which, though troublesome, apparently hadn't slowed the man down. According to an officer who had gone to question him, Zellman was insisting upon returning to work at the hospital.

Stone inwardly snorted as he thought the supercilious jerk would have to eat a good portion of crow.

Others hadn't been so lucky as the shrink. Just ask James Cosmo Danielson, Stephanie Wyman, Madeline Turnbull, and Conrad Weiser, the security guard still lying in intensive care at Halo Valley. Even though Weiser wasn't dead, he hadn't come out of his coma, and there was speculation that he might never. When he did, who knew how well he'd function. Whether a primary target or not, Weiser was a victim one way or the other, as were the others.

He turned to his computer and worked his mouse to show the pictures of Justice Turnbull's victims. Jesus, the psycho was cutting a deep swath, and so far, he hadn't reached his goal of destroying the women of Siren Song.

Stone leaned back in his chair until it creaked. Justice Turnbull had a history of attacking the women associated with the Colony. Some had escaped; others hadn't been so lucky during his previous rampages.

Now it was only a matter of time. Turnbull had almost gotten to Laura Adderley last night. An intended victim. One of the women of Siren Song. She was one of Turnbull's prime targets.

Scratching at his chin, he studied a map of the area that included marks where evidence of Turnbull's crimes was noted. Everything from the location of vehicles to bodies, or sightings, the most recent being Laura Adderley's house. He'd noted the old motel that Madeline Turnbull had run and the lighthouse where Justice Turnbull had made his lair. On Whittier Island, known by the locals as Serpent's Eye, the old, unused lighthouse was hard to reach unless it was low tide. Two deputies from the department had made the torturous boat ride and reported back that it looked as if no one had been inside in years. The only evidence of life had been a colony of rats and bats.

"Perfect place for a Halloween party," one of them had joked, "except no one can get there."

Now Stone also marked Siren Song on his map and, in another color of ink, areas that Turnbull had lived in or frequented during the time before his arrest. He'd read the thick case file on the maniac and pinpointed the spots of interest from his previous crime spree.

It all centered around the Colony and the women there. He considered Laura Adderley, a woman who had lived the first part of her life—the formative years—at Siren Song but then had been allowed to make her way in the outside world.

Only to be dragged back because of the psycho.

He tapped his pencil on his desk, frowning as he studied his map. He'd had his run-ins with the women behind the big gates before, and it seemed he was going to have to have another meeting.

He spent the next half hour writing a report, then turned away from the computer monitor and punched the number of his own home into the cell.

He smiled when Claire answered.

"Hey, where are you, Detective? Dinner's cold." He imagined her at the desk she'd set up in one of the spare bedrooms, reading glasses perched on her small nose, dark hair twisted into an unruly knot on her head. She was petite, but strong, a psychologist who had stood toe-to-toe with some pretty class-A crazies, though she would hate to hear him classify her patients as such.

"I'm not biting, Doctor. You had patients tonight, if I remember right. Group?"

"Good memory."

God, it felt good to talk to her. He remembered meeting her at Halo Valley and how they'd clashed so violently. But there had been reasons for that. He'd been forced to deal with her during another case, which had put him at odds with her over his sister's death and had also touched on the Colony of Siren Song. He never would have believed that he could fall for her, and he'd had his reasons not to trust the pretty psychologist, but during the course of that investigation, he'd fallen hard and deep. Recently, they had moved in together and planned to marry before the end of the year.

"Are you on your way home?"

He scanned the files strewn over his desk and glanced at the computer monitor, where crime scene pictures were flickering. "I'll be there in half an hour."

"Really?"

She knew his ways at work. Glancing at his watch, he

said, "Twenty minutes," then grabbed his jacket, thinking he was one lucky son of a bitch. Savvy Dunbar was just leaving as well, and he met her at the door. "What do you say we take a trip out to Siren Song in the morning?" he asked, shrugging into his jacket, then shoving open the door to the outside.

"Sounds like a blast."

"Yeah." He was nodding, turning up his collar to the bite in the clear, cold night. Summer came late to this part of the coast. At least it did this year. "Let's see what Catherine, the keeper of the gates, has to say."

"You've had so much luck with her before," Savvy pointed out.

"Yeah, well, surely my luck's about to change."


In the passenger seat, Laura shivered as Harrison pulled into the driveway of Laura's little house. The cottage was dark, no beckoning lights streaming from the windows, the exterior illuminated only by the wash of the Chevy's head-lights.

Despite the fact that Harrison walked her to the front porch, her nerves were strung tight as bowstrings, her heart racing as she fumbled with her keys and unlocked the front door. Images of the night before flew before her eyes, Justice with her knife outside the window, his heavy footsteps as he chased her through the house, the brush of his finger across her skin.

Her knees nearly gave way.

Inside, she flipped on the lights.

Eyeing the interior, her skin crawling, she made her way to the kitchen, where she noticed the sprayed glass across the floor and the broken window of her back door. As Stone had said, the door was sealed tight with plywood. "The landlord's going to love this," she said, the soles of her shoes crunching on the broken shards.

"What a mess. I'll double-check that it's secure."

She walked into her bedroom, remembering her fear of what or who was hiding in her closets the night before. From the dresser she grabbed underwear, a clean pair of jeans, and a couple of T-shirts, including one that was large enough to sleep in. She stuffed them into a small overnight bag that she kept on the closet floor.

As she snapped out the light, she glanced at her bed and wondered if she'd ever feel safe enough to sleep here again. Probably not.

In the bathroom, she found a ziplock bag and stuffed it with a few essential toiletries, dropped it into her bag, then returned to the kitchen, where Harrison was on one knee and fiddling with the lock on the back door. "Still works," he said. "Maybe the damage isn't as bad as it looks."

"Maybe not," she said, but the house didn't feel like home. Yeah, her stuff was here, her coffeepot and pots, her dish towels, her herbs growing in the window over the sink, but now that it had been invaded by a madman, the once-cozy bungalow felt cold and empty. Without any soul.

Then again, maybe it always had. Maybe she had been kidding herself, because this small cottage had been the home she'd shared with Byron and that hadn't endeared the house to her. Maybe it was time to move on.

Harrison straightened, dusting his hands on his jeans, and Laura decided that when Justice was caught and the lease was up, she would move.

She didn't know where or how, but she would make a fresh start.

For her.

For her child.

She swallowed hard and slid a glance at Harrison, who snagged the bag from her fingers. "Ready?"

"Yeah." She had told him so much, confided about her childhood, but had kept her pregnancy a secret.

From everyone.

Except Justice. *He* knew.

Her blood chilled when she thought about his proclaimed ability to sense when women from the Colony were with child. She would have laughed it off, except he'd certainly zeroed in on her. And in so doing, he'd lost control, decided to go on another murderous spree, and now not only were she and her unborn child at risk, but so were all her sisters.

She would have to do something about that. They couldn't live in fear forever and her baby . . . her baby had to survive.

Locking the door behind her, she decided that she and Justice were destined for a standoff.

Harrison hadn't gotten through to his sister to tell her that he was returning with Laura, but he pulled into her drive, parked, and decided against ringing the doorbell. "Hello?" he called through the door, as he usually did, and he heard his niece squeal in delight.

Didi, on her way to bed, was thrilled with the prospect and used Harrison and Laura's arrival as an excuse to avoid brushing her teeth and slipping between the covers. She insisted on being toted around on Harrison's shoulders and giggling uproariously, then having Laura read her two books before Kirsten put an end to the stalling and hauled her protesting daughter off to her bedroom.

Only Chico seemed unhappy with the situation and snarled at Harrison from behind the rocking chair.

"Yeah, yeah. I know," Harrison told the dog as his phone rang, and seeing that it was Geena Cho, he took the call outside, on Kirsten's small patio, where he could smell and hear the ocean only a few blocks away. He sat on a bench beneath a macramé hanger that surrounded a large Japanese float. Light from the porch lamp bounced off the bluish glass.

"Thanks for nothing," Geena said with a pout in her voice.

"Sorry," Harrison apologized. Then, "It didn't work out with Alonzo?"

"Alonzo," she repeated, as if suddenly remembering. "The bartender. Uh. No. It definitely didn't work out." She hesitated. "Actually, I called to apologize. I think I was a little over the top last night."

"Maybe a little."

"My hangover today suggests that it was more than a little. Even a lot."

"No big deal." He watched as a bat swooped past, just over the top of the fence.

"Good thing today was my day off. But . . . well, thanks for offering to pay for the cab."

"I'll make good on that later."

"I heard about what happened with Justice Turnbull," she said cautiously. "Be careful, would ya? I wouldn't want anything to happen to you."

"I will." They talked for a few minutes more, then hung up amicably. Standing, he nearly hit his head on the suspended artwork, then slipped through the slider and into the eating area, where Kirsten was plating up some day-old ham and cheese rolls from the bakery, fruit, and decaf coffee while Laura set out three plates.

"Next time maybe I'll get you to barbecue."

"That'd be a trick." His attempts at grilling were legendary—burnt chicken, raw hamburgers, you name it, he'd ruined it.

They ate quickly, tried to focus on some summer-replacement television shows and, eventually, decided to go to bed, just as they had the night before. Harrison planned to check his e-mail, then take the floor, giving Laura the couch, but he knew it would be a struggle leaving her by herself.

"You mind if I shower?" Laura asked Kirsten.

Kirsten was already walking toward the bathroom. "Not at all. There are towels in the hall closet. Here. Let me get some for you."

Harrison turned his attention back to his story, polishing it as Laura made her way to the bathroom.

Before he'd trimmed the piece, he heard the pipes groaning and the water running. Kirsten appeared from the bedroom wing and grabbed hold of Harrison's arm.

Surprised, he said, "Hey, I've got to put this to bed, or it won't run tomorrow."

"Tough." She pulled him outside, onto the small patio, where the dull roar of the sea reached his ears. She slid the slider closed and stared up at him.

"Sorry to keep intruding," he said.

"It's not a problem," Kirsten assured him. "Really. At least not for me. Or Didi. Maybe Chico, but he doesn't have a vote."

"Then?"

"It's you, brother dear," she said, eyeing him in the half-light spilling from the eating area inside the house through the glass of the sliding door.

"I'm fine."

She snorted. "You know that she's in love with you."

"What?" He glanced back at the house.

"When your back is turned, she stares at you, and it's not just a friendly, 'oh, gee, aren't we great friends' look. She's falling for you, Harrison, and, I suspect, pretty damned hard. She doesn't strike me as the kind of woman who falls quickly and shallowly, or has had a lot of boyfriends. We talked a little bit. I gather her marriage wasn't all that great."

He'd put those pieces together himself. "Her ex is a prick."

"That may be, but tread carefully, okay? She doesn't need her heart broken. I kinda think she's going through enough without that on top of it." The pipes groaned, indicating

Laura was twisting off the taps. Kirsten took a step toward the door. "And there's a lot going on with her, all that Colony stuff. Yeah, I did a little research about it on the Internet today. So . . ." She beseeched him with her eyes. "Take it slow, okay?"

"Slow? I'm a snail, Kirsten."

"Yeah, you're . . . something. Laura's not the only one who's falling in love, now, is she?" With that she walked into the house and said, "Good night."

Following a moment later, Harrison scraped back his chair at the kitchen table and reopened his laptop. He connected to Kirsten's wireless Internet and, before checking his e-mail, did some research on the Colony. Laura's vague answers about her life at Siren Song and the women who lived there had bothered him. He tried to find out all he could about "Mary," who seemed to have daughters with different men. Not only had she been indiscriminate, it seemed, but somehow she'd managed to birth only girls, although Laura had mentioned several brothers.

Still, it was odd.

Then there was her death and the closing of the gates of Siren Song. He checked his notes, the ones he'd taken from the book he'd read at the historical society, and found that he had no real answers.

Checking his e-mail, he found nothing of interest and was closing his computer when Laura stepped into the living area. She was towel drying her wet hair, her face devoid of make-up, and she was walking to the couch, the oversized T-shirt she was wearing giving him a view of her long legs, the action of drying her hair lifting the T-shirt's hem even higher, providing a glimpse of pink panties.

With an effort he dragged his eyes away, but the image lingered. God, she was sexy. And she didn't even know it.

An interesting, intriguing woman.

A woman with more than her share of secrets.

He looked up and found her smiling at him, a wistful, al-most melancholy smile. "You okay?" he asked and felt a hard-on starting to form.

"Yeah. I guess."

"You're safe here," he said, and felt the overwhelming need to comfort her.

"With you?"

He inwardly groaned. *Not on your life,* he thought but didn't say it as she put the bed together on the couch and slid between the sheets. It was all he could do to stay seated. "Of course," he said and wondered how the hell he'd get through the night with her sleeping less than five feet away.

# CHAPTER 35

She felt as if she hadn't slept more than five minutes at a stretch. Thoughts of Justice, her sisters, and Harrison filled her head most of the night. She listened to him softly snoring not three feet from the edge of the couch and wondered what it would be like to make love to him every night, to feel his arms surrounding her, keeping her safe, and then to wake up the next morning, his body warm, his eyes sleepy, his smile so crookedly irreverent, they would make love all over again.

*Silly fantasies,* she told herself and rolled off the couch to sneak into the bathroom, where she flipped on the light and caught a glimpse of her reflection in the mirror. She was pale, her hair a mess, and her lack of sleep was evident in the dark smudges beneath her eyes.

Not exactly a sexy seductress.

She felt a twinge in her abdomen and frowned, then used the toilet, feeling slightly better before returning to the living area.

The rooms weren't completely dark. The sun was rising, dawn slipping through the windows, gray light seeping inside.

Harrison wasn't on the floor.

His bedding was mussed, but he was missing.

She felt a breath of cool air and noticed the sliding door was open a crack. Harrison, barefoot and shirtless, wearing only low-slung jeans, was outside on the patio, on his cell phone. His hair was at all angles, and it wasn't helped by the fact that he was raking the fingers of his free hand through it as he spoke in low tones.

He was staring toward the west, his back to the house's open doorway. Laura watched for a moment, noticing how his skin stretched taut over broad shoulder muscles, then tapered over his back to disappear below the waistband of his battered Levi's.

She caught a glimpse of white, a strip of flesh that hadn't been tanned, and her stomach did a slow, sensuous roll. She imagined running her finger down the cleft of his spine, then pressing moist lips to the same path. . . .

*Stop it!*

He cocked his head into the phone and muttered something under his breath as she stepped through the doorway.

"Okay. That's it then," he said and turned, catching her in his gaze before he hung up. For just an instant, his expression remained dark and guarded. Sexy as all get out, his chest bare, dark hair visible over the rock-hard muscles, his abdomen a washboard, the top button of his fly left open.

So damned male.

As if he read her mind, he grinned, his teeth a slash of white in his beard-darkened jaw.

"Important call?" she asked, the back of her throat dry as the Sahara.

"Umm. Making sure the follow-up story on the bandits made it in."

"And . . . ?"

"We're golden." He slid the cell into his pocket. "And why are you up at the crack?"

"Couldn't sleep. Too much on my mind."

He cocked a dark brow. "I could make coffee . . . or . . ." His eyes glittered in the half-light.

"Or?"

To her surprise, he slid his arms around her waist, the T-shirt bunching, and he rested his forehead against hers. "Well . . . it's still early. We could go back to bed."

"Back to the couch and the floor," she reminded him, and he snorted a little laugh, his breath warm against her face.

"Not the best situation." The tip of his nose touched hers.

"And then there's Didi and Kirsten," she said a bit breathlessly. "They'll be getting up soon."

"I can be incredibly quick."

She smiled. "That's just what a woman wants to hear."

"Foreplay is so overrated," he said but chuckled deep in his throat, and his hands slid up her bare arms, silently telling her he was kidding, that their lovemaking could last for hours.

Her blood was running hot.

And then he really kissed her, gathered her closer still and pressed his lips to hers. They were warm and supple, promised sensual pleasures that made her head spin with images of wet skin, and hot desire. She thought of where he would touch her and how she would return the favor.

Closing her eyes, she let herself go and leaned closer, felt the length of his body against hers, the heat from his torso permeating the thin cotton of her T-shirt.

*Don't do this,* her mind warned. *This is dangerous, Laura. You know that you're already treading in emotional and perilous waters.*

But she couldn't stop and let herself get lost in the feel of him. His male scent filled her nostrils. One hand twined in her hair; the other pulled her tight to him.

She responded, opening her mouth, feeling his tongue

slide deftly between her lips. Her breasts tightened, her nipples stiffening, desire pulsing deep inside.

"Lorelei," he whispered, and she groaned softly, felt her knees weakening.

Before she could say a word, he'd scooped her up and carried her through the open door.

"Mommy?"

Didi's voice was like a splash of cold water.

Harrison froze.

Laura scrambled onto her feet, straightened her T-shirt, and turned to the kitchen, where she grabbed the coffeepot and switched on the water just as the sound of tiny feet hit the floor.

Three seconds later Didi appeared, dragging her blanket. Chico was on her heels. He glanced up at Harrison, then made a funny, snarling face before streaking outside.

"Hey, kiddo," Harrison said and scooped her into his arms. "Got a kiss for your favorite uncle?"

"No!" she said, scowling at him, but he blew a horse kiss on her arm, and she began to giggle, her bad mood disappearing.

"What gives?" Kirsten stumbled out of her bedroom and glanced at the kitchen clock. "It's only six," she groaned.

Harrison said, "I thought people who worked in a bakery were up at two in the morning."

"Old school," she mumbled, yawning and stretching one arm over her head. "Coffee on?"

"Just about." Laura, sensing that her cheeks were hot, turned toward the cupboards and poured the carafe of water into the coffeemaker. Kirsten was already digging in a cupboard near the stove. She came up with a filter, lined the basket, then found beans and measured some into a grinder on the counter. With a press of a button the grinder shrieked into action. She poured the ground beans into the coffee machine, hit a button, and in less than a minute coffee began to drizzle into the glass pot.

"Now we're cooking," she said, then plucked her daughter from Harrison's arms. The aroma of freshly brewed coffee filled the room as Chico returned and Kirsten closed the door behind him. "So what about you?" she said to her daughter. "What do you want for breakfast?"

"Pancakes!" Didi said brightly.

"Big surprise. Get dressed and I'll make a batch." She glanced at her brother, then swung her gaze to Laura. "For all of us."

Didi was off like a shot, and with a nostalgic smile twisting her lips, Kirsten said, "Oh, to have her energy," slanting Harrison a knowing look. "And your damned passion."

Laura flushed, but Kirsten waved off any protests and warned her, "Just be careful." She found three cups in the cupboard and set them on the counter, near the slowly filling carafe. "My brother is a helluva guy who has this problem thinking he has to protect everyone close to him."

"That's a problem?" Harrison said.

"That you don't know it, that's a problem," Kirsten said.


Savvy Dunbar drove past the motel that Madeline Turnbull had called home before Justice's vicious attack on her that had sent her to the nursing home. The place was a shambles, individual cabins falling in on themselves, porches sagging, the fence barely existent on this cliff overlooking the sea. The land had to be worth a fortune; the dilapidated buildings were not worth a plug nickel.

She pulled into the once-gravel drive. Now weeds and beach grass choked the rutted lanes, and her squad car bounced and jostled through the potholes. No other police cruisers were nearby; there was only so much surveillance possible on the department's limited budget. Twenty-four/seven just wasn't in the cards.

After checking the grounds and peering into the few

windows that weren't boarded over, she drove along the highway to a turnout where she could spy the lighthouse where Justice had squatted before his incarceration. It had been abandoned for years, aside from harboring the killer a few years back. Now, from the shore, it appeared empty again, a lonely, graying tower on a rocky island in a white-capped sea, a solitary reminder of an earlier era that brought up thoughts of clipper ships and wrecks upon the rocky shoals.

"Where are you, you miserable son of a bitch?" she said as the wind, fresh with the scent of the ocean, caught her hair and slapped at her face.

She was tired, as was everyone working for the TCSD these days. With their increased workload, the officers were running on empty.

And still Justice Turnbull ran free.

Somehow, someway, she and the department had to catch him.

Before he started killing again.


The sun was climbing high overhead when Laura finally stood at the gate of Siren Song. Her heart was pounding, her nerves stretched tight. Harrison was leaning against his car, eyeing the grounds beyond the wrought-iron barrier.

"Are you sure about this?" he asked and she forced a smile.

"I'm not sure about anything," she admitted. *I wasn't even sure about spending last night at your sister's house, with you staring at me from the floor . . . and then that kiss . . .*

She cleared her throat, dragged her gaze from his. "But this is where it all started," she explained. She'd decided she couldn't let Justice rule her life. For most of the past week, she'd been dodging him, fearing him, calling him, then running away.

No longer.

She couldn't stand being terrorized, and it wasn't fair to everyone inside these gates. After breakfast, she'd asked Harrison to drive her here. He hadn't argued, only insisted that they stop and assess the damage to her house before they drove to Siren Song.

Neither of them had mentioned their kiss and what might have happened if Didi hadn't come bouncing in from the bedroom. Laura figured it was just as well. She wasn't going to pretend the kiss and her response to Harrison hadn't happened; she just didn't want to think about it too much.

For now.

At her little cottage, he'd come up with the name of a glass company that would drop by later to replace the shattered window. He figured he could replace the lock on the door himself. Laura had left a message for her landlord on his voice mail; then they'd driven the remaining miles to the lodge, and now she stood on the outside of the gate, wondering what answers lay on the other.

"I guess it's now or never," she said.

Since there was no bell to call the inhabitants, she wrapped her fingers around the thick wrought-iron bars and jangled the gate and chain, while calling, "Catherine! Catherine!"

Before the words were out of her mouth, Isadora appeared at the front door. Long skirts rustling, she race-walked across the porch and quickly along the stone path to the gate. "Lorelei," she whispered, clearly distraught as she unlocked the chain and yanked hard on the bars. With a groan the gate opened, and she flung herself into Laura's surprised arms. "We heard what happened," Isadora said, her throat obviously thick. "I was so worried . . . so . . . oh, dear God." She was shaking under the canopy of trees, light from a pale sun piercing the leaves to dapple the ground. The ground was still damp, smelled of earth and water, and the scent of the sea wafted through the old growth that surrounded the lodge.

"I'm fine," Laura said. "Really, Isadora, don't worry."

"I can't help it. He's a madman!" As if realizing they weren't alone, Isadora looked over Laura's shoulder to spy Harrison standing near his car. "Oh . . . sorry."

"Harrison's trying to help."

Isadora shook her head. "No one can." Her suspicious gaze cut to Harrison as he walked forward and extended his hand to her. "Harrison Frost."

Isadora reluctantly took his fingers in her own. "You're the reporter."

"Yes."

"But more than that," Isadora said aloud as she let her hand drop and her pale eyebrows slammed together thoughtfully. "He's the one Cassandra talked about. The truth seek . . . ?" she started to ask before seeing the warning glance in Laura's eyes and let her voice fade. Isadora had been in the room when Cassandra had made the prediction. She'd also heard about the pregnancy, and Laura fervently willed her sister to be quiet.

"I need to see Catherine," Laura insisted and was vaguely aware of the sound of tires crunching on the sparse gravel of the lane, the sound of a smooth engine.

Isadora looked up and cried, "Justice . . . !"

Harrison and Laura both stiffened, staring down the drive.

"Come inside," Isadora instructed. "Hurry!" To Harrison, "You, too!" She was already stepping through the open gate, intent on slamming it shut, when the nose of a Jeep appeared through the trees and Laura saw a tall man behind the wheel, a man with dark hair and a grim expression, the shadow of a beard darkening his strong jaw.

Not Justice.

A woman sat in the passenger seat. She, too, appeared worried, and before the Jeep slammed to a stop and she climbed out, Laura knew who she was. This woman was related to her, her sister. Fascinated, she noted the newcomer's large hazel eyes. Streaked blond hair. Firm, pointed chin. And that certain, indefinable resemblance in her carriage.

The gate was creaking shut when Isadora suddenly stopped the motion. "Becca?" Isadora whispered, her eyes rounding as Catherine walked from the open door onto the porch.

"Isadora?" Catherine called out to them.

"Who's Becca?" Harrison asked.

"One of my sisters," Laura said as the man behind the wheel climbed out and rounded the Jeep. She'd never met Becca before, but she knew she was her sister. She'd read about Becca Sutcliff and Hudson Walker a couple of years earlier, during Justice's last bloody rampage.

Becca, who had been adopted away from Siren Song before Catherine had closed the gates forever, had never lived at the Colony, nor had Catherine ever spoken of her, but the sisters had whispered between themselves about those who had grown up on "the outside." Even though Becca had been adopted, Justice had discovered her and she'd been the object of his deadly rage once already.

Now, as sunlight pierced the towering fir trees, Becca lifted a hand and flashed an uneasy smile, her hazel eyes worried. The man with her, presumably Hudson Walker, opened the back door of the Jeep, and Becca reached inside only to retrieve a curly-headed girl of about two who had been strapped into her car seat.

*He smells them when they're pregnant.*

Justice's terrifying claim sizzled through Laura's head, and she felt a new, chilling fear. Had Becca been pregnant with this little dark-haired girl when Justice had been tracking her down? Was that why she'd been his primary target?

Laura's blood turned to ice as she looked at the toddler. Pale. Wan. Listless. Oh, God . . .

Becca gathered the child in her arms, but her gaze found

Laura's and she stopped dead in her tracks. "You're Lorelei," she guessed. "You're the one he's after."

"You know?"

She hesitated, seemed to want to lie, then finally nodded. "I have visions," she admitted carefully. "I saw him chasing you . . . Lorelei. . . ."

"What the hell are you talking about?" Harrison asked her.

"We all have 'gifts,' " Becca said. "Didn't Lorelei tell you?"

"Well . . . yeah, but . . ." He looked nonplussed.

"She's not the only one." Becca was walking forward again.

"Isadora!" Catherine yelled. Spying the group gathered at the gate, her back stiffened and her face lost all color. "Oh, Lord!" Holding her skirts high, she stepped off the porch and marched purposely toward them, her linen-colored dress rustling, her hair pulled back in a silver knot pinned at her nape. "What is this?" Anxiety twisted her features.

Laura sneaked a peek at the house and saw the faces of her sisters in the window—Ravinia and Cassandra. Lillibeth had wheeled her chair onto the porch, her face turned toward the gate.

A prisoner.

Of the chair.

Of Siren Song.

Of fate.

Catherine came blistering through the gate. "What're you doing here?" she demanded, her face a mask of concern as she glared at Becca. "Don't you know he's loose again? Haven't I warned you that you can't come here? That it's not safe?"

"We couldn't wait." Holding her daughter protectively, she glared at Catherine.

"It's more dangerous now than ever," Catherine declared.

Becca was shaking her head. "You've stopped me long enough. I don't care about your secrets." Catherine tried to say something but Becca wasn't finished. "Too many have died already, Catherine. Too many of us, too many others. This has got to stop!" She was shaking, fighting tears. "And now . . . and now Rachel," she said, squeezing her eyes shut as the child stirred in her arms.

Catherine glanced at the little girl and her face softened.

"I know you want to protect us but it hasn't worked!" Becca visibly gathered herself, dispelling her tears and glaring at the older woman. "I've been here time and time again, trying to get answers, and you've shut me down. Sent me away!" Her voice was rising with injustice. "And now . . . now my daughter is threatened again." Clinging to her child, she whispered, "Let me in, Catherine. We need to talk. We *all* need to talk."

"I don't think—"

"Now!" the man with Becca said, his eyes flashing blue fire as he stepped forward. From over six feet he stared down at her, and he, too, was racked with emotion, pain in his eyes.

Catherine hesitated, then glanced again at the sluggish child. "Fine," she said to Becca. "But no men. Bring your child with you. Just hurry up." She glanced at Laura. "You, too." Standing in the path of the men, she ordered, "Stay here. This is between us," then she and Isadora guided Laura and Becca and Rachel inside Siren Song's grounds with the others, closing the gate behind them.

"Bullshit!" Harrison said, trying to shove himself forward, but Hudson placed a staying hand on the crook of his elbow. "I'm not leaving Laura to—"

"Let it go," Hudson said.

"The hell with that."

"We'll be right here," Hudson called after Catherine. His lips were a thin blade. "If there's trouble, we'll warn you."

"What the hell is this?" Harrison demanded of Hudson.

"Let's just see if they can help my daughter," he said. "I don't have any problem waiting at the gate in case that sick bastard should show up."

Catherine gave a curt nod to Hudson and seemed suddenly ten years older than her years. Becca, holding Rachel close, walked briskly up the path, and Laura wondered how desperate she was to bring her child here, knowing that Justice was nearby. Waiting. Lurking. Breathing death for every one of them.

Sliding her key into the hidden pocket in her skirts, Catherine shepherded them along the path, keeping one eye on the gate, as if she expected to see Satan and his legions marching up the drive.

Once inside the house, introductions were made quickly. Becca met her sisters as if for the first time. She explained that the man who was with her was, indeed, her husband, Hudson Walker. The women who greeted her offered up their names: Isadora, Cassandra, Ravinia, Ophelia, and Lillibeth, all blond or ash brown, all blue-eyed, all curious. There were still others, too, and some like Laura and Becca, who hadn't spent all their lives here; some dead, some missing, but all ghosts who seemed to be a part of these old timbers.

This time Catherine didn't shoo the younger girls upstairs but led the visitors into the large gathering room off the front hall, opposite the dining room and dominated by a stone fireplace that rose two full stories to the gallery above. A fire was banked, the smell of smoldering ashes heavy in the air. The furniture was old, a hodgepodge of pieces gathered over the last hundred years. Everything from Victorian settees to sleek midcentury sofas.

Catherine closed the heavy drapes and waved them into the ancient chairs and sofas that were spread around the room. She turned on a few lamps, old Tiffany style, which gave off muted, colored light, then stood near the grate. Lillibeth hung near the doorway, and Ophelia, whom Laura hadn't seen the last time she was here, took a seat on the hearth. Her eyes were round with fear, and she rubbed her arms constantly, as if chilled from the inside out.

Catherine's gaze fell upon the girl in Becca's arms. Rachel's hair was darker than her mother's, but her eyes were a deep green, her skin white as porcelain. Her expression softened. "You're concerned because Rachel is fussy and feverish," she guessed, "though there is no medical explanation for her condition."

Becca nodded, surprised and encouraged. "Everything was fine for the first fifteen months of her life and then . . . then things changed. Now she can't sleep at night. I find her staring off into space during the day. She . . . is warm to the touch. . . ." Gently she brushed a strand of Rachel's hair off her chubby cheek.

"But you suspect that she might be like you. Or one of your sisters," Catherine whispered, and Becca, tears forming in her eyes, nodded again.

"Yes."

"Would that be so bad?"

"I just want my daughter to be safe and happy," Becca said. "It would be difficult if she were different. I'm not sure Hudson would understand, but more than that, I just want to know, I mean we both want to know, that she's all right."

"Of course she is," Catherine said, her voice strangely soft. "She has the gift, that's all." She smiled with a bit of melancholy. "She'll be fine."

"I need to know more," Becca urged as, cradling Rachel, she lowered herself onto a worn claw-footed settee that looked as if it was nearly a hundred years old. "You've tried so hard to keep the secrets here, but now . . . because of Rachel, I have to know everything."

"It's best that you don't."

"I have questions and she will, too."

Catherine sighed.

"I'm afraid . . . I'm afraid, *he'll* find her." Becca's voice broke and Laura felt a pang of guilt. "I need to know what happened to my mother. How did Mary die?. And I don't even know my father's name." Becca glanced at the women who were her sisters, and all of them, including Laura, turned to Catherine, hoping for answers.

"Harrison . . . he's the man outside, read the history that apparently a man named Herman Smythe wrote," Laura said.

"So did I." Becca was nodding. "But there's so much that isn't in those pages."

Catherine restlessly walked to the windows, parted the draperies, and looked through the glass. "I've dreaded this day. I've only kept the secrets here at Siren Song to protect you, and I can't explain everything. There isn't enough time, and I don't even know all the truth. What I can tell you is that you all have the same mother. My sister, Mary. You know this. She . . . was . . . promiscuous." Her lips tightened. "And perhaps . . . not completely sane. I don't know who your fathers were. I'm sorry. Mary probably knew, but she didn't love men. She used them." Catherine gazed through the slit in the draperies, but, Laura guessed, she wasn't seeing the grounds outside or the wall surrounding the complex, but was staring at something in the middle distance, something only she could envision . . . images from a different past. "And not long after the youngest of you was born, she died. Mary was walking out on the bluff, which she'd done often. She took a misstep and fell onto a rocky ledge about twenty feet down. The fall shouldn't have killed her, but she struck her head on an exposed root or rock. By the time we realized she wasn't returning, that she was missing, it was late, and dark. We found her, but it was too late. She'd already passed."

There was silence for a moment while they absorbed this information. Then Becca said, "I couldn't find an obituary. Or a death certificate."

"Because there were none. We buried her in the family plot, here at Siren Song, with the previous generations."

Becca stated flatly, "I think that's illegal."

Catherine shrugged. She was rarely threatened by what was legal and what wasn't in the outside world. "You mustn't keep digging into the past, looking for answers, uprooting scandals." She looked at Becca. "There's no reason for it. No good will come of it."

Laura remembered Mary's grave. She'd seen it as a child, a moss-and-lichen-covered, graying tombstone marking the final resting place of the woman who had borne her, a woman she barely remembered.

"I'd like to see the cemetery," Becca said, but Catherine closed the draperies tight and shook her head.

"Right now we have to concentrate on staying safe, making sure Justice is captured. I've known him since he was a boy and probably realize better than any of his doctors just how sick he is, how twisted." She worried the draperies' edge with her fingers. "Rebecca, you and your daughter can stay here. You, too, Lorelei. He'll suspect you're here, but this place is a fortress."

"Even the strongest fortress can be breached," Laura said. "And what do we do? Just wait? Hope the authorities catch him?"

"What else?" Catherine asked, her gaze finding Laura's.

Laura shivered inside, wondering if Catherine suspected that she not only had the ability to "hear" Justice's mental rantings, but that she could call to him as well, taunt him, flush him out. "I don't know."

"I can't just hide here," Becca argued.

"No one asked you to come, Becca. You insisted," Catherine reminded her.

"I had to come. Not just because of Rachel, but . . . Justice and all of this. I've been having visions again, and this time it's Lorelei he's after." Becca regarded Laura a bit guiltily. "And then I knew he'd attacked you and . . . I should have come earlier." She held her daughter closer. "I was just so frightened for Rachel."

"I'll be all right," Laura said. She was already feeling pent-up, as if they were all huddled in a storm cellar, waiting for a devastating twister to threaten them all. She knew she couldn't just sit here and wait.

Should she tell Catherine that she could talk to Justice? That it was possible to goad him into some kind of trap? Catherine and her sisters might believe her, whereas the sheriff's department wouldn't.

She walked to the settee where Becca was seated and placed a hand on Rachel's forehead, which was a little warm, perhaps, but smooth as silk. "I'm a nurse," she said. "If there's anything I can do . . ."

Becca smiled. "Just tell me she's going to be all right."

"Of course she is," Laura said, though they both knew, as long as Justice Turnbull was alive, it was a lie.

# CHAPTER 36

*So close.*
*I came so close.*

*I can still feel the knife in my hand as I chased her through the night. My hand throbs from where she stabbed me; the cuts upon my skin are shallow and stinging from breaking the window of her door.*

*How had I let her escape when I was so close . . . ?*

*It was because of the man she was with, not her husband, but the reporter! I'd sensed him through her mind, the one she thinks of as "the truth seeker." It was easy enough to identify him and find out where he works, where he lives . . . all compliments of the library computers.*

*At first I thought I'd been recognized, but my disguise and the librarian's obvious myopia allowed me free access.*

*But my failure to kill Lorelei and her growing bastard is an onus, one I must throw off.*

*Her smell is overpowering. A stench that burns through my nostrils and burrows deep in my soul. There are more of them now . . . The one who got away . . . Becca . . . is back, her child in tow. I feel her and know she is afraid.*

*Good. This is good. They, too, must be destroyed. . . .*

*It took hour upon hour to make my way back to the bait*

*shop and the rat's den where I reside, but I'm here. I'm back.
And there is a vehicle I can "borrow," one never used and
parked near the boat landing, owned by that blind old fool
Carter. . . . It's parked far from the security lights. . . . I only
have to wait until darkness falls. . . .*

A headache pounds behind my eyes and my stomach
rumbles, reminding me it's been hours since I've eaten. The
money I found in both Cosmo's wallet and the van driver's
jacket is nearly gone. . . . I will need more.

My mind wanders back to that reporter. He wants to fornicate with Lorelei. My fists clench. Fornicate with the
witch whose seed is already growing inside her!

*I need to kill her . . . kill them all. . . .*

My thoughts are scattered . . . falling away, and I have
to work to snatch them back, pull them together. I breathe
deeply, but here, locked in my soiled room over the bait
shop, I feel confined and weak. . . . I find the hilt of the
butcher knife, *her* knife, and run my fingers along its
smooth shaft.

Now, in my mind's eye, I can see them, Satan's whores,
gathered together, plotting, scheming, thinking they can
outwit me. . . .

Their images run together.

Ashen hair . . .

Steely blue eyes . . .

Sharp little chins . . .

Rosebud lips that curl back to reveal tiny, needlelike
fangs . . . cat's teeth . . .

As ever, they hurl their childish taunts and razor-sharp
insults at me:

"Bastard!" one says with a high-pitched giggle.

"Idiot!" another cackles, delight sparking in her blue,
blue eyes. She feels naughty and oh, so smug.

"Cretin!" another rejoins to twitter at how clever she is.

"Changeling!" they cry in unison, as a chorus that re-

*sounds in my head, echoing with their wicked laughter.
"Changeling! Changeling! Changeling!" Their malicious
glee sends them into uproarious gales of hurtful laughter,
and I run, faster and faster, away from them, along the
ridge over the sea, to the cabins . . . and the lighthouse beyond. . . .*

*The call of a seagull brings me back to this, my wreck of
a room reeking of fish and diesel. My hands are knotted in
the grimy folds of the stolen coat on which I am lying. I stare
out the cobwebbed window high overhead and see a seagull
whirling in the cerulean sky.*

*It's time to end this.*

*Forever.*

*"Ssssissttters," I hiss, but the effort is weak and my own
words ricochet back to me, bouncing through my brain.
Lorelei has put up a wall against me, just as Catherine has
secured the walls around Siren Song. . . .*

*But I will get through. I have a plan. . . .*

*I need to go to the sea.*

*To feel the caress of the salt air and hear the roar of
waves thundering against the shore in my heart.*

*I will be restored.*

*I will be strong.*

*And I will kill.*

*I feel a thrill at this, a sizzle of anticipation, and I run
my finger along the knife's long blade. A line of scarlet
blooms along my fingertip, which I examine carefully, then
suck the wound, tasting the salt of my own blood.*

*Yes, yes. It's time. . . .*

Laura and Becca walked along an overgrown path where
sunlight, piercing the lacy branches overhead, dappled the
ground. Beneath their feet curls of mist rose from the damp
forest floor and through the trees; glinting along the hori-

zon was the steely Pacific Ocean. Becca carried Rachel, and the little girl eyed her surroundings suspiciously, though she didn't say a word.

In the past few hours, Laura had become reacquainted with most of her sisters again and gotten to know Becca, whose name had only been whispered while she was growing up. More than that, she'd been able to hold Rachel, even scaring up a smile on the little girl's face. To think that Justice would want to harm any of them, especially this innocent child, was incomprehensible.

Before she and Becca had started their walk through the grounds of Siren Song, she'd left her cell phone number with Catherine, in case they needed to get in touch. Just to ensure her aunt didn't misplace the number, she'd given it to Isadora as well.

Catherine hadn't written it down.

Isadora had.

"Here it is," Laura finally said when she spied the short fence that surrounded the small private cemetery on the eastern side of the lodge. As Catherine had told them, their earliest relatives rested here, those who died before the turn of the *last* century. The graveyard was all but forgotten by everyone except those who lived at Siren Song. Hidden deep in the old growth, high on a ledge, with a rickety fence covered with berry vines and offering little barrier, the cemetery boasted only a smattering of tombstones, marble monoliths or slabs that had grown gray and had disintegrated over time, the names and dates blurred with dirt. There were small, plain crosses and more elaborate stones decorated with angels or rings or flowers, even the Bible.

"I'm just amazed I'm finally inside," Becca said, picking her way through a winding blackberry vine that nearly covered the gate. "The sound of the ocean is closer here."

"Just your imagination."

"Peony Jane," she said aloud, reading the small headstone. "Darling daughter, birth March seventeenth, eighteen seventy-

three, died October thirty-first, eighteen seventy-five." She
held tight to her own little girl and said, "A child. How awful."

"The worst." Laura wended through the markers, some
decorated with crosses or angels or an open Bible, and the
smaller headstones, indicating the plots of children who
had passed in an earlier century.

"Here it is," she said as she reached the moss-covered
plot where Mary was buried. The headstone, that of an
angel looking down, wings folded, was chipped and blackened; part of one wing, cracked. The inscription was simple: MARY RUTLEDGE BEEMAN, LOVING MOTHER, then the
dates of her birth and death.

"I hardly remember her," Laura admitted. "I was about
ten but the memories I have are blurry and I'm not sure if
they're real or dreams or even something someone told me
about that I turned into memory."

"I never knew her," Becca said softly.

Of course she hadn't. Becca had been adopted as a baby
and had grown up in a "normal" family and attended St.
Elizabeth's Catholic School in Portland. She'd been unaware of Siren Song, of the old lodge of a house, of the surrounding walls, of this very cemetery until just recently.

"Why are there no public records of her birth and
death?" Becca asked.

"Because everything here is a secret."

"Or a lie," Becca said, staring down at the final resting
place of their mother. "All we know is what Catherine
deigns to tell us and the haphazard ramblings in that book
by someone named Smythe. Who's to say if it's accurate, or
even partially true? All we really know is that we're related,
that mostly only women survive, and that all of us now, if
Catherine's correct, including Rachel, have some telepathic
gift." She shook her head and sighed. "And then there's Justice Turnbull."

Laura glanced at Rachel, the girl's eyes round as she

squirmed in her mother's arms. "And then there's Justice," she repeated.

"I wish there was some way to find him, to catch him . . . to . . ."

"Kill him?" Laura asked and felt a frisson of fear touch the back of her neck. She remembered how he'd chased her, how intent he'd been on destroying her, the feel of him so close. . . . The sound of the ocean's roar reached her ears.

"He's planning to kill us. All of us. Including . . ." She stopped herself and looked away. Laura understood that Becca was speaking about her child, and she thought of her own and how Justice wanted nothing more than to snuff out her own child's life before she was even born.

Becca's gaze was troubled, but she stated passionately, "I would do anything to save my child, Lorelei. *Anything*. And if it means going up against Justice and taking him down, then so be it." The set of her jaw was determined; her lips flattened fiercely. She meant it.

A squirrel chattered from somewhere in the higher branches, and at that moment, Laura heard Justice's voice. That horrid sibilant rasp seeming to slide like snakes through the surrounding trees and into her brain.

*Ssssisstersss.*

Plural.

Damn. He knew that Becca was near her, and though his voice was weaker than she remembered, she closed her eyes and pushed up the wall around her mind.

"Laura?" Becca's voice came to her as if from a long distance. "Hey! Laura!" Sharper now.

Laura blinked and found her sister staring at her. Becca's eyes were round with worry as she touched Laura's shoulder. "For a second, I thought . . ." She didn't finish the sentence.

"He just tried to contact me."

"What?"

"I think he knows that you and Rachel are here."

"Oh, God." Becca's face paled.

"You have to leave. Go far away." Laura was insistent. "Take Rachel back to Laurelton, somewhere safe. Somewhere Justice doesn't know about. He won't go there, at least not until he's dealt with me. He'll be looking for me first."

*He smells them when they're pregnant.*

"I can't just let you face him."

"I won't. The police will handle it. I'll be safe," she said firmly. "You have visions. I hear him. You can call me anytime, but really, it's best if you leave." She glanced around the cemetery and beyond. Even the walls of Siren Song weren't strong enough. "It would be best. For you and for Rachel."

Becca seemed about to argue, but her daughter started to squirm and fuss.

"Let me deal with him," Laura told her.

"I think it's better if we stand together," Becca said, but at that moment Rachel, tired of being hauled around, cried, "Down!" Laura's gaze skated to her niece, then returned to Becca. The unspoken question—how would you feel if something happened to her?—filled the silent space between them.

Laura said softly but strongly, "You know what he can do. You've seen it firsthand. So, please, leave. I'll keep in contact with you. Promise. But you have to go home. Or somewhere very far from here."

"Down, Mommy!" Rachel insisted.

"We're going back now, honey," Becca said and started walking swiftly out of the cemetery, Rachel squirming in her arms. Only when they were in the clearing again did she turn to Laura. "Okay," she said, "but you have to keep in contact with me. You've got my phone number."

"I will," Laura promised.

They saw Hudson and Harrison, both still waiting outside the gate. Becca headed that way, and Laura gave Harrison a high sign, signaling that she was going back inside to say good-bye to Catherine and her sisters but would be out soon.

She vowed inwardly that she would find a way to thwart Justice. That he wouldn't stop hunting them until they were all dead was a foregone conclusion, and it was a miracle that, so far, since his escape, no one associated with the Colony had been harmed.

But it was only a matter of time.

Unless she got the better of the bastard.

"I don't like us being separated," Harrison said as he pulled into the employee lot at Ocean Park Hospital. Laura's Outback was where she'd parked it the day before, and in broad daylight nothing appeared sinister.

"I'm just going inside and straightening things out with my supervisor," she insisted and placed a hand over his, and he remembered how close he'd come to making love to her. "I'll meet you back at my house and tell you all about my family."

"You better."

She glanced at her watch and frowned. He noticed then the dark circles under her eyes, how white her skin had become. "The glass guy is gonna be there in less than an hour."

"Fine." Harrison took the hint. "I'll meet him."

"I'll be there soon." She reached for the door handle, but he caught her wrist.

"You're okay?"

She laughed without humor, and her gaze, when it found his, was troubled. "What do you think?"

"We'll get through this," he promised.

"One way or another," she said, then leaned forward and kissed him. Her lips were warm and supple, and he drew her into his arms, sliding his tongue between her lips and feeling his blood temperature become elevated.

"Hurry back," he said and she actually smiled.

"I will."

Then she drew away and was out the door, hurrying toward the front doors of Ocean Park.

Once he saw that she was inside, Harrison drove out of the parking lot to the highway. He'd spent most of the morning pacing outside the gates of Siren Song, getting to know the rancher Hudson Walker, husband to one of Laura's half sisters, and certain that somehow, someway, Justice Turnbull would know that Laura was inside. He couldn't shake the feeling that somehow Turnbull would find her and harm her. Hudson Walker couldn't have agreed more. He'd expected the rancher from Laurelton to scoff at his anxiety, but that hadn't been the case. Hudson, too, was worried, had seen close hand what damage the maniac could wreak, and wanted no part of it.

Hudson had driven to Siren Song under protest; he wanted his wife and child as far from Justice Turnbull as possible. But Becca had been insistent, and Hudson had agreed, only if he came with her. He admitted that his wife could be "mule-headed" but didn't have to explain any further. Harrison knew firsthand how stubborn a woman from the Colony could be.

Which was odd, he thought as he drove through the S curves high above the Pacific. The ocean was calmer today, sunlight shimmering on the shifting water, but along the horizon he noticed a dark swelling, clouds rolling inland and promising another storm.

Harrison had known Laura—Lorelei—less than a week, and yet there was something about her that touched a part of him he hadn't known existed, something about it that seemed emotionally dangerous in its own right.

The house was just as they'd left it. Quiet. Secluded. *Too secluded,* he decided as he found his tool belt in the trunk and, using her key, began cleaning up, then working on the lock. The repairman for the glass window showed up about forty-five minutes later, surveyed the damage, and shook his head.

"It's gonna need a little more work than I thought," he said. "The sash is busted, so it'll cost ya about the same to fix as a new window." He pointed to the area that would have held the pane of glass in place, his finger running along the broken piece of wood.

"Just fix it so that it's secure," Harrison said, and the guy got to work. While the window was being replaced, Harrison finished with the lock on the back door and double-checked every window latch in the house. He figured the landlord wouldn't mind the changes, and it really was too damned bad if he did.

Laura straightened things out with the shift manager by promising to work a double tonight and tomorrow morning. The woman was still a little miffed but turned her attention to the coming week's schedule and made the necessary adjustments.

It hadn't been as rough a meeting as Laura had expected, yet she still felt a little off, not quite right. Just as she had all day. She blamed her malaise on the events of the last week, her brush with Justice, the emotional highs and lows of visiting Siren Song. Her pregnancy also was a factor, as were her conflicted feelings for Harrison.

She needed to tell him about the baby. Come clean. She remembered kissing him and wanting so much more.

"Laura!"

She was walking toward the lobby when she heard Byron's voice seeming to boom down the hallway.

Inwardly groaning, she turned and saw him, dressed not in scrubs, but slacks, jacket, and open-necked shirt, as he strode toward her. The expression on his face was accusatory, his jaw so hard, a muscle was working overtime beneath his chin.

"What happened?" he demanded almost angrily.

She thought of everything she'd been through in the past few days. Had he heard Justice had attacked her? That her home had been broken into? That she was spending a lot of time with Harrison?

"You didn't return for your shift last night, and the damned shift nurse called *me*. She wanted to know where you were, said you'd abandoned your patients—"

"She didn't say that," Laura cut in, too tired of his BS to listen to another word. "I had the shift covered and she knew it."

"But why?"

"I was with the sheriff's department. Explaining that the house had been broken into, that Justice Turnbull had tried to kill me."

"What?" All the wind was suddenly out of his sails. "Turnbull's after you? Why?" he asked; then his expression darkened. "Because you're part of that Colony."

"You knew?"

"Suspected," Byron snapped. "My God, I can't believe this. You're a professional and I'm a doctor. I can't . . . defend . . . all of that."

"We're divorced, remember?"

His lips tightened. "You're still connected to me, Laura. And if you're carrying my child, then things are even stickier. And, for the record, you even still have my last name. So be careful. Some people think we're still married!"

"Then make sure you let them know we're divorced. Wouldn't want to tarnish your rep." She was shaking her head as his cell phone beeped and he glanced down at the number. "Me being from the cult and all."

# CHAPTER 37

Mike Ferguson wasn't about to wait around for his dickhead of a brother to grow a pair. Not when Justice friggin' Turnbull was on the loose. He lay on his bed and tossed a tennis ball upward, seeing how close he could come without actually hitting the ceiling and catching it, only to toss it again.

How cool would it be if he could get a picture of the psycho? Or grab some kind of memento from one of his lairs? Or even help bring the bastard down?

He snapped the ball from the air, then let it drop as he rolled over and hopped off the bed to look at the wall over his desk. He had cut out articles about Justice Turnbull and had pictures tacked to the wall. Justice Turnbull's mug shot, a picture of the shabby old motel where he'd nearly killed his mother, and the lighthouse perched on the island known as Serpent's Eye.

Man, would he love to go there. Just to look around. Maybe climb the steps to the top and look out to sea . . . and take some pictures, of course. He could do it easily on his iPhone.

He'd impress a lot of kids at school then.

Maybe even James.

The jerk.

Mike kinda knew that he was suffering from what James had called "nerdy delusions of grandeur," which said something as those were pretty big words for James's vocabulary. But Mike wasn't about to be thwarted. His parents would be returning home over the weekend, and then the opportunity to go to the coast would be over. No way would they let James drive over to Deception Bay for a day.

If only he had his license. He wouldn't wuss out like James.

He could steal the keys, he supposed, while James was sleeping, but he'd eventually be caught, and it wasn't like he had a driver's license or even a learner's permit. But really, how hard could it be to drive? Stick in the key, twist on the ignition, find the right radio station, and put the car into the gear. Then all you had to do was hit the gas, right?

His mother did it while on the phone and eating a snack bar, so Mikey figured he could handle it.

But he'd rather not add grand theft auto or anything near it to his growing list of sins. His mom would kill him.

No, the best thing to do would be to try and convince James that the trip was necessary, but James had been in a real bad mood the last few days. Still, Mike tried again, walking into his brother's bedroom and finding James lying on his bed, flipping through channels on the televison while playing a game on his iPhone.

"No!" James said before even looking up at Mike in the doorway.

"You don't know what I'm gonna ask."

"Sure I do. You wanna go to the coast and me to drive you. Well, forget it." He frowned as he stared at the phone in his hand.

"I already told you how cool it would be. And we have to go right away. In two days the tide is going to be the lowest of the year."

"So what?"

"So then it's easier to get to Justice Turnbull's lighthouse. We can walk across the rocks, maybe."

"How do you know all this crap?" James grumbled. "And why do you care? Oh, I forgot. Cuz you're an obsessed freak."

"I'm not—"

"Are you kiddin' me? Listen to yourself. You want to wade out in the ocean to go to an abandoned lighthouse where a serial killer used to live. Wait, no, make that a serial killer who's currently on the loose again and killing people." James rolled over onto his back. "Do you know how nuts that is?"

"He won't go there. The cops will be all over it."

"Then the cops'll catch you!"

"They won't be looking for me."

"You're a moron, you know that?" James threw his brother a look of pure disgust. "I said, 'No way,' so leave me the hell alone."

"But—"

"Look, dickwad, it's not gonna happen." His phone must've vibrated, because he picked up the call and got caught up in it.

Mike took the hint and headed back to his bedroom. If James wouldn't drive him, he'd find another way. In fact, he was already making a plan. "You're just scared," he called over his shoulder.

"You're just a dumb shit." A football rocketed out the door, and Mike dived to the floor. The ball smacked against the hallway wall, leaving a mark. Mom would be pissed. But then she was gonna be really mad, anyway, if she ever figured out that Mike intended to hitchhike to the beach.

Catherine stood at the bedroom window on the west end of the lodge. From her vantage point on the second floor, she was able to see through the trees to the ocean, glittering in the afternoon sun. Far off, on the horizon, a stubborn bank of clouds threatened to roll inland, bringing with it drizzle and fog, staving off summer for a few more days.

Things had become complicated again, perhaps more complicated than before. There was the visit from Becca and Lorelei; that in and of itself was disturbing. And Catherine had witnessed the expressions on the rest of her charges, especially Ravinia, who was forever stroking her long blond hair. She'd glowered a bit, and Catherine sensed she was readying to leave. Cassandra had warned her, and Catherine could see the rebellion in Ravinia's expression, the way she'd listened hungrily to Becca and Laura. With Ravinia, who had always been disobedient and questioning, it was only a matter of time before she bolted. Catherine wouldn't be able to stop her.

Ophelia had appeared a little wary, but then that was her nature.

Lillibeth was the most troubling, as the girl, confined as she was to her chair, desperately wanted her freedom, yet she was slow to develop, filled with innocence and naïveté, the kind the outside world took advantage of. Still, she knew there was something out there beyond the walls of Siren Song, and she was chafing at the bit, expecting a world of joy, excitement, and answers, perhaps even help for her condition. She had no knowledge of society's cruelty, how even in times when people were supposed to be "enlightened" and "politically correct," there was still so much hatred, hostility, and distrust.

And then there was the very real, very physical threat of Justice Turnbull.

Catherine, though sometimes considered a jailer, was a pacifist. The old shotgun hidden in the attic had been left there for years; now, however, she'd gone so far as to clean and polish the gun and kept it ready at her bedside. She also had a smaller weapon, garnered from one of Mary's lovers, and she'd placed that handgun in the cabinet in the dining room, hidden behind the silver platter that was used only on special occasions. It was loaded and ready. Pacifist or no, if Justice came for them, she wouldn't think twice about blowing the bastard away.

Anyone who intended to harm any of the women she cared for would have to go through her to get to them. That was just the way it was.

Or had been.

She sensed the life she'd carved out for herself, for the others, was about to change. She only hoped all the girls would be able to adapt to life outside these carefully tended walls when the time came.

Most of the girls were in their rooms now, before dinner. Studying or reading, talking to each other, but observing the quiet time Catherine had insisted upon since she'd been in charge. She took advantage of this time now to hurry down the stairs and outside.

Into the forest she walked. Briskly through the thick ferns and clumps of salal, past berry vines that stretched forward with their thorny vines and under the looming, mossy firs, their branches spreading wide, squirrels scolding from the branches.

Earlier she'd seen Becca and Lorelei walk this same path to the cemetery, watched as they'd huddled over Mary's grave.

Oh, Lord.

That was the trouble with lies, Catherine thought as she passed through the gate and into the small cemetery. If one began to unravel, the whole fabric would soon fray and the ugly truth would be revealed. She eased around some of the plots, images of those who had died sliding behind her eyes, then stopped at the spot where Mary's grave was marked, where once, years before, the earth had been turned and a coffin lowered into a dark hole.

Though some of her children might have been too young to remember the lowering of the ornate pine box, or dropping flowers onto the glossy lid as rain began to fall from the sky, they had stood and watched the loamy earth and sand being shoveled over the coffin.

Catherine remembered.

Once again she felt that old animosity, that depth of fury boiling through her blood, as she thought of her sister's callousness, her disregard for those children she had brought into the world.

Mary, in her own way, had been a monster.

And so, Catherine had killed her. Oh, not physically, of course. Killed her memory. And that was when the lying had begun, here, in this forgotten graveyard where Mary's casket now rotted, nothing inside it but stones.

Mary, or what was left of the woman whose mind had slowly soured upon her, was still very much alive.

In exile.

Trapped on a solitary little island beyond the rocky dot of land known as Serpent's Eye, where the lighthouse stood. Mary's island was just as small and even harder to reach, so no one ever bothered but Catherine, in Earl's boat.

Mary lived there in a life of solitude, and none of her daughters knew it.

Now Catherine peered through the surrounding stands of fir and hemlock, to the peekaboo view of the ocean. Here, where large rocks, capricious winds, and high tides made travel difficult at best, it had been easy enough to get rid of her sister. Her gaze centered on her sister's island, the one that had been named Echo Island by the locals for the way the sound refracted off the island's sharply planed rock walls. Earl, who had worked for the Colony most of his life, had been there the most recently to drop off supplies.

Catherine couldn't remember the last time she'd seen Mary.

"Dear God," she whispered, closing her eyes and praying that none of Mary's daughters ever learned of what she'd done.

* * *

The first cramp cut through Laura's abdomen as she stood in line at the deli counter of the Drift In Market, the store where she'd worked as a teenager. One second she was peering through the glass case in the deli department and trying to decide between the turkey on sourdough or the ham on rye sandwich, and the next a dull, swift pain was searing through her.

"No," she said aloud, and the girl behind the counter glanced up, her knife poised over the hero she was about to halve.

"Excuse me?"

"Nothing." Laura held up a hand and made her way to the restroom near the back of the market. Fortunately it was free. She bolted the lock and tried to convince herself that she was wrong, that she hadn't felt the contraction, that she wasn't miscarrying . . . but the evidence was there.

She was spotting.

*Oh, please . . . no . . .*

The sharp pains, cramping as if from a heavy period, slicing through her lower torso weren't a good sign. She knew what was happening, and she also knew it wasn't uncommon to miscarry within the first two months of pregnancy. Still, it shocked her just the same, and she wanted to deny it, to fix whatever was broken inside her, to save the precious life that had barely begun to form.

But there was too much blood. She waited as long as she could, buying supplies inside the bathroom, crying silently. Empty and alone, she experienced a piercing grief to the point that she couldn't move for almost an hour. People jiggled the door handle but she didn't answer.

When she could, she walked numbly out of the store, lunch forgotten, and drove straight to her house without consciously being aware of the other cars and bicyclists traveling along the road.

All her thoughts were concentrated on the tiny life that she'd so desperately wanted. But it was too late . . . too late. . . .

Harrison had just finished with the lock on the back door, and the new window was in place when she arrived. She managed a weak smile for him but dodged a longer embrace. "Give me a sec," she said, then grabbed some clean clothes from her closet and locked herself in her bathroom, where the signs of her miscarriage continued.

She'd lost the baby.

Tears filled her eyes and her throat swelled shut.

Sadness clamped around her soul.

She'd only known she was pregnant for a week, and yet she'd felt such a bond with this baby, such hope for their future.

Twisting on the handles on the shower, she bit back her sobs. Stripping out of her clothes, she stepped under the needles of hot water; then, once the water was loud enough to muffle her voice, she let go, crying softly as the warm spray washed over her muscles.

*No! No! No!*

*This can't be happening!*

*Please, God, spare this poor little innocent!*

Her shoulders shook with her sobs.

With everything that had happened to her in the last week, losing the baby was, by far, the worst. She'd wanted a child for years, and even though she and Byron were divorced and she would have to raise the little girl alone, she hadn't cared. But . . . oh, dear God . . . She leaned against the tiles and felt the water ease her muscles. A part of her wanted to deny what was happening, but she couldn't.

She wasn't just spotting; she was having a full-blown heavy period.

There was nothing to be done but accept her loss.

It would take time.

A lot of time.

She slid down the wall and sat, arms over her knees, on the floor of the tub as the water ran over her.

"You bastard," she said, as if Justice could hear her. "You damned son of a bitching bastard!" Her fist curled and she called to him again. Using all her strength, she closed her eyes and sent out the warning.

*Come and get me, you freak. Just try to come and get me!*

And then, spent, she shut him out. If it weren't for him, chasing her down the hill, terrifying her in her own home, sending out his hate-filled, hissing messages, she might not have lost the baby.

Fury and grief twisting her insides, she turned off the taps and, shivering, wrapped herself in a huge towel.

*Bastard! Bastard! Bastard!*

The mirror over the sink was fogged from the steam in the bathroom. Even so, she saw her reflection through the mist. Wan skin, eyes that were puffy and red, a mouth that was a line of sadness, grief etched in the small lines of her face—and something more. Something deeper and darker than her sadness was the fierce determination to destroy the monster who had tried to ruin her life, the maniac who had taunted her for almost a week.

*No more!*

*Never again!*

Placing her hands on the sink's rim, she forced herself to take in deep breaths as water from her wet hair dripped into the basin.

She heard a tap on the door. "Hey," Harrison said, his voice filled with concern. "Are you okay?"

"Fine," she lied, loud enough that he could hear her. "I'll—I'll be out in a second."

*Pull it together, Lorelei. You have to pull it together. No matter what.* She squeezed her eyes shut and tried not to think of the little life that hadn't made it, and as she did, the fury, in a full-blown blood red cloud, filled her mind.

"Okay," he said uncertainly, and she felt a fresh onslaught of hot tears burning the back of her eyelids. She fought them off as she dried off and stepped into fresh clothes. New underwear, jeans, and a V-necked sweater. She wiped the condensation from the mirror so that she could better view the damage, then pulled her hair into a ponytail, slapped on lipstick, and tried to hide the damage tears had done to her eyes with liner and mascara. She knew she should probably contact her doctor, but what was there to be done, really? Her body had done its part. It was over.

Eventually, she pulled herself together and walked out of the bathroom to find Harrison seated on her couch, his laptop open on the coffee table.

"Big story?" she asked.

"Yeah, I've almost made it to another level of backgammon." He cracked a smile, and she forced one in return but turned away, not ready for his scrutiny. There was a part of her that wanted to tumble into his arms and cling to him, to blurt out the truth, to tell him of her pain, but she had to hold back. She hadn't told him about the baby when she'd thought she'd be a mother; there just was no reason to bring it up now. One question would lead to another, and another, and eventually they would end up discussing her ex-husband and how she'd gotten pregnant.

"Hungry?" he asked, climbing to his feet.

"Starved," she lied.

"Me, too." He glanced around the house. "Maybe you should pack some things. I changed the lock and the window's back in the door, but until Turnbull is caught, this place isn't secure."

"It is my home." She looked at the living room with its worn matching chairs and couch with sagging pillows. Books lined the shelves around the fireplace, a few pieces of abstract art splashed color on the walls, and the faded rug covering the hardwood floors gave the place what she thought of as eclectic chic.

"I know, but if you insist on staying here, I'm moving in."

"Okay," she said. He was clearly surprised by her rapid capitulation, so she said, "Justice tried to contact me earlier, while I was with Becca in the graveyard. I shut him out. But today I called to him."

"What? Without me?"

"I'm tired of running, Harrison. Let's face the bastard. I'm ready."

# CHAPTER 38

"**A**re you out of your mind?" Harrison demanded, double-checking that the locks were secure. "You called that psycho?"

"It was originally your idea, remember?"

"That's before I thought you could really do it," he admitted.

"When you were trying to get info for your story."

"Well . . . yes . . ." God, he'd been such a fool. Now she was on the warpath, determined to come face-to-face with the maniac who had nearly sliced her to ribbons. "But then he came here and nearly killed you and . . . now you're calling and taunting him again? Laura, you don't have to do this." He put a hand on her shoulder, but she shrugged him off.

"Don't try to distract me. It won't work. I can't live the rest of my life in fear," she said evenly, and he wondered what had transformed her. Had it been meeting with her sisters at Siren Song? Visiting Mary's grave? Something Catherine had said? Whatever the case, now Laura was on some kind of mission.

At least that was what it looked like to Harrison.

Gone was the frightened, worried Laura he'd first met,

and in her place was a determined, fire-in-her-eyes woman who was ready to do battle, it seemed, at any cost.

"When I was talking to Becca, I heard his voice. It was weaker, maybe because I was with one of my sisters, I don't know, but he found me, and I'm sick of it, sick of living in fear, sick of him being able to terrorize me. Sick of *him*."

"The police—"

"Don't know him like I do and they don't know that we communicate." Before he could even suggest that she confide in Stone or Dunbar, she held up a hand. "They wouldn't believe me if I told them, so don't even go there. They've promised me protection, and I'm pretty sure they're keeping this house under watch, so I'm safer here than a lot of places."

"Not twenty-four/seven, they're not," Harrison reminded. "This is no sanctuary."

"Agreed. Not for me. Nor my sisters. Any wall around Siren Song isn't strong enough to keep him out, either." She leveled her calm gaze at him. "He has to be stopped."

He wouldn't be able to change her mind. He could see that clearly. "I've got a gun," he admitted. "And a license to carry it. It's locked in my apartment."

"Why the hell don't you have it on you?"

He thought of the violence he'd seen in his life; how his brother-in-law had been gunned down, an innocent victim, one homicide victim among the hundreds across the country in recent times. "I didn't think we needed it, until the other night."

"And now?"

"I'll get it."

"Good."

Harrison gathered up his laptop and belongings while she, grudgingly, packed an overnight bag. Then they drove to a restaurant in Cannon Beach, where they ate chowder served in hollowed-out sourdough bowls and watched the sun play tag with the clouds. She told him more about the meeting at Siren Song and that she had to work a couple of shifts, but he felt that she was holding back, that there was something more, a secret, behind the sadness in her gaze and the determined set of her jaw.

Once back at her house, they split up. She headed to Ocean Park, and he, though he didn't like it, drove on to Seaside to put in some hours at the *Breeze,* then to stop by his apartment for his pistol. All the while he was nervous and on edge. He told himself that Laura was safe at the hospital, that Justice wouldn't risk an attack where there were so many people around, so many cameras, a place the police would be monitoring.

He pulled into the lot of the *Breeze.* He'd been kidding, of course, when he'd told Laura that he'd been playing video games online. He'd really been working on the Justice Turnbull story, for two reasons: one, because he wanted to write it, but also two, because it was a puzzle that needed solving and Justice was a killer who needed catching. He wanted to be a part of that.

Currently, there was one piece of the puzzle that was nagging him. Justice's escape had been because he'd complained of some ailment that the staff at Halo Valley wasn't able to diagnose or treat. So he was being transferred to Ocean Park Hospital on Dr. Zellman's orders. Justice's illness now seemed more of a ruse than a reality. But how had he fooled the staff, and especially Zellman?

That conundrum was on his mind as he made his way to his desk, walking by the newsroom, where a television was mounted and Pauline Kirby's face was plastered all over the flat screen. Looking seriously into the camera, she was talking about the band of Seven Deadly Sinners and their crimes.

"She's really running with this," Buddy said from his cubicle.

"Whatever." Harrison wasn't really interested.

"Y'know, you really punched Noah Vernon's old man's

buttons. The guy is going berserk! He's called and complained but Connolly loves it. Likes all the attention the *Breeze* is getting! Believes any publicity is good publicity. And Pauline hasn't let up an inch. Your story about Envy is just the beginning. She'll probably feature each of the kids involved, stretch it out, and get up close and personal, the whole human interest angle."

"Let her," he said, glad he was done with that particular article.

"Maybe she'll take some of the heat from the leader's old man. Bryce Vernon is threatening a lawsuit."

"Sounds just like him."

Harrison found himself wishing the Turnbull story would come together and, more importantly, the whack job would be caught and put behind bars forever. Until then, Harrison felt that Laura wouldn't be safe.

As Buddy took a call on his cell phone, Harrison tried to work, but he couldn't get Laura off his mind. He wondered how she was doing at the hospital.

*She's fine,* he told himself but couldn't shake the feeling that something was wrong. Really wrong. She'd been so different today.

Then again, her life was totally out of control.

He put in a couple of hours on the computer, adding information to Justice Turnbull's file, printing out articles and blogs about the killer from his earlier spree, then drove to his apartment.

Traffic was thick and the sun was just setting over the western horizon, streaking the sky in shades of orange and magenta, leaving deep ribbons of color on the calm Pacific. He pulled into his parking space, between two faded yellow lines in the worn asphalt, grabbed his laptop, and hurried to his unit. From the long porch, the building offered a peekaboo glimpse of the sea, but he was so lost in thought, he made only a cursory note of nature's brilliant display.

Once through the front door, he realized he'd barely

been in this—his home—in almost a week. In that time, his situation hadn't improved. In fact, more dust had settled, and the leaking kitchen faucet was still keeping up its slow dripping tattoo. The unopened boxes and crates seemed to mock him; the camping chairs with their cup holders were a joke. He compared his place to Laura's cozy little bungalow, and this cold, empty space that couldn't even come close to a bachelor pad came up short. Cream-colored walls with not a picture upon them, only nail holes left over from the previous tenant; a beige rug that showed wear down the hall; a bathroom so white, it was hard on the eyes, the strip of bulbs over the mirror and sink nearly blinding; his travel shaving kit and a faded green towel hung over the shower door the only signs that anyone resided here.

If you could call it that.

The one sliding door off the cracker box of a kitchen had a set of vertical blinds with several slats missing, and the almond-colored appliances were circa 1972.

"Retro," he muttered, walking to the bedroom, where the blow-up bed was covered with his rumpled sleeping bag. He'd managed to put some of his clothes into a small dresser. His one suit and a couple of sports coats and jackets were hung in the closet. On the top shelf, surrounded by boxes, was his locked gun case. He pulled the metal box down, unlocked the combination, and saw his pistol, a Glock he'd bought a few years back and never used. He picked up the 9 mm, loaded it, made sure the safety was on, then stuffed it into the waistband of his jeans.

"Locked and loaded," he muttered as he found a leather jacket, slid it on, and saw that it effectively hid the weapon. "Just like on TV."

He phoned Laura's cell, and his call went directly to her voice mail, so he didn't bother leaving a message, just left the apartment and locked the door behind him as he stepped outside.

Night had fallen. The security lamps were humming

and casting the parking lot in a blue-tinged light. A few stars were just beginning to wink high overhead as he reversed out of his space and nosed his Impala toward the street. He planned on finding out when Laura's next break was, then meeting her in the hospital cafeteria. Just to assure himself she was okay.

He wended through the traffic and headed south along Roosevelt Drive, which was essentially the part of Highway 101 that wound through Seaside. On the outskirts of town, his cell phone jangled. Expecting to hear Laura's voice, he answered, "Hey."

Across the wireless connection, he heard a rasping, ominous voice. "You've been with the witch!" the caller intoned, turning Harrison's blood to ice.

"Who is this?" he demanded and, with a quick look in his rearview mirror, cut into the empty lot of a bank.

"Sssshe's the spawn of Sssssatan," the caller hissed, and Harrison's pulse started hammering. The caller was Justice freakin' Turnbull?

"Who the hell are you?" Harrison demanded, staring through his windshield and seeing nothing. His gaze was turned inward; his concentration on the caller.

"They all will die . . . all the witchesss who hide in their fortresss," he scoffed. "Sssssiren Ssssssong . . . The sssisters think they're ssssafe." Then Harrison heard a smile in the caller's voice. "But they never will be, not until all of Satan'sss spawn are dead, their black sssouls going sssstraight to hell!"

"Turnbull?" he asked.

*Click!*

The phone went dead in his hand.

Jesus, what was that all about?

Immediately, he recalled the number, then hit the dial button, but no one answered. No voice mail picked up.

"Damn!"

Had he really been talking to Justice Turnbull?

Or could it have been a prank?

No way . . . The voice was too low, too deadly, too damned weird.

*Psychotic.*

Even now, his car idling in the bank lot, traffic rushing by on Roosevelt Drive, Harrison's skin crawled. Where the hell was the bastard? Why was he taunting him? Of course, he knew that some criminals, including killers, got off on the replay of their crimes in the press. They loved the notoriety. But it surprised him that Justice Turnbull knew him, had his number, for Christ's sake.

Then again, who really knew what went on in the mind of a psychopath?

Even those who purported to understand them could be fooled. Dr. Maurice Zellman was a case in point. He'd been so sure of himself, of his understanding of the maniac, that he'd let down his guard. And nearly lost his life in the process.

A little calmer, Harrison grabbed his wallet and found Detective Stone's card. He punched in the number of the offices of the TCSD, only to be told that the detective had left for the day. Not missing a beat, Harrison next dialed Stone's cell number. On the first ring, voice mail answered, and Harrison was forced to leave a short message telling Stone that Turnbull had called him and he had a cell number for the bastard.

Once more, as he pulled out of the lot, he dialed Laura. Once more, she didn't answer.

He tried to convince himself that she was fine, just busy, that she wouldn't take his call while on duty. He also assured himself that if Justice Turnbull had done anything to her, the maniac would have bragged about it in his call.

Right?

"Son of a bitch." He pushed on the accelerator and risked a call to the hospital. An operator answered and he asked to speak to Laura Adderley.

"Just one second," the receptionist said, and a few minutes later a smooth female voice said, "Nurses' station, second floor."

"I'd like to speak to Laura Adderley. This is Harrison Frost."

"Ms. Adderley's with a patient right now. If you would like her to call you back . . . oh, wait." Her voice became more muted as she said, "Laura, there's a Harrison Frost on the line. He wants to talk to you," then, more loudly, "If you'll just hang on, she'll be with you."

Relief rained over him.

"Hello?" Laura's voice was a balm.

"Hey. Just thought I'd check in. Was wondering if we could have lunch or dinner or whatever your next break is."

"I just took lunch . . . I won't have another break until one in the morning. You still on?"

"About that . . . ," he said. Then, though he didn't want to worry her, he thought she deserved to know what was happening, so he explained about the call he'd received, finishing with, "It was anonymous, of course, but I've got a call into Stone, to find out to whom, if anyone, the phone is registered. It could be one of those throwaway cells."

"He's targeting you?" she asked, sounding coldly furious.

"I think he's looking for a little press, and that worries me because his need for publicity, to be on page one, might ramp up his anxiety, his need to *do* something to draw attention back to him."

"Like kill," she whispered.

"I'll keep you posted on what I find out, but be careful. I think you're safe at the hospital. So call me when your shifts are over, and we'll take it from there."

She hesitated.

"Laura?"

"You be careful, too. He's got *your* phone number."

"I told Buddy to give it out. I don't think Turnbull's interest in me is personal. It's you he wants."

"And my family."

"Yeah." He almost said, "I love you," but caught himself, surprised by how it had seemed so natural to say.


"You won't believe this," Stone said, an edge to his voice as he drove south toward the Zellman estate.

"What?" Dunbar asked, sounding far away wherever she was on her cell phone.

"The reporter, Harrison Frost, the guy we saw earlier. He claims he got a call from Justice Turnbull."

"What? Why?"

"Maybe he wants some publicity. Who knows? He's a psycho. But get this, Frost got the guy's cell number and I ran it. Guess who it belongs to?"

"Just tell me, Stone." She sounded exasperated.

"Dr. Maurice Zellman. I'm on my way there now. Should arrive in fifteen minutes. Frost is probably going to show up, but I told him to stay back. Who the hell knows what's there."

"Did you try calling the number?"

"No answer."

"What about Zellman's home phone?"

"That's the kicker. They don't have one. Everyone in the house has his own cell, and an answering service takes after-hours calls for the doctor. Helluva deal."

"No kiddin'. I'll be there in twenty. I'm—" There was a little gasp, and Dunbar sucked in a shaking breath.

"What?" Stone demanded. "Dunbar?"

"I think I'm going to throw up again," she said on a sigh. "I'm gonna have to pull over."

"You sick?"

"Probably pregnant. I'll let you know."

"Well, don't come to the Zellmans. I've got this one," Stone told her, surprised.

"Okay," she said and hung up.

Stone didn't have time to think about that as he took a corner a little too fast, his tires screeching a little. Was Turnbull holed up in Zellman's house? Had he stolen the doc's phone? Or had someone else called?

It seemed to take forever before he pulled into the drive and past the stone pillars guarding the gate which was still dented and lying open, the result of some unfortunate crash. Carriage lights blazed against the stone house. Cars were parked in front of the huge garage, and he wondered vaguely why they weren't locked inside it, especially after the son's Range Rover had been stolen.

He parked behind a BMW, then called again, trying both Zellman and his wife's cell. Again, neither call was picked up.

For a few seconds he surveyed the place, but it looked quiet and occupied, the lights glowing through tall windows. He phoned in his position with the department . . . just in case, then climbed out of the car and eyed the premises again. Still nothing looked out of place, the darkness shrouding the huge house on the cliff over the Pacific was to be expected. A porch light was on, so warily, with one hand on his sidearm, he walked up the front steps and rang the bell.

From within he heard the sound of classical music, then quick footsteps. A few seconds later a woman he recognized as Mrs. Zellman peeked through the windows near the door, then unlocked the dead bolt and pulled the door open slightly. A chain still kept the door from swinging free.

"Detective Langdon Stone, Tillamook Sheriff's Department," Stone said and flipped open his badge.

"Oh . . . yes." She managed a tight, worried smile. "What can I do for you?"

"I tried to call. Neither you nor your husband answered."

"Oh, my . . . well, the music is on in the house, and I was watching television in the den. I must not have heard my phone."

"Is your husband inside?"

"Yes . . . oh, and I'm sure you didn't reach him, because he's misplaced his cell. It's been missing for a few days now. . . ." She let her voice trail off, then asked, "Is something wrong? Oh, dear, it's that patient of Maurice's, isn't it? He's killed someone else or stolen another car or God knows what else!"

"Ma'am, I'd like to speak to your husband."

She was just rattling the chain when headlights swept across the drive, and Stone recognized Harrison Frost's old Chevy. The reporter killed the engine and sprinted across the lawn into the light cast by the exterior lamps.

"Oh!" Mrs. Zellman gasped; then her brows pulled into a knot. "Mr. Frost?"

"I thought I told you to stand down," Stone said.

"And I thought I told you I'd be here ASAP."

"Well, come in, come in," Mrs. Zellman insisted, anxious to close the door and bolt it shut again, as if a chain lock or dead bolt could keep out a psycho like Turnbull. "Maurice," she called over her shoulder. "We've got company!"

"Is your son here?" Stone asked, but she shook her head as she led both men down a short hallway.

"Brandt's out with friends. Something about a late movie, I think." She opened the double doors to a wood-paneled study, where the doctor was sitting behind a massive desk, notes spread upon the top, books piled in the corners, the music much louder within the octagonal room. Through the windows, Stone guessed, was an incredible view of the ocean, though now, with the night, all that was visible was darkness.

Zellman looked up over the rims of his glasses and

blinked, then reached behind him and pushed a button on a console and the music ended abruptly. His neck was still bandaged, and he didn't look pleased to see them.

"Maurice, this is—"

Scowling, he waved impatiently at her and nodded. He knew who they were. But, obviously, he still didn't speak.

Stone said, "We want to talk to you about your cell phone."

Zellman wrote: *It's missing. Haven't seen it for the better part of a week.*

"You lost it?" Stone said.

Mrs. Zellman cut in. "I told you this already," she said and opened her hands to the ceiling, as if to explain to her husband that she was sorry for the disturbance, that she'd tried to intercept the visitors before they bothered him.

Frowning, as if the detective were stupid, Zellman wrote: *Obviously I misplaced it.*

"Then you've made no calls on it in the last twenty-four hours?"

*No. How could I?* Zellman shook his head and, somehow while seated, appeared to look down his nose at them. *Why?*

"Someone called me from it," Harrison said, "and he hissed a message that made me think it was Justice Turnbull."

Mrs. Zellman whispered, "No!" and clasped her hand over her chest, and even Zellman's facade of superiority dropped as Frost relayed the conversation.

"Oh, my God, Maurice!" Mrs. Zellman said, walking behind the desk to put her husband between herself and the disturbing news. "But how? And why?"

Zellman began typing furiously. *You think my phone was stolen?* And then before anyone could answer, he added, *By Justice Turnbull? When he took the car?*

"We don't know."

"No . . . oh, no . . . I was afraid of this," his wife said, her eyes wide, her skin an ashen color. "When you deal with all of those mentally unstable . . . murderers. And that . . . maniac. He's the worst! I told you, didn't I?" she said to her husband. Frantically, she looked out the windows to the darkness beyond and worried aloud. "He could be here now. . . . Oh . . . and what if he got the keys to the house? From Brandt's ring? Oh, dear God!" She began walking to each of the windows and drawing the drapes.

*You're sure it was Justice who called you?* Zellman typed, then looked up at Harrison Frost.

Frost answered, "I've never spoken with him but he said some things that were pretty freaky and he said them all as if he were hissing. He said things like 'sssisster.'"

Zellman looked away. Closed his eyes for a second. Shook his head almost imperceptibly, as if denying what he knew to be true.

"Dr. Zellman?" Stone asked.

Zellman sighed. Guilt crossed his features as his wife walked into the next room and started lowering blinds and pulling drapes frantically, the zip and clatter of the closure filtering into the study.

*He doesn't always hiss,* Zellman wrote, his fingers nearly trembling on the keyboard. *Only when he's agitated, when he's talking about the women of Siren Song, his sisters. Justice Turnbull refers to the women who live there as his sssissstterss.* He paused, then wrote: *Is that what you're talking about?*

"Yes." Frost's voice was stone-cold, serious as a heart attack.

"How did he have Mr. Frost's cell number?" Stone asked.

*I put it into the phone menu.*

Stone asked, "Is there any chance he could have a set of keys to the house?"

The psychiatrist's brow furrowed as he shook his head. *I don't think so. The keys were returned with Brandt's car, and the house key was included.*

"He could have made a copy," Stone said, though he doubted it. There just hadn't been enough time. Then again, anything was possible.

*Justice Turnbull isn't that patient or organized. He works off emotion and opportunity.* As he wrote the last line, Zellman flushed and grimaced. Stone guessed the psychiatrist was thinking of how he'd played the doctor for a fool out of emotion and opportunity. *He's also off his meds, so he's even more unpredictable, more out of control.*

"Son of a bitch," Frost muttered, staring at Zellman's computer screen.

"Someone else is here!" Mrs. Zellman said, her voice rising as if she was about to panic.

"Probably my partner." Stone walked out of the study and told the nervous woman, "Let me get the door."

"Thank you," Mrs. Zellman said gratefully. "I'm afraid all of this business with Maurice's patient has me beside myself." She lowered her voice. "I warned Maurice about him, you know. To no avail. Even after that maniac threatened Maurice with his life, it didn't matter. Not to my husband and his damned job." She threw a dark look in the direction of the study, then rubbed her arms as if suddenly chilled before turning away.

Savvy Dunbar entered a few minutes later and the discussion continued, but Stone didn't learn much more. The doctor appeared embarrassed that Justice had somehow stolen his phone—probably because he'd left it in an unlocked car. When asked about his health, Zellman said he already had speech therapy scheduled and planned on returning to work early in the morning. Stone told him not to shut his cell phone service off; there was a chance that they could locate Justice by GPS. If he made any more calls, they could zero in on the killer, hopefully before he struck again.

Shaken, Zellman agreed.

Mrs. Zellman seemed a little calmer by the time they all left, but she vowed she was changing the locks on every door and having the gate to their estate fixed as soon as she could get a repairman out.

"Good idea," Stone told her and only hoped it wasn't too little, too late.

# CHAPTER 39

*Sisssttterrr!*

Laura nearly dropped the thermometer she was holding for her patient. She'd let her guard down and Justice was calling her.

*It's gone, isn't it? The evil incubus . . . you lossst it!*

*How does that feel, bitch? It'ssss gone!*

There was a snarling sound of satisfaction in his hiss. Her knees nearly buckled. She closed her eyes and threw out her own taunt: *Come and get me, you sick freak. Just try.*

And then she slammed up her mental wall. Fast. Hard. Before he could respond.

"Hey!" her patient said, a man who'd had his appendix removed the day before.

"Sorry." She forced a smile just as the electronic thermometer beeped, showing that Mr. Greer's temperature was perfectly normal. He glowered up at her as she gave him the good news, then demanded more ice in his water glass and a change on his menu, one he'd chosen the night before, when his pain meds had, apparently, colored his options.

"I'll see what I can do," she said, "but I can't promise anything."

How could Justice know that she wasn't pregnant any longer?

Just how deep was her connection to him?

"Time to end it," she muttered under her breath as she left fresh ice with Mr. Greer before heading to the nurses' station. Sooner or later she'd have to come face-to-face with Justice, and that thought both terrified and galvanized her. She had to be ready, both mentally and physically strong.

Somehow she had to shake off the melancholy of losing her child and let anger burn through her, directed at her tormenter. But today . . . today she just felt sad and overwhelmed.

By the time that Laura was through with her double shift, she was ready to tumble into bed and never wake up. She needed to regroup, then somehow get the drop on Justice.

How much easier it would be if the police would catch him.

But she was losing faith in the authorities as the days since his escape wore on. Wherever he'd holed up, it was a dark, well-concealed hiding spot.

"He can't hide forever," she reminded herself as she clocked out.

Grabbing her purse from her locker, she headed toward the main doors of the building. Working in the hospital had helped take her mind off losing the baby and Justice's attack and her conflicted emotions about Harrison Frost. Falling in love with him was definitely not on her agenda, but then neither had been getting pregnant, suffering a miscarriage, or fighting her mental and physical battles with a homicidal maniac.

A week ago, her life had seemed boring. In a rut. Predictable.

But now . . .

She clicked on her cell phone and saw that she had half a dozen messages, mostly from Harrison. She was about to phone him back when she rounded a corner and nearly ran into Carlita Solano heading the other direction. Carlita was carrying a patient intake packet but stopped short when she spied Laura. "Hey! You outta here?"

"Uh-huh." Laura kept walking.

"That reporter, the guy who was here from the *Seaside Breeze,* he's been waiting for you."

It was amazing to Laura how Carlita's nose could smell out gossip. Rarely did anything go on within the walls of Ocean Park that the nurse didn't know about. Right now Carlita's dark eyes flashed, as they always did when she sensed gossip. She fell into step with Laura as they passed a visitors' lounge where several people were leafing through dog-eared magazines.

"Have you heard anything about Conrad?"

Laura shook her head. "Still comatose, from what I hear." What she didn't admit to was going to the ICU and checking the man's vitals herself early in her shift. Conrad lay on the bed, eyes closed, tubes running in and out of his body, his heartbeat monitored by a computer screen.

"That's what I heard, too. It's all just so weird," Carlita said. "It seems that every time I turn on the local news, I see Ocean Park on the screen. Or at least that reporter who's been hanging out around here. Pauline What's-her-name."

"Kirby," Laura supplied as she passed the admissions desk, where several patients, insurance cards and forms in hand, were seated in plastic chairs by a few strategically placed ficus trees while waiting to be admitted.

"Right. What a bitch." Laura didn't comment and Carlita asked, "So, what's the deal with you and the guy from the *Breeze?*"

Laura shrugged. "He's probably after a story," she said and forced a smile she didn't feel as she pushed through the doors just as Nurse Solano's pager went off and she bustled away.

Harrison was parked next to her in the lot, near one of the security lamps. Gone was the good weather. A soft rain was falling, causing the lamp's light to look a little fuzzy and creating a slick sheen over the pavement.

He climbed out of his car as she approached, and she felt a little jolt in her heart at the sight of him. His beleaguered jeans, T-shirt, and beat-up leather jacket, along with his scruffy hair and beard shadow, added to the I-don't-give-a-damn allure. Something she'd thought she was immune to.

"Don't you have a job or anything?" she asked as she approached him.

His smile was brief. "Doin' it."

"Hmmm."

"Look, there's a lot we need to talk about."

She glanced back at the hospital and wondered if anyone, including Carlita Solano, was taking note of their conversation. "Not here. How about at my house? I'm really beat."

"You know you can't stay there."

She didn't want to hear that, but she knew he was right. "Then how about a five-star hotel, somewhere with room service, decadent desserts, and a Jacuzzi tub . . . ?" she suggested with a wan smile.

He laughed. "In your dreams."

"Yeah, well . . ."

"I have an idea. A little B and B owned by a friend of mine in Astoria. He owes me a favor."

Out of the corner of her eye, Laura noticed Byron striding out of the hospital. Her stomach did a nosedive. She wasn't in the mood.

"Laura!" Byron called, loudly, zeroing in on her.

"Want me to get rid of him?" Harrison asked.

"He *is* a doctor here. Could be considered my boss, in a way." When Harrison's brows slammed together, she touched his arm. "I know," she said, then reluctantly turned to meet her ex-husband halfway across the lot.

"I'm off duty," she told him curtly.

"I know." He seemed a little less hostile than before. "Look, I'm sorry about what happened at the house, about that maniac chasing you down, and I know I've been kind of rough on you lately."

"Really."

He held up his hands in mock surrender. "Okay, I know. A jerk, but I wanted to make sure you were okay."

"Yeah, that's what it is."

He struggled not to argue further but said instead, "And the baby?"

"Oh, for the love of God. How many times do I have to tell you, I'm not pregnant! Seriously. Forget about any delusions you have. There is no baby!" Her heart cracked at those last words, and she felt a rush of tears, which she somehow managed to blink back.

Byron stared. "I almost believe you."

Laura silently counted to ten, then left him to stalk back to her car and a waiting Harrison.

"What was that all about?" he asked.

"Another misunderstanding," she bit out. She heard a car door slam and then a powerful engine roar to life. Byron was gunning his Corvette. A moment later he shifted into second before reaching the street, where he tapped his brakes, then sped onto the highway.

Harrison's gaze followed Byron, too. "I can't believe you were married to that guy."

"I was young." *And stupid. So easily and ridiculously impressed.* Clearing her throat, she said, "Let's get back to you trying to convince me not to go home."

He turned his attention to her again, and she noticed his hair starting to curl and darken in the mist. "I did a feature on the B and B when I first moved up here, and the owner got a lot of free publicity. He said I could stay anytime. I think this qualifies as anytime."

She was so weary. So, so weary. Seeing her waver, he touched her shoulder as he reached for his phone with his other hand. "You're gonna love it."

She wasn't so sure but climbed behind the wheel of her

Subaru as he stood outside his Impala and made arrangements for the night.

"We're set," he said. "The name of the place is Heritage House. You want to follow me?" He gave her the address before climbing behind the wheel of his own car and starting the engine.

Like an automaton, she headed after him, north to Astoria. She hoped he didn't have any thoughts of romance, because it just couldn't happen. With a sigh, she said, "I'll jump off that bridge when I come to it."

*I sneak down the stairs to the bait shop's parking lot and drink in the scent of the sea. It's foul here, rank with the scents of oil and dead shellfish and diesel, but still, there is a hint of brine to fill my lungs.*

*I wonder if the van will still work. Faded letters advertising Carter's Bait Shop, along with a phone number and an image of a sexy mermaid, cover the driver's side. The plates are expired, so I quickly switch them with those of a Toyota parked in the corner. The Toyota belongs to Carter's daughter Carrie, but she leaves it whenever her boyfriend picks her up in his winched-up 4x4.*

*It's a simple matter to change out the plates and hotwire the van. It starts easily, which is good, and the gas gauge indicates the fuel tank is nearly a quarter full. Enough for tonight.*

*Slowly, not bothering with the headlights, I cruise out of the bait shop's lot and up a short rise toward the highway that snakes along the coast.*

*I have business to attend to. . . .*

James Ferguson stared in disbelief at his brother's empty room.

He was gone? Seriously?

Mikey had really taken off?

James searched his brother's room for the third time, then the garage and the family room and the whole rest of the house. He'd called Mikey's phone a dozen times and left him messages as well as a kazillion texts. Desperate, he'd even called some of the dweeb's friends, but no one copped to knowing where Mikey was.

"Great," he growled as he flung open the slider door off the kitchen dining area and stepped onto the covered patio. Rain dripped down from the corrugated plastic roof to puddle around the edges of the concrete pad and soak the yard. Where the hell was that little jerkwad? Mom and Dad were due back in a couple nights and James was in charge and now that little freakoid was gone! James hadn't seen him at all after school, and he'd thought maybe Mikey had cut out early with friends. After all it was the last week of classes . . . but . . .

"Shit! Fuck! Hell!"

James thought about the little jerk's fascination for that psycho at the beach, the escaped whack job. Mikey couldn't get enough info on that sick dude. He was really pushing James to drive over to the coast before their folks returned and . . . oh, son of a bitch! The douche bag had taken off on his own.

Standing on the back patio, looking into the wet night, his stomach already a rock-hard knot, he worked up the nerve to call Belinda Mathis. She was on his speed dial, though he never called, or hadn't until right now. He hit the button and waited impatiently for her to answer. Just the thought that he was trying to contact her caused his palms to sweat. He thought of her pretty pixie-like face and incredible long hair. Then there was her tight ass and . . .

Her phone went to voice mail. He didn't leave a message and texted instead:

does your sister know where my brother mike is?

There was a few second gap as the rain plopped steadily

on the ground, and James noticed the neighbor's Siamese
cat skittering quickly across the top of the fence, only to
look his way and hiss before gathering itself and jumping
to the far side.

"Perfect!" As the testy cat disappeared, James's phone
chirped to indicate he was receiving a text.

Belinda Mathis's phone number, along with her pretty
face, appeared on the screen of his cell.

Her short reply was: k says at the beach she thought
he was with you

James's stomach dropped as he typed quickly, his fingers flying, his head pounding with about a million questions.

James: im at home how did he get to the beach
Belinda: dk

dk—Don't know. Crap! If she didn't know, who would?
James: when did he go
Belinda: k says maybe 2nite

"Shit!" he said aloud, but typed: thx
Belinda: tell him to call k

"Oh, sure that's what I'm gonna do," he said aloud as he
texted Mikey again and felt another wash of embarrassment that the only way he could talk to the coolest girl in
school was because of his dumb shit of a brother.

He curled his fist and jammed it into the metal post that
supported the overhang. *Bam!* Pain erupted in his hand.
Water splashed off the roof. There wasn't so much as the
tiniest dent in the post.

He knew what he had to do. If he didn't get his brother
back here, ASAP, Mom and Dad would kill them both!

And it would be the little creep's fault. All Mikey's god-
damned fault!


Laura had to hand it to Harrison.
He hadn't been lying.

She did like the bed-and-breakfast. In fact, she liked it a lot. Situated on a steep hillside, the old Queen Anne–style home was poised to look out over the mouth of the Columbia River. Inside, the house had been renovated, with interior plumbing in each of the suites, though the rooms held their original charm, Tiffany lamps glowing warmly on gleaming woodwork, a runner protecting the stairs, tables and settees scattered around a foyer.

Their room was on the third floor. A bay window looked over the roof of the carriage house and the lights of the city to the black waters of the wide river. Lights glowed on the waterfront and shone upward on the massive Astoria-Megler Bridge, which spanned the wide Columbia River as it linked the two states of Oregon and Washington. The Oregon end of the bridge rose to the heavens, making it tall enough for freighters to pass in the deep channel; then the span dropped suddenly to flatten over the rolling waters as it stretched to the Washington shore.

"That must've been quite a favor," Laura said as she dropped her bag on the four-poster bed. In her mind's eye she saw Harrison under the thick covers, his dark hair mussed on the linens, his naked body stretched next to hers. They would touch and kiss and . . .

*And it was too soon . . . too soon. . . .*

A deep sadness welled inside her, and she dropped into one of the side chairs near the window. "Justice reached out to me again, but I closed him out."

"Don't think you're so special. Remember, he called me, too," Harrison said.

"This is getting worse and worse. So many people." She found his gaze. "It's not just me, or my sisters. Justice is terrorizing everyone he's ever dealt with. I saw Conrad Weiser today, the security guard who was supposed to help transfer him, and his condition hasn't improved."

"When the bastard uses Zellman's phone again, the police might locate him and figure out where he's holed up."

"There could be so many places," she said. Even though Justice had an attachment to the ocean, Tillamook County was only a portion of the Oregon coastline. If he headed north, as they had, he could travel into Clatsop County and into Washington State, or to the south into Lincoln County and beyond. And that didn't count on the fact that he could head inland, if he followed Becca and Hudson, which she believed, hoped, was a long shot.

"I brought protection," he said and slid the gun from the waistband of his jeans.

She stared at the gun. For a moment she'd thought he meant something else, and she had to fight to keep her emotions from showing on her face.

"You know how to use it?" he asked.

"Only from what I've seen on TV."

"It's not too heavy, but it's got a little kick to it, so if you have to use it, use both hands, okay?" He handed her the gun, came around behind her and, placing his hands over hers, leveled the pistol.

She quivered. "I hope it doesn't come to this."

"Me, too. But here, let me show you." He pointed out the parts of the gun. "Tomorrow we'll go to a range and you can practice."

She held the 9 mm in one hand, then the other, then with both, frowning at the weapon as she tested its weight.

Harrison pressed it onto the table. "For now, it's peace of mind. Tomorrow it might become something more. Let's just leave it."

She nodded but every once in a while glanced at the gun, safety on, lying on the antique table.

They talked for a while, getting nowhere; then Harrison offered to go out and bring back some kind of dinner.

"It's ten o'clock," she protested, but he waved off her concerns, promising to be back soon. As soon as he stepped out of the room and locked the door behind him, she stripped out of the clothes she'd worn through both her shifts, twisted her hair onto her head, and took a hot shower. She was still bleeding, but already her flow had slowed. She didn't break down. She almost did, but once again she channeled her emotions into anger, plotting how she would face Justice.

What the hell was Justice doing calling Harrison on Dr. Zellman's cell phone?

She toweled off and put herself back together, tossing on an oversized T-shirt to sleep in. Hearing the door to the suite open, she grabbed the thick robe left hanging on the door and slipped her arms through the wide sleeves, then walked into the living area.

Harrison, his hair wet and windblown, was just walking through the door from the hallway. In his arms was a cardboard pizza box and a bottle of wine. "Pepperoni and Merlot," he said. "Pretty high class."

"Very." She couldn't help the smile that tugged at the corners of her mouth.

"What could be better?"

"Nothing," she said simply, her voice cracking a bit.

Harrison threw her a look. "We're going to get him," he said as he placed the box and bottle on a lacquered pedestal table, then served up the pizza on napkins. There were wineglasses and a corkscrew tucked into a small glass-fronted cupboard. Harrison found what he needed, uncorked the wine, and poured them each a glass, then set the bottle near the open corrugated box. "Anyone 'call' while I was gone?"

"If you're talking about Justice Turnbull, the answer is no."

He clicked the rim of her wineglass with his. "Here's to catching bad guys."

"Real bad guys," she added.

"Real bad guys," he agreed.

It was all Harrison could do to keep his hands off her as she fell asleep on the bed beside him. She looked sexy as hell in the oversized T-shirt, with her hair piled on her head, her long neck exposed, but he stayed on his side of the bed and simply watched as her breathing grew regular.

He knew she cared about him, had felt her response the last time they'd kissed. Her blood had heated as fast as his had, but tonight she was a little withdrawn, and his sister's words echoed through his brain.

*Take it slow, okay? Laura's not the only one who's falling in love. . . .*

Much as he hated to admit it, Harrison grudgingly decided that he was feeling something deep for Laura. And whether she was truly falling for him was yet to be determined; she seemed to run hot and cold. Then again, maybe she was riddled with the same doubts he was. He'd started out intending to write a story that would blow the public away. Now he was embroiled in some kind of creepy mind game with a psychopath while falling for the monster's latest intended victim.

He watched the rise and fall of her chest and softly brushed a strand of hair off her cheek. His heart twisted and deep inside he felt a male response. He tamped that down as best he could but risked brushing his lips over her forehead. She moaned in her sleep, and he watched as her lips twitched.

That was it. He couldn't do this.

Sliding off the bed, he grabbed his pillow, found an extra blanket in the armoire and, still cold, slipped on his jeans before lying on the floor. The settee in the room was just too small for his six-foot frame.

This, him sleeping on the floor, either at Kirsten's or his own damned apartment, on the Aero Bed, was getting to be a habit.

Pain in the ass.

*The bait shop van is mine for the taking. Risky, but I need to hurry. My mission cannot wait any longer. Care-*

*fully, I pull around to the road and turn, out of view, and then I'm gone.*

*The witches are slumbering.*

*It doesn't take long and I'm there, but I park far away from their lair, hiding the van on an unused driveway, then walk more than a mile through the darkness to the fenced grounds.*

*Though the main gate would be the easiest to breach, it could be watched and is far too risky, so I ease around the corner, deeper into the forest, the surrounding trees a canopy, their branches heavy with the rain. Through the Stygian darkness, I move, and I feel that quick little frisson of anticipation, the soul-jarring excitement that comes before a kill.*

*For a split second, my mind wanders and I nearly stumble. Voices call to me. Voices from my youth . . . or are they nearby?*

*I whirl and stare at the gloom behind me.*

*Is it a creature of the night? Some rodent stirring the brush? Or just the rain?*

Or your imagination . . . You know you've seen things that can't be.

*But I'm dizzy for a second, and I think with fury of the one who dares call me . . . Lorelei. Her scent is faint now . . . farther away.*

*I grip the rough bark of a nearby fir, squeeze my eyes shut, and slowly count to ten, forcing a calm through my center, trying to capture that bit of reality that, I'm told, sometimes escapes me.*

*Slowly, I recover. I release the tree and slip my weapon, Lorelei's knife, between my teeth as I scale the fence, away from the front of the grounds, toward the back. There, in the shadows, I stare up at the huge edifice where lights still glow.*

*They are inside.*

*Unaware.*

*While the sea pounds the shore far below. I draw deep breaths, filling my lungs with the salty air, listening to the thunderous cadence, imagining the crash of waves against the rocky shoals. Rain runs down my face. Clears my head. Helps me focus.*

*There is so much to do. And it must be done tonight. All of it.*

*In my mind I hear the taunts of the witches . . . "Bastard," "Imbecile," "Freak," and my blood rages, thundering in my brain, their cruel taunts like a drill with a dozen heads piercing my brain. Hateful, evil spawn of Satan! Whores who procreate like their sinister bitch of a mother!*

*My head throbs, and then I remember the doctor who thought he could treat me. Fool! Sanctimonious, supercilious, arrogant idiot! How dare he think he can determine my fate?*

*But I fooled you, Zellman. Proved you to be unworthy, a charlatan. But that's not enough. You need to feel my pain. . . . You need to feel the same depths of despair. . . . Oh, there is so much to do, so many things to do.*

*Tonight . . .*

*In my mind I see the doctor in his office, his eyes knowing . . . his smile false and forced, and he thinks he knows me. . . .*

*I blink. Feel the rain on my face. Return to the moment.*

*There is no more time for planning. No seconds left to savor my intentions. Staring at the house, I see movement behind the windows, and I smile as I recognize her glancing worriedly through the panes before she draws the shades.*

*My fingers curl around the hilt of my knife, now in a death grip in my right hand.*

*She peers through the small space where the curtains don't quite meet.*

*Too late, bitch.*

*Far, far too late.*

# CHAPTER 40

His cell phone, tucked inside the front pocket of his jeans, vibrated, and Harrison was instantly awake. The first streaks of dawn were piercing the windows, and Laura was still sleeping soundly, breathing deeply, dead to the world while he had barely been asleep. He glanced at the clock. Six a.m.?

He fumbled for the phone, checked the screen, saw that the number belonged to Zellman's cell phone.

*Justice!*

Scrambling to his feet, he flipped the phone open and slipped through the door to the upper landing.

"Frost."

"They're dead," the rasping voice declared. "Zzzzellman and his family!"

What the hell was he hearing? "Zellman? Dr. Zellman?"

"Along with his evil sssspawn! And they're not the lassst," the voice assured him in its hissing, sibilant tone. "You can write about them all. And don't forget the ssisssterss!"

Full-blown panic struck Harrison. Hard. "Wait! No! Turnbull! You can't—"

But the monster had clicked off.

"Damn!"

Desperately, Harrison called back.

No answer.

"Don't do this . . . for the love of God. . . ."

He tried again.

Nothing.

"Jesus, Joseph, and Mary," he muttered under his breath, adrenaline pumping through his veins. Was this serious? Had Turnbull slaughtered Zellman's family and then called to brag?

He punched in the cell phone number for Detective Stone. "Come on, come on," he muttered when the phone rang four times and went to voice mail. "God damn it." He waited impatiently for the voice mail to answer, then left a message. "This is Harrison Frost. I just got another call from Turnbull. He says he killed Zellman and his family. I'm on my way to their house now, but I'm in Astoria, so it will take a while. Call me." He snapped the phone closed and walked into the room.

Laura was still sleeping.

He noticed the gun on the table and grabbed it; then he found his shoes, shirt, and jacket and slipped out, locking the door behind him. If he bothered waking her, she'd insist on coming with him and he didn't want to risk that. There was a chance—a good one—that Turnbull was screwing with him, maybe even setting a trap, so it was best to leave Laura here, where she was safe. He'd call her later, as soon as he knew what was really going on.

The owner of the B and B was already awake, working in the kitchen, where his wife was baking some kind of cinnamon rolls for breakfast, when Harrison reached the foyer. Harrison pulled him aside, told him that he'd left his girlfriend sleeping and, if anyone came looking for her, to please call him immediately.

"Is she in some kind of trouble?" the guy asked.

"No. She's just really tired. When she wakes up, have her call me." He didn't have time to explain further and dashed through the rain to his car. He backed around Laura's Outback and hoped by the time she woke up, this would be sorted out.

Flipping on his wipers, he wound down the hillside to hit the highway. It was early enough that traffic was thin as he drove south, pushing the speed limit, passing slower cars and trucks. All the while he thought about Turnbull's call and his sudden interest in Harrison.

Why call him? To get his story out there? Why not Pauline Kirby, where Justice Turnbull would get television attention?

*He knows you're with Lorelei. That's what it all comes back to. You're with one of his "sssissters."*

He shuddered as he thought of Turnbull's twisted mind. Through Seaside and past the interchange for Highway 26 he drove, the cloud cover and rain seeming to keep morning at bay.

He was just on the south side of Cannon Beach when his phone rang again. Steeling himself for another call from the monster, he glanced at the phone and realized it was Detective Stone's cell.

"Frost," he answered.

"Stone here. I got your message. I'm on my way to the Zellman house now. What's going on?"

"I'm going through the tunnel at Arch Cape. Hold on." Harrison gunned it through the darkness, the sounds of the truck barreling the opposite direction echoing against the cavern-like walls, his headlights cutting through the dark.

Once he was through the tunnel, he gave Stone a quick rundown of the last few hours. For his part, Stone listened intently, only interrupting to ask a question to clarify things.

"So I left Laura at the inn, called you, and started driving."

"You haven't tried to get hold of Zellman at home?" It was more of a statement than a question.

"Turnbull said he was dead." Harrison said. "And he has the doctor's cell so I can't get through."

"He could be lying about the Zellmans."

Harrison remembered the sound of the maniac's voice, the barely suppressed delight in the killings. "Maybe," he said, unconvinced.

"The guy's completely off his nut. Off his meds, too, according to Zellman. What the hell's he doing?" Stone muttered. "Why go after Zellman?"

"I don't know."

"Okay, thanks. Now, I want you to back off. Don't come down here. Turn around, go back, and wait. I'll get in touch with you later. This is either a sick prank or police business, but you're out of it."

Harrison's answer was a short laugh. He wasn't backing off now. Not when there was a chance of nailing Justice Turnbull.

"Listen—"

"I'll be there in half an hour, Stone!" He gunned the Impala's engine, up past the viewpoint on the rim of Neahkahnie Mountain. "Turnbull's dragging me into it whether I want to be or not."

"Did you hear me, Frost?" Stone demanded, his voice tight. "This is the sheriff's department's bus—"

But Harrison had switched off. No way was he backing off. No damned way.


*Son of a bitch!*

Stone glowered through his windshield. The bullheaded newsman wouldn't do as he was told. Not when there was a story as big as Justice Turnbull's escape and killing spree to cover. Luckily, Stone knew that he could beat the reporter to Zellman's estate.

He half expected to find the family gathered around the kitchen table, eating breakfast, or already heading to their cars: the kid off to one of the last days of school, the wife ready to run errands, and the doctor on his way to the hospital. Hadn't he said as much two night's ago—that he was going into the office? An attack by a psychotic killer wasn't about to keep Dr. Maurice Zellman away from his work with the other nutcases at Halo Valley.

He called Dunbar on the way to the Zellman residence and told her, a little reluctantly, what was going down and where he was going. She was all business and said the troops were on their way. He wanted to ask more about the pregnancy but decided if she wanted to say more, she would.

On a whim, he called Zellman's work. "Halo Valley Hospital," an even voice answered. "How can I direct your call?"

"I'd like to speak to Dr. Maurice Zellman," Stone said, then identified himself.

"Dr. Zellman was out for a medical leave and . . . wait. That's odd." He heard her clicking buttons, a muted quick conversation with someone else, and rustling papers before she said, "I'm sorry. I was mistaken. It looks like he came in early this morning." Clearly, she wasn't trusting whatever it was she was seeing. "I'll try to connect you."

Stone turned off of the main road and wound up the smaller lane leading toward the Zellman estate. The rain was coming down in sheets now, blowing in from the west on a gusting wind that was tearing through the branches.

A second later a barely audible voice whispered, "This is Dr. Zellman."

Stone felt instant relief. "Detective Stone, Doctor. Sorry to bother you, but Harrison Frost claims he received another call from your cell phone."

"I'm not surprised," he said with effort.

"The caller claimed he was Turnbull and said he'd attacked your entire family."

Silence.

"He claimed you were included in the attack, and obviously you weren't."

"No . . . I . . . I couldn't sleep and came into the hospital early. . . ." His voice, already weak, faded out altogether.

"I'm almost at your house. It could be a ruse." Stone saw the lane turnoff for the Zellman house and wheeled in. The gate, still unrepaired, hung open, and through the trees, in the gloom, the house lights glowed warm in the gray dawn.

"That bastard's toying with me. He always resented me." Zellman was struggling to get out the words, and Stone had to strain to hear. "Please . . . check on Patricia. . . . I . . . I have her cell phone with me, so I can't call her. I brought hers with me to work since mine is missing. . . ." There was a pause and then the doctor forced out, "Oh, God, tell me she's all right." His voice, faint, cracked with fear.

"I'll call you right back."

Stone snapped off as he pulled into the driveway. The garage doors were down, no vehicles visible. Everything seemed fine, but as he stepped out of his car, he unbuckled his holster and pulled out his sidearm. No reason to take foolish chances.

Through the drizzle, he walked briskly up the walk, pausing only to look through the windows at the front of the house but seeing no one, only perfectly decorated rooms that were empty of life. The living room and dining room were in shadow, lights coming from the back of the house.

He rang the bell and waited, his hand over the butt of his gun. If Turnbull was hiding in the shrubbery or behind a tree, he could rush Stone and he might not hear him over the constant, dull rumble of the sea.

No one came to the door.

He rang the bell again, heard dulcet tones peal inside, but no answering footsteps. "Mrs. Zellman?" he called loudly, pounding on the thick door with a fist. "It's Detective Stone. Mrs. Zellman!"

Nothing.

He tried the door. Locked tight. Then he started walking around the big house, past rhododendrons shivering in the rain, under the wide branches toward the rear of the estate, where the forest opened up to the cliff. His boots squished in the puddles collecting on the ground, and he felt the hairs on the back of his neck lift as he rounded a corner and stepped onto the patio off the family room and kitchen.

The French doors were ajar.

Stone's stomach tightened.

Eyes trained on the warm interior, where the blinds Patricia Zellman had insisted on closing were wide open, he saw a pair of feet, one bare with toes painted a deep cranberry, the other still half inside a black slipper.

"Mrs. Zellman!" Using the nose of his gun, he pushed the doors open farther and stepped inside. The house was utterly still, and there, lying in front of an L-shaped sectional, Patricia Zellman lay in a pool of blood, red stains blooming through her silk pajamas.

"Damn . . . oh, damn . . . ," Stone whispered, angry.

Checking her pulse, knowing he would find none, he snapped up his cell phone with his free hand. As he speed dialed, he leaned forward, listened for her breath. Nothing.

"Nine-one-one," an operator said. "What is the—"

"This is Detective Langdon Stone," he said, his gaze sweeping the rooms. What if Turnbull was still in the house? He snapped out his badge number, then ordered, "I need backup and an ambulance." His gun in his right hand, he began moving through the rooms as he gave the operator the Zellmans' address. "I've one victim dead, Patricia Zellman, and I'm searching the rest of the house now."

"I'm sending a backup unit now, and the EMTs are on

their way," the 911 operator said just as he heard a noise from the hallway.

Spinning, his heartbeat accelerating, Stone held his pistol with both hands.

"Come on, you bastard," he muttered through clenched teeth.

Something dark moved in the shadowed hallway.


Trying to save time, Harrison raced down a back road that wound through the Miami River valley, avoiding some of the small towns and their speed limits. He sped through Tillamook and drove south, all the while his heart thudding. This could be it. Turnbull could be captured and the nightmare could be over.

He and Laura could be together.

He almost missed the turnoff to the Zellman estate and stood on his brakes just as he heard the sirens and saw, in his rearview mirror, the lights of police cruisers strobing the morning gloom. He didn't doubt for a second the emergency vehicles were heading for Zellman's address as he wrenched the wheel and sped into the lane ahead of them.

Passing the open broken gate, he set his jaw. His hands tightened over the wheel and his gut wrenched. Something was going down. Something big.

And it wasn't good.

He slid the Impala to a stop behind the police vehicle parked near the garage—Stone's car—then cut the engine and scooped up his 9 mm from the passenger seat.

Clicking off the safety, he crouched and started for the front door.

The first police vehicle sped down the drive. As the car slid to a stop, both front doors flew open and he heard, "Police! Drop your weapon!"

Harrison did as he was told. His gun fell to the wet lawn.

"Turn around!"

He did and saw he was staring into the barrels of two guns, both leveled straight at him.

"Get on your knees," a young man in uniform demanded.

"Hey, I'm the guy who called Stone! I—"

"Get the fuck on your knees and keep your goddamned hands in the air!"


Heart thudding, Stone aimed at the man looming in the darkened hallway. *Go straight to hell, Turnbull!*

"Dad?" a deep voice rasped. "Mom?" The dark figure stumbled a step, then pitched forward, falling into the light of the family room.

"Oh, no." Stone flew across the thick carpet to the spot where Brandt Zellman, wearing only boxer shorts, bleeding from wounds to his chest and neck, collapsed. But he was alive. Dragging in shallow, gurgling breaths.

"Jesus . . . Hang in there!" Stone said to the boy and heard the sound of sirens approaching. *Oh, God, will they make it in time?* "You hang in there." There was so much blood running from the jagged cuts on his chest and neck. Brandt had twisted onto his back, his eyes open, staring up at the ceiling. Stone held the kid's bloody fingers. "I'm here. Help is coming."

The kid seemed to be fading away.

"No way, Brandt. You hang in there."

Stone heard the sound of tires screeching to a stop.

*Thank God!*

More sirens. Close now. Screaming.

Voices. Shouting. Angry commands.

Maybe they caught Turnbull outside. *Get in here! Get the hell in here now!*

The boy was fading away, his skin blanched white, showing the acne of his youth amid the thin stubble of his whiskers. "Brandt! I'm right here. Don't you let go." He gave the boy's hand a squeeze. "Help is here." *Why the fuck aren't they coming inside?* "You hang on. . . ."

He yelled toward the front of the house. "In here! For Christ's sake . . ."

From the corner of his eye, he saw two officers hurrying through the shrubbery, their pistols drawn. Then, as Dunbar looked through the window and caught a glimpse of the bloody scene inside, she sprang forward, through the open French doors.

"Holy . . . ,"she whispered.

"We need an ambulance!" Stone said.

"They're here." She was already heading to the front of the house.

As Stone gripped the teen's hand and kept offering up words of encouragement, he heard the welcome sound of footsteps.

"We've got him," one of the EMTs, a slim, dark-haired, small-featured woman, said.

"I don't know if the house is secure," Stone admitted, and two other cops began searching each of the rooms.

"We've got the reporter in cuffs," Dunbar said. "Found him outside with a nine millimeter."

She glanced at the body, turned a little green.

"He called in the crime. Turnbull phoned him."

"Still, he stays in cuffs in the back of the vehicle, till we sort this all out." She took a deep breath, then slid her partner a glance. "Let's let Clark Kent cool his jets for a while."

# CHAPTER 41

Harrison was gone.

Not in the bed, not on the settee, not on the floor, where a pillow and blanket had been left, not in the bathroom.

He was missing.

As was the gun.

Laura's heart went cold. She threw off the covers and noticed on the bedside clock that it was after nine in the morning. Quickly, she tossed off her sleeping shirt and yanked on her jeans and a sweater. With the distinct feeling that something was very, very wrong, she was starting out of the room when she heard his vile hiss:

*You're nexxxt, Ssisster.*

She nearly tripped on the stairs outside the room.

She slammed up the wall before Justice could terrorize her any further, wasn't ready to get into a telepathic shouting match. . . .

Her throat was dry as she raced down two flights to the main level, where the scents of brewing coffee and cinnamon tantalized her nostrils. Three couples and a single man were already seated in the dining area. Two of the couples were laughing and talking, planning a trip to the nearby Astoria Column, a historic tower on the highest hill in the city, while the other couple was just finishing up, sitting across from each other at a small table for two and sipping coffee over their finished plates. The sixtyish single guy perused the sports section of a newspaper through reading glasses while absently picking at a gooey cinnamon roll.

*Normal people, with normal lives . . .*

Cloths covered the six tables; a bud vase with a single rose adorned the center of each. Upon the long sideboard, carafes of chilled tomato, apple, and orange juice stood next to the coffee urn and teapot. A woman wearing an apron and a bright, welcoming smile carried in plates filled with some kind of quiche, sausage, and the rolls.

"Excuse me, have you seen Mr. Frost, in three-oh-two?" she asked as the waitress left the plates on the table.

Her smile faltered and she shook her head as she headed toward the kitchen. "Sorry."

"Thanks." *Don't panic. Just because he's not in the room doesn't mean . . . But the gun, he took the damned gun!* Laura's heart was knocking, her mind racing to all kinds of awful scenarios as she stepped barefoot onto the front porch and jogged to the corner that overlooked the parking lot.

Rain was slanting from the heavens and gurgling in the gutters. Clouds were hanging low over the wide chasm that was the Columbia River, adding to the gloom.

Shrubbery fronds were dripping; the ground was sodden; the asphalt of the parking lot, slick with rain.

And Harrison's car was gone.

"Damn it," she muttered and turned on her heel. She hurried through the thick front door and raced up the stairs, running up the two flights to their room. Finding her cell, she checked for messages. . . . Nothing. No voice mail, no texts. She punched out his number and, after four rings, heard his voice mail message. "It's me," she said, going quietly out of her mind. "Where are you? I'm—I'm still here at the B and B, but . . . just call me." She clicked off and felt a knot in her stomach.

Why would he have left without waking her or leaving a note or calling? "Come on, Harrison," she said, anxiety twisting her guts as she stared at the cell. "Come on!"

With the phone in her pocket, she packed her things, twisted her hair onto her head, and added a little make-up. Justice's vile message rolled through her brain. *You're nexxxt, Ssisster.*

She caught the edge of the sink to steady herself.

What the hell did that mean? Next? Did the monster have Harrison? Her heart filled with a new, dark fear. If Justice had wounded Harrison . . . or *killed* him . . .

Spurred by her thoughts, Laura grabbed her things and headed to her car. She thought of calling Kirsten but didn't want to worry Harrison's sister. Nor did she want to leave a message at the paper.

Climbing behind the wheel, she tossed her overnight bag into the backseat, then jammed her keys into the ignition.

Only to stop.

See her reflection in the rearview mirror, witness the mind-numbing terror in her own eyes.

*So where are you going to go? What're you going to do? Harrison thinks you're here. If he comes back and misses you . . .*

"He can damned well call!"

She turned on the car, flicked on the wipers, and rammed the Outback into reverse. Her heart was a drum, every muscle in her body tense, as she hit the brakes; then, before her vehicle had stopped rolling backward, she shoved it into drive and sped down the hill.

Harrison heard his cell phone ring but couldn't answer it, as his hands were cuffed and he was locked in the backseat of a sheriff's department cruiser that smelled of some kind of lemon cleaner, which couldn't quite mask the scent of vomit, probably from an arrest the night before.

He didn't have to see the readout to know that the caller was Laura.

She was awake and wondering where he was. New panic assailed him.

*Stay put. Don't go anywhere. You're safe in Astoria.*

Desperately, he yelled through the glass and tried to get someone to talk to him, to tell Stone that he was here, but he was left by himself as more cars arrived and, to his horror, he saw a vehicle from the medical examiner's office.

He did kill them! That whack job killed the Zellmans!

It seemed like hours before he saw detectives Stone and Dunbar walking out the front door, when it had been less than twenty minutes.

Serious faces, deep in conversation, they didn't notice. Dunbar said something Harrison couldn't hear. They stepped out of the way as a collapsible gurney was pushed through the front door to a waiting ambulance.

Harrison craned his neck as the gurney passed.

Zellman's teenaged son, Brandt, was lying pale as death, an EMT in attendance and holding an IV bag as the boy was loaded into the back of the waiting ambulance. Thank God. At least he was alive!

Stone looked up, spied Harrison in the car and, with a quick word to his partner, strode over. He unlocked the back doors. "Come on out," he said and, as soon as Harrison was on his feet on the drive, unlocked his cuffs. "You don't listen," the detective said, "but it's what you should expect if you show up at a crime scene brandishing a weapon."

"I know." Rubbing his wrists, Harrison heard the sound of a car's engine racing and looked up just as Dr. Maurice Zellman's black Lexus, headlights glowing, squealed to a stop.

"Oh, hell!" Stone was already heading toward the doctor's sleek car. "Stay put," he ordered Harrison over his shoulder as the doctor threw open the door of his car.

"Brandt?" Zellman whispered brokenly, his face ghostly pale, his eyes round in horror. "Oh, no, oh, no!"

"Doctor Zellman, if you'll get back into your car until we sort this all out." Stone was all business.

"Not Brandt. Oh, God, not Brandt. He'll be all right!" Disbelieving, he collapsed across the hood of his car. "Not Brandt. I . . . I have to go with him! I'm a doctor," he rasped weakly as Detective Dunbar crossed the drive to the Lexus.

The doors to the ambulance slammed shut, and an EMT got behind the wheel. Sirens shrieking, lights flashing, the ambulance took off, roaring down the drive.

Zellman appeared confused. "I don't understand . . . Brandt . . . son . . . I have to go with him. I should never have left. . . ." His eyes were dark with guilt. And then he swallowed hard, with difficulty, it appeared. He seemed dazed, almost a zombie. . . .

"Dr. Zellman," Savannah Dunbar said and touched him lightly on the shoulder.

"Oh." Blinking several times, he looked around. "Patricia? Where's my wife?" He cleared his throat and his eyes glittered. "What the hell happened to Patricia?" His gaze was nearly accusatory as he glared at the detectives. "What did that bastard do to her?" He glanced from one of the cops to the other, then collapsed to the ground. "He said he'd 'get me.' That's what he said. And I knew . . . oh, dear God." His voice was nearly mute.

"He threatened you? You never said?"

"Patient-doctor confidence," Zellman snapped, sitting on the wet pavement, rain plastering his hair. Then, less angry, he added regretfully, "And I didn't believe him. . . ."

"He was a convicted murderer," Stone said in disbelief.

Zellman's eyes closed. Then he seemed to gather himself and, with Stone's help, climbed to his feet again.

"Where's my wife?" he whispered. "Patricia. I want to see her."

Harrison felt that little tickle of apprehension that was innate, an inborn response that came right before a devastating blow. Maurice Zellman felt it, too. His head was already shaking when Savvy Dunbar said, "I'm sorry, Dr. Zellman. I'm afraid I have some bad news."

Laura's cell phone rang just as she was driving through the north end of Seaside, trying to determine if she would attempt to locate Harrison's apartment or stop at the offices of the *Breeze* to see if someone had heard from him.

Eyes on the road, she dug through her purse, retrieved it, and flipped it open. Ignoring the fact that it was illegal to talk on a cell phone without a hands-free device, she answered, "Where are you? I was scared out of my mind that something happened . . ."

"Lorelei?" a fragile woman's voice said.

Laura's heart dropped like a stone.

"It's Catherine. You said to call if there was trouble."

*Oh, no!*

"What's he done?" Laura demanded, fear jetting through her blood as she remembered Justice's threat.

*You're nexxt, Ssisster.*

"It's Ravinia and Isadora," Catherine admitted, her throat catching. "Justice attacked them."

Laura's heart froze as she braked for a red light.

"He had a knife. . . ."

*My knife,* Laura thought, remembering her missing butcher knife in Justice's hand as he stood outside her kitchen door.

"I've been so wrong," Catherine said, her voice, barely a squeak, catching.

"Are they all right? Isadora and Ravinia, are they okay?" Laura demanded.

"I don't know."

"But they're alive?" *Oh, please God.*

"Yes."

"Call the sheriff's department. Detective Stone. No, better yet, call nine-one-one. Have you done that?"

"No, we're private here, you know—"

"Damn it, Catherine! He attacked my sisters! Your nieces! In the one place they were supposed to be safe! Where is he now?"

"I—I don't know."

"Look, I'll be there in . . . ten minutes, maybe fifteen. Hang on." She hung up and then, before she thought twice, dialed 9-1-1. To hell with Catherine and her secrets, her need for privacy, the gates, and the whole damned thing.

Until Justice was either locked up forever or killed, no one would be safe!

Paying no attention to the speed limit, hoping she would pick up a cop who was in some unseen hidey-hole and waiting for speeders, she blasted on toward Siren Song. Was that where Harrison was? Where was he?

No police car followed, only a guy in a low-slung Porsche, who sang past her as she pulled into the turnoff to the lodge, swerving to a stop. For the first time in memory she saw the gate open and a man standing on the far side.

"You Lorelei?" he asked, eyeing her and nodding to himself as the front door to the lodge swung open and Cassandra flew down the steps, her blond hair flying out behind her.

"Yes, Earl. This is my sister. Come on!" Cassandra's pretty face was twisted with worry, her eyes round, and she paid no attention to the fact that the hem of her skirt was taking on water and dirt as it skimmed the wet ground. "Hurry, Laura!"

"Where's Catherine?"

"Inside."

Laura glanced at the man. "Who's—?"

"Earl's our groundskeeper. You don't remember? He's been gone for a week or so, but he's back. It was his cell phone Catherine used to call you."

The groundskeeper was tall and slightly stooped, with a thin swatch of gray hair. He wore an open rain jacket over a flannel shirt and overalls and boots caked in mud. He was nodding his agreement as he closed the gate behind the two women.

"Don't lock that!" Laura ordered. "And please, stay here. I've called the police."

"Oh, no!" Cassandra sent her a panicked glance as they reached the porch. "Catherine will kill you."

"She'll have to stand in line. What happened?"

"It was Justice!" Cassandra shuddered. "He climbed over the wall and tried to kill Ravinia. If Isadora hadn't been there . . ." She shuddered again. "I don't know what would have happened."

They walked through the open front door and into the parlor, where a fire smoldered and Ravinia was lying upon one of the long couches that had been draped in white sheets. Isadora was seated in the rocker, bandages surrounding each of her forearms, while Ophelia and Lillibeth hovered nearby.

The smells of ashes, smoke, and something savory, like stew, were partially hidden by the acrid scent of antiseptic. Bleach and iodine, Catherine's answer to ridding germs from everything.

Catherine, ashen faced, was filling glasses of water from a pewter pitcher Laura remembered from her youth, something that had been passed on for generations, or so she'd been told.

Her hair pulled into a long, solitary braid that snaked between her shoulder blades, Catherine looked up as Laura and Cassandra entered. "Thank God you're here," she said, hurrying to greet Laura. "You're a nurse. I was hoping you had your own kit with you."

"Let me see how bad it is, but no, I don't have a kit." She noticed gauze strips and patches, in sterile packets, along with a role of adhesive tape that had to be a quarter of a century old. "Don't suppose you have any butterfly bandages or . . . never mind."

A bandage was over Ravinia's shoulder, the white gauze turning scarlet. "What happened?" Laura asked and Ravinia looked away.

"She was trying to escape," Catherine said, not bothering to hide her accusatory tone. "And she ran into Justice."

"He was here?"

"*Inside* the fence," Ravinia clarified, her voice low, her lips turned down at the corners. Obviously, her run-in with Justice and brush with death hadn't lessened her rebellion. Her gaze flicked to Catherine, as if the older woman were a jailer. "It wasn't safe here. If he hadn't seen me, he might have come into the house and slaughtered all of us. All he had to do was wait until we were asleep."

"She's right," Cassandra said.

None of the other sisters were in the room besides Ravinia, Cassandra, and Isadora.

"Tell me what happened," Laura said to Ravinia as she knelt beside the couch on which her sister lay, "I'll take a look at your wounds."

"He tried to kill me."

"You were outside?" Laura was unwinding the bandage. Blood was still seeping a bit.

"I'm just so sick of this place." Ravinia threw her aunt a look. "We never get to do *any*thing, not even socialize with other home-schooled kids, and no computers or telephones, and television only once in a while. . . ." She cast a look at an ancient bubble-eyed console that stood in the corner. "It's a weird, weird life."

"That's because we're weird-weird," Cassandra murmured ironically.

"But you got out." Ravinia glanced up at Laura as she

unwound the last bit of blood-soaked gauze. "You and Becca. She even married and had a kid. And you, you were married, too. You got to have a real *life!*"

Laura's lips flattened. Real life, be damned. She lifted the bandage, and Ravinia sucked in her breath as the gauze pulled away from her wound, a deep, nasty cut that might have been deeper if the knife hadn't been partially deflected by her collarbone. Fortunately, her artery hadn't been nicked, but she thought Ravinia's muscle might be damaged. "So you were outside. . . ."

"Then he was there! I stepped around the corner and caught him looking at the window. I gasped and he saw me and just leaped." She outwardly trembled. "I saw the knife in his hand and tried to run away, but he caught up with me and whirled me around. He hissed at me! Called me names and I was kicking at him when he swung the knife down. Then . . . then Isadora came running."

"I'd been looking out the window," Isadora said. "Pulling the curtains shut when I saw him. It was dark. I didn't know what was happening, but I grabbed the first thing I could find, which was the cast-iron skillet, and ran outside. I screamed and hit him over the head with it, and his knees buckled for a second. . . ."

Laura watched as Isadora swallowed hard, her lips moving silently as she relived the horror. "Then," she said, her voice softer, "he turned and I saw his eyes. There was light. . . . The moon? I don't know, but they were *glowing!* Ice blue. Horrible! He sprang at me, swinging his knife. I put my arms in front of my face and was screaming and running backward when Catherine came with the gun."

"Gun? You shot at him?" Laura asked, reaching for a fresh roll of gauze.

Catherine shook her head. "I couldn't. It was too dark. I was afraid I'd hit Ravinia or Cassandra. . . . I shot into the air and he bolted. Disappeared into the night."

"And you didn't call the police? When you knew they

were looking for him?" Laura accused as she began to cover Ravinia's wound with a fresh bandage.

Catherine's jaw was set, her eyes narrowing, as in the distance the sound of sirens split the air.

"Looks like I didn't need to, now, did I? You took care of it."

Before Laura could respond, her cell rang. She saw on her caller ID that Harrison was finally calling her, and she felt instant, gratifying relief. "Hold this," she said to Ravinia, placing the fingers of her unharmed hand over the sterile gauze patch. "Hold it tight." Then, "Hey," she answered.

Harrison was terse.

"Sorry about running out on you. There's been trouble down at Zellman's house. Turnbull was here."

Laura glanced in surprise at her sisters, all of whom were staring at her and eavesdropping on her conversation. "Then he's been busy, because he came to Siren Song last night. Wounded a couple of my sisters. I called nine-one-one when I heard about it, and I think the cops are just showing up."

"Don't go anywhere. I'm on my way!"


Harrison snapped his phone shut and headed for his car. Stone was standing near one of the police cruisers, cell phone pressed to his ear, his eyebrows drawn together in a hard scowl, while Detective Dunbar was still dealing with Dr. Zellman, trying to reason with the man as they all stood in the rain. While the detectives and deputies of the department were wearing caps emblazoned with the sheriff's department logo, Zellman and Harrison were bareheaded.

"Are you sure you're all right?" Dunbar asked the psychiatrist, who, after watching his wife's body bag being placed in the back of the medical examiner's van, had somehow pulled himself together.

"I need to go in and change." He tugged at the bandage at his throat.

"Sorry, not until the investigators for the crime lab are finished."

"I need to go in—"

"It's a crime scene now."

"But—"

"Is there anyone we can call to be with you?"

"No," he said, his tone rasping with the effort. "I need to get to Ocean Park, to see my son! Brandt, he was injured and . . . I'm leaving!"

"I don't think you should be driving alone."

Zellman pulled himself together and breathed down his nose in that superior way of his. "I said, I'm fine. I'm a doctor. I should know."

Without another word, he turned on his heel and strode to his car. Seconds later he was wheeling out of the drive. Dunbar caught Harrison watching and just shook her head.

Harrison turned to witness Zellman's Lexus streak through the trees and rain. What kind of a man acted like that just after learning his wife was murdered and his son brutally attacked and fighting for his life? Something was definitely off with the good doctor.

But then Zellman always had been a prick.

A tech came through the front, carrying a plastic bag of bloody bedsheets.

"From the kid's room?" Dunbar asked.

"Yeah. Someone left him for dead."

She took one look at the blood-soaked sheets, then turned quickly and doubled over to vomit in a stand of rhododendrons just shedding their blooms.

"You okay?" Harrison asked.

"Yeah." She wiped at the back of her mouth with her hand. "Nothing to do with this."

One of the officers overheard and grinned like a ghoul.

"Sure, Dunbar. It couldn't be blood and death and violence. Must be some other reason."

Spitting into the ground, she stood up and regarded him coolly. "I'm pregnant," she said.

The officer started to laugh uproariously, then cut himself off when he saw her expression. "You're kidding." Then, "Who knocked you up?"

Stone joined their group at that point, just in time to hear her say, "Don't worry about it. It isn't mine."

He did a double take, and he and Harrison exchanged a mystified look. "Uh . . ." Stone had momentarily lost his train of thought, but then he shook himself out of it and said, "That was the boss. Seems our boy was busy last night. An attack was reported at Siren Song. Two of the women injured. A unit and ambulance have been dispatched."

Harrison said, "I heard. I just called Laura. She's there."

Stone was already striding to his car. "I'm on my way."

"I'll wrap things up here and then head north," Dunbar said.

Harrison didn't wait. He was already jogging to his Impala. He figured the detectives would try to talk him out of driving to Siren Song, but they might as well save their collective breaths. He was going to see for himself that Laura was all right.

"Hey!" Stone yelled at him. "You might want this." He was holding up the 9 mm. "You do have a license. I checked."

"Told you."

Stone handed him the gun, then slid behind the wheel. "It's nothing personal, Frost," he said. "It's just I don't trust reporters."

# CHAPTER 42

Mike Ferguson found the old motel fascinating as hell. He'd hitchhiked to Deception Bay first with an elderly couple in a pickup that looked like it was from the sixties. They took him as far as the cut-off to Jewell and Mist at a crawl. Then two teenagers picked him up in a hot Toyota 4 Runner. They didn't believe in going less than sixty-five, which was fine by Mike. He got to the turnoff to Seaside in that cool rig, then had to walk a couple of miles before the ride to Deception Bay with a guy who claimed to be a cook at some place called Davy Jones's Locker. The driver of the Ford Focus had dropped him off in the middle of town, and Mike then worked his way to the old motel that Mad Maddie, Justice Turnbull's mother, had once called home. Ignoring the chained fence with its faded NO TRESPASSING sign that creaked with the wind, he'd soldiered on through the rain to the front of the motel.

The place was a wreck, but Mike couldn't help from poking through the old dilapidated cupboards and closets of the units. There really wasn't a lot left. It looked like someone had camped here at some point and left an old rat-eaten sleeping bag in the living room of the manager's unit, the best one of the whole sagging stream of cabins. Strung together with carports, each individual cabin was falling apart. The roofs had gaping holes in the shingles, and bricks had fallen off the chimneys. A couple of doors had been nailed shut, and there was plywood over most of the windows. The fence surrounding the place was like Old Man Ramsby with his mouth of gaps where teeth were supposed to be.

And it was loud here. Overlooking the ocean.

But there were a few things that he considered cool enough to shove into his backpack. An old license plate from the sixties, way older than Justice, he thought; and a small picture of Jesus charred into a piece of driftwood, which had once hung on the wall and had fallen from its nail and down through a hole in the floor; and a dog collar with a tag that read SPORT. He'd even found a tarot card and remembered that Mad Maddie had been a fortune-teller of sorts. So the death card was a real treasure.

But what was there of Justice Turnbull's? What little bit of his boyhood had he left in this wreck of a building?

Mike thought Justice had lived a good part of his childhood years here, but he couldn't find anything that proved it. He knew only that this place was where he'd tried to kill his mother and that other woman a few years back. But he found no evidence of the crime; it had been too long ago.

Sitting cross-legged on the dirty floor, he listened as the wind howled. Low tide was still a few hours away, so he'd hole up here for now. Maybe he'd find something really cool, something that might impress James . . . or even Kara Mathis, at the lighthouse. How badass would that be?

He found his phone and turned it on. Belinda had texted him, saying that James was looking for him. Yeah, well, he knew that much. James had left a ton of texts and voice mails. Mike thought about phoning him back, then decided he didn't want to be called an idiot. Let him stew. Served the jerk right!

He'd be home tomorrow, anyway.
After visiting the lighthouse.

There was something about Zellman that really bothered
Harrison. As he raced to Siren Song, he tried to figure out
what it was. Something more than his super-inflated opinion of himself. There was something manipulative about
the man. It was as if Zellman, in reveling in how brilliant he
was, thought he could maneuver people to do his bidding.
Except it had backfired with Justice Turnbull. Zellman had
misread his own patient.

What had Zellman said when asked about the threats by
Turnbull to the doctor? Something about patient/client
privilege? But Zellman wasn't always so eager to play by
those rules. He'd let a lot of things slip in a previous interview with the man, even typed it out on his computer, as it
was difficult for him to speak.

Harrison flipped his wipers to a higher speed and
squinted as the rain picked up and the roof of the sky seemed
to lower, the clouds thick and gray. One of the things Zellman had mentioned was that Turnbull believed he could
smell the women of Siren Song when they were pregnant.

Crazy talk.

But then wasn't telepathy between Laura and Justice
Turnbull unbelievable?

And something else burned in his mind. Seeing Detective Dunbar throw up in the bushes at Zellman's house had
triggered thoughts of when he'd first met Laura and she'd
lost the contents of her stomach.

Hadn't Laura's ex, that jerk Adderley, accused her of
being pregnant? Wasn't that what he'd said in the parking
lot?

An uneasy feeling crept through his mind. She was
tired. Pale. Dark circles under her eyes. And she'd been distant as well. He'd chalked it all up to the newness of their

relationship and all the pressure she was under with Justice Turnbull on the loose. But maybe there was something more that was stealing her sleep and worrying her mind.

"Stop it," he muttered, disgusted with himself. He braked for a corner, scaring up a crow picking at the carcass of something indistinguishable on the pavement. The crow, disturbed, flapped his wings and flew to the shoulder.

Harrison barely noticed. The tires of his Chevy sang over the wet pavement as he drove and his thoughts grew as dark as the heavens. Surely Laura wasn't . . . She would tell him if she were . . . what? Carrying her ex-husband's child?

"Don't listen to that asshole Adderley," he told himself, but his reporter's gut instinct that something was very wrong in a relationship that had just barely begun wouldn't leave him alone.

Coming up on the turnoff to Siren Song, he slowed to a crawl. The twin ruts of the lane were riddled with puddles, the grass mashed from the tires of several vehicles parked near the open gate. No chain nor taciturn woman in a dress right out of the eighteen hundreds was blocking his entrance.

Instead a row of police cars, lights flashing, and armed officers kept the onlookers and curious at bay. No amount of talking would get Harrison inside the walls of the estate, though he tried his damnedest. The police were conducting a thorough search of the grounds and the area outside the gates, trying to discover where Justice Turnbull had entered.

Even Stone, who'd arrived before him, wouldn't come out and give Harrison the green light. But Laura, who had obviously been waiting for him, must have spied his Chevy, as she came hurrying from the house and along the path to the gate.

He hadn't seen her since morning, and the sight of her chased away his doubts. She was shoving her arms through a lightweight jacket. She smiled and waved as her gaze met his, and he remembered kissing those lips and being so disturbed by her closeness the night before. There was just something so damned alluring and sexy about her, something that touched him in a spot he'd never really known existed.

*Lorelei*, he thought.

"It's all right," she insisted, cocking her head at Harrison and speaking to the cop. "He's with me." She looked tired, the dark circles under her eyes still visible, as if she was battling insomnia or the flu. He'd thought he'd understood. Now he wasn't so certain.

But he did know that Justice's reign of terror was taking its toll on her. Now the madman had not only chased her down and nearly killed her, but he'd attacked her sisters. Here. At Siren Song. Where they were supposed to be safe. No doubt she would be all the more ready to "call" the psycho telepathically for a showdown.

A bad idea if the carnage at Dr. Zellman's house was any indication of what the murderer was capable of.

It was obvious Justice Turnbull was escalating, going off the rails. Patricia Zellman was dead, Brandt Zellman clinging to life, and as he understood it, two of Laura's sisters were seriously wounded, though from what he could determine, they hadn't suffered life-threatening wounds.

All in all, a busy, bloody night for Turnbull.

The officer in charge of the crime scene, a twentysomething with short red hair and a hard expression far older than his years, shook his head. "I've been told no one goes in, and unless the sheriff himself says this guy can come inside, then he stays out."

"I'll get Detective Stone to okay it."

The officer, whose name tag read CRAMPTON, was unmoved. "I said, 'The sheriff.'" His eyes narrowed on Harrison. "I know you," he said. "You're that reporter. The guy who blew up the story on the murders around that club in Portland. Boozedog."

"Boozehound," Harrison automatically corrected him.

"Yeah, well, you just stay where you are."

"How are your sisters?" Harrison asked.

"They'll be okay. I'll be out in a sec," Laura said, obviously deciding that arguing was pointless.

He had no choice but to wait outside. The rain had slowed to a steady, skin-soaking drizzle, and there was talk of a storm rolling in that night, but for now, the wind had slowed, and the old lodge, visible through the stand of mossy old growth, looked dark and formidable. He called the offices of the *Breeze,* checked his e-mail, and left a message for his editor that he was working on the Zellman murder story as well as an assault that happened at Siren Song.

Connolly called him back about half an hour into his wait to basically tell him to "keep on it," then went on to gleefully say that since the Seven Deadly Sinners story had broken, the paper had had a 30 percent increase in new subscription requests from the same time period the year before. The change might be coincidence, but Vic Connolly wasn't betting on it. He was happy with Harrison. Happy, happy. None of it made the waiting easier.

It was another half hour before Laura returned, this time, it seemed, ready to leave. In the meantime Harrison had watched an ambulance and EMTs arrive, and again his thoughts had turned to Adderley's accusation that she was pregnant.

He simply couldn't get it out of his head.

"Let's get out of here," Laura said as she walked past the guards at the gate and looked into his eyes. He reached for her, but she caught his arm and said in a low tone, "Why don't we meet somewhere?" Her gaze, with her beautiful, intelligent eyes, held his for a second. "How about the Sands?"

"Okay."

Then she let go of his arm and Harrison saw that the red-haired cop was watching them, as were two of Laura's sisters, one of whom was in a wheelchair. They were both outside, under the overhang of the porch, their eyes trained on Laura and Harrison.

He knew she'd suggested the Sands of Thyme Bakery, but anyone could interpret it as the bar in a hotel in Seaside named the Sands or a small lunch counter in Cannon Beach.

He drove the few miles and kept her taillights in his line of vision. Though it was only early afternoon, the day was gray and the clouds, instead of breaking up, appeared to be darkening. The Outback's taillights were small red beacons through the drizzling rain.

He followed her into the main road cutting through Deception Bay. At the west end of the street, past the store-fronts and shops, was the ocean. Dark and shifting, white-caps visible, the waves tumbled and rolled. Laura turned into the tiny parking lot for the bakery. Harrison slid his Impala into a parking lot across the street. He locked the car, then jaywalked, his collar turned up against the rain, the crash of waves louder than usual. He caught up with Laura just as she reached the front door.

The bell over the door tinkled as they walked inside to the warmth and smells of baked bread and old coffee.

"Hey! We're about to close," Kirsten called from the back of the shop before she stepped to the counter and spied her brother. "Make that we *are* closed." She offered them a smile.

"You're telling me that you don't have one lousy bear claw left?"

"Nada, brother."

"You alone?"

"My afternoon to close. The barista just left ten minutes ago."

"What about something from the lunch menu?" Harrison suggested, studying the chalkboard mounted over the deli case. "You said you were expanding it."

She came around the counter. "Oh, well . . . I guess I can make an exception *this* time and stay open a few more minutes."

After locking the door behind him and Laura, she flipped the OPEN sign to CLOSED in the window, then, wiping her hands on her apron, said, "So what can I get you? I've got a great roast beef/tomato/mozzarella sandwich, and if you ask nicely, I'll add bacon and broil the whole damned thing."

"You're on," Harrison said. "And a beer."

"Ha-ha. You can pick anything you want from the cooler. Unless you want coffee, then grab it from the pot. It's still hot." Turning, Kirsten lifted her eyebrows at Laura. "What about for you? The same? Or I've got a killer Caesar salad topped with prawns."

"That would be perfect." Laura was nodding as she took a seat at one of the scattered tables.

Harrison poured them each coffee and brought over the creamer and a tiny basket of various sugar packets. "Pick your poison," he said, trying for a little levity, though he had dozens of questions for her.

She told him of waking up to find him gone, then getting the panicked call from Catherine and the subsequent hours at Siren Song.

Kirsten brought their meals, the sandwich and a cup of coleslaw for Harrison, the salad and a small loaf of sourdough bread for Laura. She refilled their cups, then told them she was officially "off duty." When they were finished, Harrison was to bring the dirty dishes to the back, where she was cleaning up. They could hear her rattling around—water running, pots clanging, a radio playing pop rock from the eighties.

Laura pulled off a piece of bread, buttered it, and sank

her teeth into it. "God, this is heaven," she said, closing her eyes as if she'd truly entered the pearly gates. "I missed breakfast this morning."

"And lunch." He took a bite of his sandwich. True to her word, Kirsten had come up with a "killer."

"Your turn to tell me," Laura said, her eyes serious. "I heard from Detective Stone that Mrs. Zellman was killed and that their son is in the hospital. You got another call?"

"Yeah. From Turnbull." Between bites of his sandwich, he told her about deciding to let her sleep and to leave her somewhere safe while he drove like a maniac to the Zellman house. "The doctor was at work. Early. Despite the fact that he still can't talk very well."

"So Justice told you they were all dead. But Zellman wasn't there?" She jabbed her fork into one of the prawns atop her salad.

"Yeah." Harrison was nodding. That had bothered him, too. Then again, so many things did.

They finished their meal. "He's escalating," Laura finally said. "Getting bolder. Taking chances. Making bad choices."

"And killing people."

"Isadora said she wounded him," Laura said, picking up her cup with two hands. Her eyes narrowed a fraction. "Cracked him up the side of the head, but who knows if that did anything other than save Ravinia's life."

"Too bad it didn't kill him."

"I've never been one to wish anyone dead, but Justice . . ." She sighed and pushed her half-eaten salad aside. "He's a special case."

"Amen."

"I wonder how badly he's wounded. Where would he go?" She sipped from her cup. "Somewhere he'd feel safe."

"Wherever he's holed up," Harrison thought aloud, "the police will find him. He has no money or credit cards, no job or car. He's not got friends or family other than Siren

Song, and his face has been plastered all over the news-papers. It's only a matter of time."

"The sooner the better," she said, then looked at him over the rim of her cup. "And the next time you get a call, would you mind waking me up? Is that too much to ask?"

He remembered how peaceful she'd looked lying on the big four-poster, how his heart ached at the sight of her. Had she been lying to him? "There's something I need to ask you," he said, carefully picking his words. "A couple of times during this investigation, there's been mention of pregnancy." His gaze was locked with hers, and he noticed her lips tightened almost imperceptibly. "Zellman, when he was explaining about the relationship between Justice Turnbull and the women of Siren Song, his victims. Turn-bull bragged to Zellman that he could find them more eas-ily when they were pregnant."

She looked away, twisted her coffee cup on the table.

"And then, when you were talking to your ex . . . in the parking lot. He—"

"He accused me of being pregnant," Laura said, cutting in, turning her gaze a dark, angry blue. "So you're asking me if I am. I told him that I wasn't and it's not a lie. I'm not, Harrison." He felt a second's relief, until he saw a bit of guilt in her gaze. She took in a long breath and sighed. "But in the interest of honesty, yes, I was. Recently." She bit her lip. "I was pregnant when I met you, had just found out, and yes, that's how Justice found me so easily, but that's over now." Her eyes glimmered with unshed tears. "I just suffered a miscarriage. In the last few days."

He felt his entire world begin to rip apart.

"I didn't plan it. . . . Byron and I got together just to try and give our relationship another try. Obviously, it didn't work, but I found out I was pregnant just a little over a week ago and I . . . I didn't tell anyone. The only person who knew was Justice."

Harrison couldn't think of one thing to say. He hadn't really expected to be right, so he just sat in shocked silence.

"I was still sorting everything out. I'd wanted a baby for years, and now . . . now I was bringing her into this world of madness."

"Her?"

"I assume. There are very few men in my lineage, and . . . one of my sisters at Siren Song could tell."

"So she knew, too."

Laura looked at him. "Well . . . yeah."

"I don't understand any of this!" He suddenly exploded. He was mad as hell that she hadn't told him, hadn't confided in him. Mad at himself. He'd found himself fantasizing about her, about sharing a life with her . . . and this basic lie had been there all along!

She read the fury burning deep in his soul, the pain. "I was trying to do what I thought was best to protect my child. And I wasn't sure what that was. Run away? Hide as far away as possible from Justice? Look over my shoulder, her shoulder, for the rest of our lives? Or face him and try to destroy him? And then you were there . . . the truth seeker, I thought . . . and I believed I might be falling in love with you." She blinked and scraped her chair back. "Obviously that was a mistake."

"Yeah," he said coldly.

His anger crushed her. "Should I have bared my soul to you?"

"Yes!"

"Well, I didn't know how." She slung the strap of her purse over her shoulder, strode to the front door, unlocked it, and stepped outside.

He jumped up and caught the door before it slammed shut and took off after her, striding through the puddles and across the tiny lot, where she had already hit the remote lock for her car and was yanking open the door.

"You should have trusted me!" he called as he reached her, then forced the door shut with his body.

"You ask too much!" Lips trembling with anger, she tugged hard on the door's handle again. "Get out of my way." When he didn't budge, she looked up at him and said, "What the hell is it you want from me?" Rain drizzled down her face and under the collar of her jacket.

*I want you. All of you. Heart and soul.* But the words wouldn't come. When he didn't immediately respond, she tossed him a hard, knowing look and ordered again, "Get out of my way."

"Laura—"

"You don't listen! Get the hell out of my way!"

All he wanted to do was kiss her. To drag her into his arms and gather her close, press his mouth onto her wet lips, and try to roll back the hours and days, to start over. But she'd lied to him. And it was a big one.

She pulled on the door handle, and he stepped to the side, watched as she slipped behind the wheel. "Tell Kirsten thanks," she said, twisting on the ignition and backing up before jamming her Outback into drive and nosing out into the street.

And then she was gone.

# CHAPTER 43

She wouldn't cry.

Laura drove away from the restaurant and bit her lip, but she wouldn't cry.

She'd made a mistake with Harrison Frost, thought he was somehow different from the other men she'd muddled her life with, but, of course, she'd been wrong. She saw the repressed fury in the set of his jaw, the accusations in his eyes as he'd asked her about the pregnancy.

You should have told him.

"How?" she asked herself, her gaze flicking to her rearview mirror. "When?" It all would have ended up the same, though it might have ended faster.

What kind of a fool was she to fall so hard and so fast? "Idiot," she accused and caught a glimpse of her reflection, shimmery blue eyes from her struggle against tears, brown hair growing out with her lighter blond roots.

She needed a change. To get away from here. From all the memories of her weird childhood, her disaster of a marriage, the loss of her unborn child, and finally, to get away from Harrison. She thought of their last few nights together, camped out at Kirsten's or the bed-and-breakfast. . . . It seemed as if they'd shared a lifetime in little over a week.

Boy, oh boy, was *that* stupid.

She flicked on the radio, heard a newscast about the attack at Siren Song, then found a station that played a blend of pop and rock. Not that she really noticed. She was concentrating on her next move. As long as Justice was on the loose, no one was safe. Not her, not her sisters, not anyone close to her. Nor innocent victims that got in his path. Currently, no one could find him.

She alone could communicate with him.

She alone would have to find the son of a bitch. She didn't have to worry about her baby's life anymore, nor did she really have concern that he would zero in on Harrison now that they had split. Justice would probably know that about her, like he knew everything else.

She said under her breath, "It's just you and me." She wasn't foolish enough to think she could kill him or try to arrest him, but she might be able to find him or flush him out, and then, once she knew where he was, she planned on calling the police with an anonymous tip, one that had enough information that they would follow up.

Afterward, once he was no longer a threat to Siren Song and her sisters, Laura would figure out what the hell she planned to do with the rest of her life.


"Don't tell me, you screwed it up," Kirsten said when Harrison walked into the bakery-cum-deli and carried their dirty plates into the back area. "I saw through the window."

"She's mad."

Kristen leveled her gaze at her brother. "So apologize."

"You don't even know if the argument was my fault."

She took the dishes, placed them into the sink, and began rinsing them with an industrial hose and nozzle. Steam rose as she sprayed the plates. "Sure I do." Letting the hose retract, she leaned her hips against the stainless-steel counter. "I saw how she looked at you and you looked at her." A small smile touched her lips. "It was the same way Manny and I used to look at each other, Harrison. She's a smart, beautiful, funny woman, and you're letting her slip through your fingers."

"You don't understand."

"What I understand is that I would do just about anything to bring him back, to recapture what we had . . . and I never will." His sister shook her head. "Okay, I get it. Laura didn't tell you she was pregnant. Big deal." When he just stared at her, she said, "So I eavesdropped a little."

"She *lied.*"

"Seriously? That's what you think? With all the hell you two have been going through? And what does it matter? Even if she was still pregnant now. Does that make her a different person? Well, yeah. She'll be a mother, and that changes women, usually for the better. But she's still Laura, and you're in love with her whether you admit it or not. Do you know what she's going through? She just lost a baby. Maybe one she didn't know about for long, didn't plan, but let me tell you, that woman is hurting, and you, brother dear, only made it worse. I wouldn't blame her if she never takes you back."

"Hey, whoa . . . we weren't going together."

"Really? You aren't crazy nuts in love with her? You don't fantasize about her day and night? You haven't thought about what it would be like to live with her?" She shot him a glance that accused him of lying to her and to himself. "And think about it from her point of view. What's she going to do the minute she meets you? Say, 'Hi. I'm Laura, and I'm pregnant with my ex-husband's child'? I don't think so. How did you find out, anyway? From her ex?"

Harrison didn't answer.

"It doesn't matter, anyway," Kirsten said, warming to her topic as only she could. "Once Laura didn't tell you from the get-go, when would there have been the right opportunity? And then she loses the baby. . . . God, Harrison, quit being so tunnel-visioned, such a *man,* and think about her, what she's going through! Take your damned male ego out of the equation, would you?"

Harrison had heard enough. "Thanks for all the sisterly advice."

"Anytime. It's free. Oh, and another thing, you weren't seeing someone else, were you? Some blonde?"

He shook his head. "What are you talking about? I'm not seeing anyone. I met Geena Cho for a drink the other day, but that was really about work."

"Is Cho Asian? 'Cause this one's definitely not. She came in today, ordered coffee. Asked if I was Kirsten Rojas and my brother was Harrison Frost. When I said yeah, she asked where you lived. I didn't tell her, just directed her skinny ass to the *Breeze."* She leveled her gaze at her brother. "But she's not worth losing Laura over."

"I don't know what the hell you're talking about," he muttered again.

She cupped her hands around her mouth. "I'm saying don't lose Laura."

He shook his head and walked out the door again, skirting mud puddles on the way to his car. His head felt heavy with unwanted information, and Kirsten's voice echoed through his brain. *You aren't crazy nuts in love with her?* "Hell," he muttered and climbed into his Impala. He needed to think things through, and he usually did it best when he worked. He had an inside look at Turnbull's last rampage, so he'd start there. He had direct quotes from the maniac and could use the phone calls as his hook into his piece.

He cut through the back roads of town and hit the main road as his cell phone rang. Hoping that Laura was calling him, he glanced at the display. Not Laura. Not Justice. But a number he recognized as belonging to the cell phone of Pauline Kirby. She'd probably heard of his involvement at the Zellman murder scene.

He wasn't in the mood to talk to her and instead let her leave a message.

On the drive to Ocean Park he tried to dismiss all of Kirsten's pointed remarks.

*You don't fantasize about her day and night? You haven't thought about what it would be like to live with her?*

*How did you find out, anyway? From her ex?*

The words kept turning over in his mind.

*You aren't crazy nuts in love with her?*

*How did you find out, anyway? From her ex?*

Well, yeah, but the more he thought about it, the more it bothered him that he'd really twigged to her pregnancy thanks to Zellman. Despite patient/doctor privilege, the psychiatrist had let it slip that pregnant women from the Colony were Justice's primary targets. At the time, Harrison thought Zellman was just showing off, trying to impress him with his knowledge of the maniac.

*The maniac who he'd unintentionally helped set free.*

His thoughts took a dark turn, his fingers tightening over the steering wheel.

It was almost as if Zellman had seeded the information about the pregnancies to him. Had the doctor slipped it in on purpose? But why? Zellman couldn't have known Laura was pregnant. Only she knew. *And Justice.*

What the hell was Zellman's game? Harrison felt that same old distrust for the man again as he took a corner a little too fast and corrected, the Chevy's tires sliding a bit.

Had it really been Justice on the phone to him?

With that disturbing thought gnawing at him, he pulled into the lot at Ocean Park Hospital and remembered the last time he'd been here, to pick up Laura, to see that jerk of an ex-husband accost her before driving off in his Corvette. It had only been one day.

One helluva day.

Inside the hospital, he inquired about Brandt Zellman

and was told only that he was "stable." He asked about the patient's father, but the information desk had no information about Zellman, and in a quick scan of the partially full lot, he didn't see the black Lexus. He tried another tack and asked if Conrad Weiser was well enough to have visitors, but was met with a stony glance and a shake of the receptionist's head.

He wanted to see Laura but she wasn't here. With an effort, he shoved thoughts of her aside and concentrated on Zellman. So where would the doctor go? Either to his home or his office.

Climbing back in his car, he headed toward the *Breeze* offices, a place where he could do some research. Then he was going to find Zellman and confront him. Something was very, very off with the guy.


"I knew I'd find you here, stupid ass!" James eyed his brother with pure disgust. Mike had been searching the cabins again and had come back to the manager's unit to have another granola bar, the only thing he'd taken from the house before he'd snuck out.

"You didn't have to come after me."

"Of course I did! Mom and Dad are gonna murder us when they find out!"

James was really mad, his jaw working just like Dad's when he was about to hit the roof, his eyes glittering, as if it was all he could do not to take a swing at his little brother right here and now. So let him.

"Let's go," James ordered.

"No."

"Hey, dickwad, did you hear me? We're leaving and we're leaving now." James glanced around at the rotting boards and crumbling mantel and shook his head. "You can't really want to stay *here*."

"Just a few more hours. The tide'll be out around eight

. . . at eight eighteen, to be exact, and we can get to the lighthouse easily then. It's light till nine at this time of year, too."

"You're certifiable!"

"It would be cool for you, too. Think what your friends would say if you showed, I dunno, something like . . . uh, a shoelace from Justice Turnbull's boots."

"Everyone would laugh their asses off! How could I prove that?"

"With this?" Mike pulled out his iPhone. "I'll take pictures."

"They'll all say it was photoshopped, or digitally corrected."

"Not if I send 'em to Facebook while we're still out there . . . you know, a whole series?"

"It's a stupid idea." But he wasn't as adamant.

"What'll it hurt?"

"What if the dude shows up, eh? What then?"

"He won't."

"What if we get stuck out there . . . ?"

"Only if we're morons."

"Well, there's the question." James eyed the broken-down couch as if he might sit down, then changed his mind. "We could be. We probably are."

At least he'd said "we." "What if we found something out there that breaks the case wide open and leads the police to Justice Turnbull?"

James snorted.

"It could happen!" Mike insisted. "Look. We go out there. Stay only fifteen minutes, or maybe, maybe half an hour. Then we come back, and . . . and I'll go straight home with you."

"Oh, sure."

Mike pulled out the ace he had up his sleeve. "I'll even tell Belinda Mathis that you were the one who made me go out there, that I got chicken at the last minute."

"Big deal."

"Kara thinks it is and she's been talking to Belinda. You can see it on my text." He scrolled through a zillion texts on his phone. "Here."

that's so cool bring us back something.

Mike looked up at his brother. "She means her and Belinda."

James scowled. "I don't care what Belinda Mathis thinks."

*Liar.* Mike backed off. The hook was set. Now he just had to reel him in. "Well, okay, but I'm going out there. And then I'll go home. But not before. And *I'll* bring something back." He didn't add, "For Belinda," but he could see that James was already making that leap.

"Then you won't put up a fight?" James demanded.

"Uh-uh."

"And you'll tell Mom and Dad you ran off and I had to come and bring you back?"

"Yep."

James sighed and looked through a dirty pane to the outside, where, Mike knew, he could see the ocean. "I must be nuts," he muttered. "And I want your Mariners' tickets!" The Mariners were the Seattle baseball team, and Mike had scored a couple of tickets for his birthday.

"Deal," he said quickly. He wasn't into baseball, anyway.

In just a few more hours . . . he'd finally get to see into Justice Turnbull's lair.

*My head pounds. The knot on my crown is tender. The pain in my shoulder is excruciating, burning. . . .*

*It was all I could do to drive back to the bait shop, leave the van in its parking place, and stagger to my room.*

*How could I have been so careless?*

*I remember clearly the exhilaration of being inside the*

*forbidden walls, of plotting all their deaths, and then see-ing the one out of the corner of my eye.*

*Ravinia—horrid, scurrilous creature—trying to escape.*

*I smile as I think how I thwarted her escape, aborted her attempt for freedom. And I would have killed her, too, slit her fine white throat and watched her blood spray and pump from her body. I imagined the surprise in her eyes, the fear, the anguish when she knew she was about to die . . . and then the other one attacked. Smashed something hard that nearly cracked my skull. Before I could turn around, another hard blow. That glanced off my shoulder.*

*Bitch! You will pay!*

*Inside my room, I take off my jacket gingerly. The pounding in my head throbs, and my shoulder is nearly useless. But my arm still works.*

*I need to heal. To recuperate.*

*Food and sleep and the sea . . . I have to return. . . .*

*And then, the spawn of Satan will feel my wrath . . . all of them.*

*And Lorelei will understand she cannot save them.*

*She is weaker now. Battered from the loss of her child. I sense no wall stopping my thoughts from reaching her.*

*It's your fault, sssisterr, I think. They will all die because of you. . . .*

*In a blink, her wall is up again and I can't break through. But she saw . . . she witnessed her doom.*

*I take great comfort in the future and will my body to heal.*

*Lorelei will die.*

*Slowly.*

*Painfully.*

*Forever silenced.*

# CHAPTER 44

Harrison leaned back in his desk chair at the *Breeze,* ignoring its squeaking protests as his mind traveled along several pathways. He had been researching Zellman for about an hour and had developed a very unflattering picture of the man.

It was weird. He'd learned Zellman was in his office right now. Working. As if nothing had happened. As if his son weren't in the hospital, clinging to his life. As if his wife weren't dead.

It didn't make sense.

Unless . . . Harrison called Stone, who, for once, picked up.

"Stone."

"It's Frost. Hey. I've got a question for you. The cell phone calls I've been getting from Justice Turnbull on Zellman's phone? Have you tracked that phone down? Made sure it's in someone else's possession?"

"I can't discuss the details of this investigation with you, Frost. You know that."

"Off the record?"

"Doesn't matter. Why? You don't think it was Justice who phoned you?"

"I don't know. Look, I'm going to want to ask you a few more questions about what happened at Siren Song for a story. Can we meet?"

"I'm a little busy right now." There was an edge to Stone's words.

"Will you call me when you locate that phone? I have a personal interest in it, you know, since I'm the one who gets the calls on it."

"As I said, I can't discuss the details of the investigation."

"I tipped you to the Zellman house," Harrison reminded the detective. "Because the lunatic called me."

"When we're ready to go public with everything, you'll be the first person in the media I contact. Now, I've got another call."

Stone hung up and Harrison listened to his other messages, both from Pauline Kirby, wanting to interview him as a "witness" to the Zellman murder.

As he headed out, he lifted a hand in good-bye to Buddy, who yelled at him, "Where you going?"

"Got an interview," Harrison said.

"You got a story for Connolly? 'Cause, man, I'm not staying here all night."

"Work it out with the boss."

Harrison was out the door, in his car, and on the road to Halo Valley, thinking about the phrase that he'd said to Stone: *because the lunatic called me.*

Why was that? Why hadn't Justice called Laura and harassed her? Why him, one step out? At the time Harrison had thought it was because Justice preferred to contact Laura mentally, throw his taunts out into the atmosphere and scare the bejesus out of her. But she claimed to have shut him down on more than one occasion . . . so why not threaten her on the phone as well? If that was part of his MO, why not call Laura the usual way?

Zellman had claimed he'd added Harrison's name to his

list of contacts in his phone, that it was an automatic thing with him. He'd wanted a journalist's number at hand?

He didn't buy it.

He thought about the raspy voice on the phone, one he assumed was Turnbull's hissing threats, but really? The doctor knew Turnbull's speech patterns, what irritated him. . . .

And asking for press? Turnbull? That just wasn't what made him tick.

So, why call Harrison Frost?

A tense feeling settled in the pit of his stomach as Harrison considered the possibilities. By the time he reached Halo Valley, he'd convinced himself that Dr. Maurice Zellman was not the victim of anything other than his own deceit and treachery. In fact, in the whole dark scenario that filled his mind, Harrison felt Zellman could have been pulling the strings of everyone involved in the investigation from the onset. How else did they know anything about how Justice Turnbull thought or acted? Only from his psychiatrist, the one man who was his confidant, his only contact with the outside world.

The more he thought about it, the more the pieces of the puzzle fell into place, and he could hardly believe it had taken him this long to see it.

It was only a matter of proving it.

"You son of a bitch," Harrison said, as if the psychiatrist were in the car with him.

An hour later he was angling his Impala into the Halo Valley Hospital lot. He gazed with a locked jaw at the redwood and concrete building, that bastion of good intentions and failed results, at least in Justice Turnbull's case. Side A, Side B, it didn't matter. Just like a bad LP.

Slipping his pocket recorder and cell phone into his pocket, Harrison considered his Glock, then decided against it. Too many security cameras and even metal detectors in the mental hospital. He left the 9 mm in his locked glove box, then locked his car and walked into the hospital.

The receptionist on Side A was cool. "Dr. Zellman's actually not seeing anyone," she said, obviously starstruck by her boss.

"I realize he's still recuperating, but please let him know I'm here." He slid his card across the desk. "Tell him I think I have new information and want to run it by him, get his professional opinion."

She stared at him a long second, then sighed and hit a button on her phone.

Zellman's voice, a rasp Harrison recognized, answered. "I thought I told you I didn't want to be disturbed."

"I'm sorry, Doctor," she said, "but there is a Harrison Frost from the *Seaside Breeze* who wants to talk to you." Sliding Harrison a dubious look, she relayed the rest of his message, and to the girl's wide-eyed surprise, Zellman said, "He's here? Well, then, I guess you'll have to send him in. Remind him I'm a busy man."

"Oh, he knows, Doctor," she said and clicked off. She buzzed Harrison through and gave him instructions that guided him to a skyway where private offices and conference rooms were located. Those he could access without a security code; Side B, where Justice Turnbull had been housed, was off-limits.

He clicked on his micro-recorder and kept the device in his jacket pocket.

Zellman was seated at his desk, where he was typing on his laptop while scanning a couple of green-jacketed files lying open on his ink blotter. His camel's-hair jacket had been tossed onto a hall tree; his shirt collar, left open. The bandage around his throat was visible, as was his irritation.

Shoving away from his desk, he motioned Harrison into one of the two visitor's chairs facing the desk. "I'm busy," he said with effort.

"I thought you were at the hospital with your son."

"He's doing well. . . . Cuts were surprisingly superficial, thank God."

"Too bad your wife didn't get so lucky."

"Yes," he said, his face clouding. Was it with grief? Guilt? Fear? He sighed. "Is there something you wanted?"

"I'm surprised you could come into work."

"I know. It's difficult but I'm not good at waiting around."

Harrison decided to take off the boxing gloves. "I did some research on you, Zellman."

The doctor narrowed his gaze and said in a whisper, "Doing an article on this mess?"

"Mmm. Your wife filed for divorce two weeks ago."

Zellman blinked. "A misunderstanding." But he was more wary now.

"Your marriage was over a long time ago."

"Mr. Frost, I loved Patricia. Still do," he said, affronted. "This is preposterous. If you've finished harassing me, you can go." He seemed to struggle to talk, but Harrison wondered. Was it all a crafty, malicious facade?

"You wanted her out of your life, and you saw a way to get rid of her. Even if it involved hurting your son."

"What?" Zellman was on his feet, appearing agitated and, for the first time, dangerous. Harrison kept his eyes on the doctor as he sputtered, "Get out! Before I call security!"

"Call them." Harrison settled farther down on his back and stared up at the psychiatrist. "Did Brandt get in the way? Try to save your wife?" he asked, a quiet rage seething through his blood.

"You're insane!"

"You should know."

"Get out of my office, now!" Zellman ordered, his voice clearer, the skin over his reddened cheeks drawn taut. Beneath the cultured reserve was a fierce, angry man.

"Did she want all your money? Or, was it that she just wanted out? Big ego slam." Harrison narrowed his eyes, as if he understood. "Oh, I get it. There's someone on the side, right? A girlfriend? You couldn't risk the chance of losing your rep or your fortune."

"I have never been unfaithful to my wife! It was Patricia—," he started to say, then backpedaled quickly, trying to recover. "It's true. She wanted a divorce. She didn't care a whit about how that would affect Brandt, at his age." He added icily, "It was she who had affairs, Mr. Frost. She who didn't understand the boundaries of marriage, the responsibilities of raising a son . . ." He was stock-still, his anger having crystallized into something clear and cold and deadly. "Patricia couldn't possibly see what a divorce would do. Her plebeian upbringing was always coming into play." He sneered down at Harrison. "She didn't even finish college."

"Because she got pregnant with your son."

Zellman's eyes flashed a rage that had been seething for years, possibly decades.

"And that's why I'm here at Halo Valley. Instead of teaching at Harvard, doing research at Yale . . . whatever."

"So you killed her?"

"I told you—"

Harrison kicked his chair back and leapt to his feet. He towered over the shorter man. "You pretended to be Turnbull! You called me, played me, pretended to be that twisted nut job so that I would call the police and we would all buy into your pathetic act!"

"That's enough!" Zellman reached into his top drawer and pulled out a Taser.

*Whoa.* Harrison focused on the weapon. It wouldn't kill him, but it would render him helpless so that Zellman could use something else to kill him . . . the knife that he'd used to carve up his family. "Do you think you can really get away with this?" Harrison asked, knowing that there was no way to avoid the shock of thousands of volts if Zellman decided to use the weapon he must have been issued for extreme cases in dealing with the criminally insane.

"You're deluded, Mr. Frost." Zellman was calm again as he pointed the Taser at Harrison's chest. "I assume you know the meaning of incapacitation via neuromuscular shock? Or maybe compliance via pain is more your style. Either way, this weapon is guaranteed to shoot enough voltage through your system to make you convulse and gasp, and squeal in pain like a pig being slaughtered." He offered Harrison the coldest smile he'd ever seen.

"And you're a fuckin' murderer, *Mr.* Zellman."

"It's *Dr.,*" Zellman spat back, his voice clearer than ever. "I've earned my degree and title, and people like you and Patricia never understand." The weapon quivered a little in his hand. Zellman's stun gun was without a cartridge. He wouldn't be able to shoot Harrison from a distance or create the neuromuscular havoc he mentioned, but he could sure as hell zap him with enough electricity to send him to the floor. But he could do it only if he actually touched the weapon to Harrison's body.

No way would he allow that.

Nor would he back off.

"Did you let Turnbull go on purpose? Fake your injury? Did you let that monster out in the world just so you had a cover to murder your wife and son?"

"Brandt is alive! He's . . . going to make it! His wounds are only superficial!" A darkness gathered in his eyes, and Harrison realized he was hoping that Harrison would make the first move, jump him and force him to take defensive measures. The man's lower jaw was trembling in rage or fear. Harrison couldn't tell which it was.

"You could have killed him," Harrison charged, ready to spring at a second's notice. He kept his gaze locked on the psychiatrist's eyes.

"I would never!"

"Sure you would. You'd take care of anyone who got in your way. Including Brandt!"

"You don't know what you're talking about!"

"How many times before were the police called to your place for domestic violence, huh? Just because the charges were dropped doesn't mean it didn't exist. What did it cost you to keep Patricia from leaving? Flowers? Diamonds? Or maybe a white BMW—"

"She was never satisfied!" Zellman roared, his voice strong as it quivered with fury. "Never." He re-aimed the Taser to make a point. Threatening. "Come on," he goaded. "Come on, attack me."

"So you have a reason to use that thing?" Harrison said, though he was sweating bullets.

"I don't need a reason!" Zellman snapped. He lunged, the teethlike prongs of the stun gun glinting.

Harrison leapt to the side.

Zellman missed. Nearly fell over.

"You self-serving fraud!" Harrison vaulted over the chair and grabbed Zellman's arm, forcing the guy down. Was it his imagination, or did he hear footsteps? "In here!" he yelled toward the open doorway.

Zellman twisted and, teeth bared, forced his hand around.

Harrison shifted but felt Zellman press the stun gun against his arm.

*Oh damn!*

*Zzzzzzztttt!!!!!* Pain, so excruciating he screamed, shot through Harrison's left forearm.

His knees buckled and he fell, knocking over the chair and dragging Zellman to the floor. Writhing, he rolled over the smaller man and was rewarded with another jolt of two hundred thousand volts.

"Stop! Police!" a deep voice said from the hallway, and to Harrison's immense relief, Deputy Langdon Stone, weapon drawn and aimed at the doctor, strode into the room. "Maurice Zellman, you're under arrest."

* * *

"I don't like this," Catherine said sternly as she relocked the gun closet and handed Laura the little revolver, a .38 Smith & Wesson snub nose that had some years on it.

"I don't either, but I think I need a weapon. A serious weapon." Laura knew what she had to do. Justice's last missive, a horrid image of all her sisters writhing in their death throes, convinced her.

She had to stop him.

She was the one.

"I didn't tell the police I fired it. None of us did," Catherine said.

Laura and Catherine walked outside and stood a moment on Siren Song's front porch. The rain dripped steadily off the roof, and a brutal wind was kicking up. The door was closed behind them, no one else had been allowed to know what Laura wanted, but she noticed the curtains in the living room move and a pair of eyes—Cassandra's, she thought—peeking through. Then there was the shadow of a wheelchair visible through the narrow window near the front door. Lillibeth was hovering, hoping to catch a phrase here or there.

It had been hours since Laura had seen Harrison, and in that time she'd formulated her shortsighted, if necessary plan, eventually calling in sick to work, then loading her car and driving back to Siren Song.

"You don't have to do this." Catherine's face was grim, the lines in her face more pronounced than ever, and her hair, in the drab day, was an equally drab gray.

"Something has to be done, and I'm the only one who can contact him." Laura said it without inflection, and the older woman gazed at her in worry.

"This has been such a nightmare."

"Hopefully now it'll be over."

Catherine didn't appear convinced as she reached into a pocket of her voluminous skirt and came up with an old box of bullets. "God help me," she whispered, handing over the ammo and folding her fingers over Laura's. "Please, be careful."

"I will." She forced a smile.

"If you're not calling the police—"

"I'm not." She wasn't going to spook Justice before she had the chance to confront him.

"Then, please, take that reporter, Harrison Frost, with you. He seems strong and sturdy, and Lord knows he loves you."

*Oh, Catherine, if you only knew.*

Laura nodded because she knew there was no way Catherine wouldn't keep harping at her until she agreed. The older woman frowned, obviously wondering at Laura's quick capitulation, but Laura left her to her thoughts. "I'll see you soon," she promised and hugged the woman who had tried her best to raise her.

"Take care."

Laura released Catherine and hurried away, along the puddles of the pathway to the main gate, where Earl waited to bolt the gate after her. She climbed into her Subaru with the rubber raft strapped to its roof rack, an earlier purchase, one she'd made on a whim but one that could very well prove to be a necessity if she kept with her plans.

She knew facing Justice bordered on lunacy, but she didn't care. This had to end. And it would. Tonight.

Harrison watched as Zellman was led away, his hands cuffed behind his back. It had taken fifteen minutes to read the psychiatrist his rights and haul him out of his place of business, but now Harrison and Detective Stone were alone in the doctor's tidy office.

"How did you know?" he asked Stone.

"Same as you. The domestic violence charges were dropped, but there were the accusations. Zellman's half nutty himself. Thought his wife was having affairs when she wasn't. And then the knife wounds on Brandt and Patricia Zellman? Inconsistent with the wounds on the two women at Siren Song."

"So Turnbull was attacking the women at Siren Song while Zellman attacked his own family?"

Stone was nodding. "The timing seemed too close, so we had to start looking at Zellman as the possible doer. He planned it all along. I even checked with his physician. He was faking his injuries, or at least making them appear worse than they were. He pretended he couldn't talk, then mimicked Turnbull on the phone when he called you. We did find the phone. In a garbage can near the Drift In Market, close to where the last call was made according to the cell phone company tower records. I'm betting my badge the only prints we find on it are the doc's."

"You came at the right moment. I think he was going to claim I was attacking him and he shot me in self-defense."

"How're you feeling?" Stone asked.

Harrison moved his arm, which was down to a dull throb. "Electrified."

Stone smiled thinly. "Good thing you don't have a weapon on you. Or a recording device, because we wouldn't want anything to compromise nailing Zellman for his wife's murder and his kid's assault."

"Good thing," Harrison agreed with a straight face. "I can't believe the bastard attacked his own kid."

"He never meant to really hurt him. It was a cover. He had to make sure the kid didn't get up during the attack. But Brandt didn't sustain any deep cuts. He didn't recognize his dad, either, as he was attacked in the dark while he was sleeping. Or, at least he says he didn't. By the time he was conscious and thinking, Zellman had barricaded him in the room by shoving a hall dresser in front of the door. Brandt was too weak to get out and then passed out, we think. Still working on that." Stone exhaled heavily. "Zellman had to have had a pretty bad moment there, at the house, when it looked like Brandt was hurt worse than he thought."

"Good," Harrison stated coldly.

They were walking across the skyway. From the glass crossing, Harrison looked down on the parking lot, where emergency vehicles and police cruisers were parked, lights flashing, the night settling in. An officer was helping Zellman into the back of a car.

Stone said, "I'm not kidding, Frost. Don't mess up my arrest, okay? Zellman may be crazy as a loon, but he's still wealthy, can afford a good lawyer. This case has got to be pristine. If you have a recording or notes, I don't want to see them. Ever. In exchange, once it's over, you'll get first crack at interviews with the department and Zellman." He slid a glance at Harrison. "And this conversation never happened. You need to come down to the department and make a formal statement." Then he walked swiftly away, calling the elevator.

Harrison waited until he saw Stone in the parking lot; then he reached into his pocket, withdrew the microrecorder, tossed it onto the floor, and squashed it with the heel of his boot.

That accomplished, he picked up the pieces, stuffed them into his pocket, and pushed the call button for the elevator.

He glanced at his watch. Seven p.m. Now that Zellman was behind bars, he had to concentrate on Turnbull.

He thought of Laura, of course, but didn't go there. Not yet.

Once outside, he jogged to his car, turned on his cell phone, and read through his texts before he got behind the wheel.

The message that made him take notice was from Buddy, sent fifteen minutes earlier.

Blond chick here with info on Manny Rojas killing at Boozehound.

He stared at the screen, disbelieving. The anorexic blonde? Was this some kind of a joke? The same "skinny blonde" who had stopped into the Sands of Thyme and talked to Kirsten? That was who that was? The one with information on *Manny's death?* He felt that quick little rush of adrenaline pump through his blood he always felt when a story was coming together. And this one, about his sister's husband, was more than just something he found interesting. It was life changing. For Kirsten. For Didi. For him.

Sliding behind the wheel, he called Buddy, who answered on the second ring. "Is the woman still there?" he demanded.

"Yeah, but it's late, y'know? I convinced her to wait, but we're trying to go home here." Then, "She is kinda hot, though, in that super-skinny model way."

"Is she legit? I mean her story."

"You tell me."

"I'll be there in twenty," he said. "Tell her I really want to talk to her." He hit the gas. Was this possible? After all this time, she just came forward?

But there had been a thin blonde the night of the shooting. . . .

He slid into a parking spot at the newspaper in fifty minutes, then hurried inside. Sure enough, seated in front of Buddy's desk, wearing a short skirt, boots, and a long-sleeved T, was a really thin woman with platinum hair feathered around her sculpted face, which had a bored expression. The smell of cigarette smoke surrounded her as she saw him enter. "You're Harrison Frost," she said, and Harrison knew, from viewing the tapes from the security cameras surrounding Boozehound, that this was indeed the woman who'd witnessed the murder of his brother-in-law. "I've been following what's been happening with you."

"And your name is?" he asked.

"Marilla Belgard. I was at the club that night, and I know who killed your brother-in-law."

"You would make a statement to the police?"

"Sure."

"Why now?"

She snorted. "Does it matter?"

"Yeah. It does."

"Guilty conscience, I guess. I saw that you lost your job and well"—she fiddled with the gold cross danging from a chain around her neck—"the Lord found me and I've been atoning . . ."

Harrison grabbed his notepad and said, "Go." After a halting start, she gave him the whole story, which included admitting to knowing Bill Koontz, working for him as a party planner, overhearing him talking one night about how to "get rid of Rojas." She hadn't known he'd planned to have Manny killed until the shooting. She'd disappeared after the doer shot himself, afraid for her life; then, finding a new faith, she'd decided to come clean to Harrison.

"I should have done it earlier," she said, still fingering the cross that dangled between her protruding collarbones.

"Let's just deal with the here and now. I'll call Detective Langdon Stone with the Tillamook Sheriff's Department. He's a friend of mine." Well, that was probably stretching the truth a bit. "It's not his jurisdiction, but he used to work with the Portland Police Department, so he'll know where to steer us."

"You'll . . . you'll be with me, though, right? I'm not really cool with cops."

"Isn't Jesus?"

Marilla eyed him speculatively. "Are you making fun of me?"

Harrison shrugged. "I'll call Stone and we'll head down in my car together."

She relaxed a bit. "If you let me smoke in your car." She looked at him ingenuously. "I'm not kidding. Cops kinda freak me out."

"It'll be fine," Harrison said, the bigger problem being

the time that was passing and the fact that he was beginning to worry about Laura. He'd let his temper get the better of him, and now, after he'd been beat up by and lectured by Kirsten, zapped by Zellman, and confessed to by Marilla Belgard, he was beginning to cool off and realize how much he missed her, how much he worried about her.

Escorting Marilla to his Impala, he checked his phone, saw no message from Laura, and figured she had to be still angry. Well, she had a right, he supposed. As soon as he squared Marilla Belgard with Stone, he'd find Laura and they would work this thing out. Of course, he had a story to write, telling the truth about Manny's death, vindicating himself. But that story could wait a few more days, once Bill Koontz was arrested.

But Justice was still out there, and Laura wouldn't be safe till he was caught.

# CHAPTER 45

Harrison walked out of the Tillamook County Sheriff's Department into a cloud-filled June evening, feeling as if a final page had been written on a chapter of his life that was now closed. He'd introduced Marilla Belgard to Detective Stone, who had listened to her story and called his ex-partner at the Portland Police Department. It looked like Koontz would soon be arrested and finally, finally, Manny's killer would be brought to justice.

*Justice.*

He felt a frisson slide down his back. The bastard may have been wounded, but he wasn't dead. He was still out there, still on his mission. And Laura still wasn't safe.

Harrison had called Kirsten and broken the news about the new evidence in her husband's death. Kirsten had been overwhelmed, asking a million questions, and though Harrison shared her relief, he had to put her on hold for a while.

"I gotta connect with Laura," he told her, and she reluctantly let him go.

He'd left Marilla in Stone's care. The detective had promised to return her to Seaside and the car she'd left at the offices of the *Breeze*.

Deciding it was time to eat a major helping of crow, he punched the speed dial button that connected him to Laura's cell phone, but the call went straight to voice mail. "Hey, it's me. Call me back. Please."

He wondered if she would. A bad feeling settled over him, and he drove straight to Laura's house. Her Outback wasn't in its usual parking spot, and the house was dark. He stopped, anyway, and let himself in with his key, as he'd kept one after changing the lock in the place. But, of course, she wasn't inside.

But she'd been there.

He recognized the T-shirt she'd slept in the night before, left on the foot of the bed, the small bag she'd brought with her on the bathroom floor, the clean scent of the perfume she wore lingering . . . So she was planning to stay here? Just went out to . . . grab a late dinner?

He searched the cottage, making note of the touches that were Laura, the books and plants, the comfortable furniture, eclectic lamps, a haven invaded by a madman. She wasn't here, of course; he knew that. But he even searched the basement, going outside to the exterior steps, but there was nothing but old boxes and forgotten memories.

He tried to call her again, and got nowhere.

So where was she?

His mind raced to several possibilities, and he was locking up, wondering how to track her down, when his phone rang and his heart lifted.

*Laura!*

But the number printed on the screen of his cell was one he didn't recognize. He answered, "Frost."

"Oh, Mr. Frost," a woman said, her voice uncertain. "I'm glad I caught you. This is Catherine Rutledge . . . from Siren Song."

Harrison's heart nearly stopped beating. His fingers curled over the cell. "Yes?"

"I was sworn to secrecy by Lorelei, but I thought you should know . . . she left here and . . ."

Harrison braced himself for the worst.

"And she's taken off after Justice. She's been gone about an hour. She's heading to the lighthouse. She's convinced that he'll return there. I tried to talk her out of it, but she was adamant. Oh, dear, I really shouldn't have let her go, but there was no talking her out of it. I . . . I, uh, just thought someone should know."

And then she clicked off.

Low tide had exposed rocks and tide pools with starfish, barnacles, and mussels. Crabs scuttled away, toward the receding ocean, while the seagulls squawked and wheeled over the sand as they searched for their next meal on the exposed seabed. The rain had let up for a while. A crack in the cloud cover over the horizon showed the last rays of a lowering sun as Laura, hauling the small raft, headed for the island, a rocky ridge bearing the lighthouse, which hadn't been used for years, except as Justice Turnbull's lair a few years ago.

And he'd go back to it; she felt it as surely as she felt electricity in the air, the warning of a gathering storm.

She had to work fast, get to the island, hide the raft, and then wait. She was as prepared as she could be, had provisions for a couple of days, but she knew she wouldn't have to spend too many hours on the island. He would come to her. He couldn't wait.

*Well, hurry up, you bastard,* she thought, paddling in the low tide, where thankfully she wouldn't get tossed around like a cork. She could have walked across the exposed rocks now, but she might need the raft for later, so she cautiously oared over, her mind on her mission.

Ignoring all the nagging questions, her fears screaming

through her brain, she reached the island and made her way to the dock, a dilapidated pier that jetted three feet above the current waterline. It was empty and bleak, covered with seagull droppings. An ancient surfboard, or part of one, had beached upon it. She tied the raft to one of the pilings, said a prayer and, using a flashlight, found the path that switch-backed up the sheltered side of the small island of rock.

As she climbed, the wind gathered force and blew at her hair, the clouds roiled overhead, and she wondered neutrally if she would ever leave this island alive. Rain slanted from the sky, and she thought of the baby she'd lost, her sisters huddled in fear at the Colony, and Harrison. . . . Her fingers reached in her pocket and she cradled her phone, though she wasn't certain there was reception on the island.

Her heart twisted as she thought of Harrison.

She'd loved him, despite knowing him such a short time, and now she wondered if she'd ever see him again.

Carefully, she put the phone back. She wouldn't think of that now. Maybe not ever again.

James's heart was a drum. He was scared out of his mind and wondered how the hell he'd let his dumb shit of a brother talk him into this. They weren't alone on this island, like Mikey had said they would be. The little creep had been wrong.

*Oh, Christ.*

James saw the guy. Tall, his hair blond as it whipped around his face, he stood like the lunatic he was, his feet planted shoulder length apart, his arms flung wide, a long coat flapping around him. He was facing the damned ocean and saying something James couldn't hear, like maybe praying a sicko's prayer. And in one hand, his fingers clenched tight around its hilt, was a mother of a knife.

Mikey hadn't noticed yet, so James grabbed him by the

arm and, with a finger to his lips, pointed with his free hand.

Mikey looked irritated and opened his mouth to speak, then closed it again as he recognized the freak. His eyes widened and he blinked, as if he was trying to dispel the image. James pulled him down to the ground so they could hide behind a rock and some tall beach grass that rose higher than the patchy ground at the base of the lighthouse.

The psycho was standing between them and the only path leading back to the old dock, where they'd ditched the surfboard that Mikey was certain would help them float back to the mainland if need be.

A crazy idea, James now knew, because the tide was turning, and if they wanted to leave and not have to try their luck with the furious, frigid sea, they'd have to leave now.

But of course they couldn't.

Damn, he'd been a fuckin' idiot to listen to his little brother with his ridiculous plans.

Mikey touched him on the shoulder, then pointed to the house that sat at the base of the lighthouse, its back wall nearly abutting. The kid actually thought they could hide in there. . . . It was insane, but they didn't have too many options. Aside from this rise on the hilltop supporting the lighthouse, there wasn't any cover, so . . .

Before he could think it through, Mikey took off running. James caught a glimpse of the psycho, saw that his back was turned, and sprinted behind his brother. Twenty yards, fifteen, ten, five—oh, shit, the madman was rotating slowly, his face in horrific profile.

*Shit! Damn! Fuck!* James leapt the final yard or two, landing behind Mikey, who'd flattened himself against the building's exterior wall. Now all that separated them from the killer was this small house, but it was something.

Carefully, James inched to the door on the far side of the building. He tried the handle. Locked tight.

He nearly pissed his jeans.

Now what?

A quick peek around the corner confirmed his worst fears.

The psycho was striding to the house.

Had he seen them? *Oh, God . . .*

Mikey, eyes serious, pointed a finger at the lighthouse itself.

James shook his head. *No!*

He reached for his brother, but Mikey was off like a shot, streaking behind the house, cutting across the small open space, and then, to James's horror, pushing on the lighthouse's front door and somehow slipping through.

He glanced around the corner again.

*Shit!* The freak was less than twenty yards away.

But his view of the base of the lighthouse was blocked by the building.

James had no choice.

He took off running as fast as he could.

He hoped to hell that the freak didn't see him.


"God damn it!" The minute Catherine hung up on him, Harrison flew to his car and slid inside, where the odor of Marilla's cigarettes still lingered.

What was Laura thinking? No way should she be going to that island!

Wheeling out of her driveway, he headed to Cape Dread, a spot where surfers often camped and the access to the old lighthouse would be the easiest.

It was raining again, almost dark, and he nearly missed the turnoff to the beach at Cape Dread, the closest to Whittier Island. Spying the sign at the last second, he slid across traffic, the RV riding his ass behind him nearly rear-ending him. The driver laid on his horn, but Harrison barely noticed. He hit the gas and drove along a short lane to the lot closest to the park.

Laura's Subaru was parked, nose in, by a short two-rail fence.

His heart sank.

He'd hoped Catherine had been wrong, but now . . .

And there was another car as well. A Dodge Charger parked at an odd angle, taking up nearly three of the faded marks delineating individual spots.

Justice's latest vehicle?

*Jesus, no!*

Harrison's insides curdled with a new, unending dread as he reached into the glove box and extracted his 9 mm. He checked the magazine and, satisfied, climbed out of his car.

Were they both on the damned island, at that lighthouse? Had Laura called the bastard, taunted him, urged him to come and find her in some deadly game of hide-and-seek? Oh, hell . . . Harrison stared toward the spot where the horizon would be, that line where sky meets sea, but that line was invisible, blurred by clouds and darkness. The only good news was that the tide was so low, it looked as if it was almost possible to hike to the island now.

And what then?

*What if you get out there and can't get back?*

He glanced at Laura's car again, absently rubbing his arm where Zellman had shoved the stun gun against it.

To hell with it. Heading toward the ocean, he called Detective Stone's cell phone and left a voice mail about his position and what he thought might be going down. Heart in his throat, he pocketed his cell, held tight to his Glock, and started jogging through the exposed rocks toward the island Justice friggin' Turnbull had once called home.

\* \* \*

Rounding a final curve on the trail up, Laura sensed the storm shifting, a malevolence brewing.

And somewhere Justice could be nearby. She felt it. Her fingers clamped around the .38 as she narrowed her eyes against the rain. It was coming down steadily now, the drops cool against her face.

At the crest of the path, the lighthouse was in full view, a narrow tower that knifed upward and seemed to pierce the darkening heavens. Standing on a rocky tor, with thick patches of beach grass, the tower loomed over the squatty, dilapidated house at its base.

*What horrors have you witnessed?*

Had Justice ever brought anyone here?

Or had he hidden in solitude, his mind disintegrating with the passing of time?

It didn't matter what had happened here; it was only important that it was finally over. She flipped off the safety of her gun, then dashed to the door of the keeper's house, but it was locked tight. No entrance here. Slowly, still wary, she eased around the building and kept her body flush against the crumbling walls. The windows were boarded, a back exit locked as well. No way to get inside.

She had brought a few tools with her and could break in if she needed, but first she wanted to make certain she was alone. Cautiously, she hurried to the attached lighthouse, the monolith that Justice, according to what she'd read, had called home. Where he'd found peace. Or whatever it was he'd been looking for.

The latch on the door wasn't fastened.

The door itself was slightly ajar.

Her heart turned to ice.

*He's here!*

*Inside!*

*Oh, dear God.*

Fear turned her insides to water.

*Wait! You don't know that he's inside. The door could have been left open long ago.* Suddenly she wondered if she'd made a deadly mistake, if she should turn around, call the authorities, save herself. . . .

Instead, she drew in a long, steadying breath, then pushed the door open farther with the revolver's short nose.

As the door creaked open, Laura stepped into the yawning darkness.

*She's arrived!*

*I smell her and her empty, malodorous womb. Foolish, foolish woman. So easily tricked to come here to my lair. I feel a smile curve over my lips as the spray from the ocean caresses my face and the wind plays with my hair. I heard her pathetic voice trying to reach me, to tempt me to this, my home, but I had already arrived.*

*As ever, I am a step or two ahead of her.*

*I take in a long, healing breath of salt-sea air, dragging it into my lungs, feeling its glorious healing powers. I look toward Cape Dread, that crooked finger of land that stretches into the Pacific, where it lures the tidewaters and foolhardy sea captains to a certain and deadly fate.*

*Tonight no lights glow on that cape; there is no sign that the narrow expanse of land is inhabited. That evil lurks within the densely forested cliffs. Which is just as it should be.*

*I feel my strength returning.*

*Earlier this day I was weak, recovering. I'd let my guard down with the vile ones. Been foolish.*

*But now . . .*

*I'm whole again.*

*And anxious.*

*For Lorelei.*

*Get ready, whore.*

# CHAPTER 46

On silent footsteps Laura climbed, one hand on the rusted circular rail, the other gripped over the butt of her gun. The old staircase groaned with her weight, thick, blistering paint peeling beneath her fingertips. Could Justice hear her over the thunder of the sea? She didn't know, but she kept mounting the rickety stairs, her heart pounding an erratic tattoo.

She had two choices. To kill him or wound him badly enough to disable him and wait for the police to arrive.

Otherwise, she was dead.

She knew it.

So did he.

Up, up, up. Her legs beginning to cramp. While the storm picked up and the sea raged, she moved inside and around the lighthouse walls, ever ascending. Her pulse was pounding; her body drenched in a thin layer of perspiration.

Was he waiting for her?

Hidden in the shadows?

Her throat closed in fear at the thought that he could toss her headlong down these narrow stairs or, with his strength, could throw her over the fragile rail and down to the concrete floor some sixty feet below. . . .

*Do this, Laura. Do it now.*

Gritting her teeth, she kept climbing.

Squinting into the darkness, ears straining at every sound, her fear palpable.

But she didn't stop.

Frigid water, cold as the Arctic, swept into the small cove as the tide shifted, each wave creeping farther inland. The wind had become a battering ram, pushing him backward with every step forward.

Harrison kept diligently moving onward, making headway regardless. He stopped only once to try and reach Detective Stone one more time. Still no answer. Was the cop ignoring his calls? Or just busy with Marilla? He left a second message outlining what he knew and hoped the detective got it.

*It's late. Stone might have called it a day.*

He considered calling 9-1-1 but thought better of it. What if it wasn't an emergency? What if when he got to the island, he found no one? What if Laura had just parked her car there and . . . and what?

No way!

She was out here. In danger.

He knew it.

Could feel it.

The sky was darker now and he still had a lot of ground to cover before the turning tide rushed in, so he kept moving forward, determined not to fall, intent on keeping his body dry and his gun ready to fire.

With each step over the slippery rocks, his gut tightened a little more. Like notches in a belt that was already too tight. Cutting off his breath. Reminding him that he was only human.

Still he moved forward.

Crossing from one flat rock to another.

Making his way to the lighthouse.

He tried to stay focused, but with each step to the next rock, his insides tightened and he thought of Laura and what she might be going through.

*Don't go there.*

*Concentrate.*

He hopped to the next rock, nearly misjudging the distance, and his feet slipped a little. He caught himself.

*You can do this.* Only a little farther, five or six more rocks.

But the tide was rising, the top of the rocks disappearing under the wildly swirling foam of each wave. He had to center all his concentration on crossing the inlet. Time his steps. Pick out the rocks that were the most exposed, ignore those that were beginning to submerge.

And all the while time was passing. Minutes ticking by. Darkness settling.

He thought of Laura's car and the other one . . . the unknown.

*Don't go there. Don't give in to the panic. Concentrate, damn it!*

Rain was falling steadily now, the wind screaming and above it all, loud as thunder. The ocean threatened, moving ever inland, destroying the land bridge, making certain that whoever was on the island would be trapped. . . .

His cell phone jangled.

Stone! Thank God.

He tried to snag the phone from his pocket.

And his right foot slipped.

He tried to catch himself, grasping at only air, teetering crazily.

A wave slapped the rock. Cold water splashed over his ankles. His balance, already compromised, gave way.

No!

He slid farther, falling wildly and scraping himself on

the rock as he sank, his body sliding beneath the bitter cold water.

His gun fell from his hands and he panicked, tried to regain it, felt it tumbling end over end in the sea. No! He couldn't lose the only weapon he had! Shit! He hit bottom and realized he was still in only six feet of water, the crevice near the base of Whittier Island just deep enough that he couldn't stand.

For now.

With the passing of time, the turning of the tide, the water would rise farther.

He dived down. Cold water surrounded him, moving and shifting, pushing him against the rocks. He felt the bottom of the sea. Nothing! His lungs were on fire, so he stood, sucking in air.

He should go on. Forget the weapon. He was losing precious time, and his arm that had been shot with the stun gun earlier was throbbing. But he needed that gun, damn it! He took in another deep breath, and as the restless water washed over him, he submerged, running his fingers on the sandy bottom, feeling rocks, and a fish that slid away, then seaweed that curled over his wrists like a lover's hands.

His lungs were tight. He needed air. But he kept at it, until he felt as if he would explode.

His fingertips scraped against something metal.

He grabbed hold and dragged the object up with him, gasping and gurgling as he stood on tiptoe. The Glock, probably useless now, was firmly in his hand again.

*Move it, Frost. You're running out of time.*

He forced himself forward, toward the dock, his clothes sodden, icy weights, his skin colder than it had ever been in his life. It was like slogging through mud, and the sea forever tore at him, pushing against his shivering, battered body. There was no ladder, but an inflated raft was tied to the dock, and he knew now, for certain, he wasn't alone on the island.

Was Laura hiding somewhere here? Or had Justice found her? He couldn't think that she might already be dead, wouldn't let his already anxious mind go there. Using all his strength, his wounded arm practically useless, he hauled himself onto the worn, rotting boards while the rain peppered his already drenched body.

He figured he might freeze tonight.

But he didn't care.

As long as he found Laura and she was safe.


Stone was shrugging into his jacket before heading home when he checked his voice mail. He listened to Frost's messages about Justice Turnbull being holed up on Serpent's Eye and Laura Adderley tracking the killer down at the abandoned lighthouse.

No way.

They'd checked the lighthouse. As best they could, anyway, as most of the time it was inaccessible by land.

Didn't make sense.

But he checked the license number of the Dodge Harrison had phoned in and discovered it belonged to a Ron and Francie Ferguson. Who lived in the valley. Huh. Not reported stolen. Maybe not related to the Turnbull business . . . and yet . . . he reached for his sidearm and his holster. In the last few days Stone had garnered a grudging respect for the reporter. Frost had helped nail Zellman and hadn't printed anything he'd promised not to. He'd brought Marilla Belgard to the police before penning the story that would be his ultimate revenge, a way to clear his name of the huge black spot from supposedly mishandling that mess outside Boozehound that had resulted in his brother-in-law's death.

Yeah, all in all, Frost was okay.

Not one to sound the alarm when there wasn't trouble.

So why the hell wasn't he picking up his phone?

Stone hesitated. Thought of Claire, who was waiting for him with dinner prepared and warming on the stove.

Again.

He had sent Savvy Dunbar to take the Belgard woman back to her car in Seaside and had intended to go straight home. . . .

Oh, hell. It wouldn't kill him to go out to the cove and have a look.


Out of breath by the time she ascended to the top of the lighthouse, Laura found herself in the small room that housed the huge long-dead lamp. Her heart was pounding in her ears and her skin crawled with the feeling—the sense—that Justice was here. She remembered the rage in his last attack, how his finger had scraped her back, how his fury had palpitated from him.

A bona fide lunatic.

She felt as if he were watching her, sensed hidden eyes somehow scrutinizing her every move. Could he see her? When he sent his horrible threats to her mind, was he able to visualize her, too? Watch her like a sadistic voyeur?

She threw off the image and scanned the room. The glass windows were cracked, but intact, the view of the ocean barely visible through layers of dirt and grime. The glass walls were curved, and there was an exit door through one of the windows that led to the metal outside balcony and railing. The lamp itself, long extinguished, filled the center of the circular room, a dead relic of an earlier era.

An era that Catherine, with her long skirts and avoidance of all things modern, tried vainly to re-create.

Laura's skin crawled as she thought of how many times Justice had climbed those stairs, how many times he'd stood in the very spot she now occupied. She imagined him on the platform, arms wide, face turned toward the west as he embraced the sea.

Fear crawled up her spine, its icy fingers clutching at her soul.

*Don't go there,* she told herself.

Then she heard it.

Over the roar of the surf and the rush of the wind.

That horrid scraping rasp that was Justice's voice.

*Sssissterr . . . ,* he threw out at her and she nearly dropped the gun. She spun, expecting him behind her, but the top of the stairs was empty.

*Sssissterrr!*

The sound only she could hear reverberated through her mind.

And it was close.

"Where the hell are you?" she demanded and thought she heard a squeak of fear. From behind the lantern? Really.

And then the heavy step upon the uppermost stairs.

She snapped her head up, saw the huge, dark figure looming in the doorway. "Oh, God," she whispered, the gun in her hand shaking.

Justice stepped into the dome, his face a twisted mask of hatred, his icy eyes damning. She stared face-to-face with her mortal enemy as Justice, filling the doorway to the stairs, smiled with a menacing, satisfied grin.

"Foolish, foolish woman," he snarled.

She raised her gun at him. "It's over." The barrel was pointed at him.

He glanced down at her weapon. "Lorelei . . ."

"Don't move, Justice."

"You can't kill me, Lorelei."

"Watch me." Her teeth were starting to chatter.

His grin was pure evil. His eyes cold as a demon's soul.

She heard a whimper and glanced to the side. Was there someone else up here?

Oh, God—

In a split second, Justice lunged. "Sssisterr . . ."

She pulled the trigger to blast him to hell.

# CHAPTER 47

Breathing hard, shivering, Harrison hauled himself to his knees. He couldn't slow down. Had to push forward. Up the steep path that wound to the crown of this tiny scrap of land. He had to climb over a sagging, useless chain-link fence, but he kept moving, the salt water in his jeans squishing and feeling like dead weight.

He reached the top of the trail and stared through the dark to the lighthouse. No one in sight.

But she was here. She had to be.

And someone else. The owner of the Dodge Charger.

He crept forward, Glock in hand, breathing hard, squinting in the darkness, staring at the lighthouse.

*Blam!*

The sound of a gun blast rocked the island.

"Shit!"

A quick fire flash flared bright in the windows of the dome.

Then it was dark again.

Eerily so.

*Laura!*

In his mind's eye, Harrison saw her, bleeding from the bullet wound in her chest, staggering and pitching over the railing, her hair streaming behind her, blood spraying as she fell to her death.

He took off at a dead sprint.


All hell broke loose!

With a roar, Justice fell backward, blood blooming on the shirt visible beneath his open coat.

Two boys, hidden by the huge lamp, screamed and leapt to their feet, exposing themselves. Oh, Jesus! Kids? There were *kids* here?

Laura pointed the gun at her attacker again but couldn't shoot, not with the boys in the tiny room. The bullet could ricochet. . . .

Unless she got close enough to him to jab the gun under his ribs.

She didn't have time to think. He caught himself on the door and, glowering at her, raised his damned knife and lunged again. "Run!!!" she screamed to the boys as she backed up, her fingers finding the latch to the window exit. If she could get him outside, she'd fire every damned bullet she had into his filthy flesh.

Justice, stunned, eyed the kids.

She aimed. "Leave them alone, you son of a bitch!"

He glared at her from the doorway, and the blind rage she'd seen before entered his eyes. "Sssisterrr! Filthy whore!" He took a step forward, and she backed up, holding her .38 as steady as she could.

"Run!!!" she screamed again as Justice raised his knife and reeled forward.

The boys were huddled against the far wall, behind the lamp.

Her fingers scraped against the rusted latch. *Please open . . . please . . .*

She pulled on the latch.

Nothing!

She was trapped! The only way out was behind Justice, down the stairs the way she'd come up. Unless there was a ladder on the exterior of the lighthouse . . . *Come on, come on!* Her fingers coiled over the window's latch, and she gave it another hard tug. Something creaked, started to give way, but at that moment, Justice raised his knife and swung, throwing himself forward.

The blade sliced downward.

She dived to one side and Justice was thrown off balance. He fell against the lamp.

With a shriek the boys ran behind him, throwing themselves through the open doorway and clattering down the stairs. Their voices echoed upward, their footsteps ringing loudly on the weak metal steps.

Justice lunged again and she pushed her gun into his gut, but he grabbed her hand and thrust it aside as she pulled the trigger. The bullet went wild, pinging back and forth through the small space, shattering the lamp in a deafening blast.

Glass sprayed. Justice threw his weight onto her, pressing her to the wall, twisting her arm back at her wrist.

Pain rocketed up her arm.

She sucked in her breath but couldn't let go. Wouldn't! Scrabbling backward, she pushed against the outer door.

With a shrieking groan, the latch gave way and the window exit flew open. Rain and wind burst into the dome as the window opened. They toppled together onto the rickety metal platform surrounding the dome. It shimmied and creaked under their weight, barely attached to the lighthouse. Her back was to the rail, and Justice's body, heavy and smelling of sour sweat, pinned her tight.

She fired another shot and it went wild, into the air.

*Snap!*

Pain screamed through her arm.

The gun went sliding away, across the mesh platform.

"No!"

She watched in horror as the Smith & Wesson slid over the edge, spinning down into the darkness.

Gasping for breath, Harrison ran up the stairs. "Laura!" he yelled, his voice echoing within the hollow tower of the lighthouse, the wind screaming outside. "Laura! Hold on!" If that sicko hurt her . . . oh, hell. Up he ran, holding onto the rail, taking the steps two at a time.

He heard the footsteps hurrying toward him, and he flattened against the wall, his gun drawn. "Laura!" he cried.

"She's up there!" a boy's voice cried, and then he saw them, two kids in their teens. "He's got her!" the younger one said, staring into the muzzle of Harrison's gun. "Justice Turnbull. He's got her!"

"Get out of here!" Harrison yelled.

They plowed past him, running, tumbling, racing to the bottom.

Harrison hurtled upward, adrenaline fueling him, rage burning in his soul. "Turnbull!" he yelled. "Come on, you son of a bitch! Come the hell after me!"

And then he heard Laura scream, a piercing shriek of pure terror.

"Die, Ssissterr!" Justice hissed, the stench of his breath fanning over her face. He raised his blade high, and she screamed, flinging herself upward, trying to throw off his heavy weight.

The blade glinted wickedly above her.

The platform groaned, metal twisting over the shriek of the wind.

He swung downward, intent on slicing her throat, but she kicked him hard. Brought her knee fast to his groin and the blade struck his own leg.

Bellowing, he convulsed, and she rolled away, the railing of the platform against her back.

She sprang for the open window to the inner dome, but the platform shifted, ancient bolts giving way. Her wet hands slipped. Rain pelted her. The metal footing listed and she began to slide, toward the place where the platform had torn from the wall and dangled precariously over the rocks below.

Justice leapt for her, clawing on top of her. She kicked again, swinging hard! Her booted foot jammed into his crotch.

With a shriek, he doubled over. His knife fell from his hands, skittering across the metal flooring, sliding toward the edge as it listed, then falling, as if in slow motion, to be swallowed in the darkness below.

Justice's fingers, slick with his own blood and the rain, scrabbled for purchase on the railing. His weight dragged him downward. Laura held on to the platform with her good arm, trying to inch toward the open window, praying the platform would hold. Its groaning metal hurt her ears. She clawed her way upward, grabbing, struggling. She wrapped her good arm around a rusted metal post, wedging it against her shoulder, flattening her body over the flooring.

With a horrible scream of twisting metal, the entire platform tore away from the wall of the lighthouse. Part of the flooring gave way and fell to the sea. Laura closed her eyes, held tight, and prayed. Then she felt the clamp of steely fingers around her ankle.

Justice had grabbed her, his weight too much, dragging her downward.

*No! God, help me.* She struggled upward. Her leg felt as if it would pop out of its hip socket. The world started to spin, darkness threatening to shroud her, the wind gusting and keening.

Her boot began to slip from her foot.

God, the pain.

She struggled to hang on, to stay conscious, to not give in to the desperate need to let go.

Setting her jaw against the agony clawing through her, she kicked back with her free foot and connected with the monster's arms. *Bam!*

He howled again.

She kicked again, but he twisted. She missed, and it was all she could do not to black out.

"Laura!" For a moment she thought she heard Harrison's voice. Oh, God. Her heart wrenched at the thought of him. Again, the blackness came, luring her to let go . . . to fall to the sea like her namesake.

"Laura, hang on!"

The world seemed to swim before her eyes. Clouds roiling above, sea swirling below. The blackness tugged at her consciousness, dragging her under.

*Hang on,* she told herself, *for God's sake . . . oh, but the pain.* Her body felt as if it were being ripped in two.

*Fight, Laura. Do not let him win. For the love of God! Do not let Justice win!*

"You miserable bastard." One more kick! *Smack!* She connected with his wrist.

He screamed, a piercing, soul-splintering cry.

Suddenly the hand clasping her ankle gave way.

"Sissterrr! Nooo!"

She glanced back. Justice tumbled into the night, arms and legs kicking wildly, down, down, down into the darkness. Through the mesh of the platform she watched him disappear to the rocky shoals below.

He cast out one final threat. *You will never be rid of me . . . Lorelei . . . Sisst—*

"Laura!" She looked up and saw Harrison in the open window of the lighthouse. He stood before the dark hole, his gaze on hers, his face white with terror. "Hang on. Do you hear me? Hang on!" He leaned forward, one hand holding on to the broken latch, the other stretched far as he could reach.

His hand caught only air. "Grab my hand!" he ordered.

But she couldn't lift her bad arm. Her wrist throbbed and wouldn't respond as she flailed.

His fingers brushed hers.

"Harrison!" she cried, but it was too late.

With one final deep, echoing groan, the final bolt gave way and the platform ripped free, wrenching away from the lighthouse.

Laura, still grasping the rail, began to tumble and fall, spinning out of control. Sky and ground one dark, horrifying blur . . .

"Lorelei!" Harrison called, his voice drowned by the surf.

The platform swung downward, then released, Laura with it. The wind rushed. There was a sense of flying. She closed her eyes, expecting death.

She hit the water so hard, every bone in her body screamed. Arctic cold water poured over her as she sank into the salty depths. Waves crashed and tossed her, yanking her free of the platform. She scraped on rocks and looked up through the watery depths, seeing a light, bright and round, above her.

*Harrison . . . love . . . I'm sorry . . . . so, so sorry . . . I should have told you. . . .*

The blackness came again, seducing her, dragging her under, salt water seeping into her lungs.

She let go.


"No!" Harrison watched in horror as Laura fell away, her body disappearing into the sea. He didn't think twice but took a running start and threw himself out of the lighthouse. He could miss and hit the rocks, or hit the sea and die from the impact, but he didn't take the time to second-guess himself.

Through the night he sailed, arms out, down to the ocean that he couldn't see. At the last moment he tucked himself into a straight arrow and hit the surface tension of the water feetfirst, a wave immediately catching him and tossing him closer to shore.

He surfaced, treading water, spitting salt water, spying a light . . . on the ocean, a beam illuminating the whirling, foaming surf. In the middle of the beam, he saw her. Limp. Lifeless. Laura.

He was too late.

*No!*

He swam for her, intent on reaching her, fighting the strength of the surf, forcing himself closer, into that wide swath of light. As he reached her still form, he realized that the light was from a hovering helicopter that battled the buffeting storm as a basket was being lowered.

"Laura," he gasped, his voice a whisper, the sea a roar in his ears. He'd lost her. God in heaven he'd lost her. He thought of how he'd reacted when she'd told him she'd been pregnant, how callous he'd been. What a self-serving idiot.

His soul seemed ripped from his body as he held her, watching her hair fan around her white face as the waves undulated. Her eyes fixed and staring, her skin as cold as the sea, the rain like the tears of the gods. "Lorelei . . . don't die. Please . . . please . . . don't die!" The words were torn from him and lost in the thunder of the seas. "Lorelei, I love you! Oh, God . . . you can't die. You can't. If you only knew . . ."

She awoke in a private room at Ocean Park Hospital.

She remembered hitting the water and a bright light, and Harrison hanging out the yawning window of the lighthouse. In the ensuing moments of lucidity, she recalled images that were more like postcards than a movie. A helicopter ride over the ocean, landing at the hospital. Harrison with her . . . or was that a dream?

She blinked. "Am I in the north wing?" she asked, getting her bearings.

The window ledge was covered in flowers, but she was pretty sure the view outside the window was on the north side of the building.

"Good call. North one-twenty-six." Harrison's voice was a surprise. She turned her head and found him seated in one of the chairs that stretched into a bed. It was mussed, as if he'd camped out here. "Lucidity at last," he said with a smile.

She tried to lift her arm and found it strapped down, an IV running into it and, she guessed, from the way she was feeling, some pain meds flowing through her bloodstream. She attempted to sit up.

"Slow down," he said and was at her side, staring down at her, looking guilty as hell. "Here . . . I think I can work this." He found the button to raise her head.

"If you can't manage, I'm pretty sure I can."

"Hey! Look who joined the living!" Carlita Solano, dressed in blue scrubs, came bustling up to the bed. "How're ya feeling?"

"Like a train ran over me, then backed up and went at it again."

She grinned. "That's about right. But you're tough and it looks like you might just live. Let me take your vitals and then you and he"—she cocked her head in Harrison's direction—"can catch up."

Carlita explained her injuries, that Laura had suffered a broken wrist, sprained elbow, concussion, and pulled hip flexor. "All in all, it could have been worse," Carlita said, then finished with her temperature, pulse, and blood pressure, entering the data into a computer by the bed. Once she finished, she said she'd call the doctor for a more extensive examination, then slipped out of the room.

"Okay, so tell me," Laura said as the door closed behind the nurse. "Why are either of us alive?"

"Just lucky."

"That's a long way down."

"Tell me about it."

She slid him a glance. "I do remember you in the water . . . right?"

He nodded. "I got a little beat up, scraped and bruised, but that's about it."

"No hypothermia?"

"As I said, lucky."

She drew a long breath. "Justice?"

"Dead. Fell on the rocks. Not even he could survive that. Broke his neck and a dozen other bones."

She closed her eyes for a moment. She didn't feel any remorse that he lost his life. Too many people had died or been terrorized and wounded because of him. Harrison filled her in on the crimes Zellman had committed against his family. When he finished she asked, "How's Conrad?" The last time she'd checked, the security guard was still co-matose.

"Awake. Was released yesterday. And Zellman's still cooling his jets in prison. His son is talking. Seems as if it wasn't too dark for Brandt to recognize that his own father was trying to wound him. The kid thinks he was supposed to die that night. His father swears not."

"My God."

"Zellman used Justice's escape for his own means. He's as sick as any of 'em."

Laura absorbed that. "How long have I been out of it?"

"Just a couple of days. You've surfaced, only to submerge again."

"I think I'm back."

He smiled, relief sketched on his face.

"Have you heard from anyone at the Colony? My sisters?"

"Actually, this . . ." He walked to the window and touched a small pot holding a live tea rose, bright yellow and bursting with blooms, the same kind of small roses that were grown in a sunny spot at Siren Song, as old-fashioned as the women housed there. "It's from Catherine and your sisters." He handed her the card. A simple get-well note signed by the women of Siren Song. "I think Catherine may have had a change of heart since Justice breached her walls and some of the girls are itching to get out."

"Ravinia," Laura guessed, running her fingers over Ravinia's bold scrawl, a large signature next to Lillibeth's rounder, more feminine one. Lillibeth dotted her *i*'s with a heart. Ravinia didn't bother dotting them at all.

"And this one"—he indicated a large bouquet with tropical flowers, a bird-of-paradise the focal point—"is from Hudson, Becca, and Rachel."

"You've been going through my mail."

"Guilty as charged. And Becca's been calling." He handed her a yellow envelope with a funny card. It was signed in a woman's handwriting—Becca's—with a wild, multi-colored felt pen scrawl covering most of the message inside.

"Looks like Rachel's going to be an author. She's pretty proud of her signature." Laura smiled, thinking of Becca's daughter. The last time she'd seen the toddler, she'd been listless. "How is she?"

"Better, I think. From what Becca said. But she seems worried."

"About the gift," Laura said aloud. "Becca understands." Growing up being different was difficult enough for Laura and her sisters. Rachel would have more than her share of battles to fight. Another thought struck her. "There were some kids in the lighthouse that night?"

"The enterprising Ferguson boys." Harrison nodded. "The younger one had a fascination with all things Justice Turnbull. Mikey—he felt some kind of weird connection to him, wanted to see his lair for himself, and maybe to impress his friends or a girl, I'm thinking, find some kind of memento, proof that he'd been there. But I think he got enough of that at the lighthouse."

"And you know this how?"

"I got to write their story, gave them their fifteen minutes of fame while their parents intended to give them their thirty days of no car or cell phone."

"Death to a teen," she observed.

"Yeah, well, hopefully they'll think twice before they chase down psychotic killers again." He touched the back of her hand. "And what about you? Are you done 'calling' homicidal maniacs?"

"Let's hope," she said. "One personal serial killer is more than enough, don't you think?"

"Way more."

In her mind's eye, she saw Justice in the ocean at the lighthouse again, witnessed his terror; and then, when she was nearly lost, was filled with a sense of giving up and letting go, she'd heard Harrison's frantic voice, felt his warm arms around her in the frigid water. He'd brought her back. "So, you saved my life?"

"I don't think I can take credit." When she raised her eyebrows, encouraging him to explain, he said, "It was actually the Coast Guard. Lieutenant O'Neal. I've thanked him for you."

"I think I'll talk to him myself."

"That would be good. And then there was Detective Stone. He called them."

"Who called him?" she asked, watching the shift of emotions upon Harrison's handsome face.

"Me."

"But you were in the water." She was thinking hard, remembering him beside her, talking to her, insisting she not let go. . . . "You jumped!" she cried, absolutely astounded, and when he didn't respond, she added, "You're crazy, Frost. And that's something coming from me. I know crazy."

He couldn't scare up a smile.

"What?"

"I think I owe you an apology."

"For saving my life?"

"For being angry with you about the pregnancy."

"Oh." She sighed, not wanting to go there yet.

"I'm in love with you, Lorelei. I'd just figured that out and it scared me. But then . . . thinking I might have lost you." His jaw slid to the side and his throat worked, but he didn't break down. Instead, he slid his fingers around her nape, leaned over, and placed a kiss on her lips. "If you only knew how sorry I am."

"I should have told you. . . . I didn't know how. I was pregnant by my ex-husband, with a baby I intended to keep." Her throat caught as she remembered the pain of the miscarriage, the loss of the baby. But there was more. He was being honest, and now so was she. "The truth was, I was falling for you. Hard. Fast. I couldn't believe it was real. It . . . it just didn't make a lot of sense."

"I know."

She stared at him long and hard, saw the depth of his pain, a mirror of her own, then reached up to draw his mouth to hers once more. "Maybe we should start over."

"Think that's possible?"

"Anything is if you want it badly enough," she said, knowing her eyes were twinkling.

"Then, how bad do you want this?" he asked.

"Bad. You?"

"Even badder," he said, a slow smile curving his lips.

She laughed. Then she kissed him. Hard. Just as he expected.

# EPILOGUE

She'd made a mess of things, Catherine thought as she rode in Earl's motorboat to Echo Island.

With all her good intentions, in trying to save her charges from heartache, ridicule, and pain, Catherine had fouled up.

In the two months since Justice had died, their life at Siren Song had never returned to what Catherine proclaimed was normal.

The gates of Siren Song were closed and locked again; the work and rules restored. But there was a restlessness with the girls, and Catherine knew the order she had preached, had tried to instill, was forever broken. Ravinia was chomping at the bit to leave; the others would follow.

They had seen Rebecca with her husband and little girl, had witnessed firsthand Harrison Frost's dedication to Lorelei. They'd all been swept away by the fantasy and romance that he'd risked his life for her.

As Earl guided the boat to the small dock here on Mary's island of exile, her "Elba" she'd once said, Catherine wondered what she would say to her sister, how she would explain her change of heart. Could she admit that she'd been wrong? That perhaps Mary should return to

Siren Song and, as far as anyone knew, from the grave? Of course that wouldn't work. There were laws about those kinds of things . . . laws similar to faking someone's death, she supposed. And now that Lorelei spent more time with her sisters, and that fiancé of hers had a nose for news . . . no, it would never work.

She would have to think of something else.

The sound of the sea was louder here, the tides splashing around the rocks and shoals. Mary had always said she'd found it comforting.

Catherine wondered.

But if she was happy, so be it. Of course, Mary had always been delusional. . . . It ran in their family. . . .

"I shouldn't be too long," she said to Earl as he cut the engine and tied up. "Half an hour, maybe."

He nodded. "I'll wait. Got my pole."

With his help, she climbed onto the dock, and left him opening his cooler of bait. Holding her skirts so that the hem of her dress wouldn't skim the dirt and bird excrement on the old boards, she bustled to a sandy, overgrown path that wound a hundred feet to Mary's home. The cottage was little more than a one-room cabin, even more austere and cut off from the world than Siren Song. It was a wonder no one had ever found her here. . . . But then, Catherine knew from her own experience that even the most bizarre circumstances did exist . . . how else to explain all the gifts the girls had received.

There were rumors in town of a hermit who lived on the island, an old hag that ran sightseers off, but if anyone had made the connection between the recluse and Mary Beeman, Catherine didn't know about it.

She swatted at a fly as she walked, felt a bead of sweat on her brow. It was late summer now, going on September, the August sun hot against her face.

*A fly?* she thought. *Out here?*

Odd.

Then again, what wasn't odd these days? Everything about her sister had been "out of sync," "a little off," or "odd" since her birth. Upon her exile, the cover story was that Mary had fallen to her death on one of her solitary walks, while the woman sometimes seen on Echo Island was the bereaved, reclusive wife of one of the lighthouse caretakers from Whittier Island who had died, but no one really paid attention. Everyone today was all caught up in their own lives, too interested in themselves to do more than gossip about the weird old lady of Echo Island.

Catherine hurried on. Squinting against a lowering sun, she noticed that Mary's garden, usually so perfect, was untended. Beach grass had taken over, and the tea roses were leggy, the blooms dried and dying. "Mary?" she called as she walked to the door and saw the boxes of supplies on the porch. The cardboard was sun bleached, the fruit and vegetables gone bad, the stink of rotting meat overpowering.

What the devil?

"Mary!" she called again and pushed on the door. How long had it been since she'd been here?

It was unlatched and from within the stench was worse. It hit Catherine with the force of a malodorous tidal wave. The buzzing of swarming flies competed with the sound of the surf. Catherine's stomach revolted as her eyes grew accustomed to the darkened interior. On the bed was a corpse, what was left of her sister, little more than dried, rotting flesh and exposed bones. Mary's face was unrecognizable, her eyes gone, two dark exposed sockets where those beautiful blue orbs had once been. Her hair was long and splayed around a skull of darkened, dried skin, her teeth exposed as she had no lips, her cheeks gone. She looked like a zombie with a ghoulish, wicked grin.

The hilt of the knife rose from her chest. The skeletal fingers of Mary's right hand surrounded it, as if she'd tried to yank the blade out and failed. Hanks of old flesh hung from her fingers and arm.

A scream boiled to the heavens. A wild shriek of pure fear.

It took Catherine a moment to realize it came from her own lips.

"Holy mother of God!" she whispered, retching, backing away.

But the vision of Mary was burned in her brain as she scrambled backward, nearly tripping over her own skirts. Trying not to scream, she turned and ran for the door.

What in God's good name had happened to her sister?

Dear Reader,

I hope you enjoyed reading WICKED LIES. My sister Nancy Bush and I had a great time writing about The Colony again, just as we did in WICKED GAME, the first book where members of Siren Song were introduced. We always like returning to the Oregon Coast as it's truly one of our favorite places to visit.

Next up, I've written BORN TO DIE, the third in my series featuring Detectives Selena Alvarez and Regan Pescoli of Grizzly Falls, Montana. It will be in bookstores in August 2011. This time, a killer is on the loose and he's targeting a certain physical type.

All the victims are pretty and resemble each other, and they look a lot like Dr. Kacia "Kacey" Lambert, with her long auburn hair and green eyes. It's unsettling for Kacey, especially when one of the victims is the ex-girlfriend of a single father in town, Trace O'Halleran, the father of a child she's treating. It all seems surreal to Kacey, but she can't deny her own case of nerves, that somehow, someway she's come into a diabolical killer's sights!

I've always had a lot of fun writing about Alvarez and Pescoli and the interesting if odd characters that pepper Grizzly Falls, and I think you'll enjoy this new book.

I've included an excerpt and if you want even more information about BORN TO DIE or any of my other books, please log onto www.lisajackson.com or join me on Facebook. I look forward to hearing from you!

Keep reading,
Lisa Jackson

*Sometimes you win; sometimes you lose.*

Tonight, Shelly Bonaventure thought, she'd come out the loser. Make that a loser with a capital *L*; the kind kids made with their thumb and forefinger held up to their foreheads.

She was feeling queasy, the pain in her abdomen intense.

Either she'd drunk too much, eaten the wrong thing, or her period was coming a few days early. She would take some Pepto if she had it and if not, just suffer through until morning. As she tossed her purse onto the couch, she glanced around for her cat and made her way to the bathroom. Nearly tripping on the rug she'd bought—oh, God, had it really been seven years ago—she called out, "Lana? Kitty? Momma's home."

Had she lived in this one-bedroom apartment for nearly a decade, watching the years tumble past and the roles she'd hoped to land be handed to someone else?

Ever since her divorce from Cameron . . .

She wasn't going to dwell on *that*. Not tonight. A positive attitude, that's what she needed. She'd just had a little too much to drink at Lizard's, the bar down the street. Cut-

ting loose, telling herself she was going to embrace the big
3-5 that was bearing down on her, she'd overindulged.

But just a bit.

How could she help it, when the guy she'd met had
heard about her birthday and bought her several Mai Tais
and had seemed really interested? She'd been flattered and
flirted as she sipped drink after drink.

A mistake, she now realized.

But he'd been so damned hot! She'd even mentioned to
him that he had a killer smile and he'd found that comment
amusing.

*Yeah, but you left him in the bar, didn't you?*

Of course she had and it was probably a good idea,
really, considering the fact that she was feeling ill and had a
five o'clock wake-up call. She was auditioning for a role on
a new drama to be aired on Fox in the fall. The casting call
was being held early tomorrow and she intended to look
her best. Better than her best.

If she could just shake this lousy feeling. Good Lord, was
she actually perspiring? That wasn't good; not good at all.

After all, this television series might be her last shot,
considering Hollywood's attitude about age.

How depressing was that?

Shelly Bonaventure had to make it, she *had* to. She
couldn't very well go back to that podunk town in Montana
with her tail between her legs. Hadn't she been prom queen
of Sycamore High, voted "Most Likely To Be Famous" her
senior year? Hadn't she taken off, shaking the dust of that
small town from her shoes as quickly as possible? And
hadn't, in the beginning, her star shined brightly, rising
with promise and a few plum roles? A recurring role in a
soap opera before she was twenty! Hadn't she worked with
the Toms—Cruise and Hanks—and Gwyneth and . . . and
even Brad friggin' Pitt? Okay, so they were small parts, but
still, they were legit! And she'd been a double for Julia
Roberts! Then there was the vampire series *What's Blood*

*Got to Do With It,* on cable. She'd paid her dues, by God. But, she realized, those flashes of fame had been a while back and lately she'd been relegated to corpses on *CSI,* a few commercials, and voice-overs for low-budget animated films.

If she didn't land the part of Estelle in that new series, she could kiss her B-listed career good-bye.

Hollywood, she thought, the land of worn-out casting couches and broken dreams.

She kicked off her heels and padded into her small galley kitchen where she opened a sparse refrigerator, retrieved the half-full bottle of Pepto, unscrewed the cap, and took a swallow of the pink ooze. Shuddering, she replaced the top and put the remainder of the bottle back on the shelf, then looked around.

Where the hell was the cat?

Well, certainly not on the counter where three days worth of coffee cups, dirty glasses, and Lean Cuisine trays littered the chipped tile.

She winced, her stomach still aching and, as she walked to the bathroom, told herself she couldn't let the town beat her down.

Hadn't she suffered through bulimia?

Hadn't she done whatever it took?

And even if she wasn't classically beautiful, she'd been told her face had "character" and "intelligence." Her auburn hair was still vibrant, the skin around her green eyes and full lips without too many tell-tale lines.

With a glance in the mirror over the sink she cringed as she wedged herself into the tiny room that was the only bathroom in her apartment. Despite the pep talk to herself, the years were beginning to show, if only a little. She used a ton of products to keep her complexion flawless and she wasn't into Botox. Yet. Though she wasn't ruling it out. She wasn't ruling anything out that would help push Father Time back into the closet.

But he was a persistent son of a bitch, she thought and pushed the flesh on the sides of her jaw backward in an attempt to see if she really needed to be "tightened up."

Not yet, thank God. She didn't have the money for any kind of "work."

Noticing the whites of her eyes were a little bloodshot, she removed her contacts, then found the bottle of Visine she kept in the medicine cabinet and after unscrewing the bottle cap, tilted her head back, blinked in the drops and resealed the bottle. She closed the mirrored front of the cabinet and caught a glimpse of a shadow behind her.

*What?*

Her heart clutched and she turned. The room was empty, the door behind her open to the living area and the sliding door to her patio, but no one was in the apartment.

She would know.

The unit just wasn't that big; barely larger than a studio.

And yet her flesh prickled.

"Lana? Is that you?" she called as she stepped into the living area again, the edges of her room blurry from her myopia and the drops that hadn't quite settled. "Kitty?" Where was the damned cat, a calico she'd named after her favorite movie icon? "Come out, come out, wherever you are," she sang, but decided the cat, who often played a game of hide and seek, was lurking in the shadows somewhere, ready to pounce. More than once, Lana, leaping from behind the framed pictures set upon the book case, scattering the photos, breaking the glass and, plumped up to twice her size, had startled Shelly. It was the cat's favorite pastime. "Here, kitty, kitty . . ."

True to her independent temperament, Lana didn't appear.

Shelly kicked off her high heels and stood barefoot in the living room. There was something about the apartment, a stillness that suggested no one, not even the cat was inside.

Which didn't make sense.

Shelly had left Lana sleeping on the back of the couch when she'd gone out earlier. She was certain of it and remembered the cat only flicking her tail as she lay curled in the soft cushions.

So why did it feel as if the rooms were empty, devoid of life?

Shelly felt a nervous little twinge in the pit of her stomach.

"Lana?" she said and noticed the slider door was open, just the tiniest of cracks.

Hadn't it been shut?

Absolutely. She remembered sliding it closed, though of course it didn't latch because that stupid super, Merlin, hadn't gotten around to fixing it.

The hairs on the back of her neck lifted and her heart began to knock, though she told herself she was being paranoid. No one was in the apartment, lurking inside, lying in wait for her.

*You've been auditioning for too many victims in those cheap horror flicks.*

Still . . .

Ears straining, heart thudding, she looked at her bedroom door, open just a crack. She took two steps in the direction of the open door when, from the corner of her eye, she saw movement, a dark figure at the slider, on the other side of the glass.

"Wha—?" She bit back a scream as she recognized the hot guy from the bar. "Oh, God, you scared me half to death!" Her heart was racing, her pulse a sharp tattoo. She could barely breathe as he pushed open the door and stepped into the living room. "What the hell are you doing out there?" she demanded, a little irritated now that her initial wave of fear was evaporating.

"Waiting."

"For me?" *Really?* Shelly had been around the block enough times to recognize B.S. when it was hurled her way.

"So, how did you find me?" she asked as he smiled, that sexy grin that had caught her eye at Lizard's. He really was a heart-stopper with that square jaw, dark hair, and eyes that showed a bit of the devil in their blue depths.

"Wasn't hard." Oh, God, did he really have dimples? "You flipped your wallet open when you were looking for your credit card."

She remembered, it was just for a second, before he offered to buy the next round when she'd admitted it was almost her birthday.

"Most people come to the front door and knock."

His lips twitched. "Maybe I'm not most people."

She couldn't argue that and wasn't about to try when another pain, sharp enough that she had to double over, cut through her. "Oh . . . oh . . . Geez." She placed a hand against her glass-topped table and sucked in her breath. Again she was perspiring, this time feeling a little faint.

"Are you okay?"

"No." She was shaking her head. "You'd better leave. I'm sorry—oh!" She sucked in her breath. This time her knees buckled and he caught her. Before she could protest, he picked her up and carried her unerringly to the bedroom.

"Hey, wait a second . . ."

"Just lie down."

She didn't have a choice. The bedroom was spinning, the bedside lamp seeming to swirl in front of her eyes. Man, she was sick . . . oh, wait . . . a new panic rose in her as he lay her on the bedcovers and the mattress sank. He left her for a second and she thought about trying to escape. This was all wrong. Her meeting him at the bar, the illness, him showing up on her patio . . .

Before she could move, he was back, holding her cell phone out to her. "I've already called 9-1-1," he said and she tried to reach for the phone, but couldn't. Her fingers were limp, her arm flopped back onto the bed. Useless. He set the cell next to her face on the quilt her grandmother had pieced for her when she was ten . . .

From the bed, she looked up at him and saw him grin again, and this time she was certain there was no mirth in his smile, just a cold, deadly satisfaction.

"Oh, God, what did you do?" she tried to say, though the words were barely intelligible.

"Sweet dreams." He walked to the doorway and paused.

"Nine-one-one," a female voice said crisply.

"Help," Shelly cried frantically, her voice the barest of whispers. Her mouth wouldn't work, her tongue thick and unresponsive.

"Pardon me?"

"I need help," she tried to say more loudly, but the words were garbled, even to her own ears.

"I'm sorry, I can't hear you. Please speak up. What is the nature of your emergency?"

*Help me, please! Send someone!* Shelly tried to say, now in a full-blown panic. The room was swimming around her, the words she wanted to cry out were trapped in her mind. The phone fell from her fingers, to slide off the bed and land on the floor.

Her head lolled to one side, but she saw him standing in the doorway, staring back at her. The "killer" smile had slid from his face and he glared at her with pure, undisguised hatred.

*Why? Why me?*

Evil glinted in the eyes she'd found so intriguing just hours before.

She knew in the few last moments of her life that her death hadn't been random; for some God-forsaken reason, he had targeted her. Theirs hadn't been a chance meeting in the bar.

*God help me,* she thought, a tear rolling from her eye, the mysterious stranger with his disturbing smile staring at her as she drew in a slow, shallow breath.

A voice was squawking from the phone on the floor but it seemed distant, a million miles away. She watched as he placed the vials of pills at her bedside, then slowly, methodically, began to strip her of her clothes . . .

Dear Reader,

I've been writing a series of thrillers which focus on The Colony, beginning with WICKED GAME, then onto UNSEEN, BLIND SPOT, and now the really fun WICKED LIES. It's been a terrific ride, one both my sister, author Lisa Jackson, and I plan to continue!

But for now I'm taking a detour. My next thriller, HUSH, debuts in July 2011 and it centers around a group of girls who've known each other since early grade school and who get together just before their senior year at a beach campfire and reveal their innermost deep, dark secrets. Then some of the guys from their class crash their party and before the night ends, one of them is dead: Lucas Moore, the cool, surfer-dude who most of them have a serious crush on.

Twelve years later, Coby Rendell has tried desperately to put the events of that night behind her, but now her and her friends' lives have been threatened. A killer, who's been waiting for just the right moment, has come back to take care of unfinished business—a business which includes getting rid of Coby and the other secret tellers, one by one.

I hope you like HUSH as much as I do! It was one of my most fun books to write.

For more about HUSH, and information on my other books, please visit my website at www.nancy bush.net.

Nancy Bush

**Please turn the page for exclusive
bonus material about The Colony!**

**A SHORT HISTORY OF THE COLONY**
by Herman Smythe

Introduction by Joyce Powell-Pritchett, Director,
Deception Bay Historical Society

*Let me introduce myself first. My name is Joyce Powell-Pritchett and I've been Director of the Deception Bay Historical Society for the last twelve years. A Short History of The Colony was given to the Historical Society by the estate of Dr. Parnell Loman. Though it was originally believed the account was written by Dr. Loman, subsequent discovery showed that it was really Mr. Herman Smythe, a contemporary of Dr. Loman, who actually compiled and wrote the narrative.*

*"The Colony" is the loose description for a group of women who live together at Siren Song Lodge in Deception Bay, and who are the descendants of Nathaniel and Abigail Abernathy. Mr. Smythe is honest about the fact that his account was taken from word of mouth, mostly from a colony member, Mary Rutledge Beeman, who is one of the two last descendants listed in the book. Mr. Smythe personally knew Mary Beeman before her death, as well as her sister, Catherine Rutledge, who still resides at the lodge with some of Mary's children who are unnamed in the account.*

*Mr. Smythe is still living and when I told him I was going to write an introduction for him, he smiled at me, his eyes* twinkled and he said, *"People keep acting like the book is all lore, but believe me, I was there during the seventies and eighties, and I'll stand by my words as fact!"*

Whether truth, or truth mixed with fiction, I'm sure you'll agree, *A Short History of The Colony* is a fascinating read.

*Enjoy!*
*Joyce Powell-Pritchett*

**FROM THE ANNALS OF HERMAN SMYTHE:**

The locals around Deception Bay call them The Colony. Why? Because they built a lodge in the late 1800s which was named Siren Song somewhere over the years and they've lived there together in a commune-like tradition ever since. Who are they? Well, let me tell you what I learned from Mary Rutledge Beeman, my friend, and one of the most colorful characters from The Colony's already colorful past!

It all started when Nathaniel Abernathy married his young bride, Abigail, and moved from the east coast to the west coast, about as far as humanly possible. Both Nathaniel's family and Abigail's were rumored to be descendants from the women who were condemned to die during the Salem, Massachusetts witch trials of the 1600s. Incidentally, the capital of Oregon, is Salem, and was named after Salem, Massachusetts.

Nathaniel and Abigail must have gotten a big surprise when they realized their union had spawned children with extraordinary abilities. No one knows how, but it's a proven fact that Colony members—usually women—can do amazing things. How? It's been speculated that it's in the genetic code for this tribe, the result of a mutated gene, maybe.

Whatever its cause, it has played havoc with Colony members and locals alike throughout the years.

When Nathaniel and Abigail Abernathy reached the Pacific Ocean, they decided that's where they wanted to live and set about buying up as much real estate as they could. They purchased a stretch of property along the Oregon coast and therefore amassed vast acreage that included mountain forests with old-growth timber, a large rock quarry and a hunk of coastline. In a very short period of time their holdings stretched from the foothills of the Coast Range to the east, across the land on both sides of what is now Highway 101, to the Pacific Ocean itself (though, because of later Oregon law, the beach that was their property was ceded back to the state as all Oregon beaches are now publically owned).

The Abernathys cleared smaller tracts of land, too, and Siren Song was erected in a spot that was clear-cut of timber. Stands of forest still abut the south section of the lodge and grounds, framing the lodge and a makeshift unincorporated "town" which is inhabited mostly by Foothillers. (More about them later.) Southwest of the lodge is the small town of Deception Bay, which spills across Highway 101 toward the timberland to the east, and the Pacific to the west.

From the onset, Nathaniel and Abigail bartered and bought even more adjacent lands to expand their isolated retreat. Though they no longer own that stretch of beach, or the small jut of rocky coastline directly across from the lodge called Serpent's Eye where a now-unused lighthouse still stands (an area that's islanded when the tide comes in), they do still own a larger island, Echo Island, which is about one square mile, and is located in the treacherous waters of the mouth of Deception Bay itself—the bay the town was named after, which in itself was named for the deceptive and deadly currents and waves that swallow fishing boats almost every season.

Nathaniel and Abigail got busy right away starting a family, but of their children, only two survived: Sarah and Beth (Elizabeth). All the boys died in infancy or were stillborn as were several other girls. Abigail was late in her life by the time Sarah and Beth arrived and though she lived into her late eighties, long past her husband, she wasn't much of a parent to her daughters so they mostly raised themselves. Beth, plagued by visions or sounds or sensations she couldn't handle, apparently went mad when she was in her early thirties. She had one son out of wedlock, Harold Abernathy, who was scorned by the townspeople for being both born a bastard and always acting decidedly odd. A hermit, Harold lived in sin with his young wife, an Indian shaman's daughter, who died giving birth to Harold's only child—Madeline "Mad Maddie" Abernathy—who lives in Deception Bay to this day. Beth either fell, or threw herself off a cliff, into the sea. She was presumed dead, though her body was never retrieved from the cold waters of the Pacific. Some people think she was pushed to her death, possibly by her sister Sarah who got rid of Beth in order to become sole heir to the vast property amassed by their parents, Nathaniel and Abigail.

Sarah Abernathy, the surviving daughter, married James Fitzhugh in 1909, but James died in a hunting accident on their tenth wedding anniversary. A full year after her husband's death, Sarah gave birth to a baby girl: Grace, in 1920. It's been theorized that Sarah had an affair with an Indian shaman whom she seemed to fall under the spell of sometime before her husband's death. Rumors have it that Sarah and the shaman plotted to kill James, but no one knows for certain and his "accident/murder" has never been solved. Sarah has been much vilified by the Deception Bay Townies over the years, and even her descendants are suspicious of what her intentions were.

But everyone agrees that Sarah was remarkably bright and learned about the value of land ownership from her father, Nathaniel. She managed to increase the amount of acres of timber, farmland and coastal holdings during her lifetime. Sarah raised Grace alone and modernized the original homestead into the imposing lodge it is today, although electricity and indoor plumbing only run on the main floor; the upper floors are much as they were when the place was first erected.

During Sarah's time, there was a bunkhouse on the property, left over from her parents' days of ranching and farming. Some say she enticed local men to do the work by offering up sexual favors. Others fervently believe Sarah possessed strange powers, and that she used those powers to persuade the neighboring farmers, millwrights and lumbermen to build onto the lodge and improve the grounds. Whatever the case, men seemed to come from far and wide to help out, while their wives and sweethearts stewed and gossiped about Sarah, only adding to the rumors of witchcraft which continually plagued The Colony and their supposed demon-possessed ancestors.

Members of the local community, Deception Bay, have long regarded the growing "cult" with suspicion. Fueled by gossip and the strange heritage of The Colony, the townspeople felt Sarah believed she was some kind of High Priestess. It's not clear who dubbed the lodge Siren Song, whether it was the locals or someone associated with The Colony itself, but Sarah's actions seemed to be the reason and the name stuck. Sarah's shaman lover never acknowledged that he was: a) her lover nor b) Grace's father, but his friendship and relationship with Sarah continued until her death in 1956, shortly after her daughter Grace's marriage to Thomas Durant, a hard-drinking, good-looking and hotheaded lumberjack who grew up in, and around, The Colony. Thomas was the son of one of the men/workers who seemed completely under Sarah's spell. (Thomas Durant's mother, who was known by the single name of Storm, was also a member of the same Indian tribe as Sarah's shaman lover.

Some say Storm was the shaman's sister, and that Thomas was really Grace's first cousin. This is the same tribe from which the sole member of the other branch of the Abernathy family tree—Harold Abernathy—took his young Indian bride.)

At the time of Grace and Thomas's marriage, Grace was already pregnant with Mary who was born June 21, 1958, Summer Solstice, and the town gossip is that Thomas raped Grace in a night of drunken debauchery. From the get-go, Mary was a fussy, unhappy baby—the result of "nature" or "nurture" or possibly both—as the fights between Grace and Thomas were legendary. He was a womanizer; she a fiery, angry woman who could give as good as she got. (Baby Mary seemed to absorb the fury, wrath and passion between her parents, Grace and Thomas; an unstable brew of mystical, inexplicable genetic material, she grew psychologically twisted herself. A dark personality at best, a deranged one at worst, Mary's strange behavior became legendary.)

After Mary's birth, Grace and Thomas's relationship, always tumultuous, grew even more strained. They both recognized something strange and dangerous in their daughter, though neither really addressed the issue head on. They always spoke of it in the abstract, though, even as a baby, Mary's precognitive skills were obvious.

When Thomas inexplicably disappeared bare months after Mary was born, the locals breathed a sigh of relief as he was a notorious drinker and brawler. But then more rumors swirled. What happened to him? Where did he go? Was foul play involved? No one, however, was really interested in asking a lot of questions, not even the local sheriff, as Thomas Durant was in and out of the local jail more often than not; always causing problems. People were kind of glad he was gone. Maybe he was killed, maybe he wasn't. A number of people said they'd spotted Thomas in the days after his disappearance and everyone allowed that he'd probably just taken off. It was the safest assumption. Still, like Grace's Aunt Beth's body a generation earlier, he never resurfaced in Deception Bay.

Grace, free of Thomas, married John Rutledge in 1959, regardless of the question of the marriage's legality (since no one knew whether Thomas was missing or dead). From the moment of the marriage Grace maintained that Mary was a Rutledge and never used the name "Durant" again. Within the year Grace and John had one child together, a girl, whom they named Catherine.

In 1975 Grace and John were killed in a freak automobile accident: their car missed a turn and plummeted into the Pacific Ocean at the sharp corner known as Devil's Point, a spot where the storms that rage across the Pacific hit with incredible force. The funneling waters at that cove have become the graveyard for many a boater or surfer. Grace's daughters, Mary and Catherine, were seventeen and fifteen respectively at the time of the accident. Though Grace and John had always planned to write a will naming Catherine as the prime beneficiary—and therefore leaving her in control of Siren Song and all the other property— Catherine was too young at the time of their death and they never fully formed their plans. Their eldest daughter, Mary, took over, and that's when the fun really began.

Mary treated her new position much as her maternal grandmother, Sarah, had: as if she were a High Priestess where the only rules that mattered were the ones she made herself. But Mary wasn't as innately intelligent as Sarah, and her hot anger wasn't tempered by cold calculation, like her father Thomas's could be. Mary was a very sexual being and took lovers indiscriminately. This is a fact I'm personally aware of, as I spent time at Siren Song myself; one of Mary's many willing conquests.

But this story is of The Colony, not me.

Another of Mary's lovers was one Richard Beeman whom Mary claimed was her husband. There is no record of this union, though Catherine insists the marriage was real. If Richard Beeman were truly Mary's husband, he certainly slipped in and out of Deception Bay and Siren Song without much more than a how-do-you-do. I'm inclined to believe he is a fabrication.

At the time of her parents' death, Mary, wealthy enough to do as she pleased, was beyond a narcissistic megalomaniac. Her mind was fractured, however, and self-satisfaction and even cruelty were her way of life. As far as relationships went, Mary slept with whomever she wanted and damn the consequences. She left behind a string of lovers and a number of children whose paternity has never been fully established.

Mary's sister Catherine never married. She became a mid-wife to Mary who delivered children like a mother cat, indiscriminately and without much interest in the newborns once they were a couple of months old, and she was also called occasionally by the Townies, if a mid-wife's help was needed. They feared her less than they did Mary.

The Colony had a feel of a commune after Mary took over, during the last half of the late '70s and '80s, with Mary still as sexually active as ever and Catherine managing the care of the growing brood of Mary's offspring.

Beyond Catherine and Mary, there were a number of men who lived in the bunkhouse that burned down in the mid-1980s. These men were there to service Mary, and there are tales of Catherine shooing them out time and again, and that maybe she actually struck the match that finally burned it down. There were also a number of cottages built along the eastern rim of land that leads toward the Coast Range where a smattering of families still live. These Foothillers—that I mentioned before—formed their own "town," which has never been really named or incorporated. Most Foothillers are Native American but some were shirt-tail Colony members, never fully recognized, but bound by some ill-defined relationship. Some of them exhibited extra abilities. Some of them pretended to be special. Some of them claimed to be Mary's past lovers. Mary paid scant attention to them, and the later men who cruised through the bunkhouse as she descended into a darker interior world. Eventually those Foothillers who were tied to The Colony all but disappeared.

The core of The Colony has always been women. As a rule, they possess the strongest extra abilities and seem to be the hardiest. Mary almost seemed tuned to some inner radar when it came to picking her lovers/the fathers of her children. With surprising success, she bore mostly girls and those girls all possess extraordinary abilities that seem to reach their zenith around puberty.

The Colony has tried to live in relative isolation. People in Deception Bay are wary of them. They seem to be from some other place and time, especially after Catherine took over total control, somehow wresting it from Mary. When that happened, Catherine changed everything, even her, and Mary's daughters', daily apparel. Per Catherine's decree, they all dress as if they were from a previous century wearing long skirts and calico prints and their hair in buns. The Townies live in uneasy co-existence with Catherine, and watch her closely on the rare times she deigns to go into town for supplies: food and gasoline/fuel. The enlightened locals of Deception Bay consider The Colony merely benign odd-balls, out of step with reality and the world, young women who live with their "clan." Still, there are the dissenters who consider them beyond weird, even evil, based on the lingering rumors of witchcraft, all the missing people and unexplained deaths.

The absence of men hasn't gone unnoticed, either, other than the "studs" who moved through the commune either from the bunkhouse, The Foothillers Community, or random lovers like myself. There is definitely an element of Townies who are resentful, mistrusting and envious of the women of Siren Song and their dark gifts.

Mary was born in 1958 and started having children in 1976 at eighteen. Her children are:

1. 1976—Isad

*This is where the account ends, I'm afraid. We know the eldest daughter's name is Isadora, but the rest of Herman Smythe's book has been lost. Older members of the Historical Society remember there being a leather book with notes and letters that this smaller, laminated missive was tucked within, but it, like many things associated with the women who live at Siren Song, has gone missing.*

*If you have further questions, please drop by the Deception Bay Historical Society next time you're in town. I would be happy to discuss the history of The Colony with you personally.*

*Joyce Powell-Pritchett*